To Imprison the Insane & Powerful

The Captured, The Imprisoned and The Stolen Series

C. Reader

Lit & Lore Co

Contents

Trigger Warnings

Your well-being matters. This story contains themes and scenes that may be triggering for some readers, including:

Violence and battle-related actions

Mentions of past sexual assault

Depictions of consensual sexual activity (including both MM and MF relationships — because love is love)

Imprisonment and captivity

Mental health–related themes such as grief and trauma

Please take care of yourself while reading. Find a safe space, tuck yourself in with a blanket, your favorite beverage, and let yourself enjoy the journey at your own pace.

Blurb

Olivia thought her chains were broken. She was wrong.

Jeyr will stop at nothing to bring her home.

Jethro burns for vengeance.

Caomh will sacrifice everything for family.

War is here—where power and madness collide.

Will they bow to fate...or become the monsters even gods fear?

Fates are never kind. Olivia once believed her days of captivity were behind her, yet the shadows of chains return. In the darkness, a voice whispers from the cell beside her...one that may be ally or doom.

Beyond the walls, Jeyr refuses to wait any longer for the mate stolen from him, even as a ruthless King bends all his power to keep them apart. Grief drives Jethro to the edge of madness, vengeance the only fire left in his heart. And Caomh, caught between loyalty and love, will sacrifice everything to keep his family safe.

The realm teeters on the edge of war—between the powerful, and the ones reckless enough to stand against them. But power and madness are a fine line, and only those willing to embrace both will decide the fate of kingdoms.

When the fates tighten their snare, will they bow to destiny...

Or rise as monsters the gods themselves will learn to fear?

Recap

C C. Reader recommends starting with *To Capture an Empath* before diving in—this recap contains spoilers. To fully enjoy the journey of the characters, read the first book first!

Already finished *To Capture an Empath* and just need a quick refresher? Read ahead!

In *To Capture an Empath*, Olivia—the last living empath—is thrust into a dangerous world where her very existence is hunted. After years of hiding, her solitude shatters when three Fae discover her true nature. Determined to protect her, they offer both shelter and training, while asking for her help in mastering her rare gifts.

As Olivia learns to wield her powers, she wrestles with temptation, inner conflict, and the lure of freedom. Deep bonds form with her guardians—most of all with Jeyr, whose connection to Olivia becomes undeniable. Their love grows into a proposal of marriage, promising a future filled with hope.

But on the eve of their wedding, tragedy strikes. Jeyr is called away to face the massacre of his family, leaving Olivia exposed. She is captured, tortured, and forced into a devastating choice: remain pure-hearted or embrace her darker side to survive. Harnessing her empathy as both weapon and shield, Olivia manipulates her captor and turns the tide—at the cost of her own blood.

In the chaos, she kills her tormentor but falls herself, only to be claimed once more—this time by the Great King and his Grand Duke, Bane. Her harrowing journey is far from over...

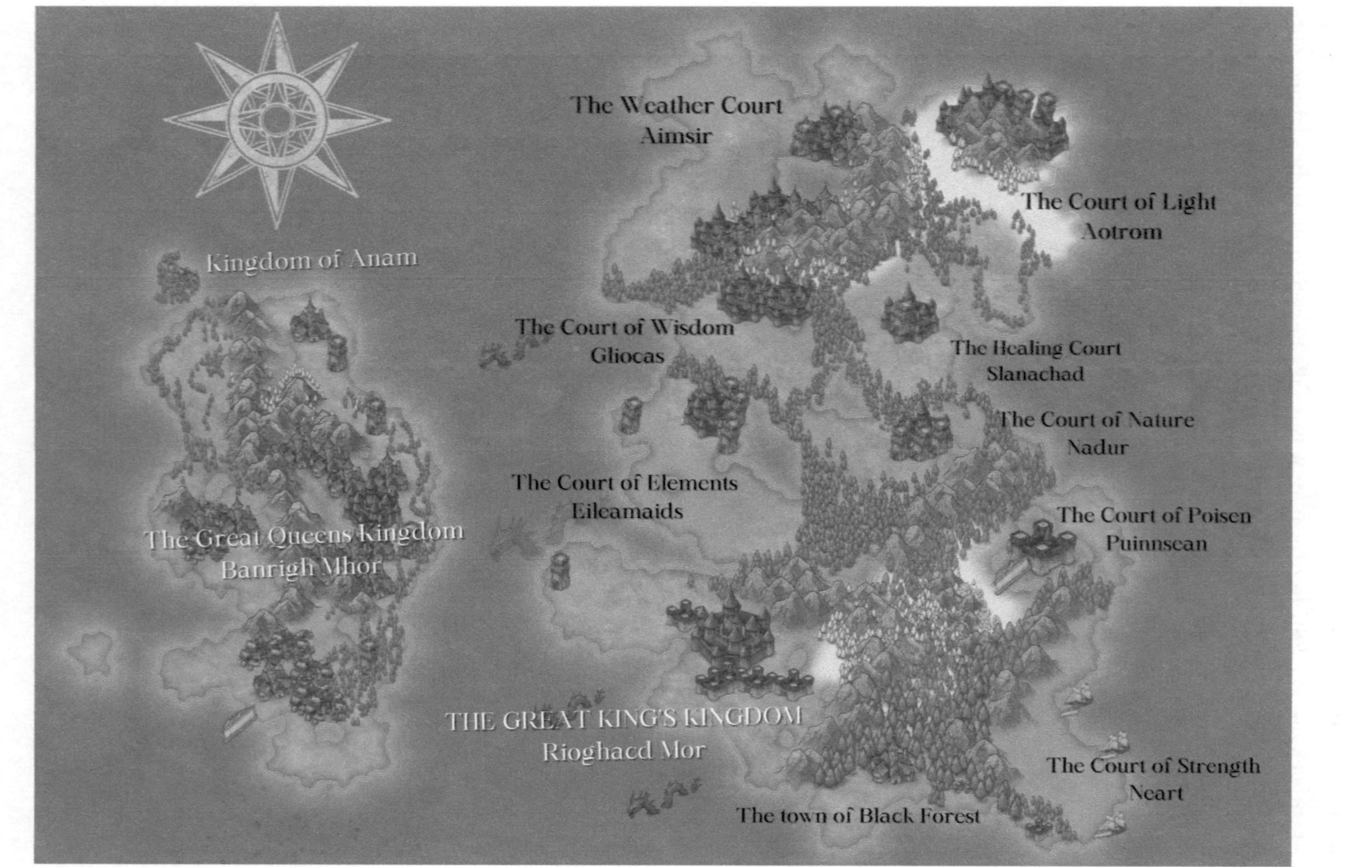

Kingdom of Anam
The Weather Court
Aimsir
The Court of Light
Aotrom
The Court of Wisdom
Gliocas
The Healing Court
Slanachad
The Court of Nature
Nadur
The Court of Elements
Eileamaids
The Court of Poisen
Puinnsean
The Great Queens Kingdom
Banrigh Mhor
THE GREAT KING'S KINGDOM
Rioghacd Mor
The Court of Strength
Neart
The town of Black Forest

The Tale Of Two Queens

The Kingdom of Anam, once radiant with unbridled magic, had collapsed into shadow. Where empaths once soothed minds, shifters roamed the skies, and witches wove wonders into the earth, only silence remained. The Great King's raids had left ruin in their wake, and of a noble lineage of the dragons that protected them.

Only three survived. They withdrew into the mountains, the stone keeping their secrets, the cold rock preserving them through centuries of waiting.

A prophecy lingered in those hollowed halls, spoken and re-spoken by voices older than memory:

Two Queens shall rise. One, the Queen of hearts and minds, who holds the tether to every soul. The other, a vessel of every gift, bearing the power of all the realms. Together, they shall shatter the Courts, unravel the King's dominion, and free the companachs from their chains. Together, they shall remake the world.

But the prophecy carried its warning too:

*If the Queens shall fail, the hope and purity of **all that is good is gone**.*

Olivia

The Prison Listens

In the tumult of my mind, lightning dances—a frenetic waltz across the canvas of the night. Its fleeting brilliance pierces the suffocating darkness, illuminating shadows that claw at the edges of my consciousness. Amid the chaos, fragments of memory flicker like dying embers, each one a whispered echo of the nightmare holding me captive.

Yellow eyes gleam with malevolence, their gaze searing into the depths of my soul. A dagger—sharp and gleaming—hovers at the fringes of my perception, a silent threat poised to strike. And then, amidst the storm of recollections, a kiss lingers—a fragile moment of solace in a sea of uncertainty.

But this isn't a dream I can shake off.

It's a labyrinth of torment, a maze I can't seem to escape. Every movement sends waves of agony coursing through me, a symphony of pain echoing from somewhere deep inside. The ground beneath me is unforgiving—a bed of jagged stones gnawing at my flesh with each desperate attempt to rise.

I fight to steady myself, but the world spins in a dizzying whirl—a kaleidoscope of sensation threatening to drown my senses. Darkness presses in from all sides, a suffocating embrace that tries to swallow me whole. Nausea coils in my gut, a serpent of dread tightening its grip, threatening to consume me.

With a defiant breath, I try to hold back the rising tide of discomfort, to stem the fear clawing up my throat. But the air is thick with rot—a sickly perfume that mixes with the bile rising in me. I can't hold it down. A primal instinct surges, and I retch, expelling the toxic remnants of my torment.

When the convulsions pass and my stomach finally settles, I try to take in my surroundings—but there's nothing to see. Just black. Endless, smothering black. The kind that makes you doubt your own shape, your own hands, your own mind. The kind that amplifies every other sense until they claw at you.

The stench hits harder now, thick and wet like rotting meat soaked in magic. My muscles protest, sluggish and aching as I shift just enough to curl an arm over my nose. It barely helps.

But it's not the smell that haunts me.

It's the sound.

The walls whisper pain. Not mine, not just mine. Ageless, layered, endless. Eons of agony etched into stone. Screams carved into silence. My own discomfort is a blink, a blip, a trivial shiver in a frozen sea of suffering.

I wish I were important enough to be worth killing. I wish they'd show mercy and just end it.

Instead—

Oh great, comes a voice, languid and sharp, like glass dragged slowly across silk, *what I need—another overly emotional, weak-willed cell neighbour.*

The words slice through the dark like they're spoken right beside me. I spin on the spot, wild-eyed, heart hammering. I strain to hear breathing, shifting, *something*, anything to anchor the voice to flesh.

I said neighbour, not cellmate, the voice drawls again. Feminine, yes. But more than that—bored. Effortlessly disdainful. She sounds like she's lounging in velvet while the world burns.

I blink into the dark, trying to pierce it. Trying to make sense of the way her words curl inside my skull.

"Who are you?" I whisper.

Please, she sighs. *I know you're smarter than to speak aloud in here. The walls have ears.*

Her frustration crackles like static through my mind.

My breath catches. My body stiffens as understanding clicks sharply into place.

She's in my head. This isn't just hearing thoughts—I'm *transmitting* them.

Panic flickers. My thoughts ping wildly between possibilities. If she's not tormenting me, not *one of them*, then... what is she? A fellow prisoner? A hallucination?

Maybe I *am* finally slipping.

The last clear memory comes in flashes—being dragged, held, bound. Wrong hands, wrong voices. Then Jeyr—his panic breaking through just before the darkness swallowed everything.

Jeyr.

I am not interested in your love life, Empath, the voice snaps.

Silence follows. Not peace—*silence*. Cold and pressurized, like the air itself is holding its breath.

White noise builds behind my eyes, a soft hum that grows louder with the passing of time—if time even exists down here. I can't tell. I only know that the dark presses tighter the more I think, as if it's listening too. Waiting.

The space between us—between my mind and hers—isn't empty. It's *charged*. Like the moment before a storm breaks. Like a secret held too long.

I don't know who she is. I don't know how she does this.

But I know one thing already.

She's not afraid of the dark.

You reached for me first. Not with your hands, no. With those spidery ribbons of power trailing out from your mind—an Empath's instinctive reach in the dark. But you... you are not like the others. Not like any Empath who's ever graced these rotting walls.

They snapped too quickly. Cracked like glass under a scream.

You, though—you crept. You slipped into the corners of my mind like water under a locked door. The first in a long, long time.

And I let you.

I try to piece things together, try to make sense of the fragments clinging to my thoughts like leaves caught in tar. But nothing moves. Every memory, every truth is sunk deep in the sludge of confusion. I can't pull any of it free.

Am I dead? The thought curls, slow and dangerous. Maybe this is some vivid purgatory—sharp enough that I can still feel the heat in my skin, the sting behind my eyes.

You are not dead, Olivia, the voice answers smoothly, before I can spiral further. *I can sense your heart. I can still taste the remnants of the poison seeping from your blood. I can...*

She stops.

The silence that follows is sudden and weighted. That unfinished sentence lingers like an aftertaste. My mind skips over tasting the poison—I'm not ready to unpack that particular horror—but the part she didn't say? That hooks under my ribs.

What else does she know?

Trying to plant something resembling trust, I push a thought outward, tentative but honest. *I don't know why I can hear you. I was wondering how you got past my shields. I'm... usually better at hiding.*

Her presence shifts in the dark—still there, but just beyond reach, like watching fire through glass.

I hear only your surface thoughts. They're loud, she says with a flicker of amusement, *but your mind is sealed. I cannot see into it the way I do with others. Your memories are closed to me. Tidy. Guarded. But my mind is always shut, and I am not under the influence of any poisons. That means...*

A pause. Deliberate.

You must possess some form of mind power.

I shake my head, jaw clenching as the fragments flash behind my eyes—flickers of things I've done. Bloody, brutal truths. None of them hint at some mental mastery. I am a weapon, yes. A killer. A creature stitched together by trauma and rage. But a mind reader? A puppeteer?

No.

Believe me, or don't, she says at last, her voice curling around me like smoke, *but this channel is of your making—not mine.*

I only let you in.

I sit with the thought, denial thick as the rot in the air.

At what point do I admit that this—whatever *this* is—is real? That the voice in my head, the presence pressing against the edges of my thoughts, isn't just another crack in my sanity? Gods know I wouldn't be the first to go mad in captivity.

The voice laughs. Not kindly. A cackle that scrapes against the inside of my skull, making everything worse.

I ask again—this time silently, as if speaking to hallucinations has become the new language of my reality.

Who are you?

Stillness answers me. But not emptiness.

I feel her hesitation, subtle but there—a swirl of emotion like dust caught in a slow breeze. Doubt. Curiosity. That sharp internal waver that comes before one decides whether to reveal the truth... or a prettier lie.

Can you keep a secret? she asks at last.

The words wrap around my mind like velvet laced with thorns.

I can keep a secret, I whisper back, low and certain in the quiet chambers of my mind.

The pause that follows is electric. A stretch of silence so taut it hums, every breath suspended. When she finally speaks again, her voice is different—no longer sharp or teasing. Just a hush. A confession not meant for ears.

I am a byproduct of testing.

Not just years. Generations.

The scrutiny began before I ever drew breath—before I even took form in the womb. They pulled me apart piece by piece, trying to map the impossible. Trying to name what they didn't understand. I was their puzzle. Their prophecy. Their monster.

Her words echo in my mind, and I feel the ache that threads through them—an ache she never intended to share. But pain doesn't need permission. Not with me. I feel it all, even when it's buried deep beneath a polished tone or a cruel smile. Her pain thrums like a bruised pulse against my own.

But it's the word *monster* that catches me like a blade to the gut.

My mind recoils, dragged backward through memory's bloodied corridors—relentless, unmerciful. Flashes of my own monstrosity flicker behind my eyes: the way I've broken things, broken *people*, the way power has warped my reflection until I've struggled to recognize the girl beneath the wreckage.

I know what it is to be feared. To be the thing someone begs mercy from.

I'm sorry, I whisper, the thought soft and frayed around the edges.

A hollow word. Fragile. I know it offers nothing. *Sorry* doesn't patch wounds. Doesn't undo the choices carved into us by other people's hands. It's a ghost of accountability—a whisper against the scream of what's been done. A threadbare offering at the altar of suffering.

But I still mean it.

Still *feel* it.

And somehow, even that small tether of shared understanding seems to matter.

You are not the one who harmed me, she says, her voice steady and unshaken, *and for those who have... they are the ones who will be sorry.*

The conviction in her words is like steel wrapped in velvet. No fury. No fire. Just *certainty.*

And in that certainty, I hear something more than anger—I hear a promise. A vow sealed in silence and suffering. A storm gathering beyond the walls, biding its time.

Something shifts.

The air grows heavy. The stone around us hums. The prison listens. It *knows*.
And just for a moment, I believe it too:
They will be sorry.

Jeyr

The King's Red List

Every report from our scouts delivers unwelcome news. The wards remain impenetrable—a truth I know too well after months of futile attempts to breach them and reunite with my mate. Frustration reaches its zenith as I toss the correspondents into the fire, my once-neglected hair now long, woven with stubborn knots that have grown comfortable in their chaos.

By the crackling flames, Jet sits, as if trying to absorb a warmth that no longer lives in him. It's been a week since his declaration of war, a week since he locked us all out. His responses are minimal—nods for yes, shakes for no. His eyes are darker than they've ever been, and his power cloaks him in living shadow.

Shouts echo from the foyer, but the voices don't stir me. If I had the energy, I'd roll my eyes. Olivia's loss has done more than shatter our foundation—it's either broken it beyond repair, or revealed the cracks we spent years pretending weren't there.

Aella's voice cuts through the air, reverberating off the marble walls like thunder. "Who gave you permission to touch our wards?"

Hecate's reply is swift, unwavering. "Jeyr said to do anything in my power to get us to Olivia. I am doing just that."

"You do not belong to this Court. I will not have you damaging wards that have survived centuries just to bring hope to someone who might well be a threat to us all. I heard what she did on that battlefield."

My hands tighten in my hair, yanking at the knots like they might anchor me. The pain is grounding—real, controllable. Aella, who once stood beside me in support of my bond with my Companach, now lets it crumble under the weight of truth. The rift between us only deepens.

But deep down, past the noise and grief, I know who my mate is.

The strongest woman alive.

What she did—what she stirred in that man, even if it was his twisted form of love—is nothing short of extraordinary. No one else could have made him falter. No one else could have made him *feel*. I wish I could say I'm not surprised. I've always known she was unlike anyone else.

And yet, somehow, she always finds a way to leave me in awe.

"What she did on that battlefield," Hecate continues, her voice rising like the spark of a blade before the strike, "was kill an unkillable monster. *While* making a field of good men and women *sleep*."

At that, the door slams over and their voices are no longer smothered by the walls.

"Enough. Just—enough." I wish my voice carries more strength, but the words escape on a breathy exhale, sounding feeble even to my own ears. Both Aella and Hecate turn toward me. Strangely, the softness I expect in my sister's eyes is absent; instead, it rests in Hecate's—the one who has woven herself into our family.

"She has been *playing* with our wards!" Aella snaps.

Desperately, I glance at Jet, hoping for some flicker of support. But his gaze stays locked on the flames, unmoving. My shoulder aches with phantom memory—the ghost of his hand, the weight of it in times like this.

"Hecate, did you improve the wards while you were playing with them?" I sigh, only half listening to the rising voices still echoing in the foyer, voices that threaten to make everything worse.

"Yes. To say they were centuries old is an understatement," she replies, calm and matter-of-fact. "But I wanted to see how yours compared to Puinnsean's. If I could crack yours, then I could crack theirs."

Her words pull me back to the present. Just for a moment, I forget the argument unraveling outside. Something sparks in my chest—small, bright, a fizz of hope daring to live again. "*And?* Did you?"

The space between my question and her answer stretches taut, like a bowstring drawn to its breaking point.

"Possibly. If we're considering the similarities between the two—both your wards allow native people to pass freely. Puinnsean's, however, includes a red list. Any Fae marked on it are poisoned on contact. Yours just alert the guards of an intruder. So... if bloodline grants passage, it occurred to me: what if we could temporarily mask our blood to mimic someone else's?"

I stare at her.

"I tested the theory here," she continues. "I created an elixir that disguised me as a civilian from Aimsir. It worked. I passed through undetected. Also—unrelated—but your wards are now stronger. If anyone not from Aimsir enters, they'll be shocked and disarmed until your forces arrive. I'm still improving the spellwork, but it's something."

I should feel reassured by that last part. Should feel relief. Instead, my mind clings to the possibility she just laid out—*a way in*. We're one step closer to slipping past Puinnsean's borders. One step closer to reaching Olivia. The urgency builds inside me, clawing at my ribs. Time is running like sand through an open palm.

"Get onto it, Hecate. And... thank you."

She starts to answer, but the voices from the foyer finally breach the study's sanctuary.

"If you think I'll let you come to the Kingdom with us, you've another thing coming, Lorkan."

"Oh? And what would that be, Commander?" Lorkan drawls, arms crossed, completely unfazed by Caomh's rage.

"I'll send you back," Caomh says, stepping forward, eyes narrowed with sharp intent.

Lorkan towers above him, gaze steady and unbothered. "And you think you have the power to do that?"

Caomh straightens even further, as if his spine alone might meet Lorkan's height. "Yes. I can. Don't underestimate me, Lorkan."

Lorkan chuckles, low and rumbling. "Oh, I've never underestimated you, *Cay*."

I see it—the steam curling off Caomh's anger, the clench of his jaw like a vice.

"Alright, you two. What is this about *now*?" I sigh, rubbing at my temples like it might stop the wreckage that is my life from swirling just a little longer.

"The King has called for a Courts meeting."

You'd think my heart would be used to unsavory news by now. That it would stop its habitual pause in my chest every time something goes wrong. But it doesn't. It halts—just long enough to make my chest ache.

This moment has been coming. Ever since the discovery of illegal forces in the Dark Forest. Ever since the capture of an Empath. There's only so much time before the King moves to reassert his power over the Courts.

Three Courts' armies had already been sighted—no signs of allegiance to the illegals, but we did stand beside them regardless. Even if the majority of our forces were subdued by Olivia—if you can call it that. *Put to sleep*, as Hecate would so delicately phrase it.

I nod, already knowing the score.

I've been lucky to avoid these meetings before now. Niall was always the one at my father's side. And before Niall, it was my mother.

"Lorkan wants to go as Jethro; he thinks it's best Jet stays here, since... Bane will be there." Caomh's tone bites—sharp and clear that he doesn't think this is a good idea.

Jet, a statue until now, lurches at the enemy's name—a flicker of life breaking through his frozen exterior. But when I brace myself for words, *any* words, he retreats back into silence, leaving me stranded in the void of his unspoken thoughts.

I glance at Caomh, silently pleading for a telepathic bridge, some thread of understanding between us. But he meets my gaze with only a stoic stare, his silence a stern demand: *Jet must speak for himself.*

The air crackles with unspoken tension, heavier than the shadows that cling to the room.

"Not happening. You're not going into that kingdom without me. Who knows what that fucking King wants, but I know for sure it won't be good," Lorkan booms, his large body towering over Caomh. My presence remains invisible, a ghost caught in the heat of their clash.

"I can handle myself," Caomh snaps, pride bristling like a shield.

"Spare me the bravado," Lorkan scoffs. "Hiding me won't last forever. I'm done with exile. Done watching our family die like flies."

Caomh's anger flares, ready to ignite.

Jethro's voice cuts through the tension, voice smooth despite its disuse. "Meeting's soon, Caomh. You go. Lorkan, your magic's needed with Hecate on the wards."

Relief flickers across Caomh's face, quickly replaced by a tense nod from Lorkan.

"This isn't over," Lorkan growls, jabbing a finger at Caomh. "I've stayed silent long enough."

"And I've kept you safe, shifter," Caomh counters, his voice laced with weariness. "What's another century?"

"Another century of your *control*?" Lorkan roars.

His form ripples—unstable, shifting. In two heartbeats, his clothes tear, feathers erupt, and a raven explodes into the air. With a rush of wind and the whisper of wings, Lorkan vanishes.

"Guess I'll follow the feathered fury," Hecate mutters, stalking toward the door.

Aella trails behind her, but not before shooting me a glare sharp enough to cut.

A heavy sigh escapes me.

I ache for the quiet of the manor. For my mate's laughter. Even for Kyzan's ever-chaotic presence. He hasn't returned. Last seen near the Great Kingdom's borders In silence, my brothers and I gather what we need, bracing ourselves for the Great Kingdom.

The brownstone buildings of the Great Kingdom lean into one another like gossips whispering in the dark, their narrow windows glaring down at me as if they know I don't belong here. Every step deeper into the city tightens the vise around my chest. Too many walls. Too many eyes. Too little sky.

Crowds press in from all sides, the crush of bodies and heat making it impossible to draw a full breath. A sweaty shoulder collides with mine, and I bite back the urge to bare teeth. Claustrophobia blooms sharp and hot in my ribs, but I school my face into indifference, weaving through the chaos as if I don't want to claw my way back to open air.

The castle looms ahead, all brownstone and mortar stacked high on its hill, its towers stabbing the sky like a warning. It doesn't just sit at the city's heart—it strangles it, every crooked street bending to its will.

The air is thick, oppressive, as though the kingdom itself sweats with the people. Scents layer and curdle together: the sour tang of unwashed skin, the sweet bite of fruit left too long in the sun, the sharp bite of manure as horses jostle through passageways never meant for hooves. It is a tapestry of stench and sound and heat, one that makes me long for the clean bite of mountain air, the wildness of rain against my face.

I hate it here. Every brick, every breath, every heartbeat of this kingdom reminds me why.

"Remind me again why we are entering by foot and not winnowing or, you know, by wyvern or *at least* horse," I moan. It's not even the method of entry that bothers me most—it's just one more irritation in a rising of unknowns.

"Because arrival by wyvern isn't allowed," Caomh answers, tugging at the collar of his shirt like it's choking him. "The castle wards prevent it. Same goes for winnowing. His security is tight—obsessively so. I also think he enjoys making royals walk among civilians. It's a power trip."

The top buttons of his shirt are done up, and for Caomh, that's equivalent to being waterboarded by fashion.

We reach the base of the palace entrance, and I stifle a groan. My eyes travel up—way up—the tall expanse of stairs.

"You have got to be kidding me. At least tell me we can winnow *up* the stairs, right?"

As I speak, sweat trickles down my spine, and the air feels even thicker here, like the very base of the steps is cursed to be suffocating. Something tells me this is the King's sick joke, and I have *no* doubt he's up in his tower right now, laughing at the sight of his royal subjects dragging themselves up hundreds of steps like commoners.

Normally, I wouldn't mind. But in this heat?

This is my own personal hell.

A thought comes to mind, and I send my power out, calling for a shift in the weather—but nothing stirs.

"Don't even bother trying; he controls the weather here. And the wards," Caomh adds, tugging at his shirt like it's choking him.

I glance up and spot Coran Conroy making his way up the stairs, his suit nearly identical to Caomh's.

"Come on, let's follow Father dearest up the stairs," Caomh drawls.

I let out a scoff-laugh at the dryness in his tone.

We start the climb, and though the air gets lighter with each step and the mountain breeze begins to cool our skin, our footfalls grow heavier. It's like the stone itself resists us. I make a mental note to add stairs to our training regimen—clearly, we're woefully underprepared.

Jet stays silent and unmoving the entire time. I try not to look at the darkness in his eyes.

And I pray—quietly, urgently—that he stays in line.

Just for now.

Stepping onto the gated bridge, the air thickens with judgment. No words, no accusations—just the weight of it pressing on my shoulders as surely as the damp heat of the city. Royals drift in clusters, silk sleeves brushing, eyes flicking, lips curving into tight, bloodless smiles. Not a single warm greeting. Not here. Not with the new Grand Duke close enough to see.

I recognize faces among them. Men I stitched back together when the war was still bleeding us all dry. Women who once clutched my hands with thanks after their wounds closed. Now their eyes skim over me, their gratitude curdled into suspicion, their warmth replaced by something brittle and cold.

Are you surprised, brother? Caomh's voice slips into my mind, low and steady, though I feel the tremor beneath it. *Bane made sure the world knew of our transgressions.*

I don't answer. Because no, I'm not surprised. Not anymore.

The grand courtyard yawns ahead, vast and open, its marble polished to a cruel gleam. Above, balconies sag under the weight of tapestries—each one immortalizing the King at different stages of his eternal reign. Always alone. Always the same face. The same smirk. Ageless. Untouchable.

But he is still one man. And me? I carry the loyalty of those who would bleed for me. Friends. Family. The love of my mate—my mate I will tear the world apart to reclaim. Bonds are a power the King will never understand.

My teeth grind loud enough that Caomh prods at my mind, his voice clipped. *That's enough. Shoulders back. Pretend you belong here.*

Right, I shoot back, biting down on the smirk tugging at my mouth. *Says the one who hasn't stopped tugging at his shirt for the past ten minutes.*

His mental snarl is immediate. *I curse the fool who decided clothes were appropriate. I look better without them. I fight better without them.*

You have a problem, Caomh. Truly. Deeply.

He hums like he agrees, then adds, *Yeah, my problem is we need to get Olivia back, end this war, so I can finally get laid and maybe sleep longer than three fucking hours.*

You know, I murmur into the thread between us, careful not to let my lip curve in the open courtyard, *the getting laid part doesn't necessarily have to wait for the war to be over.*

His disgust is instant and delicious. *Like I'm getting laid in your cursed Kingdom.*

I refer you to my original statement, I counter smoothly. *You have a problem.*

Fuck off.

A throat clears—sharp as a blade—and slices through our back-and-forth.

I look up.

A steel door groans open at the far end of the courtyard. From its shadows emerges a

Fae so slight he looks carved from glass and will. Lime-green eyes blaze under a fall of black curls, his pristine white velvet suit gleaming like fresh snow against the stone.

His voice, when it comes, is smooth as honey and just as cloying. "Dukes. Duchesses. Emissaries. Welcome."

And every head bows, save mine and Caomh's.

"Good evening, royal members of the Courts. Your Great King appreciates your attendance. Please make your way up the grand stairs toward the briefing room," the Fae announces, his light, twittering voice floating just above the hush of the courtyard.

I study him as he speaks. Too innocent-looking to be working for *this* King. Too bright-eyed, too unweathered. It's almost laughable—like he wandered into the wrong life.

Shame he works for the King; he looks like a treat, Caomh hums through our mental link, and it takes everything in me not to roll my eyes.

You know there are tons of willing Fae in my Kingdom who would scratch that itch, I reply. *I even know one who can shapeshift to look exactly like the man you say looks like a treat.*

Not even funny. At all, Aimsir.

I cover my mouth, discreet as I can, to hide the smile tugging at the corners. It's a small mercy—having something left to smile about. But guilt follows quick, as it always does.

What? I can let Lorkan know. My thought cuts through, teasing even in this place.

I do not have sex with shifters. End of.

I hum back, letting it fade, focusing on one step after another—up yet another cursed flight of stairs. The whole castle is a labyrinth designed to wear visitors down. Fatigue is the King's chosen form of hospitality. I try to summon a breeze to cool my sweat-slick face, but the wards drink it down, leaving the heat to choke me.

The briefing room opens into a cavern of polished stone and glass. From here, the city sprawls below, brownstone and smoke, factory stacks coughing grey into the sky. The streets choke with bodies pressed shoulder to shoulder. Congested. Breathless. And somehow that makes me more grateful for the scraps of freedom I still hold.

"Dukes, please take your labeled seat. Duchesses, please have your consort or emissary seated in their nominated position," the steward drones, his voice smooth, practiced.

I catch it then—the way Duchesses Elomonia and Gia step behind their consorts without a flicker of defiance. If they're insulted, they hide it well. But I see the moment Grand Dukes Aison and Bliant slip quiet hands to their shoulders, subtle as shadows. The women bow their heads just enough for me to notice. Just enough to tell me they still see.

Gia's tunic clings sheer, the fabric whispering against skin, chains of gold and bone dangling like trophies at her collarbone.

That's it. I'm moving to Naidure. They respect my views on clothing, Caomh mutters.

Oh, shut it. You can take a cold shower when we're home.

Oh, I will. And I'm not wearing a shirt for a week in protest of surviving this oven.

As if not wearing a shirt for a week is anything new, Cao. I scoff, though my lips twitch.

We take our seats, the weight of the court heavy as chains. Coran—his mirror, his shadow—sits beside me. The resemblance is uncanny despite the whispered stains on Caomh's birth. Buzzed golden hair against Coran's wild beard. Stubble and mane against rigid discipline. A curt nod, nothing more. A mask of stone answering Caomh's mask of iron.

Across the table, Lumineer leans close to Jethro. A hand at his neck, a whisper into his ear. Concern flashes in his eyes, blue hair glinting like sunlight on water. "So sorry to hear about Raiden and Niall," he murmurs. "My thoughts are with you and the girls."

I manage a nod, a glance, gratitude raw in my chest. His face echoes Jethro's, and that only deepens the ache.

"Thank you, Royals, for meeting me on such short notice."

The voice snaps my head up.

The King stands at the far end of the room, cloaked in suffocating red, his presence filling the chamber like smoke. Heat clings to him as though it bows to his will, not daring to touch him. His gaze moves slow, deliberate, pausing on each face as if weighing souls.

Then it finds me.

That smirk. Small. Knowing. A knife twisting at the base of my spine.

Anger sparks, sharp and bitter, even as fear claws through me. Does he know? Can he taste the defiance that thrums through my chest, the thought of my mate, of freedom?

For a heartbeat, the world stills, and it feels as if he already has the answer.

"As you may know, there has been some unrest of late; the civil wars are growing, and the armies of Illegals have begun attacking our own."

He pauses, scanning the room, assessing everyone's expressions. No one moves—except for Bane, who looks almost moved by the King's words. *Teacher's pet.*

"The latest battle, as you may know, saw both our own Commander Lord Tierney and multiple others taken down by a force so evil it tried to eliminate them—and nearly succeeded. But it seems one last of their kind still exists. This species has powers so strong they can take out entire armies in seconds, as we saw on the battlefield last week."

Behind the King, an Illuminary flares to life, light spilling across the obsidian table. The battle unfurls in miniature—men and women falling like wheat before a scythe, their bodies crumpling beneath a single devastating force.

Olivia's smirk beside Tierney burns like acid in my gut, her face framed by the carnage she wrought. The King's voice rolls through the chamber, deliberate and cold.
"You see, the Empath has evolved beyond what we believed it to be. It is now what we always feared it could become."

Silence suffocates the room. No one shifts. No one dares meet another's eyes, as though to look is to share blame.

"I have our Grand Duke of Aimsir to thank," the King continues smoothly, "for taking her down. However briefly."

The image shifts. Lightning. My lightning. It scorches across the field, slamming into Olivia. Her body convulses, her scream ripped away by the roar of the storm. The Illuminary flickers cruelly, etching the scene in fire and smoke, replaying my sin for all to witness.

My stomach knots, bile crawling up my throat.
It wouldn't have killed her, I whisper to myself. A mantra I've repeated night after night, but it rings hollow against the truth. I could have been the one to end her. My mate. My heart.

Yet the nightmare lingers. The storm hissing, the scent of charred air. My arm outstretched, power sparking at my fingertips. The horrifying image of myself—weapon aimed at the very soul I was meant to protect.

Forgiveness? A foreign country, a place I will never set foot.

The King's voice cleaves through the quiet. "But it seems," he says, eyes pinning me like a hawk pinning prey, "that you had ulterior motives, Young Duke."

Every head turns. The air thickens, pressing against my ribs. I hold my breath beneath the weight of their scrutiny, beneath the King's sharpened smile.

He does not linger. "Which we will return to." A blade unsheathed, then sheathed again. Suspense left to fester.

His tone hardens, every word meant to be carved into history.
"My true concern lies elsewhere—the number of Fae carrying more than one power. Though we court a handful, far too many escaped. And so, hear me now: my armies will patrol your lands, and the Black Forest, for Illegals. Any discovered will be execut-

ed—publicly. Citizens will watch as they burn, so all will know the price of defiance."

Thud. Thud. Thud.

My pulse hammers, drowning out thought.

"In every Kingdom," he goes on, voice slick with certainty, "execution sites shall rise as monuments to our dominion. Each of you, as representatives of my Courts, will conduct these rites yourselves. You will show our people that mercy has no place here. That rules are not to be bent, but obeyed."

A ripple of unease whispers through the chamber, though none dare speak it aloud.

The King leans forward, eyes glinting like a predator who has already tasted blood. "Leniency has weakened us. But the Illegals breed like rot in the dark, a plague gnawing at our reign. No longer. We will prove to the world that we are unyielding. That power is pure. And that those who would stain it are not only traitors—" His smile spreads, cold and cruel.

"—but a threat to existence itself."

The King's voice coils through the chamber like smoke, deliberate and suffocating. "The establishment of execution sites across the Kingdoms is no act of cruelty," he declares, light gleaming from the Illuminary at his back. "It is strength. It is preservation. These sites will stand as monuments to order. Our citizens will look upon them and remember: to harbor an Illegal is to invite death. To defy us is to meet it."

Murmurs die before they're born. No one dares shift in their chair.

"Fear is the foundation of obedience," the King continues, his tone smooth as steel. "And through fear we will secure the prosperity of our realm. Together, we will scour the Illegals from every corner of our lands. Together, we will remind the fates themselves of our supremacy."

The silence that follows is absolute. My chest heaves with the weight of it. And before I can think better, before Caomh's warning can still my tongue—words spit out like blood from a wound.

"And what of me, King?"

A ripple of unease flares through the table. His head tilts, that serpent's smile curving. "And what of you, Duke of Aimsir?" His voice sharpens, savoring the provocation.

My pulse thunders in my throat, but I press on, reckless. "I am an Illegal, am I not? I hold more than one power. Not from birth. The fates themselves gave me what I am. By your decree, I should be put to death."

The King's gaze darkens, shadow swallowing the glint in his eyes. A chill lances through

me.

"I am aware," he says softly, cruelly. "But you pose no threat. You are a healer—proof of the fates' flaws, not their favor. Elevated as Grand Duke only because you were paired with that Companach abomination. You, Young Duke, are my greatest weapon against fate itself. A living reminder of its fallacy."

The room spins. Heat drains from my face, leaving me hollow. Dozens of eyes bore into me, watching the tremor I cannot hide.

The King hums, as though savoring my dread. "Hmm. I suspected as much. But let us be certain."

The Illuminary flickers, the image shifting.

And she is there.

Olivia. My mate. My heart.

Stripped bare in the prison's darkness, swallowed by shadows. My breath catches, my body straining against the invisible chains of the sight. No wounds. No chains. No lash marks carved into her skin. Relief flares, sharp and fleeting—but the truth is worse. Untouched. Preserved. A kindness that reeks of cruelty, a cell that still suffocates.

A guttural roar tears through my chest, but the sound chokes off as unseen hands seize my throat. Air vanishes. My lungs claw at nothing. Panic sears me raw.

Her eyes snap wide, her body convulsing as she gasps in the same silence. The same invisible vice crushing her.

It strikes me like lightning: he controls us both. Pain, yes—but worse. Helplessness. The despair of watching the one you would die for suffer and being powerless to stop it.

I collapse to my knees, agony clawing through me. She mirrors me in that darkness, the echo of my torment writ on her body.

This is how he will break us. Not with iron. Not with flame. But with each other—our love twisted into a blade, our bond weaponized until the only mercy left is madness.

Caomh

BUTTONS AND BURDENS

Jeyr's neck bulges with every strangled gasp, veins standing out like cords as his lips darken to a frightening shade of blue. His eyes roll, wild with pain, and the sound—gods, the sound—isn't even a sound at all. Just silence wrapped around his choking.

Instinct shoves my hand out, catching Jet by the chest before he can draw steel. *Don't*, I plead silently, locking onto him with a force that burns. His raw anguish mirrors mine, a perfect reflection of helplessness, of rage we can't unleash.

And through it—through the horror of watching Jeyr convulse, Olivia thrash under the King's invisible grip—a shameful flicker twists in my chest: gratitude. That Lorkan isn't here. That his brother's torment, this grotesque spectacle, isn't carved into his memory.

The buzzing in my ears grows, drowning the war raging inside me. Self-preservation snarls at one side. Kinship bleeds on the other. But deep down, I know the truth: stepping in now is suicide. And yet—

I need you. The words thread through my mind, soft, broken. A plea I slam the door on before it roots itself too deep. My throat burns as I whisper the apology no one will hear. Then I draw my sword.

Gasps ripple through the chamber as if I've already struck. The Illuminary sputters, Olivia's image flickering once, twice—then gone. Snuffed out like a flame. Jeyr collapses, dragging in ragged breaths, his whole body shuddering from the force of the King's unseen hand.

My eyes snap to the King. Fury boils through me, scalding, but I bury it deep, layering my shields like stone. His gaze finds mine across the table, dark with satisfaction, as though he can already taste my breaking.

Jeyr? Are you okay? I test the bond, but only static answers, empty and crackling in the back of my skull. I look at Jet—his face is carved from rage, no attempt at hiding the truth written there.

Jeyr? I try again, desperation gnawing at the edges of me.

Silence.

The chamber turns tomb-like. Every person is an island, untouchable, watching as if afraid to breathe. Then the King speaks, his voice a venomous whisper that slices through the silence like a blade.

"And now my suspicions are confirmed. How difficult it must have been to be bound to such a monster—controlled, manipulated, through a myriad of emotions."

Jeyr's shoulders rise and fall, his breathing ragged, but it's his hands—fists clenched white on his lap—that betray the fury boiling inside him. Fury that could level this room, this palace, this realm.

And I know, with bone-deep certainty, that if he unleashes it—

It won't be just this room that burns.

It will be the world.

"In a week, once we are done with her, you will be the one to execute her. Save our Kingdom. And yourself," the King declares.

Jeyr lifts his head at that, the motion slow, deliberate. His voice emerges husky, roughened by restraint, yet it does nothing to mask the thunder that rumbles beneath. Though his gaze doesn't meet mine, I know the skies over Aimsir are raging now—clouds split open, winds lashing, storms bleeding their fury in answer to his silence.

The King's laughter rolls through the war room, a cruel echo that tightens every spine like a bowstring drawn to the breaking point. The sound crawls beneath my skin, suffocating. My prayers rise—not for mercy, not anymore—but for a day when one man's power no longer strips us of kin, of freedom, of hope. But the wish dies before it can take root. I've seen too many crushed beneath his boot to believe.

He's stolen from us over and over, reducing us to pawns on a board none of us agreed to play.

Now the choice looms before Jeyr, and I feel it humming down the bond I share with him—the same impossible weight that has stalked us for years. Family. Kingdom. Or the one he loves. The King forces him to bleed for it all, again and again.

"If you don't," the King says, poison dripping from every word, "I'll not only charge you with treason, but your family too. The Court of Aimsir will lose its last reigning heir, and the only two left to carry its name. I wonder then..." His smile slices like a blade across my skin. "Who will the fates choose to rule next?"

Jeyr nods. Not weakly, not brokenly—resolutely. "I will do what is right for our Kingdom, my King."

The predator's smile that follows is worse than the threat. He's savoring the cornered prey, gorging on our helplessness. Fury sparks wildfire in my chest, every thought turning sharp with the temptation to end him now. Here. To make this chamber his tomb.

"Good," the King says, final as a blade sliding home. "I will have my army stationed at every Court. We begin the cleanse of the Illegals—for the safety of us all. This meeting is adjourned."

He leaves as though he hasn't just sentenced thousands of our kind to die. As if executions are a trivial matter, another stroke of quill across parchment.

The weight presses down, crushing. My lungs burn with it as I fling my mind wide, my voice threading through every bond I command. *Hide. The King has issued a kill notice for all Illegals. Get every man, woman, and child to the safe zones. Now.*

Responses flood back—panicked, sharp, desperate. Each cry twists deeper. Each plea lodges like a shard of glass inside my chest. My heart clenches even as I whisper to myself that I don't have one left to break.

When does it end?

When does this mask I wear finally become the man beneath?

The screech of chairs scrapes me back to the room. I reach without thought, my hand finding Jeyr's shoulder, seeking to tether him.

Don't, he snaps, shaking me off with a force that cuts deeper than the rejection itself. His voice is raw, serrated, every edge honed by pain.

He storms past, Jet close behind him. Most avert their eyes as they pass—sympathy flickering there but wisely unsaid. Not all, though.

"The King might've shown mercy this time," Bane sneers, oily venom dripping from every syllable, "but don't count on it again, Commander."

"It's Marquis Caomh Conroy to you," I say, my stride unbroken, my body angled so not a finger of him brushes mine. My composure holds—barely—beneath the tide of fury that begs me to turn back.

Jeyr and Jet descend the palace steps ahead, their movements sharp, brittle with tension. The descent is easier than the climb, but my fingers fumble with the buttons of my shirt, clumsy against the need to look composed when I feel anything but.

The capital swallows us. Clamor rises—fae and creatures and humans threading through their own tangled rhythms, the pulse of the city heedless of the noose tightening above it.

I fix on Jet's shoulders as he cuts through the crowd, black tunic threaded with silver glinting in the light. Jeyr moves just beyond him, nearly lost to the throng in his navy suit, swallowed by bodies that have no idea they walk beside ruin.

But I feel him.
The buzz of his energy thrums against me, jagged and erratic, a current on the brink of snapping loose. He's teetering—dangerously close.

And I know, bone-deep certain, that once we pass beyond the King's wards—
Jeyr will break.

I land outside his castle just as the storm churns to life around me, lightning splitting the jagged peaks of the Aimsir ranges. Thunder rattles through my bones, shaking loose every ounce of control I've been clinging to. The glass doors loom ahead, black and gleaming, a mirror to the fury burning in me.

But before I can reach them, he's there.
Lorkan.
Running straight toward me.

His eyes rake me head to toe, frantic, searching. And the anger already seething in my veins spikes higher, because I can't—won't—take what's written in those eyes right now. I shove past him. His hand clamps around my forearm, solid, unyielding.

"*Cay?*"

That voice. Gods, that voice. Weighted with the edge I know too well—an edge that drags me back to a past gilded in naivety. A past where things were easy, golden, where I was stupid enough to think happiness wasn't temporary. But that illusion shattered long ago, and all that's left are the jagged pieces.

"Not now, Lorkan," I snarl, spitting venom even as the nickname slices me open. "I just watched my best friend—my brother—choke on the brink of death. My army, my family, condemned. And you think I've got room for your drama right now?"

His posture stiffens, jaw tightening like stone. "No one ever forced you to *deal* with me, Caomh," he growls, the sound rough enough to scrape. "I never asked for your pity. Never begged for a seat in this mess you made."

I turn on him then, locking hard onto those violet eyes—furious and soft at once, too much like the lavender fields I once knew. Their glow flickers in the storm light, lashes dark, lashes too thick, too unfairly beautiful.

No. Not beautiful. Not anything.

I rip my arm free, tearing myself from his pull. "Good. Then shift into a fucking fish and swim home. Get as far from me as you can."

He laughs—low, bitter, dangerous. And he closes the distance I'd tried to put between us, step by step, until his breath is hot against my skin.

"You'd love that, wouldn't you, Cay?" His voice is a rasp that hits bone. "To not have me here. To drown yourself in meaningless sex, to throw yourself into death for your family and friends. But me? No—you'd keep me safe, wouldn't you?"

My steps eat up the space between us again, defiance tightening my chest. The air crackles, thick, violent. A heartbeat of silence hangs—sharp, loaded—before I rasp, final as steel:

"You're right. I don't want you here. I don't need your guilt, your temper, or your half-fucked loyalty. So go. Leave. Be the one thing in my life I don't have to bury."

His eyes flare, but I don't give him the chance to answer. I tear myself free, shove through the doors.

The slam echoes behind me. Loud. Brutal. Final.

Just like my words.

Dust motes swirl in the lamplight, tiny galaxies spinning as if they, too, are trapped inside the suffocating stillness. Jeyr's pacing scrapes through the silence, his boots a steady rhythm against the stone, his body moving like a predator pressed against bars—searching for a way out, finding none. Jethro tracks him with weary eyes, the taut line of his shoulders betraying the same fear clawing inside my chest.

At last, the silence shatters.

"Jeyr," Jet rasps, voice rough, breaking through the fragile stillness. "This plan... will it hold?"

Jeyr halts, his back to us. Shadows carve his face when he turns, the weight of sleepless nights etched into the hollows of his eyes. "It's the best I've got," he mutters, each word steeped in exhaustion. "Kyzan says their eyes are everywhere. Guards on every inch of wall. If the damned potion works... if Jet glamours us..." His voice falters, doubt flickering, dimming the fire that once burned unshakable.

"The potion lasts twenty-four hours," Hecate cuts in, tone flat, final. "When it burns out, the wards will scream the instant they sense a foreign soul. He'll know."

"Twenty-four hours is all we need." Jeyr straightens, resolve snapping into place like a blade drawn. "Jet, armor on. Caomh, you too. Lorkan—I need you to wear my face. I'm getting my mate."

The words strike me like a blow, panic rising like a tide that crashes hard against reason. "No." The word rips from my throat, raw and unyielding.

His gaze snaps to mine. And for the first time, I see the toll of his desperation—the bruises coiled like violet shadows around his neck, remnants of battles his healing can't erase. They mark him as mortal in a way Jeyr never allowed himself to be. Emotion slams into me, chaotic and consuming. This plan—this fragile, reckless hope—holds everything we are in its trembling grip.

"What?" His voice is thunder, rolling and heavy, daring me to defy him again.

"If the King sees him," I press, ignoring the tremor threatening to splinter my words, "that's it, Jeyr. You know it as well as I do. Torture, interrogation, the end of him—and us. It's too dangerous. Let him come with us. *You stay.*"

The muscle in his jaw ticks, his teeth flashing like a predator ready to strike. "Don't even think it," he growls, low and lethal. "You think I'll sit here—sit on my throne—while there's even a sliver of a chance to save her? Don't push me, Caomh. Rank doesn't mean a damn thing here."

I swallow hard, my chest a knot, eyes pleading before I can stop them. The vulnerability I bury so deep cracks wide open. "Jeyr... the King mustn't see him. I swear—I'll get Olivia to you. Just like I brought your sister back. Don't you trust me?"

The room tightens around us. His stare pins me, searing, the silence stretched thin as wire between us. And in his eyes, I see it—the resentment simmering like coals, the impossible weight of the choice I've forced into his hands.

"If she returns harmed," Jeyr warns, voice carved from steel, "even a hair out of place—you'll answer to me. Do you hear me? No more failures. No more pain inflicted on her because of me. Because of my weakness. This is the one and only time I will step down. Understand?"

The weight of his words crashes into me—merciless, inescapable. His desperation mirrors my own, twisted into a knot of duty and fear. In that moment, the lines blur between protector and protected, between commander and kin. And I know—with a certainty that hollows me out—that this mission holds more than Olivia's fate.

It holds our bond. Our trust. Everything we have left.

A wave of relief threatens to buckle my knees. My head dips, the words slipping free like a vow. "I would sooner die than fail you."

Jeyr scoffs, the sound cold as winter steel. He stalks forward, sapphire eyes blazing with a fury that sears hotter than any sun.

"Don't you dare think about sacrificing yourself until she's back here—in my arms, alive and breathing. And when you return," he bites, every word clipped with venom, "remember this: I'm done sacrificing my love, my duty, my everything for someone you refuse to claim as your own. This is your last chance, brother. Do you hear me?"

The knot in my throat swells until it feels like it will choke me. My gaze clings to his, searching for even a trace of the boy I grew up with—the boy who once lit halls with laughter, who loved brighter than anyone I'd known. But he's gone. In his place stands a Grand Duke—shoulders scarred by grief, spirit forged in fire and shadow.

And I'm the one who pushed him there.

"Yes, Your Highness," I rasp, the title heavy and bitter on my tongue. "I hear you."

He closes the distance in a blur, shoving me back with enough force to make me stumble. I gasp, scrambling for balance—but before I can recover, his arms seize me, brutal and unyielding, hauling me flush against him. My shock freezes me, nerves dulled, muscles useless, as he leans in close and growls into my ear.

"Don't you forget it," he hisses, low and dangerous. "I may be Grand Duke to this kingdom, but I'm still your family. Remember that. You wouldn't be standing here if you weren't. Now get your head out of your ass and go. Save my mate."

His arms vanish as suddenly as they trapped me. One last shove sends me staggering, and then he's gone—thunder in his retreat, lightning simmering just beneath his skin. His footsteps echo down the corridor, dragging a thousand unspoken things in their wake.

Jet shadows him without a word, silent and loyal, the steady weight Jeyr no longer allows himself to show.

I stay rooted, my head bowed, the phantom heat of Jeyr's grip still seared against my ribs. The air feels thin, brittle. It takes me a moment to register the tug at my shirt—the slow, deliberate unfastening of buttons. My chest locks, caught in the haze of everything just traded: trust, command, pain. The weight of it presses down, anchoring me to the stone floor.

Lorkan's fingers never brush my skin. They only ghost over fabric, deft and precise, pulling my shirt free and tossing it into the fire. The flames catch, a spark leaping up to mirror the one flaring—unwanted—in my chest.

"What if I wanted to keep it?" My voice is hoarse, uneven, a whisper scraped raw.

A beat of silence stretches, taut as a bowstring.

Then his voice cuts through, cool and steady. "The two buttons you ripped off said otherwise. Get ready. We have a princess to save."

He turns, steps sharp, purposeful, retreating toward his chamber.

I watch him go, the realization settling heavy and cold in my gut.

The burden Jeyr carries isn't his alone.

It's mine too—etched deep into me with every missing button, every scar, every word we never speak.

Olivia

Not Waiting to Be Saved

Her questions ricochet inside my skull, a relentless volley of confusion and fear. My own voice, rasped raw, joins the cacophony as I groan and clutch my head, certain it will split open.

The glint catches me first. A simple black band sits where the ornate serpent ring once gleamed—the mark of Lady Tierney stripped away. Beneath the surface, pressed against bone, lies the sigil of my mate. The proximity to his suffering rolls through me like sickness, each wave a vice around my throat.

I need to get out. The words scrape through my cracked lips as I scan the cell. Stone. Barred window. Nothing sharp enough, heavy enough, real enough to be a weapon.

Then let's get out, a voice hums, smooth, amused. *Don't waste your time with rocks. You are the weapon.*

The words freeze me. Ice slides down my spine. Not again. Not that. I won't be the weapon. I won't hurt, won't destroy. I killed the monster who made me into that—didn't I? Freedom was supposed to be mine now.

You are in prison, the voice counters, dry and cruel. *Does that look free to you?*

Frustration bursts, raw and loud. "Stop talking! Stop talking! I'm trying to think!"

You're thinking like a victim.

The snap of it cuts me deeper than I want to admit. *I need to get to my mate. That pain—that was him. Someone's hurting him, and I need him.*

Silence follows. Heavy. Suffocating. My pulse slams against my ribs. I wait, chest heaving, hope flickering like the last ember of a dying fire.

Please, I whisper inside, desperate. *Answer me. Someone. Anyone.*

You should be thinking about saving yourself, the voice returns at last, colder. *That pain? That was nothing. What waits for you here—it doesn't stop. Your mate isn't the priority.*

I close my eyes, drag in a shuddering breath. *He's the one person tied to me—mind, body, soul. He's mine.*

A scoff slices the quiet, sharp and scornful. *Ugh. That sounds awful.*

A laugh rips out of me, cracked and half-hysterical. *It's not chains. It's... like something missing clicks into place when he's near.*

The idea of being bound to anyone is my nightmare, the voice mutters, cynical, edged. *But if it makes you happy... we'll find him.*

The words land strange, but warmth stirs anyway, quick and sharp, catching in my throat. "We?" I breathe.

Shh. Yes, we, the voice purrs, smoke curling into my mind. *Gods, finally. I've been waiting for someone like you to claw us out of this pit. You and I—we want the same people dead.*

Ash settles heavy in my lungs. I press a hand to my chest. *I don't even know your name. How do I trust you? How do I know you won't bleed the people I love dry the moment you're free?*

A pause. Then—soft, reverent.

I had a friend once, she called me Lia.

The way she says it unravels me. It smells like baked apples and cinnamon. Like hearth smoke woven into wool. Like love that lingers even after the body is gone. Something cracks open inside me. My hands press harder against my chest, like I could trap the echo of my mother's strength pulsing beneath my ribs.

"Okay, Lia," I whisper, trembling as if the air itself waits for my answer. "How do we get out?"

Her reply coils through me, velvet wrapped in steel.

We use your power. Then we make the walls shake—for every woman this kingdom has tried to break.

Her words ignite instead of settle. They spark something I hadn't dared to name. Not just anger. Not just grief. Something sharper. Stronger.

Power.

And maybe—maybe I don't need to wait for rescue.

Maybe I was always meant to be the rescuer.

Maybe my mate isn't the only liberation waiting for me in this stone cage.

Maybe I was always meant to shatter it.

Caomh

ONE MORE DAGGER

My fingers dig into the leather straps of my scabbard, tightening until the buckles groan in protest. The bite of it steadies me—sharp, familiar—matching the coil of unease twisting low in my gut.

"Do you really have to go without the arm armor?" Lorkan's voice comes low and rough, brushing my ear like a ghost of a touch. It's meant to be practical. It lands like a caress.

"Yes," I bite, clipped and cold, though my hands tremble against the leather. "My chest is protected. That's what matters."

He snorts, dark eyes gleaming with mockery. "Right. And when someone gets clever enough to aim between the plates—what then? You planning to bleed out for the aesthetic?"

I glare at him, yanking the last strap into place. "I'm not wearing the arm guards."

"I noticed," he drawls, voice low, pointed. "Is this your grand strategy? Show a little forearm, lure the enemy in close, then smolder them to death?"

"I hate the way they feel," I snap. "Tight. Restrictive. I'd rather move properly than bake inside layers I don't need."

He raises a brow, skeptical. "So it's comfort over survival. Bold choice."

"If I die because someone grazes my arm, then maybe I deserved it," I mutter. "Besides, you're a walking antidote. Stitch me back together if it comes to that."

Lorkan huffs a laugh—half exasperation, half fondness. "You're unbelievable."

"Good," I smirk, though it tastes like ash. "Wouldn't want to be predictable."

His laugh rolls low, rumbling through his chest into mine. "The only thing you're distracting is my ability to think straight with half the armor you should have. And for the record, I can restrain myself around your biceps. Even if they are... worthy of temptation."

For a breath, the levity lingers. Then his gaze hardens. "Just... don't make me watch you get torn apart for the sake of your aesthetic rebellion, Caomh."

"I'm not rebelling," I murmur. "I'm surviving the only way I know how. Unbound."

Pressure hits my hip—sudden, solid. I flinch before realizing it's Jeyr. His jaw is iron, eyes shadowed as he slips another dagger into my scabbard.

"One more," he mutters. "Give it to Olivia when you find her. Anything's better than nothing."

I nod, but the weight in his stare drags me somewhere I never want to linger. A memory. My mother, the eve of battle. Her armor buckled tight, her eyes hollow with the same quiet dread now flickering in Jeyr's. Not fear that shakes or begs. The kind that sinks into bone. The kind that already grieves.

"Don't go," I had pleaded, my voice thick with panic as she knelt before me, her hand warm on mine.

"Your father has called upon me, and it is my duty, my sun."

"Then let me come with you," I begged, clutching at the golden gown that caught the sun in its threads like captured fire. "Let me protect you."

Her smile had been bittersweet, tender and cruel in the same breath. "It doesn't work that way, Sun. As your mother, it's my duty to shield you. You stay here. With Lorkan. He's special. And we protect what's special."

Guilt had gnawed at me, sharp as Wendigos in my gut. Helplessness worse than fear. The shadows of that sunset painted the world orange and purple, and I'd sworn then that her words—her name for me, sun not son—wouldn't die with her.

The echo slams shut. I lock the memory away and meet Jeyr's eyes. His jaw works, tight with restraint.

"Brother," I rasp, my promise heavier than steel. "I will bring her back."

He gives a single nod—nothing more. Stoic. Silent. A mirror of myself.

My gaze flicks to Lorkan and Jethro, obsidian armor gleaming with the sheen of shed wyvern scales. They wear war like second skin. In them, I see resolve—unyielding, familiar. We are all sharpened for this.

Then Hecate appears, a different kind of weapon. Quiet, precise. In her hands, three vials glow faintly, moonlight caught in glass.

"Take these when you reach the border," she says, voice low, urgent. "Not before. They'll last a day—no more. Each holds a whisper of poison, enough to pass as one of them. But one dose only. More than that, and you won't come back the same. You'll become them. The third is for Olivia. Mask her, when you run."

The ancient map of Puinnsean lies etched in my mind, lines blurred from too many desperate hands. The prison waits somewhere in its jagged teeth of ink. Centuries of fear have kept it shrouded. We walk in blind.

We exchange silent nods—the kind that carry iron vows. Blood ties. Promises you don't speak aloud because the words might break them.

Jeyr's gaze lingers last, pressing against me like a question I can't bear to answer.

I don't look back.

My mind is already walking the dark.

The acrid tang of the vial hits like a fist to the throat—metallic burn searing my tongue until my taste buds beg for mercy. I growl into the link, spitting the disgust straight at the others.

Poison, Cay, Lorkan's dry wit flickers through. *Not meant to be a fine vintage.*

The witch can morph armor, I snap back, swallowing the bitter film, *but apparently not palates.*

He snorts—humor threaded thin. *Ever consider you might have a drinking problem?*

Immortal, I answer, a hair too sharp. *Problem? Don't make me laugh.*

Mm. A discussion for later.

Later will never arrive, I mutter, picturing myself lost in some endless tavern, drowning nerves in cheap liquor and better silence.

Jet cuts through the noise, voice flat and final. "Time is not on our side."

His light rolls over us—cool, smooth—shrouding our forms like mist on midnight glass. It settles against my skin, invisible as breath, but my blood keeps thrumming a low drumbeat. I was never made for blindfolded games. This mission is a knife edge; the board keeps shifting under our feet. Strategy feels like a ghost we can't catch.

We reach the Flavian entrance—limestone arches rising like bone from the earth, the jagged silhouette of Puinnsean clawing at the canopy above. Ivy drapes the edge of the Kingdom like a noose. Guards flank each column, humanoid but wrong—carved from stillness, yellow eyes like dying stars. Their gazes sweep the trees. When they near us, every muscle in me locks; my lungs pause mid-breath. Their eyes pass... then linger. Fix. Pin.

A steady palm presses the back of my neck. I hold on to it like a rope and slip into the nearest mind.

He sees trees. Empty woods. Nothing out of place. No shimmer. No slip. Just silence.

I exhale slow. The hand leaves. Cold rushes in to take its place. Something in the air shifts—not seen, not touched, but felt.

I don't look back.

The ward's veil slides over us—silk pulled tight, breath caught mid-chest. Shadows ripple along the archways like silent sentries. Pine thins from the air, replaced by a heavy floral sweetness that clings to tongue and teeth. Too thick. Too bright.

A shiver runs through Lorkan—not fear. Distaste. *My cat doesn't like this,* he mutters. *Makes my throat scratch.*

A huff pulls at my mouth

My fingers had remembered the lay of his black pelt from high-country walks: groves and clover, quiet and wind. He had let me in, once—let me feel what it was to run with ancient precision, to see like a creature made for hunting gods. Even in skin, he had moved the same—silent, sleek, full of intent. A man made of instinct and rhythm. And I had never quite learned how to look away.

We crest a hill; sunlight spills like poured gold. Daffodils punch up in yellow ranks, bowing in the breeze. I pass a hand through the petals as if they might answer.

Behind me: tap—tap—tap. Lorkan's panther paws dance backward in irritated hops. Tail lashes. Nose twitches. Upper lip curls; a rasping cough tumbles out.

"What is it?" *I ask, already half-smiling.*

He lurches, coughs. A blink—fur becomes bare skin; he's bent at the waist, dragging air back into his lungs. "Fucking pollen," *he rasps.* "Cat didn't like it. Give me a sec."

I crouch, a useless hand hovering over his back, biting down a laugh because even choking on flowers he's unfairly beautiful. He drags one steady breath, then another, eyes sharpening. Shadows crawl higher along the city's spine.

A beat later, feathers. He folds into a raven and leaps to my shoulder. I stroke along his side; silken pinions slide under my palm.

"Better?"

"Better. Cat's still mad."

The smile fades. Heat clings to me in Puinnsean—sweet and sick, coating the back of my tongue until every breath tastes of rot disguised as honey. We press into narrowing streets where the local tongue scrapes the air, guttural syllables rising like a chant with no beginning and no end. To our left, the ravine cuts through the city's spine, the river churning below, its banks lined with men in rough tunics who move beneath a sky that refuses to blink. Their faces look carved from stone, their eyes hollow as dried wells, and still their hands keep working, pushing carts, hauling ropes, faces blank as masks.

It's the silence that sinks its teeth in. Not the scrape of sandals on stone. Not the slap of water against walls. The silence of what is missing. No laughter drifting from a doorway. No lullabies hummed through an open window. No sharp rebuke of a mother scolding her child. No women. No children. Only men, laboring like ghosts who've forgotten they once lived.

Where are they? The thought throbs once, heavy and unwanted. I know better than to give it voice. Naming it would make it real.

Dusk bends the light into long bars across broken cobblestones, shadows stretching like chains that refuse to break. We're too far in to turn back now. Beneath my boots, the city's hidden heart pulses, beating us deeper into its chest.

There's no saving them, Cay, Lorkan's voice comes, quiet as a blade sliding free of its sheath.

I shrug his words off like rain off a worn cloak. If I let them in, they drown me.

We slip between limestone buildings half-swallowed by ivy, the remnants of their grandeur smothered beneath the green. Once, gold leaf kissed these walls, bright and brazen. Now vines eat it whole, as if the city itself has been consumed by its own hunger. The crowd thickens as we near the center. Voices stack like bricks, bodies pressing too close. Jet's cloak of light is fragile, delicate; it will only hold if we move together. So we do.

Instinct shifts me sideways, my arm brushing Lorkan's as I tuck his larger frame into the sliver of shadow between us, shielding him though he hardly needs it. Still—safe.

Our pace quickens. Every footfall feels too loud, every loose pebble beneath my boots tolling like a bell announcing our presence.

Ahead, the press of bodies swells. Brushing an armored shoulder is no longer a risk—it's a promise waiting to be kept.

Eyes, I send through the bond, sharp as thought. *We need a view.*

Lorkan's gaze catches mine, violet steady and unwavering, and a ghost of a smile tugs at his lips. *You've got this, Cay.*

Then he leaps. His body folds, shifts into a hawk, feathers streaked in deep brown that burn against the last of the light. One beat of his wings, and he is air itself. Reflex drags my eyes after him, the same as when we were boys, when his shadow was the only star I ever chased.

Beside me, Jethro slides forward, winnowing in quick, short bursts, scanning every corner, his eyes tracking the hawk overhead. The tension riding his shoulders is the same coiled weight riding mine—tight, relentless, ready to snap.

The castle cuts the sky in the distance—a jagged crown of limestone rising above the rooftops. Beautiful. Deadly. A temptation sharp enough to bleed me just for wanting it. I ache to be inside those walls, only to tear them down brick by brick.

But we veer east, pulled toward the steeper streets, toward the military base and the prison. The sun hangs low, its angle a cruel omen. Too late. Too little. Time sluices through clenched fists, slipping no matter how hard I hold.

I slip, arm brushing against the vine covered stone, "bloody nettle," I hiss as the sting sears across my skin, welts rising hot and red where the stone scraped me. The burn spreads, sharp as fire beneath the flesh, and I curse the weakness of being caught unguarded by something so small. One slip, one distraction—that is all it takes to unravel everything.

And then Jet is gone.

The space where he stood yawns empty, and dread punches straight through my ribs, hollowing me. I force myself into motion, shoving into the crush of bodies—hooded figures in Puinnsean armor, their helms devouring their faces until they are nothing but shadows with yellow eyes. The guttural churn of their tongue grates through the air, wrong in a way that scrapes against bone. Every brush of cloth feels like poison waiting to seep into my skin, every breath a trap poised to undo me.

Where are you, Jet?

The crowd blurs—ash, steel, faceless bodies pressing too close. My pulse is a drumbeat that drowns thought, my vision narrowing until all I see is threat.

Then a voice cuts through it, rasping and cruel, like rusted metal dragged over stone. "Well, well... what delightful prey have we stumbled upon?"

Cold steel slides against my throat, precise and unhurried, and the scent that rises makes my stomach turn. Ammoniac, sharp—mouse piss.

Hemlock.

Fear coils hot and savage in my gut. This is not the place. Not *this way. Not yet.*

I hurl myself at his mind, only to slam against walls—brutal, unyielding, trained for this very resistance. I shove harder, scraping along the edges, searching for fissures, for anything I can pry open. A splinter-thin crack appears, and I force myself into it. His wrist jerks. The blade falters, only slightly—but it's enough. My hand seizes his, forcing inch by inch, muscle straining against his own.

Footsteps echo closer. Reinforcements. No time. I dig deeper, the blade trembling sideways until the edge skims his own throat. One more push, one more breath—

And the sky itself falls.

A hawk plummets from above like a hurled spear, wings slicing the dusk. Lorkan slams into the Fae with brutal precision, talons raking the throat wide open. Blood erupts hot, spraying the cobblestones, steel clattering as the soldier gurgles and collapses, his body folding into the stones as if swallowed whole.

I stagger back, lungs dragging air in ragged bursts, my heart hammering too fast for rhythm. Lorkan lifts his head, eyes burning feral-bright in the dying light, his feathers streaked crimson. For a heartbeat he holds me there in his gaze, wild and unrelenting—then he launches skyward once more, wings carving the dusk until he's nothing but shadow against the horizon.

Always leaving. Always returning when I need him most.

"Jethro! Where are you?!" The words rip raw from my throat, fire kindling across my forearms to mirror the chaos tearing through the streets. A hawk-screech slashes the din,—Lorkan's cry guiding me toward a narrow cut of shadow between the buildings.

There is no room for hesitation. I run, boots hammering stone, a dagger flashing underfoot. I scoop it up as I pass, the hilt a familiar curve against my palm, sheathing it with a soldier's instinct even as the shouts of pursuit rise behind me. The hemlock bastard has friends—*of course he does.*

Lorkan wheels overhead, one wing tilted in sharp command. I winnow toward the alley, magic fizzing across my skin—straight into arms that close tight around me. I brace to fight until his scent hits, halting me in an instant. Jet.

His eyes rake over me like a comrade checking kit, swift and clinical. Satisfied, he gives a single nod before yanking us through space again—higher, into another seam of shadow carved into the hillside. Below us, the city howls with sirens and shouts, the sound rising like a tide. An invisible clock ticks in my ears, each beat matched by the pounding of my own heart.

Light thins.

A shadow cleaves my path—Lorkan's wings slicing the dusk. He circles tight; his call rings sharp over the slopes. Even from above, his disapproval warms my skin like a brand.

Told you—sleeves! his voice to my mind, dry as ever. *That rash spells idiot from a mile up.*

I glance down. Nettles tattoo my forearm in angry welts. I'd stopped feeling them but at his reminder. they sting anew.

Just a scratch, I lie.

Scratches turn nasty faster than you can say wounded prey. Do me a favor, Caomh—stay alive.

I can't help the grin. *I'll manage if you do, Lor.*

He tips a wing—a begrudging salute—and rides a higher current, a shadow swallowed by the sky.

We keep moving.

The trail narrows to a scar across the mountain's face, thorn and stone clawing at our legs. Shadows stretch long from peaks tall as old gods. The castle is a memory behind us. Ahead waits the edge of the kingdom, the edge of knowledge, and the place no one enters and no one leaves, Puinnsean Prisons.

I steal a look up—Lorkan knives between clouds. Beside me, Jethro moves silent and sharp, breath steady, shoulders wired. We don't speak. Words would only load the air.

The sun slips. Light drains.

Something stirs below, but we can't stop to see what is happening.

Olivia

INVOCATION

I sit in the cell, legs curled beneath me, arms wrapped around my ribs like they might hold me together, and I wonder—truly wonder—how the fuck I'm supposed to get out of here. I spent weeks planning my escape from Tierney, clawing through scraps of information, listening to whispers behind half-closed doors, memorizing faces, steps, rhythms in the way the guards moved. I had the resources, the resolve, the desperation dressed up as courage. Back then, I thought being stuck in that manor was hell—trapped in velvet and stone, gilded lies and cruel smiles.

But this?

This is something darker.

This is the beast that sits beneath hell and calls it mercy.

And now I'm here, pressed up against the cold of a cell that groans when it breathes, beside a woman who hums with power too still to name, who I have somehow—gods help me—promised to escape with... and I have no fucking plan left.

How long have you been in here? I ask the question into the dim, not sure I want the answer. The silence that follows stretches, folds, pulls tight like a thread drawn through skin. So long I begin to think she's fallen asleep. Or worse—that she's never been real at all.

Since birth.

My breath hitches in my throat.

The words aren't dramatic. They don't carry weight in their sound. But the feeling—the way they crawl through the stone and coil into my spine, thick with regret, shame, grief that's gone stale from being buried too long—it tells me everything I need to know. Her birth was a lifetime ago. Longer than mine. Longer than most. And she has never left.

Why haven't you escaped?

The question tastes bitter in my mouth. It sits wrong in the air. Another pause blooms, and my heart picks up, thudding hard enough I wonder if Jeyr can feel it from wherever he is. My mind spirals—into the future, into the unending grind of years spent here. Cold nights that crack your bones, blistering days that boil your skin. The shivering, the sweat, the stink of myself no longer my own. The acid tang of fear baked into my senses until I forget the scent of rain or fresh air or anything soft. The idea that this could be it—that I could fade like she did—is enough to make me shake.

I have one thing that separates me from them, Olivia.

Her voice is quieter now. Measured. *One secret. And if I reveal it, I might have a chance. But even then... they will overpower me. They'll drag me back. Bind me not out of hate, not for justice—but for curiosity. I won't be a prisoner. I'll be an experiment more than I already am. Not faith. Not hope. Just alchemy.*

I close my eyes.

I know what it is to carry a secret that feels like a storm barely held behind your ribs. But Lia... Lia speaks like she was born with her storm already caged, learned silence before language, and has been holding it back longer than I've been alive.

With your power, Olivia, I can get out of here.

Her voice is still soft, but beneath it is steel. *We just need a moment. A single opening. If they open the gates, your power will stretch. You'll reach further than the cell. You can take down the guards—before they remember to drug you again.*

My pulse skips.

Because they will, she says, sharper now, more certain. *They'll poison you. Keep you quiet. Keep you locked away under layers of sedation. But they haven't yet. And there's a reason.*

My fingers trace the cracks in the stone. Everything feels suspended. As if the cell itself is listening.

Something is happening beyond these walls. I can feel it in the shift of the air, the pause in their routines. They're watching you. Not restraining. Not silencing. Which means they're waiting. For what, I don't know. But I know Bane. I know the King. They don't leave openings unless they're already closing them somewhere else.

I press my forehead to the wall, exhaling slow, steady.

I don't know why she's right. My mind still questions it, circles it like smoke. But my gut—the place where truth lives before it has words—says she is. And that means I have to do the one thing I haven't done in a long time.

Go in blind. Wait for an opening. Take it when it comes. No plans. No patterns. Just presence and instinct and timing.

It reminds me of wandering the streets of the Black Forest, cloak drawn tight against the mist, letting the pull of other people's pain guide me. Letting the ones who needed me find me. I didn't chase. I listened. I waited.

Now, my fingers trail across the stone, mapping the tiny peaks and scars etched into the wall like ancient runes. As if the ridges and cracks might whisper something back. As if the walls remember more than we do. But all they give me is the echo of what's already been lost. Pain pressed into stone. A winter without sunlight.

Then—

I feel them.

Before the scuff of boots. Before the drag of metal across gravel. Before the torches cast flickering shadows through the dark.

It starts in my bones.

It's time.

Lia's voice is dull on the surface, but underneath it hums something sharp and sweet—like citrus bursting in the back of your throat. Her excitement hums from her cell in warm, pulsing waves. Tangerine.

I reach out with my senses, brushing against the air beyond the stone. Five men. Four of them flat, predictable—dull as the rock I've memorized day after day. But the fifth... he is different.

He carries winter in his wake.

Not the punishing cold of cruelty, but the kind that stings your cheeks after too long indoors. The kind that makes you feel awake. Alive.

Recognition curls low in my belly. Dread follows, heavy and deliberate—not because of who it is.

But because of why he's here.

I force myself not to move. Not to pace. Not to press my face to the bars like I need confirmation of what I already know. I stay still, fingers pressed against the stone between me and Lia, as if we're both standing there—palms flat on opposite sides of the same breath. Granite miles thick. But somehow, we're touching.

Then he appears.

Emerging from the dark, firelight catches his features like the gods themselves are trying to paint him cruelly. The torchlight dances across the angles of his face, shadows cast by the hands of the men who surround him.

Colden.

He's held between four guards—if you could even call them that. More creature than man, their Puinnsean armor turns them into hollow vessels, faceless and stiff, like they've been carved from the same stone as the city. They hold him up like a prize. Or a warning.

At first, his eyes are empty—grey, unreadable. But then he looks at me.

Just for a breath.

A sweep from head to toe. Subtle. Calculated. The only thing he can give me. And it's enough.

Because beneath that blankness, I see it: the flicker. The fight. Resistance, banked low but burning.

And for that—I'm grateful.

One of the guards steps forward. The key slides from his belt, glinting with an unnatural shimmer as though it knows what it is—knows what it does. When it nears the lock, the air thickens. Hums. Old wards twitch awake. Sparks arc between key and iron gate, and the smell hits me: ozone, scorched magic, the scent of something ancient being broken open.

The lock exhales as it clicks, the sound sharp as a bone snapping.

That's my moment.

I bolt forward, slamming through the shift in the air where the wards once pressed. Something inside me—something I've starved and buried—snaps loose.

Power tears out of me. Raw. Wild. A wave sharp as rage, bright as fear. It crashes down the corridor, and the guards topple like brittle statues. Their grunts are cut short, stolen by silence as the magic wipes the air clean.

My hands shake when I seize the fallen keys. The metal burns cold against my palm, slick with sweat or blood—I can't tell. Beside me, Colden straightens, his storm-grey eyes fixed on the bodies sprawled at our feet.

"So, Liv," he says. His voice is dry, but too tight to be casual. "What's the plan now? Because if you don't have one... we're fucked."

I don't answer. Not yet.

Because my gaze has already shifted sideways—to the cell beside mine.

And she is there.

Sitting tall, back straight, pale hands folded with the calm patience of someone who's been waiting for centuries. Her hair is snow-white, spilling like silk over shoulders too still to be mortal. Skin smooth as glass. And her eyes—those eyes that glow faintly in the dim—fix on mine with cool amusement.

She doesn't smile. She doesn't need to. The way she looks at me—like she already knows how this story ends—is far more unsettling than a grin could ever be.

"Well?" she murmurs, voice silk dragged over broken glass. "Are you going to set me free?"

Her head tilts just enough to glance at Colden. I feel the change in him instantly—the way his muscles tense, the heat that ripples off him like steam. His worry isn't loud, but I *feel* it, curling through the air between us like smoke.

And then—I freeze.

Because I hear him.

Not spoken. Not through any bond. His thoughts. Clear. Unbidden. Thick with mistrust. Not of me. Of her.

His confusion ripples, sharp and raw, crashing into me like a stone thrown into still water. His eyes snap to mine, wide with shock. For all the time I've known him, his mind has been locked—a fortress, sealed and ironbound. And now it hums inside me, as though a door forgot to shut.

The question is etched into every twitch of his brow, every flicker of his gaze: *How did you do that?*

And beneath it, quieter, almost afraid: *Why now?*

I turn away before I can answer. Before I can even try. My eyes fix on the woman in the cell.

I move toward the bars.

Colden's hand closes around my forearm. Not harsh. Not restraining. Steady. Intent. A silent question: *Are you sure?*

His voice brushes low against my ear, rough and weighted.

Should you be letting them out? They're in here for a reason.

"I know." My whisper scrapes past the knot in my throat. I don't flinch from his grip. "But Colden... she's as meant to be in here as I am."

He studies me. Still thrown—by my words, by what I heard, by what I felt. Unsure if

I'm stepping into danger or if I've already become part of it. His grip lingers, heat biting into my skin.

And then—he lets go.

Slow. Deliberate.

That silence, that flicker of trust tangled in his confusion, is all I need.

I press the key into the lock.

The metal hums, alive, its vibration skating across my skin, raising goosebumps, singing along the fine hairs of my arms. The wards unravel in a rush, air surging like it's been holding its breath for centuries.

Click.

Final. Irrevocable.

And I stand frozen in its echo.

Then I feel it.

Not magic. Her.

The embrace comes first—arms around me, soft and startling, just for a second before the air shifts again, bending to her like it knows her name. She steps back, her eyes alight—glistening with something bright, unguarded. Almost childlike.

The change in her is so sudden it leaves me dizzy. One breath ago she was a ghost behind bars, all stillness and calculation. Now she vibrates with life, with joy, with something wild I can't quite name. We stand eye to eye for the briefest moment—two women bound, now two women breaking free.

Well... sort of.

The echo of boots slamming stone reminds me that freedom is never quiet. The sound is sharp. Pursuit. The escape hasn't ended. It's only just begun.

Colden's voice cuts through the air like a blade, urgent and close. "Go! Now!"

Lia grabs my hand. Her smile doesn't change, but something in it sharpens, and before I can speak, the ground vanishes beneath us.

We rise.

An invisible force launches us upward—no stairs, no effort—just motion. Wind rushes past, stone blurs beneath our feet. Panic clutches my chest as emotions pour from her in a storm of color and noise: wonder tangled with terror, awe threading through fear. Her magic is alive, untrained, thrashing through the space between us like lightning with nowhere to land.

"What was that?" she breathes, trembling. Her voice is small for the first time.

I swallow hard. My heart's still somewhere down below. "Winnowing," I say, steadier than I feel. "You think of where you want to be... and your power takes you there." I look at her—and really look—and for a second, I forget the danger. Her eyes shimmer like watercolor bleeding across a page, like someone discovering the sky after years in the dark.

And that's when it hits me.

I haven't just opened a cell door. I've unleashed something far more unpredictable. Something raw. Something hungry.

Lia's excitement sparks in the air, charged and unmistakable. She grins wide and sharp, her lips curling into a predator's promise. "Oh, I'm going to love this," she purrs—and then she's moving again, yanking me up another flight of stairs like gravity no longer applies.

Below us, Colden scrambles, his boots dragging over stone, eyes wide with a fear I know too well—not fear of failure, but of what we've just unleashed.

What... what is she? The words drift unbidden into my mind, fragile and shaken, not meant for me at all. Yet I hear them as clearly as if they were my own.

I stiffen. His thoughts brush mine raw and unfiltered, not spoken aloud, not carried on the bond, but sharp and foreign—loud without sound, heavy without weight. For a moment it unmoors me, like stepping too far into a current I hadn't known was there.

What's wrong? Is he a threat?

Lia's voice hums at the edge of me, a murmur twined with magic and motion, her concern—or her amusement—threading through every word. I shake my head before I can voice what I don't yet understand, turning just enough to glimpse Colden still following behind. His storm-grey gaze is fixed on her with a scrutiny that burns slow and deep—not on what she does, but what she *might*. And he isn't wrong to wonder.

She moves with the kind of grace that belongs to creatures who have never feared fire, her magic pulsing in quiet rhythms beneath her skin. There is a glint in her eyes that speaks of something more dangerous than mere power—something unpredictable—and I find myself hoping, foolishly, that the madness I sense in her is the kind that still carries a heart.

"Yes," I murmur, half to Lia, half to myself. "I heard his thoughts."

She exhales a long, dramatic sigh, her eyes rolling skyward as she prowls forward with effortless ease. "I told you you could do that," she says lightly. "Still, good job breaking through his little ice fortress of a mind. Too many walls in that one—it gives me a headache just thinking about it."

I open my mouth to reply, but the air shifts before I can. Torchlight flickers ahead, shadows stretching thin over the damp stone. The guards descend like a tide returning to shore, armor clanking, boots scraping, voices sharp with command. They halt when they see us—when they see *her*—as though the thought of their prisoners standing free has shattered something sacred.

And then chaos takes root.

Screams tear through the corridor as fire erupts beneath their feet, spiraling too fast, too precise, as though flame itself has chosen its prey. It climbs legs, wraps torsos, silk turned to scourge. Heat slams toward me in a living wave, violent and alive. I raise an arm to shield my face, but before the fire can consume me, Colden's arm snaps around my waist, hauling me back. His ice shields rise in a rush, encasing us in a cocoon of winter that hisses against the onslaught.

The guards' agony pierces me like venom, their pain clawing into my ribs until my knees threaten to buckle. I double over, vision blurring. And then Colden's power slips into me, cold and steady, a winter tide soothing the fever, his strength drowning the heat that seared through my veins.

He does not speak at first. But when he does, his voice is rough with awe and disbelief. "Gods above," he breathes, the dread tangled with reverence. "What is she?"

The moment blurs—the fire, the smoke, the screams—all tangled in the haze of power unchained. But beneath it, truth takes root in my gut with slow, cold certainty: the door I opened was never just an exit. It was an invocation. I didn't free a prisoner. I loosed something untamed.

The fire snuffs as suddenly as it had flared, leaving only silence and the stench of scorched flesh. Ash clings where men had stood, twisted remnants scattered on stone.

Lia turns, grinning wide and languid, the smile of someone finally permitted to play. "Problem solved," she purrs. "Let's go."

I cannot move—not yet.

Colden's voice presses back into my mind, softer this time but no less edged. *Who have you entangled yourself with, Olivia?*

The silence that follows is heavier than the ruin we leave behind. He doesn't speak again, but I feel his tension in the brush of his shoulder against mine, in the restraint of thoughts left unsaid.

Ahead, Lia moves quickly, bare feet slapping stone, white hair catching stray light as she approaches the final gate. Keys glint in her hand as though they've always belonged there. The lock yields with a groan just as the shouts of the upper guards filter down the stairwell.

"See?" she says brightly, her eyes gleaming like struck glass. "Wasn't that fun?"

It wasn't. The blood on my hands doesn't feel any lighter than hers. I reach for her anyway—not to stop her, but to steady her. A wash of calm rolls from me into her skin. She flinches, surprised, then softens, her posture loosening just enough to remind me there's a person beneath the power.

Colden nudges at my mind again, his tone edged with something that almost sounds like pleading. *Please keep doing that. She kind of scares me.*

And I almost laugh, because I've seen Colden walk through flames, stare monsters in the eye, and never once falter. Yet something in her unsettles him. Something unsettles *me.* The air around her hums like the world itself is bracing.

Each step upward brings louder sounds—boots pounding stone, orders barked in Puinnsean. Guards choke the passage ahead. Lia doesn't slow. She doesn't need to. Vines burst from the walls to snare them, frost crackles over armor, strange metals cage their limbs in silence. No screams, no blood. Just her will, reshaping the corridor with a terrifying ease.

Light seeps down through cracks above—soft, golden, brushing dust into threads of gold. It touches my face, loosening my chest. We're close. So close.

But the next wave hits. Dozens more, blades drawn, eyes wild. The corridor shakes with their approach. Lia tenses, violence sparking bright in her gaze. I act before she can.

My power unfurls like fog, creeping low and soft, wrapping the soldiers in invisible weight. Their steps falter, bodies swaying as sleep takes them one by one. They fold quietly, not slain, not torn apart, simply laid down by a gentler hand.

Lia bounces beside me, her smile sharp with glee. "Let's go! You can feel it, right? We're close."

And she's right. The end presses just ahead—the edge of stone, the end of silence, the promise of air untainted by ash.

Colden appears at my side, voice tight, urgent. "We have to move. Now."

I don't argue. Not because of what's behind us. But because of what I've brought with me.

Lia's gaze finds mine, pupils wide, rimmed in a plea she won't speak. "Show me where," she whispers, fragile as thread. "Pick somewhere safe."

The place spills out before I can stop it: sunlight through stained glass, a cliff kissed by wind, the echo of children's laughter, warmth by a hearth, the one presence that had made walls into home. I hadn't let myself remember, hadn't let myself *want*. But now it rises like a tide, breaking through.

The pull grips hard. The world splinters into color and motion, gravity gone, time unraveling. Colden's hand shoots out, his fingers locking around mine as the prison collapses behind us, falling away into nothing.

DOMINHAL AT THE GATE

I remain busy—the only thing I can do is keep my hands occupied, so I don't sit by the fire staring at my wrist for any sign that Olivia is alive, that she's feeling something. I never thought I would miss the time she was imprisoned by Teirney... but at least then I could feel her, even if her emotions were hard to handle, leaving me sick and shivering on the floor, worried beyond might that she might not come out the same. But I swore then, and I swear now, I don't care who she is when she comes out of this, as long as she's in my arms, alive. The rest we'll figure out together.

And yet... I let Lorkan go in my place. I battle with whether I made the right choice. All I can think is that having a shifter in my place would keep her safer. I'm a known man now—no longer the discarded son who spent his time in a tent healing soldiers, instead of on the covers of the press like my brother at my father's side. But now, I'm just as much a staple on those pieces of parchment, read and then used to bind the packages traded in the Great Kingdom. If I were seen, there's no doubt we would both be dead... after they played whatever tricks they had planned. And worse, if I were seen while Lorkan was posing as me... Olivia, nor Caomh, would ever forgive me for that.

The scratch of quill on parchment, the rustle of maps, the murmur of strategizing commanders—these are the sounds that do nothing to quell the worry in my mind. But what does is the sound of thundering footsteps. The boom of a too-heavy door forced open with a gust of wind.

"Jeyr, the King!" Aella gasps, her voice barely a whisper above a panicked shout. "He's on his way!"

The quill freezes in my hand, ink dripping a stain on the map that now holds a terrible new meaning. "How much time?" I demand, urgency replacing the calm rhythm of command.

"He's already at the border," she chokes, eyes wide, frantic.

The words cut through me like a blade. Gone is my map of where my brothers, my mate, might be. Thought collapses into a single instinct—move.

"Gather the commanders," I command, my voice sharper than steel. "War room. Now."

Aella nods once, regains her footing, and vanishes down the corridor.

By the time I step into the war room, the walls hum with dread. Commanders file in, armor whispering, boots heavy. Their faces mirror my own fear, though none of us dare name it.

I slam a hand onto the map stretched across the table, the inked mountains stark beneath my palm. "Here," I say, tracing the jagged edge where cliff meets sea. "There's a cove—hidden, shielded by the rock. A narrow way through the mountain that leads out past the border."

I pause, my jaw tight. "The King doesn't know of it. It was cut long ago, a path buried and forgotten—except by us. It's the only chance we have."

Their silence is brief, broken by curt nods. No hesitation. They disperse with speed, shadows peeling from the room.

Alone, I turn to the window. At first glance, the streets lie still. But then the glimmer—blades catching faint light, bodies moving swift and unseen. My people, trained to vanish, pouring through the fogged alleys in silence.

I brace my palms against the sill, call the storm inside me, and exhale. Fog unfurls into the streets, thick and heavy, curling like smoke into every corner. It cloaks the stone, the steel, the fear. A poor shield against a monarch who holds the kingdom's magic in his fist—but if it buys even a heartbeat of escape, it is enough.

I find myself by the gates of my court's town, knowing the men of my command are beside me, listening to the hush that blankets the world around us. The sound of retreat goes unnoticed, the air still, the vision low as fog curls through the streets like smoke from a dying hearth. I don't need to see the men beside me to know their expressions are grim reflections of what's coming. I feel it—like the sharp edge of a blade kissing skin, the kind of knowing that hums in the marrow before a storm breaks. Every hair on end, lightning threatening to leap from my veins.

Through the mist, he comes, the shadow who has haunted every step I've taken. He cuts through the fog with purpose, a dark figure pushing against the breeze I've conjured to buy our people time. My every instinct screams to strike him down, to unleash the fury building behind my teeth, but I hold. I hold for the lives slipping away behind us. I hold because their freedom is worth more than my rage.

"Something to hide, Young Duke?" he calls, voice sharp enough to slice bone. I straighten, jaw clenched, defiance wrapping around my spine like armor. "Nothing to hide, my King."

He doesn't even glance at me—just keeps walking. Like I'm a minor detail in his grand conquest, a stone in his boot he doesn't bother shaking out. His soldiers fan out like wildfire, and my heart drums a frantic rhythm as he lifts his voice. "Search every house, leave no stone unturned!"

They descend like crows on carrion—ripping doors from hinges, tearing through belongings, dragging people out by the wrists. The cries of my people echo through the streets, colliding with the crash of splintering wood. My guards don't draw blades, not to attack—but to shield. To intercept. To protect where I cannot.

Then I see it: the marble podium, gleaming like a tombstone beneath this leaden sky. The taste of iron floods my mouth. They drag forward two of mine—Tynon, rain-wielder, the shield who has held rivers at bay for my ranks, and Maros, water-bladed, relentless in every skirmish, his presence cutting as deep as his steel. Both known. Both proven. They marched into this war under my banner, and now they're herded toward slaughter like thieves in the night.

"My King," I say, my voice sand and stone, each word ground out through my teeth. "These men are not illegal."

Dominhal pauses mid-stride, silver hair catching what thin light seeps through the fog. He turns slowly, deliberate as a viper, until his shadow falls over Maros. He lifts a serpent-ringed finger and hooks it under Maros's chin, tilting his face upward. Those storm-bright eyes of Maros meet the King's with defiance that does not waver.

"No," Dominhal murmurs, his tone mockingly gentle, "but this one does not belong here."

I force my gaze to Tynon—broad-shouldered, steady, but his eyes betray him. Wide, frantic, begging me to intervene. Maros stands unflinching, and it is that stillness, that refusal to cower, that twists my gut. I know that look on Dominhal's face. The decision is already carved into stone. It has nothing to do with law.

"They are bonded, your Majesty and they are not a breeding pair," I press, every syllable clipped and cold. "Their union strengthens my command. I allowed it. It makes my army stronger."

A laugh slips from the King—hard, hollow, cutting through the silence like a blade. The kind of laugh meant to bruise. Tynon flinches. Maros does not. And that frightens me more than his Majesty's cruelty—because men who don't flinch are the ones Kings love to break.

"Not a breeding pair, you say?" Dominhal repeats, amusement curling around cruelty. "Oh, Grand Duke... you never fail to entertain me."

A movement behind them—then a woman is shoved forward, dropped hard to her knees. Her cry splits the air, sharp and human, before dissolving into silence. Tynon's sister. Her belly curves heavy with child, round and full, the accusation plain. A living testament to what these cobbles have endured.

My jaw locks. I force my eyes shut, but too late—the image brands into me, burned deep, carved there by helpless rage.

"This one," Dominhal drawls, his voice velvet over poison, "has played surrogate, wouldn't you agree, Grand Duke?"

His hand skims the swell of her stomach as though caressing the curve of a blade. A threat dressed in silk.

Tynon's strangled cry rends the air. Beside him, Maros finally turns, his head tilting just enough for their eyes to meet. No words. Just a look—pleading, desperate, a silent prayer across the executioner's block. Tynon's gaze flickers between his love and his sister, his whole body trembling with the violence of a choice he cannot make.

Dominhal crouches, his fingers locking cruelly beneath the woman's chin, forcing her head up. His voice drops, intimate and venom-soft.

"The child carries both abilities to wield the element of water, and the power of storms."

Tynon shatters.

"Don't you touch them!" he roars, raw and guttural, the cry of a man unraveling under grief and rage.

The sound tears through me. My fists clench. Power thrums under my skin, eager to answer. The fog thickens, heavy, waiting.

Dominhal rises, his gaze cutting to me, cold as polished steel.

"Grand Duke," he says, void of warmth, void of soul. "Exterminate the illegals."

Lorkan

THE LAST PROMISE

The sky screams above me, a discordant symphony of humanoid howls, blaring alarms, and the metallic clash of symbols calling soldiers to the shattered prison gates. Even with hawk feathers slicked tight to my frame, the sound scrapes at my senses, sharp and grating. My wings cut the air in steady rhythm, but my focus narrows, locked onto a shimmer darting along the jagged ridgeline. A flick of light. A flare off feathers. Fae.

Panic needles beneath my breastbone. Something's wrong. I feel it in the wind.

I bank sharply, climbing higher. The desolate plains unfurl below, Humanoids crawl free from the soil like maggots, limbs sloughing away as they rise. More spill from the prison mouth, a manic flood unleashed. I hold the wind, wings taut, heart thrumming, my body ready even if my mind isn't.

Stay hidden. At all costs. I send the thought down in hope that Jethro and Caomh listen. Not that Cay has ever listened to me in his life. Panic gnaws at the edges of my mind.

Something's unfolding, the unease echoed by Caomh's bristling senses.

Shifting my gaze, I scan our surroundings, sharing my view through the mental bridge of Caomh's making. Showing him, Banes Humanoid army funneling into the prison entrance we were hoping to enter unseen. More time—it's all I crave. Time to formulate a plan, to strategize, to just be able to *fucking stop* for a minute and assess what's going on in the prison before running in half mast and blind. The odds are stacked against us, thousands to our meager few.

With a caw that splits the cacophony, I dive, wings slicing through the press of bodies as I plunge into the heart of the mess. The humanoids falter at the sight of me, hesitation flashing in their eyes, but before they can recover, I vanish, feathers giving way to nothing but air.

At the entrance, power ignites. Jethro blinds them with a burst of searing light, dazzling enough to strip the shadows from the cavern walls, while Caomh moves with quiet precision, slipping his will into the minds of the guards until their limbs bend to him like puppets on fraying strings. Their cries rise sharp and ragged, echoing off the stone in a chorus of fear and confusion.

I press myself into the shadows, scales rippling over my skin as I take the form of a lizard, my body melting into the granite until I am nothing more than another piece of the cavern wall. My claws grip the rough stone, every ridge and fissure familiar beneath me as I scuttle down the spiraling stairs. Magic sparks in my veins with each breath, carrying me through the spaces between, winnowing in quick, silent bursts that keep me aligned with them

The guttural yells from below force another shift. Soundless wingbeats carry me to the cavern floor, where I hover just out of sight. Jethro, a wraith wielding an invisible blade, cuts down men with chilling efficiency. Caomh, no longer hidden, stands his ground against the tide of Humanoids flooding the entrance. I surge forward, scanning the cells, checking back on Caomh as he holds his ground, the throng thinning around him.

Reaching the end of the cell block, I find only emptiness. Two open cells stare back at me.

She isn't here. My voice cuts through the chaos.

Then that's what triggered the alarm—the princess escaped, Caomh voice grim in my mind.

We need to get out of here. Now. My thoughts scream urgency.

Without waiting, I dive into the mob of Humanoids, shifting once more. My form ripples, mimicking the mindless bodies around me, blending into the battle. "Take this!" Caomh's voice is by my ear, his back to mine. The weight of the blade, the coolness of the metal against my skin, there was a certain rightness to it, like the touch of a loved one after a long time alone. A creature lunges with a slavering snarl and the blade finds meat. The sound that rips from its throat is a sound I do not know how to name; it is keening and tearing all at once, and the thing dies in a foxfire of ash at my boots. The air tastes of metal and something like old rain.

Heavens above, what is this? I ask, a mix of fear and morbid curiosity keeping me clutching what can only be described as a death blade.

I don't know, but if it keeps you alive, I'll kiss the blade in thanks. Caomh's thoughts are laced with a tone I haven't heard from him before.

I find myself turning, eyes drawn to his profile—drawn to the glimmer of golden flames striking over his jaw, the slight bump in his nose, and those small, almost invisible scars I've memorised like constellations. Marks I've counted in silence like freckles meant only for me.

Lost in him, I flinch as his voice yells through my mind. *To your left!*

The blade sings as I swing, another screech echoing as it grazes another humanoid. The handle, already warm, pulses with an eerie heat, its gold and silver now glowing red-hot. Jet materializes beside me, his back a solid wall against the tide of enemies.

"We need to winnow out of here, Jet, there are too many of them. " I say between the death dagger disintegrating humanoids an arm length from me.

"I know, but how far could she have gone? She can't winnow." Jet grits out.

"I don't know, but if we escape, I can patrol from the skies."

"Okay, Cao, you ready?" Jet calls, his voice strained. I feel his muscles tense against my back, preparing to initiate the winnow.

"Cao?" Jet's question pierces through my focus, and I spin around, heart pounding. But where I expect to see Cay, a few steps behind me, gracefully dispatching Humanoids, there is only empty space. It has been mere moments since he thrusted me with the blade, *just moments* since I last saw him.

Cay's voice cracks through the din, a desperate plea: *Get out, get out now!* I spin around, heart sinking as I see the looming figure behind the horde of Humanoids. Pure white hair glows eerily against the sickly green gas billowing from him, tendrils creeping up the cavern walls like grasping fingers. Caomh presses on, his strikes precise but labored, his victims sluggish puppets under his control.

I'm not leaving without you! I roar, charging forward, chest pounding. A hand snatches mine, and I whirl, ready to attack, only to find Jet, his eyes pleading—not the plea I want to see.

Go, Mo Chuisle. Caomh's voice is rough, strained in my mind. *Save our princess. Keep my promise.*

The name hits like a fist. I don't want to hear it, not now, not as the ground crumbles beneath him.

Mo ghràdh, I can't lose you.

Mo Chuisle, he repeats, softer now, *you will always have me. The same way you always have. Save her for me.*

I lunge, ignoring his plea. He won't die—not on my watch. But before I can reach him, his figure blurs, dissolving into the green mist. I cry out, a mixture of grief and fury, but it is swallowed by the gas. The last thing I see in the fading light is Cay's face, contorted in pain, as the poisonous tendrils engulf him.

Cay. Is gone. Sacrificed to buy me time. Rage wells up, bitter and hot, but beneath it simmers a chilling emptiness. He is my anchor, my balance, and now he is gone, leaving me adrift in a sea of chaos.

But his words echo in my mind, his sacrifice demanding action. Save her. Our princess. It's all I have left. With a final, choked sob, I turn away, the princess's name a mantra on my lips. Escape. Find her. Survive.

Then find my Mo ghràdh.

Olivia

SALT AND SANCTUARY

The coastal wind plays its familiar tune, weaving through my hair as Lia's laughter carries on the salt-kissed air. Warm sunlight bathes the world in gold, the comforting scent of salt and pine chasing away the ghosts of burnt flesh and bloodstained memories. A shrill shriek, joyous and unexpected, shatters my introspection. Lia, a tempest of boundless energy, rockets past, leaving a trail of sand and excitement in her wake. Bare feet dance on the warm earth, skin kissed by the sun, and the waves provide the rhythm for her uninhibited escapade.

She twirls, spinning a story with her hands, mimicking the waves, the wind, the very essence of the moment. Her hair, a silken cascade, trails behind her, rising and falling like the tide's breath. The kaleidoscope of her eyes mirrors her thoughts, each colour a fleeting glimpse into the vibrant chaos within. I, caught in the whirlwind of her exuberance, watch as she becomes one with the elements. The wind, stirred by her dance, turns partner, lifting her hair and swirling sand around her ankles.

"Oh my gods, this is amazing!" Lia's voice soars, harmonizing with the ocean's song. In that moment, surrounded by the raw beauty of the coast and Lia's unbridled embrace of life, the prison's darkness fades, replaced by the vibrant magic of the present.

"She is..." Colden's voice hums beside me, filled with the same awe blooming in my chest. He doesn't need to finish the sentence. We both know—Lia is something extraordinary. A force of nature, barefoot and wild-eyed.

But beneath the surface of our wonder, a shadow lingers. Is this joy her shield? A fragile veil draped over all she's endured? How long, I wonder, can light burn this bright before the dark tries to claim it? The questions swirl through me like seafoam, unanswered melodies that drift in the tide. For now, I let myself get swept away in her laughter, letting the worries ebb with the waves. Perhaps even shadows can dance, if only for a little while.

Her whirlwind quiets, and calm settles over the water and sand. She turns to me, windblown and glowing, a smile radiant enough to hold back the dusk. "Gods, Olivia," she breathes, voice like birdsong, "has the world always been this beautiful?" The mischief is gone from her eyes, replaced with depth, an ocean's worth of voices layered into one singular gaze.

"Beauty and death, hand in hand?" I reply, letting the words hang like incense smoke between us. She laughs at that, her sound finding something beautiful in the ache of contrast.

She wanders back toward the water, and I let her go, watching as her fingers skim the surface like she's reading the language of the sea. My gaze strays, unbidden, to the familiar cliff face beyond, the edge of home. A sob curls up my throat, but I press it down, wrapping my arms tight across my chest. *Home.* Gods, how that word hurts. How it heals.

"Olivia! Come feel this!" Lia calls. She's waist-deep now, her dress caught in the water's pull, swirling like seaweed around her legs. A smile unfurls across my face, unforced. Somehow, impossibly, this girl is a mirror of something I thought I'd lost in the wreckage.

As the sun dips low, its light fading across our faces, Lia turns back with the sadness of a child being called inside after a day of play. "It's time, isn't it? To keep moving?" she asks. I nod, and with her warm hand in mine, we leave the shore behind, our footprints trailing through the sand. Colden follows, his silent presence steady at our backs. The sun will rise again, painting a new dawn, perhaps a future we can't yet imagine. But for now, the warmth beneath our feet and the echo of Lia's laughter are enough. I am home, and even with its shadows, the journey is only just beginning.

The Manor comes into view, a stark silhouette framed by the softening light. A blur of grey and white charges toward me, and I bury my face in my hands as tears finally break free. "Ky!" I choke out, my voice thick.

Lia and Colden tense, but I quickly lift my head. "He's a friend. Hurt him, and you'll regret it." Their stances ease as Kyzan reaches me, his massive frame towering, his fur warm and familiar. His whiskers tickle my cheeks.

livy, livy, livy, my alpha is home, alpha is home, his voice chants in my mind, a telepathic rhythm of joy.

Kyzan? I pull back, meeting his golden gaze.

Alpha! The surprise in him is unmistakable. OH MY GOD, I can hear you.

Wonder ripples through me. I can feel them in you, he continues.

Feel who, Ky?

Lady Avery and Lady Clarity.

I blink rapidly, confusion bleeding into awe.

Their essence, their power. You set their souls free, but something stayed behind, Kyzan answers as if reading my thoughts. Not them... but echoes. Resonance. Their knowing.

He nuzzles my shoulder, steady and sure, and suddenly everything feels too loud, too bright, like I'm hearing with more than ears, feeling with more than skin.

The thunder of hooves shatters the stillness. Ness arrives, a storm of bay fur and black mane circling the Manor.

"Is that creature a friend too?" Lia asks, her voice trembling.

I nod and rise, racing to Ness as she skids to a halt. I wrap my arms around her strong neck, burying my face in her soft fur. Her rumbling welcome vibrates through me like a song I forgot I knew. She breathes against my cheek, warm and grounding.

My queen, I have been so worried, Ness's voice is deep and otherworldly. I begin to shake my head, but she cuts me off. Don't deny it. You have her power, and her mates'. You carry the power of mind and soul.

My hand trembles as I reach for the scar on my chest, the mark left by the blade that once bound me. So much has changed since my capture. So much I still don't understand. The world hums beneath my skin, whispers that weren't there before pressing against my mind.

There is much you need to know, Ness continues, her thoughts laced with urgency. Things that will change everything.

A shiver races down my spine. Change everything? But before I can ask, a surge of emotion crashes over me — fear, anticipation, and a raw, wild sense of purpose. It calls to me now. It is sanctuary, Home that has been adrift and so out of reach.. until now.

Ness paints the image in my mind, the Kings plan to execute anyone he didn't class as 'normal.' The Grand Duke and Duchesses' to be the wielder of the blade. "Does she speak of the Jeyr?" Lia's voice floats behind me, wary. I take her hand and offer it to Ness, who lowers her head to sniff. Her eyes widen, then she steps back.

Ness lowers her great head, her eyes sharp and assessing as they sweep over Lia. *She is a tempest of power,* the mare says into my mind, *a storm that would break lesser souls.*

Lia does not flinch beneath the weight of the words. She lifts her chin, shoulders squaring as if she has carried such judgments her whole life. Her pale hair whips in the wind, but her voice is steady, cool as cut stone. "Then they will learn not to underestimate me."

The silence that follows is alive, heavy with the kind of recognition that cannot be bought or begged. I watch her, remembering the girl I first saw in that cell, still as marble, quiet as shadow. What stands before me now is no ghost. She holds herself like a queen who has decided the crown is already hers.

Ness stamps her hoof, the sound a sharp crack against the earth. Not rejection. Respect. *Confidence does not equal control,* she warns, though her tone is no longer edged with doubt.

Lia's lips curve, her smile both precise and certain. "Control will come. It always does when the will is strong enough."

Colden turns to Lia as if offering a trivial courtesy, curiosity sparking at the edge of his face.

"So, *Lia*—does that shorten something longer?" His voice is casual; his eyes are not. I watch her toy with the syllable as if weighing a blade, the small tremor in her fingers saying more than any answer.

"Amiliana, she supplies, slow and precise—"that's what my father called me."

The name strikes Colden like a thrown stone. The way his shoulders knot, the way his face hollows. Me? I am in that too-bright sitting room in a blink: lace curtains that move when no wind stirs, the smell of whiskey and older secrets. My throat tightens around a memory that tastes like iron. My eyes scan her; at the woman my mate was going to marry.

Her voice slips into me, younger than she is, frayed at the edges, *Don't take me back to him.*

It isn't something I hear so much as feel. The raw scrape of fear in her chest presses into mine, trembling through me like a plucked string. No lie could echo that true.

And yet, she holds her head high. Regal, defiant. As if the tremor running through her veins does not exist. I ache watching it, because I know the weight of pretending. I know what it is to walk tall when your strength feels like it might shatter with the next step.

My pulse stutters. Colden's protest flickers sharp in my mind, but I push it aside. We have only just left the husk of Bane's pawn behind, and now his daughter is here—her shadow woven with ours. Enemy, some part of me insists. Enemy, and yet... I do not let her go.

Perhaps it's foolishness. Perhaps it's that bone-deep intuition I can never name until too late. Or maybe it's the part of me that always reaches, even for the broken things I should not trust.

So I reach for her hand. It's colder than mine, but her fear hums through it, alive, and something in me answers. My voice is softer than I mean it to be, but it burns all the same.

"I will never let him have you."

L'orkan

WINGS OVER EMPTY GROUND

The mountain air cuts sharp, thin in my lungs as Jet pushes through the pass. Loose stone grinds beneath his boots, each step measured, heavy. I cling to his shoulder, talons buried deep in the leather of his coat. Neither of us speaks. The silence is louder here, where the wind howls against the cliffs and the sanctuary waits somewhere beyond.

Ahead, the trail narrows. The air shifts. Jeyr stands there, framed by jagged rock and mist. His cloak is thrown over travel leathers, his eyes hollowed with waiting. He doesn't look at Jet first—he looks at the space beside him. The emptiness where Cay should be. Where Olivia should be.

The silence stretches, brittle as ice ready to crack.

"Please," Jeyr says, the word pulled raw from his chest. "Tell me he got her away. That he took her somewhere safe. Tell me they're both alive."

The plea tears through me, leaves me gutted. My talons sink deeper into Jet's shoulder, my throat burning with a cry I can't release. But Jet finds his voice before I do.

"They have Caomh." His words scrape low, tight as wire. "Olivia ran—set the alarms off. But Bane reached him first. We couldn't stop it."

The mountain wind surges, scattering the words between us, but the damage is done. Jeyr staggers as if struck, his hand drifting to his wrist, a gesture so small it shouldn't matter. But it does. Gods, it does.

I can't stand it. His pain mirrors mine too closely, sharp as the air in my lungs. With a cry I bury deep in my chest, I rip myself skyward. Wings slice through the cold, beating hard against the wind. The mountains blur beneath me, but nothing I do can outpace the storm inside.

Cay is gone, sealed behind a poisoned border I cannot break.

And Olivia—

Where in all the gods' cursed realms is she?

Olivia

The Woman Who Returns

I can't believe my eyes.

Gasps echo around me, bouncing off the walls and crashing into my ears like waves. "Livy!" The name rises from a dozen voices, colliding into one breathless, joyous cry. I clap a hand over my mouth to stifle the startled squeak that threatens to escape. On the staircase landing, Claudia's expression mirrors my disbelief—her jaw working soundlessly as she stares.

Then it happens.

A dozen tiny tornadoes explode from below, limbs and laughter and shrieks of delight as the kids rush me, all at once. Their arms wrap around me, tight and fierce, their love so immediate, so total, it almost knocks me off my feet. I want to shrink away, I'm a mess: tangled hair, dirt-smudged skin, the scent of battle and fear clinging to me like a second skin, but they don't care. Their arms anchor me. Their joy strips away the grime and guilt, like sunlight dissolving shadow.

Then another sound...softer, older, deeper. A cry from the stairs. I turn just as she rushes forward.

Mary.

She pushes gently through the children and I fall into her arms like gravity's pulling me home. I hold her too tight, the tears finally breaking free, pouring hot and fast down my cheeks. "I'm so sorry," I choke, my voice strangled with guilt. "It's all my fault. Everyone—"

She sobs against my neck, her tears thick and mauve, streaking down to stain us both. Grief upon grief.

"He would've done it a thousand times," she whispers, her voice breaking with every word. "If it meant you'd find your way back."

The words are meant to comfort, but her eyes—gods, her eyes—hold the same hollow ache that gnaws at my chest. A name I had locked away in my cage claws itself free: *Cooper.* I had refused to think of him, knowing the ruin it would bring. And now, faced with her, I realize I never once imagined what she would be without him.

Guilt coils alive and cruel in my stomach. I had barely given her a thought in the months he was gone. I shake my head, drinking her in—the deeper lines carved into her face, the hollow bruises beneath her eyes. But still... still there is light. A flicker, simmering, and it is for me. Even now, when I do not deserve it.

The room quiets. Our grief drifts into the silence, settling like dust on every surface. I lift my head just as Claudia ushers the children into the kitchen, their laughter trailing after them like ribbons of sound.

Mary steps back, her hands shaking as she wipes her cheeks. Her gaze returns to me, gentler now, though shaded with something else.

Her eyes flick past my shoulder, "Who are your friends?" she asks.

Introductions flow like a strained melody, Lia and Colden's names spoken with the weight of what's left unsaid, the truth of who they are, where they've come from, and how their stories are now tangled with mine. The manor seems to listen, each syllable echoing down its bones, curious, cautious. As I lead them upstairs, the whispers begin to rise—soft at first, then swelling like breath held too long. The air thickens, turning into a chorus of Jeyr's ghost. His embraces, his murmured promises... they cling to me like cobwebs, delicate and impossible to shake. Memory pulls at me from the corners of each room. Secrets wait behind every door, and this house—this house remembers. It's determined to make me remember too.

I settle Colden into one of the guest rooms, Lia into another. And then I'm alone. Drifting.

The hallway stretches out before me like a spine of memory, and I find myself at the far end, staring at the oak door of what used to be ours. My chest tightens, my breath coming too fast, heart pounding loud enough to drown thought. One tear slips free, cold, sharp and carves a line down my cheek.

His scent hits me before I even touch the handle. *Jeyr.* That familiar blend of Storms and coastal air something uniquely his. It wraps around me like a phantom touch, and the glamour I wear shatters under its weight. I see it then—those vibrant cords of energy, the ones that bind us. They blaze in the air between us, even stretched across kingdoms, pulsing at my core.

I push the door open. The room exhales with me, sighs with me, and I stumble inside like I've crossed into a sanctuary and a grave all at once. The bed waits, neatly made, untouched. My legs give out before I mean them to, and I collapse onto the surface, tugging at the tightly drawn blankets until I can bury myself inside. The fabric still smells of him. Salt on skin. Air after rain. Him.

I wrap myself tight, cocooned in the weight of it all, and for one night I let myself pretend. That he's beside me. That if I turn just right, I'll feel his arm slip heavy around my waist, his breath against the nape of my neck. That his warmth hasn't vanished into silence and shadow.

Memories rise, unbidden. His laughter against my ear. The way his eyes softened when they found me across a crowded room. The steady rhythm of his chest beneath my cheek when I was too restless to sleep. I hold them close, finally letting them burn through me, as though by remembering I can keep him here.

Tears soak the pillow until I can no longer tell where I end and the ache begins. Exhaustion drags me under, and at last I sleep—fitful, uneasy, but closer somehow. Closer in the ache, closer in the scent he left behind. My hands reach for the hollow where his body should be, searching for him even in dreams.

The emptiness does not lift. It settles with me, heavy, unyielding, a distance I cannot cross, no matter how tightly I hold the blankets, no matter how desperately I breathe him in.

I wake to silence. The sheets are smooth beneath my palms, the bed too neat, too still. My body feels heavy, raw, my eyes swollen from the tears I hadn't meant to shed. For a long moment I sit on the edge of the mattress, staring at the floorboards, until a thought cuts through the haze.

Change.

The word hums in my chest, steady and sure. I rise, pulling on a simple shift, and pad down the hallway barefoot. The manor sleeps on around me, shadows long and unbroken, no footsteps but my own.

The kitchen is cold, the hearth dark. I strike flint to flame, coaxing a small light to life before setting to work. My hands move with purpose, pulling jars and bundles from high shelves: dried walnut hulls, a twist of sage, a flask of sharp vinegar. Supplies once meant for preserving, for steeping, now pressed into another kind of service.

I crush the hulls in a mortar, the pestle steady in my grip. Their earthy scent rises, staining my fingertips, thickening the air with something bitter, grounding. Vinegar hisses as I pour it in, the powder darkening, slick and heavy as mud. I crumble the sage last, releasing its sharpness into the mixture, a whisper of cleansing smoke before the basin of hot water draws it all together into a dye the color of earth after rain.

I gather the bowl in my arms and climb the stairs again, the steam curling up into my face as if trying to veil me already. In the washroom mirror, my reflection waits—hair falling in fiery waves down my back, too bright, too wild, too much of the girl I was.

The mirror holds a strange truth. The woman staring back is me, heart beating, eyes blinking, yet with each glance she feels like a stranger wearing familiar skin. Like a limestone cliff weathered by relentless waves, I have been sculpted, eroded, hardened. I am still evolving. I may be slender, but my eyes burn now with something new: purpose.

The scissors gleam in my hand, poised to shear away the weight of waist-length hair in one clean cut, when a voice slices through the stillness.

"Let me.".

My breath holds as she approaches, her gaze catching on the scars across my back. Her hands are steady, practiced from years of craft, yet her lip trembles between her teeth. She tries to hide it, the ache she feels at the sight of me, tries to hold her strength as she takes the scissors in hand. Once, those same hands would braid my hair by the fire in our cottage. I see it in her eyes, the memory she clings to—the little girl I used to be, blissfully naïve, untouched by what was to come.

She gathers the first strand. The snip of the blades cuts through the silence, sharp and final. Then her voice, quiet and sure, fills the room.

"When I was a wee girl, younger than you, I had the longest blonde hair. My ma and pa used to marvel at it, and braiding it was my mother's favorite pastime. But when they passed, I could not stand the sight of it. Every strand held their ghost. Every time I touched it, I felt their fingers in mine, and it broke me. It was Cooper who cut it for me, much like this. And he never threw it away. When I was ready, when I could finally stand to visit their graves, he let me bury my hair where they lay. So I could be with them in a way. Morbid, perhaps..." She shrugs lightly, though her eyes never leave mine.

I cannot look away. Her words strike deep, her truth wrapping around my own. Strand after strand falls, each one a piece of the girl I was, soft and silent as they scatter across the floor.

The door opens. Lia and Colden pause on the threshold, their eyes widening at the sight of Mary with the scissors in hand, hair spilling red at her feet. They do not speak, but understanding settles heavy in the room.

"Me next," Lia says, her tone steady.

Mary inclines her head and lifts another section of my hair between her fingers. The blades flash. A clean snip. More locks fall, curling against the stone like fallen leaves, each one carrying the weight of memory, each one whispering of the girl I used to be.

This is not just a haircut.

In the mirror, a new image takes form. Not a stranger, and not a monster either. A witch. A shifter. Someone who is done running from her own power.

Olivia

THE WANTED WITCH

I sit cross-legged on the library floor of the manor, surrounded by the quiet hush of dust and distant memory. The map stretches wide before me, its parchment corners pinned down by thick tomes of ancient texts that still hum with power beneath their worn bindings. The map smells of ink and age, the contours of our kingdom inked in curling script. It reminds me of long nights planning in Tierney's mansion.

My fingers trace mountain ranges, rivers, borders that feel like wounds. I force thoughts of Jeyr to the edges of my mind. Not now. Not yet. Our reunion will come—but right now, people are bleeding, imprisoned, waiting. And I can't let myself fall into what I miss. What I love. Not until I get them back.

Beside me, Kyzan lies coiled, his golden eyes scanning the map with that sharp, impossible stillness only he can manage. His nose twitches, following the faint lines of troop movement along the borderlands. *The army's last known position curls between the Aotrom and Aimsir mountains, near the ridge, Alpha.* It's a smart place to hide—untraceable and treacherous.

Colden stands across from us, arms crossed, brow furrowed in thought as he studies the pathways inked into the page. "So... you want to infiltrate the heart of the Great Kingdom," he says finally, his voice dry, disbelief clinging to every syllable. "You, the woman plastered on every wanted sheet from here to the northern coast."

"Absolutely," I say, meeting his eyes. There's no bravado in my voice, just iron.

He exhales, dragging a hand through his hair. "Right. Then we do it differently. We divert. No shadow-trailing the army's paths, we need to blend in. We take the trade routes to skirt suspicion. Merchants go where soldiers don't look too closely." He leans forward, pointing to a winding path that curves through a series of outer towns. "We gather supplies on the way—food, textiles. Say we're collecting for the Royal Banquet. It gives us a reason to move freely. After that, the plan's yours to command."

I nod slowly, appreciating the shape of it. Practical. Sharp. There's something comforting in the way Colden thinks—in the way he leaves room for risk but doesn't let it lead.

Lia appears in the doorway, silent but alert, her eyes tracking the map before moving to me. She doesn't say a word, but she doesn't have to. Between the two of us, we don't match the profile of the fugitives they're hunting. Not anymore.

Lia doesn't say anything, but I feel her watching. Waiting. Like she's not sure if this version of me—the one with shorter hair and a heavier gaze—is going to break or burn.

But the truth is—I don't know either.

I push to my feet, my knees stiff from the floor. The map stays behind, paper flattened by the weight of too many futures.

"We'll need to leave before dawn," I say, mostly to the room.

I start toward the door.

Behind me, the room stays quiet, but not still.

Plans settle. Tension shifts. No one breathes easy.

And somewhere deep in the walls, I swear the manor exhales.

Olivia

THE KING'S HOUNDS

The pine needle trail crunches beneath our boots, each step a quiet rebellion against the hush of the forest. Lia huffs beside me, sharp and irritated, and kicks at a clump of earth with unnecessary force.

"Why can't we just winnow there?" she grumbles, tugging her scarf higher.

"Kingdom wards block winnowing after the outskirts," Colden says, voice low, the weight of it pressing against the cold air. "Only mental powers work beyond that line. If your war commander was a mind master, you need to let his powers still work."

He trails off, and the unnamed hangs between us like a bruise. I catch the flicker of hesitation in his eyes, the echo of chains, of rooms too quiet and minds too broken. My breath stutters at the edge of memory.

Lia scoffs, sharp and dismissive. "So what? We can't just walk in and burn it all to the ground?"

Colden glances at me. He doesn't speak, but the message is clear as moonlight. Not yet.

I sigh, quiet but firm. "Lia. Fire is for the ones who truly deserve it."

She stops walking. Her mismatched eyes lock onto mine, their usual gleam dulled by something softer. "How do you know who's bad?" she asks, and her voice is small. Not childlike—human.

"I feel them first," I answer. "An empath knows when something cannot be changed. When there is no kindness, no remorse, not even the seed of it. If there is nothing—if empathy has never lived in them—I know. And if I must, I look deeper. Into their minds.

Into the truth of who they are, and what they intend."

The rest curls back into my throat. The weight of what I've done is never far. The word murderer doesn't need to be spoken. It lives in the cracks of my ribs, in the places I still flinch when someone touches too gently.

Colden doesn't flinch. He just looks at me. Solid. Steady. The same way he always has.

We don't need to speak. He knows. He's seen it. The monster I was. The woman I try to be. And he's still here.

Lia tilts her head. "Like the men in the cell?"

My stomach drops. Even through the shield she throws over her thoughts, I feel the backlash—like knives scraping bone. Her mind recoils from the memory, images too brutal to name surfacing in fragments.

I reach out. My hand finds hers, fingers wrapping around her wrist with a gentleness I don't always trust myself to offer. I send calm, warmth, anything to quiet the storm I feel brewing behind her eyes.

"Yes," I say, voice steady. "Exactly like them. And honestly? I wouldn't blame you for wanting to get a little... extra stabby."

A grin twitches at her lips, but it isn't the usual sharp, wicked thing. It's thinner. Quieter. There's something else in her eyes now—recognition. A thread of truth that binds us both to the dark.

"I'll do it," she murmurs. "If it brings you peace."

It isn't a promise. It's a pact.

We fall into silence, our footsteps the only sound for a time. Even those feel heavier now, especially Ness's. Her gait is always louder, but now it feels like a drumbeat. Like the earth remembering every step we take.

The forest narrows as we press deeper, branches clawing at our shoulders, roots twisting underfoot like traps laid in the dark. The night feels stretched too thin, every sound sharper than it should be, the crunch of Ness's steps, Lia's steady breathing, the whisper of leaves brushing one another above.

Kyzan slows first, head lifting as if he's caught a frequency none of us can hear. Colden moves next, his hand drifts toward the knife at his hip.

Something presses against the edges of me. Not yet a voice, not yet a thought but a pressure I cannot name, heavy and watching.

Kyzan halts. Ears flatten, fur standing on end, his golden eyes cutting to the trees as if the shadows themselves are shifting.

I draw a breath. The air is wrong. Too still, too expectant, like the moment before a storm breaks.

A prickle crawls down my spine, ancient instinct thrumming in my bones. Kyzan's fur bristles, his growl low and warning. I taste it too—that metallic tang of danger curling on the back of my tongue.

I reach outward with my senses. Malice slams into me, thick and suffocating, saturated with hunger and anticipation. They are not wandering. They are hunting.

My body locks tight. So does Lia's. Colden whirls on instinct, stepping into the space between us and the trees, every line of him already braced for impact. Like his body alone could shield us.

They step out of the trees together, precise and wrong. Three silhouettes at first, then features bloom—smiles stretched past kindness, skin drawn tight over rot, teeth knife-bright and endless. My mind flicks to the painted beasts in the mansion prison, the ones that used to leer down from cracked plaster like warnings. There they were only paint and mockery. Here they are bone and breath. A cold understanding curls through me: the monster who kept me was never the only thing to fear. These are worse.

"Well, well." One drawls the words, voice slick as oil. "Little empath. Thought you could hide forever?"

Colden doesn't wait. His power lashes out, cracking through the air with enough force to rattle my bones. The intruders freeze mid-step, bodies locked, jaws straining as if they might unhinge.

Found her, King Dominhall. The thought carves its way into my mind, raw and jagged, their voice cutting straight into the hollow of my skull. I stagger, breath hitching. Not from the blow itself, but from the truth beneath it. No disguise will be good enough.

Fury floods my veins. Without hesitation, I hurl myself into the thread binding them to their master, that taut, glimmering line of control and command. I seize it and tear, savage as a wolf on raw flesh. The link snaps with a scream that isn't a sound but a shockwave, slamming through me hard enough to make my teeth ache.

The intruders twitch, shudder, their frozen bodies breaking free of Colden's hold. For a heartbeat, panic fractures their faces.

Then fire roars.

The air ignites in a sudden, searing burst. Bark blackens, leaves shrivel, and their bodies become torches, skin blistering, bone cracking beneath the inferno. Screams split the night, human one moment, beast the next, before collapsing into silence. Smoke chokes the canopy, flames devouring everything they touch.

Beside me, Lia tilts her head, an expression almost thoughtful as she watches them burn. "Those were the bad ones you meant, right? If not... whoops."

A small, jagged smile curls at my lips despite the stench of ash. "They were bad."

Colden's stare finds me. Not afraid. Not furious. Just... seeing. And in his eyes, for the first time, something like awe flickers.

"We need to move." My voice is rough, urgency snapping through me as the blaze devours the clearing. "The King will feel what I just broke."

I climb onto Ness. She bolts forward, cart jolting behind her where Colden and Lia hold fast. Each stride shakes the ground, pounding like a war drum through the trees. Smoke claws at my throat. Shadows twist, racing with us.

My senses stretch wide. Bark. Root. Branches overhead. Nothing strikes—but the air hums, heavy, watching.

I grit my teeth. That was only the first stage. Just the dogs loosed to chase us down. We haven't even reached the kingdom yet, and already they bore the mark of his leash.

If this was his warning, what waits inside his walls?

Lia's laugh cuts through the dark. "So if more of them come—open season?"

Her grin is wild, sharp as the firelight on her teeth.

I nod once, iron-heavy. "If they come for us, don't hold back."

Still, the unease doesn't fade. It coils tighter the farther we run, pressing like a hand at my back, a breath against the nape of my neck.

If the King's hounds were only the beginning, what waits in the heart of his kingdom will be far worse.

Caomh

NOT MY KIND OF CHAINS

Chains do not clatter here. They hum. A low constant thrum under my skin, through the manacles that bite my wrists and sink cold into stone. They ache. I have learned not to answer that ache. It is constant. Familiar. Contained.

The cell tastes of old blood and ash and the sour smoke of burnt herbs. Enchantments hang in the air like heat over tar, pressing at the edges of thought until my memories round off and dull. I close every door in my head. I seal every window. Not even Jeyr's touch finds me here. The silence between us is a wound I pretend not to feel.

Bane paces the threshold like a vulture with manners. His boots click across the flagstone, slow and deliberate, each step a note meant to remind me who holds the rhythm.

"Marquis Caomh Conroy," he intones, dragging my name out like a rope. His finger traces a line along my shoulder and leaves fire in its wake. The motion is intimate and filthy. I do not flinch. My breath stays thin and steady. He gets no more than I give.

That is the rule now.

He circles, scenting me with his gaze. Silence pools between us and everything in that quiet is loud—his breath, the scrape of his cuff, the tiny rattling inside my own bones. I do not speak.

"Lost your tongue, mind master?" Bane sneers, slicing the silence open. "No matter. I have ways."

He crouches until his face is almost level with mine. Torchlight makes his grin a bad moon. "Tell me about the man beside Jethro. Who is he?"

The question drifts, oily as smoke. I give him nothing.

His smile thins. "A ghost in my network. Strange." He shakes his head like a child puzzling over a toy that won't behave. "No records. No past. Yet he fights like he was born for it."

Stillness becomes my armor. I press against it until my ribs ache.

Bane's eyes glitter. "A lone guard, then *hmm?* Yet, I am curious how a hawk becomes Fae."

My jaw tightens. Too much, too soon.

He leans closer. Up close the rot in his mouth smells like old cellars. "You won't tell me, Caomh? Fine." His voice slides into relish. "When your execution takes the Empath's place, I will make a show of it. I will pluck your shifter out by that tether you have tied to him. I will pull at that string until he comes, and then I will take him apart."

His fingers twitch as if plucking phantom threads. "Shift by shift. Piece by piece. Till his power is mine and whatever's left of him echoes in my halls."

I do not trust my voice to answer. I do not want him to know how the words land. So I do not speak.

He watches me for a beat longer, searching for a crack. He leans in, a whisper now, venom threaded through a mockery of gentleness. "Indifference is a clever mask, master. But the way your shifter looked at you before he vanished—ah. That was not indifference."

The manacles bite harder as my muscles clench. My pulse drums beneath the steel. He sees it. He laughs—a low, triumphant sound that winds around my ribs and settles into bone.

Then his boots fade down the corridor and his shadow peels away from the wall.

Only when I am alone do I let my head drop back against stone. Breath leaks out of me slow and ragged, like smoke slipping from a long smothered fire.

He thinks he is winning. I do not know if I can prove him wrong. I am afraid that perhaps he is right.

Olivia

HYMN OF THE GALLOWS

The city bleeds into view slow as a held breath, a smear of stone and glass beneath a translucent dome that thrums with old magic. It hums, not with life but with something colder and older, the King's will braided through it like dark veins under skin. The wards catch the sun and split it into a hundred warning shards. The towers are too pristine, too still, like teeth polished and bared.

As we draw nearer the guards fall into a rhythm that makes my bones ache. Their march is a metronome, armor flashing in an impossible, synchronized gleam. Faces are hidden behind helms. No stray thought reaches me. No stray mercy.

I reach for them anyway. Habit, duty, a need to know. Their minds hit me like a wall. They are not quiet. They are caged, humming with a single repeated command that bleeds through each step, each breath, every footfall on the ward-hardened road.

Obey and kill. Obey and kill. Obey and kill.

It is not discipline. It is not focus. It is emptiness dressed in order. Whatever they once were has been carved out and set aside, obedience hewn so deep it radiates outward like heat from stone. I try to find a scrap of memory and come up with nothing but an ache where a life should be.

Already they bear the mark of his leash.

Lia leans close, voice flat. "They're puppets."

"I can't break through their bloodlust," she says, fingers worrying at the cart rail, frustration raw in the sound.

Colden falls in beside me, eyes narrowing. "Beyond the wards, your power shouldn't—" He stops there, the sentence hanging like a stone. Surprise colors his face. He knows the rules. He knows the risk.

I feel something like a smile lift my lips. "Then let's test the rule," I say, and mean it.

I do not reach for their thoughts. I reach for the thing beneath thought, the slow, warm current that is life. It is a delicate thing to touch, like breathing on a candle that trembles under a draft. I skim that current, a fingertip of will against a flicker, and where I brush it sparks awake inside them. Confusion ripples through vacant eyes. For a stunned beat they look around as if they have woken from a nightmare.

I pry further. Beneath the command I find small rooms of memory, shuttered and dust-choked. A child's laughter by a river. A wife's hand, rough with work, clasping his own. The smell of bread straight from an oven. Faces that had been buried under the King's orders like kindling under ash.

I don't give them these memories whole. I turn the screws of longing. I feed one memory into another, knotting them tight until yearning swells like a tide behind their ribs. The King's leash tightens for an instant and frays. The mantra stutters. The emptiness cracks.

They do not turn to fight. They do not come for us. They stagger, eyes wet or bright with sudden, ugly hope, and then they run. Not toward a battle but toward whatever life waits beyond their fences, toward the echoes of love I set loose inside them. Distance does not matter. Only the pull of home. Only the need to touch the taste of what they once were.

"Path is clear," I say, stepping through the empty guard post.

Colden looks at me, his emotion threading through mine. *What you did back there is why you are not a monster.*

I ignore the words. My eyes stay on the wards humming ahead, on whatever waits beyond them. There were times, when I was a girl, that I dreamed of this place. I wanted the music, the festivals, the gilded parties I read about in the papers. How foolish I was. Now I walk in as an assassin. And the worst part is... I am starting to accept it.

Silently, I command Ness and Kyzan to stay behind. With a final nod, they melt into the trees, shadows swallowed by the forest.

"Put your hoods up," I murmur.

Lia arches a brow but pulls the coarse fabric forward, shadowing her face. Colden does the same, the rough cut of merchant garb making us indistinguishable in the tide of bodies. Shoulder to shoulder, we slip into the crowd, just three more figures swallowed by the city's thrumming heart.

The city slams into me like a tidal wave. I've only ever seen its towers in papers, neat lines inked with false elegance. None of that captured this. The heat clings to me like a second skin. The sound—thousands of voices woven together into a single, throbbing roar—batters my senses. With each step it swells, a tide of anticipation and unease that threatens to pull me under.

And then, the hymn begins.

It crashes over me louder than the vendors' shouts, harsher than hooves striking cobblestones. Even my clammy palms, slick with sweat, cannot block it out. The pounding chorus of faith and fear drills into me until it is all I hear.

This isn't a city.

It's a living thing.

In the realm where shadows fall and dance,
A king so mighty, a powerful trance.
Against illegal mix-breeds, he stands,
Protecting with power, his subjects' hands.

"Oh gods, make it stop," I mutter.

Colden's hand brushes between my shoulders, Kyzan presses at my leg through the bond. What should comfort me only tightens the air, choking. I cannot break here. Not in front of them.

Think of your anchor, Lea's voice threads through the static of the hymn.

Anchor? I echo back.

Oceans. Summer storms.

I close my eyes. My fingers trace the technicolor pulse at my wrist. The scent of salt and pine, earth washed clean beneath thunder, presses into me. It drowns the hymn, presses it out like a tide sweeping rot from the shore. I do not need his eyes. His presence alone is enough. His love steadies me. A single tear slips free, tasting of brine, a droplet of hope in the heat.

Fortified, I press on. Through the crush of Fae, humans, and creatures both, I brush skin to skin. Each touch a ripple, my ribbons prying at the King's hold. I do not break chains. I loosen them. I nudge buried memories— a lover's hand smoothing wrinkles from a sleeve, a mother's laugh, the shade of a tree in summer. The hymn falters in those I touch, replaced with confusion, with longing. We part the sea of bodies, leaving eddies of disquiet behind us.

The flags above snap in the hot wind, each one bearing the King's face, each one daring us to look away. But the gallows draw every gaze. Looming, black, hungry.

Colden's hand lingers at my back. His steady touch anchors me as the air thickens with anticipation. Lia's dark hair devours the light, her eyes bright with crimson fire. She drinks in the crowd's mutterings—hatred, suspicion, fear—and it reflects in her fury.

"All these people," she hisses, "their intent is foul. I could—"

"No." My voice cuts through hers, firm. "They are under his spell." Her fingertips smolder, heat rising like a warning. "Fire does not harden all it consumes, Lia. Nor does it cleanse everything it touches."

It takes every shred of restraint not to reach out, not to shatter the King's leash on thousands. But that would unmask us. And they are safe enough in their obedience. The ones on the gallows are not.

We push to the front row. The crowd falls into a hush, anticipation sharp as knives. A slim man is dragged forward, wrists bound raw. He stumbles, half-starved, eyes too large in his narrow face. He cannot be older than nineteen.

Chains bite as they strap him to the post. The hymn swells.

My fingers twitch. My power stirs. I could undo it all. I could unravel the spell here and now. But the King would feel it. The King would see.

So I do nothing. Nothing but breathe a whisper of memory into the condemned boy—warmth, laughter, a mother's touch—just enough to give him courage at the end.

The executioner raises his blade.

The crowd leans forward, a single creature hungry for blood.

And I stand in silence, fists clenched so tight the nails draw blood, while the hymn swallows his final breath.

Like nothing happened. Like the cheers for a young fae boy's death were nothing.

A man walks onto the gallows, his suit pressed sharp enough to cut. He clears his throat, then lets his voice carry.

"Ladies and gentlemen, esteemed citizens of the Great Kingdom, I stand before you today humbled by your loyalty in these trying times. As the King's trusted informant, it is my honor to extend his gratitude for your resilience and unwavering support.

"In the face of adversity, you have shown remarkable strength. The King, in his wisdom, acknowledges the sacrifices each of you has made for the collective welfare.

"His Majesty pledges to uphold his sacred duty to protect our Kingdom. The presence of illegal and threatening elements that lurk among us will be eradicated. With benevolent guidance, he will cleanse our land of those who defy the laws and endanger our safety.

"Those who aid them will suffer the consequences. United, we march toward a brighter and safer future. May the Gods bless us, and may the unity and loyalty we display today become the beacon that guides us through the shadows of uncertainty."

The crowd erupts. Cheers rise like a tide, forced and fevered. Lia and I clap along, the charade sour in my hands.

The man fades into the background. Another steps forward, his robes gleaming with an unnatural shimmer. The King.

Silence falls, thick as the gold chains at his throat. His eyes sweep the crowd, sharp and cold, searching for the slightest tremor of doubt. A smile curls his mouth, cruel beneath its practiced charm.

"Today," he begins, his voice smooth as silk, "marks a turning point in the history of our Kingdom. For too long, we showed leniency. We hoped our citizens would embrace the rules crafted not only to safeguard our land but to shield the Courts around us. I kept faith that purging our realm of those who do not belong would calm the storm of war. But leniency bears a cost.

"Royal citizens charged to protect you have strayed. They have raised armies of Fae, twisted with malicious intent. Yet I, your King, vow to shield you. To end the threat.

"Today begins the unraveling of these renegade hosts. Their commander now stands in my grasp. Caomh Conroy, bastard of Gliocas' Grand Duke, leads them astray. His threads of rebellion will be cut to preserve our harmony."

No

My pulse hammers a frantic rhythm, drowning out the whispers spilling through the crowd like dust in wind. All I hear is the drum inside my ribs, urging me to act. Colden's hand finds mine. The storm in me steadies against his touch.

Lia's voice cuts through the haze, sharp and unyielding. Her eyes flick between me and the figure climbing the weathered steps of the gallows. *He matters to you?*

I choke on the words before I force them free. *He is my brother.*

The manacles clang as Caomh ascends, every step echoing like a bell toll. His presence hits me like a blow—an anchor in this sea of lies, an ache I can't ignore. Fierce protectiveness swells in me until I can hardly breathe.

I came to the Kingdom with purpose, with reason. But all of that fractures now into one truth.

I am here for him.

And I will not let him die.

Lorkan

TOWER FALLEN

Look up. Just once. Look at me.

The cheers are deafening, swallowing my cries whole. Cay climbs the gallows, chains clinking as they lash him to the post like a flag meant to be broken. His eyes are shadowed by despair, but I see it—the ember of defiance that refuses to go out.

I scan the crowd, hawk-sharp, searching for Jeyr and Jethro under their hoods. We are here, all of us, but too late. No plan. No path forward. Only the King, hand raised, blue fire licking his palm. My stomach twists. That flame is meant for Cay.

Jethro catches my eye. A single shake of his head seals it—any move now is suicide.

My pulse hammers so hard it drowns the mob's roar, drowns everything except the silent plea I hurl down the frayed tether between us. *Mo ghràdh, I am here. You're not alone. Just look at me.*

But Cay doesn't. Or he can't.

The King steps forward, his presence pressing down on the square like a storm. Power radiates from him, smothering, suffocating, heavy as chains. Every breath of it makes the air harder to draw. He doesn't need to shout to command obedience; his very existence demands it.

I know what he is, what he can do. I know rushing him is madness. But still—my choice hardens. If it's suicide, so be it. Cay is worth the fall.

I brace—

And then the crowd breaks. Screams ripple outward, sharp and panicked. The King's head snaps toward the commotion, fury carving his features.

"Find her!" His voice lashes across the square. "I commanded you—find her!"

The word sinks like a blade. *Her.*

Jeyr stiffens beside Jethro, his hood shadowing the wild gleam in his eyes. He doesn't need to see her—none of us do. The King's reaction tells us everything. Olivia is here. She is the reason the crowd is unraveling, the reason his soldiers stand frozen.

And gods, the bond in Jeyr's chest drags taut like a wire. He surges forward, desperate to get to her, to carve a path through the chaos.

But the clock tower shudders, stone screaming as it begins to fall.

I launch upward as it collapses, rubble hammering down on all below. Fae and beasts stampede for the forest, their terror a tidal wave of noise.

I dive, shifting into a wyvern, my talons snapping around Jeyr and Jethro, tearing them clear as the tower slams into the square. Flames roar upward, searing my wings. Debris whips past, a rain of burning stone.

A glance back—chains dangle empty where Cay should hang.

Relief claws a ragged breath from my lungs. He's gone. He's safe. For now.

Below us, the King's fury boils, fire spitting, power tearing through the ruin. But I climb higher, twisting through smoke, my brothers clutched in my grip.

"She's here!" Jeyr shouts, voice raw and certain, as if I can do anything to get him to his mate right now.

Caomh

Mo Chuisle, Fly

Whatever you do, don't fuck this up for me, Cao, I hear the familiar voice echo in my mind. I resist the urge for my eyes to widen; my mind is a fortress. Bane and Dominhall tried in vain to breach it, but that voice, that voice slips through where no one else can.

Scanning the crowd, I seek a glimpse of red hair. *Princess?*

Don't look for me, or you will mess this up. Keep looking your arrogant self. Oh that's her.

You love my arrogant self. There's no response to that, but I can somehow sense the tilt of a smile. The emotions I experience walking onto the stage for everyone to witness my impending death are overwhelmingly bleak, even for me. Yet, even without spotting the red hair, a glimmer of hope lingers. That is until the King approaches, ready to ignite me.

Okay, please say you have a plan, or I'm about to be burnt alive. From what I hear, it's not pleasant.

Patience, Cao.

I'll see if you have patience next time someone is holding a torch to your face. I huff, the heat from the Kings hand inching closer to my face.

Were you always this dramatic?

I wasn't always about to die, Princess.

A huff of laughter, and then I feel the air snap. Screams fill the city, and faces that have looked at their King with revelry suddenly regard him as if he is death incarnate. The heat from the fire emanating from me dissipates as I watch our King lose his composure. His eyes frantically search for the cause, but like me, he can't find the empath.

He shouts at his guards, who no longer seem under his command. The clock tower, once taunting me with the time I have left, begins to crack. The sounds, barely noticeable amidst the fear-ridden racket, signal the town's impending chaos.

The tower starts to fall, and despite the feeling of someone releasing me from the chains, freeing me from my execution, all I can do is focus on him.

A choked gasp escapes my lips as two figures materialize from the smoke, their forms obscured by swirling cloaks. Even the dim light can't hide the familiar set of my brothers' shoulders, the way they stand side-by-side like an impenetrable wall. Then, a chilling roar rips through the air, piercing the cacophony of screams and shattering any lingering doubt. *Lorkan.* He is there, wings unfurling into the sky, eyes blazing with a ferocity that mirrors the fire that has nearly consumed me. Fear, cold and sharp, claws at my throat, twisting into a primal ache. Yet, it is dwarfed by the terror emanating from King

Dominhall, his raw, primal fear resonates with my own. The realization of a shape-shifter in his midst has struck him like a physical blow, his eyes darting wildly, searching for the source of this unexpected defiance.

Despite the urgency of my escape, I fight against the hands pulling me away, my gaze glued to the unfolding chaos. I have to see. Have to know if Lorkan, my brave, reckless *Mo Chuisle* will emerge unscathed. My vision blurs with unshed tears as I watch the King unleash his magic, a desperate barrage aimed at the soaring wyvern. But Lorkan is a creature of the sky, nimble and quick. He dances through the attacks, his fiery breaths illuminating the terrified faces below.

"Cao, please!" Olivia's voice, normally a calming balm, is edged with panic. "We need to leave, now! Lorkan can handle himself." I know she is right, logically. Yet, every fiber of my being rebels against the thought of abandoning him. He is my shield, my protector, and the fear threatening to consume me isn't just for my own safety, but for his.

"I need to protect him," I choke out, the words raw and desperate. "I have to keep him safe." The city crumbles around us, the clock tower collapsing in a shower of dust and debris, mirroring the turmoil within me.

"And you will, Cao, but he wants you alive. He's okay, flying fast and bordering the forest. The King is too shocked and playing sloppy."

"Why don't you kill him?"

"Need to save you first. But don't worry, he's going to die."

Swallowing the last of Olivia's reassuring words, I finally turn, expecting to see her familiar face among the throng exiting the Kingdom. My jaw drops instead, a silent scream caught in my throat.

"Liv... your hair?" I choke, the words torn out of me as if disbelief itself has teeth.

She only shrugs, as though this isn't the end of everything, as though she hasn't just walked into hell with fire licking at her heels and come out different. Nonchalant. Already pushing forward, already clearing a path through the panicked throng while I stumble after her, gawking.

The square is collapsing into chaos—screams, smoke, banners ripped down by frantic hands. Fae, humans, beasts shove against each other, fighting for space to flee. The crowd carries us whether we want it or not, bodies pressing so tight I can feel every shuddering heartbeat, every ragged breath. Olivia moves like she was born for this, weaving through them with sharp precision, and I follow, chains still clattering at my wrists as if mocking my freedom.

Beside her, from the churn of dust and bodies, Kyzan emerges—massive, relentless, carving through the press with a predator's patience. And then I see *her*.

Another woman, stepping into step as if she's always belonged at Olivia's side. My breath snags. Her hair spills dark over her shoulders, catching what little light remains. And her eyes—gods—her eyes are a kaleidoscope, colors shifting and folding in on themselves like glass catching sun. Beautiful. Unsettling. My chest tightens.

The shock must be written all over me. Olivia glances back, catching the look, and smirks. "Man, I haven't seen you emote this much without me pushing at your mind, Cao. Cat got your tongue?"

I want to retort, but the words dry up. My gaze is locked on the stranger, on the way her eyes never quite stay the same. She looks at me, steady, and I feel pinned. Captured.

The crowd bucks around us as a line of guards tries to shove through, their commands drowned in the panic. Olivia grabs my hand, fingers firm, dragging me along. Her hair—shorter now, raw at the ends—whips in the hot wind, proof of some choice she made while I dangled waiting to die. A choice I don't understand, but one that sets her apart, sharper, new.

We run. Bodies slam against us, pushing, clawing, desperate to escape the city. A child wails. A stall overturns, fruit and pottery scattering beneath pounding feet. The smoke thickens, choking, but Olivia doesn't slow. Kyzan shields us from a rushing cart, shouldering it aside like it's weightless.

The border looms, close enough to taste freedom on the air. Olivia looks back once more, green eyes sparking. "Keep moving, Cao. We're not safe yet."

Her voice slides into my mind, sharp as ever. *I know you have a preference for dark hair, but back off from that one.*

What, got something to tell Jeyr? I shoot back, forcing play into my tone even as my mind churns, trying to process the woman's presence.

No. But let's just say she isn't someone you want to mess with. Olivia's reply is laced with a seriousness that cuts my banter short.

Intrigued, cautious, I keep my eyes on the woman anyway. The gears in my head won't stop turning.

"We need to move,"a voice cuts through, sharp and commanding. His features are set with concern. "The King will regain control of his guards soon, and they'll be searching."

"Since when do you have so many hot friends?" I quip, breathless.

Olivia only shakes her head, exasperation curling into the faintest smile.

The group closes in around me, hands tugging, pulling. The world lurches.

With a jarring crash, we land sprawled in the forest's dark embrace, the city's roar fading behind us.

"What the actual—" I sputter, disoriented, still reeling from the shift.

"Sorry!" Olivia's friend gasps, her voice strained. "Too many people. Is the pony and puppy okay?"

The chaos of our escape, the stranger's unsettling eyes, Olivia's new hair—all of it blurs together in a dizzying rush. My lungs burn, my mind races.

Escape is just the beginning. And I know with a certainty that terrifies me: whatever comes next will not be short on surprises.

Lorkan

THE SPEAR AND THE STITCH

Every beat of my wings sends fire lancing through me. The iron spear still lodged in my side sears like molten stone, every flick of my tail a brand against my own scales. Jethro and Jeyr cling low to my belly, their bodies trembling with each violent turn. The city crumbles beneath us, towers toppling, walls splitting, the King's fire chasing us through the smoke-choked sky.

A fireball screams upward. I twist hard, claws carving the air. It misses by a breath, detonating against a spire and showering us with shards of stone. Pain claws through me, but pain is a luxury. This is survival. A dance with death I cannot falter in—not while they cling to me, not while the King hunts.

Below, through the haze of ruin, Dominhall emerges. His face is twisted in fury, eyes tracking me like a hawk watching prey. I push harder, higher, the thrumming of my wings matching the desperate rhythm of my heart. I can feel the wards ahead, the final cage holding us in.

And then—I sense it. The shift. Magic thinning. A seam in the fabric of power.

Now.

With a roar that tears my throat raw, I pour every last drop of strength into the motion, ripping myself through the ward's edge. Space folds. The city vanishes in a blur of fire and stone.

And then—silence. Freedom.

The air tastes different here, lighter, untainted. I let them go, dropping Jethro and Jeyr low enough to winnow to the ground. My own landing is less graceful, the shift ripping me back into a man with blood still dripping down my side.

"Lorkan! She was right there, I could sense her!" Jeyr's voice cracks through the trees, frustration and raw longing tearing through every word.

I snarl, forcing my legs to move, stride purposeful even though every muscle shakes. "What did you want me to do? Get us all killed to chase the one saving Cay? Get fucked. We were the distraction so both of them could live."

Jethro falls in silently at my back, steady as always, while Jeyr freezes, fury holding him in place.

"We could have found them both!" he shouts, voice breaking with grief.

I glance up at the roiling clouds above us. "Do you mind? That storm you're brewing? Might as well wave a flag for the King. He saw me. He'll be hunting me—and you—now. Keep your temper in check."

Jeyr grinds his jaw, and with effort the clouds thin, the threat of lightning ebbing away.

"Fuck. I can't go back." The words fall from him like stones, heavy, final.

"No. Unless you like death."

His laugh is bitter, sharp. "Ha. Were you always this sarcastic?"

The cottage rises ahead, a sagging skeleton of wood and stone, the door barely clinging to its hinges. I push it open, the stench of mildew and old blood curling out. Jet slips in first, his silence more biting than Jeyr's rage.

"Why here?" Jeyr's voice cracks again, thinner now, brittle. "Why this place?"

"Because it's close, and it's empty. For now." My words drop like iron. "Scouts will come. We won't stay long."

Inside, dust coats everything. The floorboards creak. Old stains bloom across the planks like ghosts. Jeyr drifts up the staircase, fingers brushing the frames that line the walls. Each painting—her face. Olivia, softer, younger, untouched by the war she's become.

His hand shakes as it trails the edge of one canvas. His voice breaks, low. "The emotion isn't the same. Nothing is the same."

I step up behind him, laying a hand heavy on his shoulder. The portraits stare back at us, frozen in innocence.

"We all changed to survive," I say quietly. "She saved Cay. I don't know if the girl in those paintings would've done that."

He swallows hard, eyes fixed on the ghost of the woman who once was his whole world.

His silence is thick, heavier than the air in the dim cottage. And for a moment, none of us speak. The only sound is the faint drip of water from the eaves, the echo of all that's been lost.

The silence hangs thick, broken only by the rasp of my breath.

Jet's gaze flicks to my side, and his voice hardens. "That wound."

I glance down. The iron spear still juts from beneath my ribs, runes burning faintly along its shaft. Blood seeps warm and steady. I grit my teeth.

"I'll live."

"Not for long." Jet's tone is cold steel. "Those runes will eat you alive if you leave them. Sit down."

I open my mouth to argue, but his glare cuts me off. I lower myself onto a splintered chair, hands braced on the arms.

Jeyr finally turns from the staircase, his eyes falling on me—and widening in horror.

"Lork," he breathes, voice breaking. In an instant he's across the room, crouching at my side, hands hovering but not yet touching. His power hums at his fingertips, but his face is pale, his expression twisted with guilt.

"I should have—"

"You should heal him," Jet snaps, his voice like a whip. "Save the guilt for later. He doesn't have time for your regret."

Jeyr's jaw clenches. For a heartbeat, he looks ready to argue. Then he inhales, sharp and steady, and the shift comes over him—the healer, not the grieving mate.

"Hold him," he says tightly.

Jet's hand presses firm on my shoulder as Jeyr grips the spear. With one brutal tug, he wrenches it free. Agony flares white-hot, ripping a roar from my throat. The runes flicker, sputtering as the iron clatters to the floor.

Before the pain can swallow me whole, Jeyr's palms press to the wound. Magic surges, seeping deep, stitching torn flesh and scorched muscle. The burn lessens, the bleeding slows, the fire dims to an ache.

I slump forward, sweat dripping into my eyes, my breath ragged. But I'm alive.

Jeyr keeps his hands there longer than needed, his head bowed, as if he can will the damage away completely. His power thrums steady, strong, until the last trace of the runes is gone.

When he finally pulls back, Jet exhales slowly, his gaze cutting to Jeyr. "That's what you do. Not sulking. Not looking back. You keep him alive. Understood?"

Jeyr's eyes flick up, raw but steady. "Understood."

I manage a crooked grin, my voice a rasp. "Was starting to think you wanted me gone, brother."

For a heartbeat, something like a laugh flickers in Jeyr's throat, though his eyes are wet. He presses a hand against my shoulder, Jeyr's mouth quirks, half-anger, half-relief. "No," he says, voice low and raw, "both Olivia and Caomh will have my head if something happens to you."

The words land heavy and ridiculous and true. I snort, splinter of a laugh tearing out of me, and the tension thins—for now.

Olivia

NIGHT MARCH TO EILEAMAIDS

I hit the ground with a graceless thud, the leaves answering in dull applause. My ribs complain my palms sting and I shake my head to gather my surroundings. Kyzan folds like practiced muscle; Colden rights himself with the soldier's balance—no wasted motion. While Caomh glares as if I've ruined his day and he means to hold it against me.

"A little warning would have been nice," he grunts, dust shaking from his chest plate.

Lia stamps, Her fingers ball into fists; color in her irises shifts like weather. "Some of us only learned that trick a few days ago," she snaps, jabbing a finger at him.

"I would not test me, mind master. I doubt you could winnow four bodies, and a wolf," she taunts, every syllable a blade.

Caomh's jaw tightens. "I bet I could. Better than you. Who are you, anyway?"

Her hair lifts as if answering for her. "Want me to show you, pretty man?" Lia hums, picking which power to tease him with. The air pricks with the promise of it.

"Enough. He is not one of your cellmates, Lia." My voice hits too loud, but it closes the gap between the two of them like slamming a window. They go quiet as if the wind dropped.

Caomh takes a step back and studies Lia like a problem he'd rather not solve. Hiding her will be another war of its own. Once someone ties a name to her face, I will spend favors and burn safe routes and keep her alive with everything I have. Colden watches, steady and unreadable, and then says, dry as riverstone, "I'd say you get used to it, but you don't."

Lia grins, sharp. "What did you say, Ice-man?" she goads. Colden lifts his hands and drifts away from the bait. I roll my eyes and step in, folding a ribbon of calm over the clearing like an old ritual.

"Enough. We need to move." Ness inclines her head and I swing up. Caomh's mouth quirks at the motion. "Good to see you back home, Liv."

"I am not home. Not yet," I answer, and the sentence settles in my chest like a small stone.

The forest treats us to a soft percussion of damp leaves. Colden murmurs low warnings, habit braided with caution. Lia's fingers spark and twitch. Ahead, Caomh presses a hand to his temple, trying to pry a window through the wall I keep sealed. He pushes; I keep holding.

He does not know it is me. Not yet.

Every part of me wants to sprint to Jeyr, to fall into the shape of him and pretend the world never split us. But the King hunts like us. He will drag his fury through root and stone until he bleeds a secret from someone, one of Coamh's connections who will give away the positioning of us and of Jeyr. For a while, distance is our breath.

"Why can't I reach them?" Caomh snaps, voice raw. "My mind screams, yet theirs stay quiet. This makes no sense."

"Were you drugged?" I ask, steady as stone, holding panic away from the edges of his words.

"Yes. But the haze has cleared. " He looks at me—pleading and frantic.

Before I choose between truth and lie, Lia cuts in, blunt. "I blocked you. It's too risky till we get the illegals out." She flicks a strand of hair like a dismissal.

Relief hits like a tide and I let it roll through me for one small breath. Lia does not look back. No flicker, no small sign that she is shouldering my lie for me. Her jaw is set; her eyes are already cataloguing shadows and exits. I almost want to hate her for the calm of it, and then the strap at my wrist hums and I feel Jeyr—his steady, stubborn pulse—answer me like a promise. Alive. Not severed. Not drowning.

That proof steadies Caomh beside me; his shoulders ease by the fraction of a degree that means everything. Colden goes quiet the way soldiers do—mouth closed, eyes taking measure. Kyzan paces at the rim like a taut wire. The chatter between them shrinks down, the bickering folding into small useful sounds: a boot scraped clear, a map refolded, a tinder nest tucked out of sight. For the first time in hours something like peace settles over us—not bright, not safe, but serviceable.

We move on that peace, careful as thieves. The trees press back and then two heartbeats later they part and Eileamaids pours out below us like a truth I never thought I'd touch. The river runs in silver braids, catching the sun and breaking it into a thousand dull coins. Wind-wielders spiral across the flats, their drills shining like thread. Earth-wielders crouch and press the ground until it breathes. It is loud and alive and dangerous in the way beauty always is.

I slip down from Ness. Cold soil drinks my palms. I kneel, close my eyes, and listen. Roots answer slow, patient drums. I do not command; I receive. The trees hand me a map in scent and pressure. I push my awareness outward—river, flatlands, sand until the horizon thins to a line beneath my skin.

Something tugs at the edge of that map. Not gold and warm like the wielders' light. Fractured sparks of despair shorn and ragged. Threads knotted with grief, not for the bodies but for those held away from them: mothers thinking of babes, brothers whispering names, lovers at empty tables. A thousand small terrors hum beneath the mountain's bones.

It lands in my throat like iron. I want to tear the bars open with my bare hands. I gather the threads in shaking palms, then let them fall. I draw my power home and fold it tight, because some things I carry alone.

Caomh is watching. "Your eyes," he breathes. "They were glowing."

Blink twice to anchor myself in pine and night. "illegals," I say. The word tastes like dust. "They're locked in the lower dungeons."

"How—" Shock knives him silent.

"There's a lot you don't know, Cao." I nod toward the ragged border; the castle piles up like a crown against sky. "Not yet. The prison sits just beyond the border."

Silence tightens. "Lia, find what you can about the defenses," I tell her. "Make camp. We move tonight."

Colden

BLOOD TO BLOOD, WILD TO WILD

The wards hum—off-key, foreign. Not like Tierney's. Not like the King's either. His mansion had wards like shackles, tight and unforgiving, pressing in until you remembered who owned you. These are nothing like that. These shine with welcome, a glittering mat rolled wide.

But an old witch once warned me—never leave a welcome mat. Because the ones you don't want are the first to cross it. Let them in, and all that negative energy worms itself into your walls until one day you wake and wonder why your home doesn't feel like home at all.

Lia's fingers skim the edge of the magic, dancing just shy of touch. "Different," she murmurs. "Wide open. Like an invitation you shouldn't trust." Her words echo my thoughts.

My jaw tightens. This isn't the game I know. Hell, I'm the idiot who stayed loyal to a man like Tierney. That says enough. I never moved against him—not for lack of reason, but because I knew how it would end. I'm not hard to kill. I picked the safe option.

And now look at me.

Breaking wards. Freeing prisoners. Like it's bread and water. The urge to roll my eyes is sharp—sharper still to walk. Just walk, straight through these wards, on into whatever waits. Be free. Gods knew Olivia wouldn't hold it against me.

"You wouldn't," Lia says, answering the thought I never speak.

I bare my teeth.

"You were too quiet," she presses. "But your fortress is good. You could just talk to me. I wouldn't have to dig."

"Or you could respect boundaries," I snap, voice low, cold. I want to crowd her, show her I'm not a toy. But I stop myself. Not fear of her power—fear of what made her. I know what cages do. I know what it costs to crawl out of one. I can't bring myself to corner someone already broken and rebuilt behind bars.

She recoils anyway.

"You're right," she whispers. "I shouldn't have. I'm sorry, Ice Man."

I let out a sharp breath. Don't bother correcting the name.

"You're right," I echo. "I wouldn't run, Princess."

Her gaze flicks back to the wards. "Because she's the first hope we've seen in a lifetime. Impossible not to follow that."

Her words settle. I nod once. "Fair enough, Princess."

Her head snaps toward me. "Don't mistake this for friendship. We're not friends. Just two people chasing the same goal."

I smirk. "Don't worry. I could never be friends with someone born of a man like Bane."

The strike lands. She flinches. "Then I guess we have that in common," she whispers.

I let it hang. No apology. Just silence.

Turning to the wards again, I mutter, "So. Thoughts on how we get in?"

"They don't stop us," she says, "but they warn the tower." She nods to the stone crouched between flats and lake, pressed against the limestone wall of Eileamaid's kingdom.

I imagine the answer—the fury. The flood.

"We'll be swarmed," she adds, dry.

"Perfect."

"I'd call it a conundrum. But if you like a bloodbath, sure.

She cuts me a sideways glance, but I keep my eyes on the wards, on the way the magic shivers like breath on glass.

"The elements don't bend because we demand it," I say. "They yield only to the ones they choose—and even then, it's never simple. It's alchemy. Give and take. Salt to mercury, ash to ember, a hundred small bargains made in the dark." Tierney's wards taught me that much: you can wear power like a collar and still get your throat cut by it. "Ice chose me, yes—but it still sets its terms. Misstep, and it will carve me open. Fire will throw its shield around you and then eat your hands for reaching too far. Water cradles you like a mother, then drags you under when the moon turns. Iron promises strength and blooms rust the moment you lean your weight."

The hum deepens—as if the wards are listening, as if they enjoy the warning in my voice.

"They aren't ours," I go on. "We carry them. They carry us. But they are wild, and wild things don't swear oaths they mean to keep. Across that line"—I nod at the glittering veil—"every element is kin-bound to its wielder. You can't expect blood to betray blood. At best, you barter. At worst, you bleed."

"There are other ways," I mutter, more to myself than to her. "Nadur's way. The druids don't beg fire or ice. They call the older loyalties. Beasts. Trees. The roots and rivers that remember who keeps their word. When an animal chooses, it doesn't trade you for a prettier cage. When a tree shelters you, it does so until lightning splits it in two. They choose once. They remember."

Something flickers in her face—interest, maybe wonder. Her eyes shift through blue, green, gold, then blaze into molten amber.

A screech rips the sky. My head snaps upward. An eagle wheels high, dawn fire spilling over its wings.

I curse under my breath.

But Lia just raises her arm.

The bird dives, a streak of shadow and flame. It strikes her forearm, talons digging deep. Blood beads bright. She doesn't so much as flinch.

Her eyes glow—amber and wild, lit with something untamed.

"It has an idea," she whispers.

Olivia

BLOOD, COGS, AND KEYS

The full moon thrums overhead, bright enough that my lack of night vision isn't a concern. But it also makes me wonder—how much cover do we really have?

"Are you sure this is going to work?" Caomh growls, eyes locked on the shimmering ward ahead of us.

Lia doesn't answer. She just steps forward and pushes him aside, arms outstretched. I watch as air and water twist at her command, forming a tunnel—clear and spiraling—through the ward. A moving corridor of magic and will.

"The eagle gave me a lesson in alchemy" she murmurs.

I have no idea what she means, but Colden's lip quirks like he does.

"Stay close," Lia says, her voice steady despite the weight of what she's just done. "The tunnel will get us to the gates. From there, we have limited time until I can reform it to bring everyone back."

I swallow hard, my stomach knotting. We're trusting this entire plan to someone who's never trained, never tested herself like this. It feels reckless. It feels terrifying.

"A little faith would be nice," Lia drawls, taking my hand before I can voice my doubt. Her fingers are warm, oddly steady. She pulls me into motion, the others scrambling to keep pace. Kyzan and Ness remain stationed at the border, shadows waiting.

"Can't they see us?" Colden asks as we move into the swirling tunnel of water and air.

"No. It's glamoured."

Caomh glances back at me. His lips shape the word—*glamoured*—as his mind begins its calculations, tallying powers, weighing what it means. I feel the thrum of unease in him, the puzzle forming with too many pieces. I don't offer him an answer. I can't.

We keep a swift pace, moonlight glinting off the tunnel's surface. Above, the sky churns in anticipation. The sound of waves crashing grows louder as we reach the cliff's edge. The path narrows, slick with sea spray, and then halts.

Two guards stand at the iron gate, deep in conversation.

"Come on, man," one says, gesturing to his chest with a grin. "Why haven't you asked to marry her yet? With those melons on her chest, how could you not? Plus the dowry would set you up for life."

The other guard laughs but shakes his head. "She's beautiful. Comes from a good family. But she wants kids—a lot of them. I'm always on duty. I'd never see them. They wouldn't even know me."

"You might enjoy making them," the first jokes.

"It's not what I want," the second says softly. "And the more they push me, the more I think they're going to move me. There's talk. Moving me from this post, from you, . All these years beside you... gone."

The first guard goes quiet. Then, quieter still, "Well. I suppose after all these years, you must be bored of me."

"Kitel," the man says, voice barely above a whisper, "even another hundred years wouldn't be enough to be bored of you."

I watch them. That simple moment. That quiet, aching honesty. It's so normal. A love I know well—one that blooms in friendship, in time spent, in staying.

Then I feel it—Lia's intent shift behind me like a sudden draft. Her hand lifts, crackling with elemental threat. I lurch forward, grabbing her wrist, shaking my head hard.

"Not these ones."

Before she can protest, I take it into my own hands. I reach out with my power, webbing it across the guards' minds like a silken net. I don't bury them—I gift them. I show them dreams, peace. Let them drift into the world they long for—together. No fear. No duty. Just each other.

Their eyes flutter closed, breath evening out.

Kitel and his companion disappear into a dreamscape of their choosing, and I allow myself the smallest smile.

Behind me, I can feel Caomh's glare slicing into my back. He doesn't understand the mercy in it. Or maybe he does—and just doesn't approve.

"No time to dawdle," Colden mutters, stepping forward.

The moment Lia's power shifts, I feel it—a new pull of pressure, the tunnel funneling downward toward the cliffs.

We move fast, boots silent over worn stone as the gates rise before us—etched with cogs, old symbols layered like seals meant to be forgotten.

"Well, Lia," Caomh mutters, edge sharp enough to cut. "Cat's out of the bag. You can wield the elements. Now open the gate. Each cog requires a wielder."

I glance at Colden. He meets my eyes, reading the tension I don't dare voice aloud. In return, he offers something rare—a small, steady smile.

Lia ignores Caomh's tone. She lifts her hand.

In a flare of motion, fire cracks, water coils, earth grinds, and wind shrieks through the corridor. The cogs turn one by one, groaning like ancient beasts waking from centuries of slumber. The gate begins to open, the sound of it thundering down the stone passage.

"Well," Lia smirks, her voice dripping in mockery, "any other wee comments, Mind Master, or shall we free one of your armies?"

Caomh shoves past, muttering curses under his breath.

"Not liking being the one without power, Cao?" I tease, my voice lighter than I feel. Darkness creeps at the corners of the corridor, and my nerves snap taut. Lia, thankfully, lights the lanterns with little bursts of flame—I don't have to strain to see now.

"No, Little Empath," he snaps, voice low and hot. "I don't like all these secrets stinking up the air like a whorehouse after a festival. And when we're done here—when we're not racing the clock—you and I are going to have a conversation. Because right now?" His eyes burn into mine. "I'm not even sure which side you're on."

The words hit like a gut-punch. He means for them to.

I brace myself, breath sharp in my throat, ready to bite back. Ready to unleash the truth and justify every lie I've told for a greater good—but then Colden's cool hand brushes the nape of my neck. A soft squeeze. Let it go. His voice hums inside my head, quiet as snowfall. Actions speak louder than words.

I hate how right he is.

So I breathe. Just once. And we keep moving.

The stairwell spirals downward, rough and jagged from years of wear—carved by feet, not Fae powers. Each level smells older, more rank. When we reach the bottom, the weight hits me. I stagger under it—an emotional landslide. Grief, hunger, hopelessness. The rot of suffering clings like mold to the walls.

We round the final bend and I see them.

Men. Women. Children. Packed so tight they can't move. A child's cheek is still wet with tears that dried before they fell. My stomach turns.

"Gods above," Caomh breathes, stepping forward.

"Don't touch," Lia warns sharply, catching his arm before he reaches the gate. "Unless you want to be a pile of ash."

He looks down. Scattered across the stone floor—ashes. Dust that once had a name.

Lia kneels, hand brushing the ground where they fell. Her hair begins to rise in the charged air, a pulse of light building around her as she touches the gate. Her gasp is swallowed by a high-pitched hum that drives all of us to cover our ears. The gate drinks her blood—threads of crimson spiraling into the locking mechanisms like vines. A final click echoes. The gate swings open.

And suddenly... it's as if every soul inside takes their first breath.

They rise slowly, eyes wide. They stare—first at Lia, then at me, then at the men flanking us. No one speaks.

I step forward, hands raised, voice steady.

"Please don't be afraid. We're here to free you. We'll take you somewhere safe. But we have to move. Now."

I send a wave of calm through the room, wrapping each mind in a breath of courage. I hate the push of it—hate the way it dulls the panic. But this isn't the moment for questions or chaos. Let them choose their fate once they're free.

Slowly, they begin to file out, stepping wide around the ashes of the fallen. Colden gives me a small nod and murmurs something low to the first Fae, guiding them up the steps with Lia beside him. Caomh stays at my side, waiting as the rest of the cell empties.

When the last of them has passed us, we fall in behind.

The only sound is the shuffle of feet. No one speaks. The moonlight at the far end of the tunnel draws us forward like a thread.

I see Lia break through first. Then Colden. But just as I step toward the exit, the high-pitched shriek of alarms rips through the air.

"Fuck," I swear.

"What gave it away?" Caomh says dryly. "The blaring horn, or the complete collapse of subtlety?"

He starts shouting orders, and that's when it hits—wind howling like a banshee, rain sheeting down from the ceiling, fire licking the walls, and the earth trembles beneath us.

"OLIVIA!" Colden shouts from the mouth of the tunnel.

"Get them out—now!" I scream back, and push. I send a surge of courage through the crowd, clearing a path with sheer will. They move, faster now. Some raise shields of their own. Caomh and I stay behind, holding the rear.

Flames scorch the walls. Rain becomes steam. I feel it sear against my skin—

Then, hands grab me.

I jerk back, ready to fight—until I see them. Two women. Prisoners. One raises a shield of air over us both. The other braces me with her shoulder. I glance over—Caomh is shielded too, two wielders on either side of him, holding the elements at bay.

We break into the clearing, the night exploding around us.

Colden stands at the front, striking down guards who've winnowed to the gate. Lia's tunnel holds, guarded by the very people we just saved. A handful of men and women have chosen to stay and fight.

I reach deep and unleash everything I have.

Guards drop like stones, collapsed in a rush of power. Temporarily immobilized. The fae hesitate only a second longer.

"GO NOW!" I shout. "Down the tunnel!"

They obey.

The last of them disappears inside—Colden and Caomh covering the rear. I follow. Armed guards flood the clearing behind us.

I run backward, arms out, power thrumming. Every man or woman who tries to enter the tunnel falls. Not dead—just frozen. Paralyzed long enough.

Only when I cross the threshold, safe on the other side of the wards, do I let the power drop.

And then—

A hand grabs mine.

We vanish. Winnowed into the dark, away from the wreckage we leave behind.

Olivia

THE HEART OF NADUR

I wake to the scent of fragrant herbs and simmering root vegetables, mingled with the clinks and clatter of morning labor. The sounds are distant at first, as if underwater. My eyes sting as I force them open, lashes crusted and heavy. Panic prickles through me like cold water spilled down my spine.

How long have I been asleep?

I bolt upright too quickly. My heart stutters with the guilt of rest. We should be moving. We should have moved already. My thoughts pile up, tumbling one over the other—strategy, safety, food stores, the King's reach—every single worry crashing into me all at once. I've never slept so deeply, not in the open, not surrounded by a hundred strange fae and their half-wild songs.

Then I hear her. A slow, rhythmic rasp beside me.

Lia sits cross-legged at my side, her expression unreadable, her dagger flashing in the filtered morning light. She's dragging the blade across a whetstone with practiced ease, each stroke a deliberate whisper of metal and intent. The edge gleams too bright, colours flickering along its surface like an oil sheen. Magic. Her power laces with the blade, subtle but sure. It wouldn't surprise me if the dagger dreams at her touch.

"You're fine," she says flatly, not looking up. "Your nightmares started to leak. I didn't think you'd want the new army experiencing—or worse, feeling—the full weight of an empath's trauma dump."

She shrugs like it was nothing. Not even a gesture. Just something that needed doing.

"I wrapped the memory up and told your mind to sleep."

And I did. Deeply, without resistance. That's what startles me most.

The way she says it...like it was a practical decision, like tying back hair before battle, says more than her words ever could. It reminds me of another time, a softer time. One that feels like it belonged to a different life. A certain light weaver once coaxed me into sleep with a hand pressed to my heart and a hum threaded into the threads of my mind.

Lia glances at me from the corner of her eye, her lips twitching. "Stop looking at me like that."

She turns her attention back to the blade, angling it just so. It shimmers again, like it wants to sing.

"Your grumpy, ungrateful commander says we need to move."

I almost ask which one—between Colden and Caomh, both wear the title like a crown.

"The golden one," she clarifies, smirking. "Don't tell Iceman, but he's not as straight-faced as he thinks. He's growing on me."

"He does that," I murmur, pushing upright. My limbs ache in protest, the ground's unforgiving chill still in my bones. I groan.

Lia watches me rise with narrowed eyes and that ever-present glint of cruelty she disguises as truth. "You'd think with two witches' souls and one fae in you, you'd be free of human frailty. But it clings to you like an unwashed servant child."

She rises in one fluid movement, towering over me with effortless grace. Her gaze sweeps over me, not with concern—but calculation. Like she's assessing what part of me can be carved away.

Then, as casually as commenting on the weather, she pivots and walks off. As if her jab was nothing more than a debate over tea preferences.

"Finally awake, Sleeping Beauty," Caomh drawls, sliding down beside me with prac-ticed ease. His gaze doesn't meet mine—it stays fixed on the camp. "You know, if you want to be ready for battle, you probably shouldn't sleep like the dead."

I don't answer. The urge to snipe back flickers but fizzles out before it ever reaches my lips. I don't have it in me. Not now. Not when everything around us looks like... this.

The caravan hums with quiet rhythm. The kind of togetherness that doesn't need words. Fae move as if born into the same song—passing tools, preparing food, mending gear with practiced grace. There's no shouting, no barking orders. Just shared motion, a harmony born of survival.

Children dart between legs with squeals of delight, laughter trailing like smoke behind them. Parents don't stop them, not really—they smile, they guide with a hand here, a word there. Couples pause in their chores to press kisses to cheeks or murmur fleeting *I love You's* into shoulders. As if it's second nature. As if they've always done this, though I know yesterday many of them were chained, awaiting execution.

And now? Now they live.

Not with the past clawing at their heels—but in this fragile, golden moment of now.

I don't realize I'm holding my breath until it catches. I yearn—ache—for someone beside me to witness it too. The beauty. The reason. This is why I fight. Why I keep going. For the ones who dance, for the ones who kiss, for the ones who finally get to choose joy.

"Don't go getting all sentimental, little Empath," Caomh mutters beside me. "We have to keep them alive first."

I finally speak, my voice quiet but steady. "Maybe you'd be less of a grumpy bastard if you learned to stop and feel what they feel. Even after everything—they still kiss their lovers. They still hold hands. They still *show* their love, because they know tomorrow isn't promised. They don't want to die with their truths locked away inside them."

Caomh glances at me, brow furrowed in that way of his—half skepticism, half something else. He looks back to the camp, watching the movement, the softness, the tenderness blooming in stolen seconds.

For a moment, I think I see something flicker. Reflection. Longing. A memory, maybe. Then it's gone.

"Not everyone gets to live like that," he says. "I keep people alive by staying sharp. By not softening. You call it closed-off—I call it not getting anyone else killed."

He rises, brushing invisible dust from his trousers like it offended him. "Fairy tales don't come true, Empath. Myths are just stories. Prophecies are tools used by people too scared to face life without a script. Hope and fear—they're the same spell. Just cast in different tones."

He walks off before I can reply.

But his shoulders are tense. And he's walking slower than usual.

He heard me. Whether he admits it or not.

Caomh moves through the camp like a blade through silk—sharp, precise, cutting through sleep and softness with that ever-efficient bark of command. I watch him go, calling names, giving instructions, his tone clipped but not unkind. Somehow, they listen. They trust him. The packing begins in earnest.

Ness has been haltered with a makeshift sled, vines and leather straps wrapping around her broad shoulders, the wooden frame trailing behind like an extension of her strength. The night's work is piled atop it—bundles of herbs, bundles of cloth, foraged roots, jars of what little magic we could store without drawing attention. It's not much, but who knows when we'll next be able to pause long enough to make more.

We move now with borrowed time.

"Here. Eat."

I flinch—Colden appears beside me like a whisper, holding out what looks like a roasted chicken leg wrapped in cloth.

My first instinct is to refuse. The guilt is still too loud. But my stomach overrules my mind, roaring awake like it, too, remembers how much I'd given the night before. I take the leg from him with a nod of thanks and devour it in greedy bites, my hands trembling with the hunger I've been ignoring.

Colden watches me with his usual quiet calm, then vanishes again into the crowd like smoke, always moving, always watching.

Wiping my hands, I hurry toward Ness and scramble up onto her back. From here, I can see them all—scattered but steady. Worn but ready.

Caomh looks to me. So do others. Eyes wide. Expectant. Hopeful. Afraid.

We've made only the roughest plan, drawn mostly in the dirt with a half-broken stick and desperation. The rest we'll improvise, as we always do. All we know is the next destination:

Nadur.

Gods willing, we reach it in time—before the executions. Before the King's message is carved into flesh and displayed on castle walls. We have to try.

I raise my voice, loud enough to ripple over the clearing. "To those who wish to journey with us—we go to Nadur. To free those still in chains. Those like you."

They still, listening.

"You do not owe us your fight. You can turn toward Aotom, toward the mountains of Aimsir and find safety. That path is yours to take. But if you come with us…" My throat tightens, but I hold steady. "If you come, I ask only this: know the risk. Know it truly. I will do everything within my power to keep you and your families safe. But I am not your commander. I am not your queen."

I pause. The words catch in my chest.

And then—like wind rising through trees—the voices answer.

"We stay with the Empath."

It comes not as a chant, but a vow.

A quiet, resolute thunder that settles deep in my bones.

The convoy moves in staggered waves. Those who can winnow slip ahead like ghosts, scouting the road for dangers my feet have not yet met. I hate it. The loss of control gnaws at me—knowing there are lives I cannot shield, warriors who vanish from my side into the silence ahead. But I cannot winnow. And Ness cannot be left behind. Nor Kyzan. Nor the children. Nor the injured. So I stay in the thick of it, holding the rear with the ones who still bleed, still ache, still need.

The silence is unnatural—too still, too taut. It presses down like a heavy blanket, suffocating in its quiet. Every snapped twig has our heads turning. Kyzan's ears flick. Ness's nostrils flare. Even the birds seem to hold their breath. My human hearing catches little, but the tension is thick enough to taste.

The forest shifts as we travel. The brambling pine gives way to tighter brush, the air warming, thickening, vines beginning to snake and slither from canopy to root. They brush against my skin, sticky and whispering. The scent shifts too—green things rotting and blooming all at once.

With Kyzan pacing silently beside me and Ness's careful steps crunching through fallen leaves, we slip into Nadur's true heart. The jungle.

The only sounds are the eerie, flute-like calls of unseen birds and the wet rustle of leaves underfoot. I send a pulse of magic ahead, a gentle weave of sleep laced into the wind. I don't wish to harm the beasts who dwell here—I only ask them to rest, to let us pass.

The hush that follows feels sacred.

Then—*movement*.

My breath stutters. Heart hammering against my ribs, wild and frantic. My fingers fly to the arrow nocked on my bow, instincts sharper than thought—

But a hand closes over mine. Firm. Calm. Caomh.

He doesn't draw attention to it. Just stands beside me, alert but reverent. Like he too feels it—that something ancient has stepped into our path.

From the tangle of shadow and vine, a figure coalesces.

She glides from the trees like mist, not stepping so much as arriving. Her skin gleams with the dusky shimmer of twilight—neither dark nor light, but something in between. Her eyes are white, polished pearls that glow beneath a curtain of midnight hair that ripples with starlight. Her presence dwarfs my weapon. Dwarfs *me*. I feel like a child trying to hold thunder.

She speaks, and the words drift like falling leaves, old and sacred, in a tongue I've never heard but *feel*. They touch my skin. My soul.

Caomh translates beside me, his voice softer than I've ever heard it.

The being laughs, low, warm, and knowing. Her gaze lands on me, holding fast. "Expecting fiery hair, I was," she murmurs. "But your eyes, child... they carry the same spark as your mother's."

My breath leaves me. No thought of bowing, no thought of fear. Only stunned, aching recognition.

"You knew my mother?" The words tumble out, raw. Too fast. Too full.

A smile curves her lips—tender, touched with melancholy. "I did. We spent many moons together in her youth. Long before she wore a crown. She and your other mother both. Wild things, they were. Brilliant, stubborn, full of magic and fury. Life marked them...as it has you. But I waited. The trees whispered of your coming. For decades, they have carried your name on the wind."

My heart twists, too full to hold steady. "If the trees whisper about me... does that mean others hear them too?"

The woman laughs again, unbothered, unshaken. "Heavens no, child. Most dismiss the trees as mad things. As they once did your mother. And the King?" Her eyes narrow slightly, a flicker of shadow across her glow. "He does not listen. He hears only what bleeds. He believes the earth is powerless beneath steel."

She looks back toward the trees, fingers brushing one vine like an old friend.

"But the roots remember."

I can't help the way my lip quirks as I catch Caomh's sudden stiffness, the flicker of something unreadable in his gaze. A quiet probe of power reveals a tangle of emotion I don't dare unravel—not now. Later, maybe. For now, my attention is drawn back to the being before me, luminous and ancient.

"Gaia," I begin softly, reverent. "I came here—"

She lifts her hand, a smile already curving her lips. "I know why you've come, Empath. A weapon born of chaos, and yet... one whose heart still speaks the language of the trees." Her voice is wind through leaves, ageless. "You seek to free my children. To relieve me of the burden of silencing those who carry a sliver of my essence."

When she presses a hand to her heart, the warmth that radiates from her is overwhelming. Not the warmth of a single affection, but something vast. Ancient. Alive. It wraps around me like roots and song. I meet her gaze with my own steady truth. "Yes."

"Then let us waste no time," she says, and turns without ceremony, her presence shifting the vines aside as though the forest itself parts for her passing. "My guardians slumber only so long."

I follow.

And the world opens.

The jungle gives way to something impossible—an entire city woven into the canopy. Towers of stone and wood twist together like living things, crowned in green, dappled with bioluminescent vines. Water flows through it all, threading pathways like veins. Every surface breathes with life. Two enormous manitaurs, their scales catching light in shimmering gold and emerald, bow as Gaia passes. They murmur her name like a prayer.

And within, life blooms. The Fae here wear moss and silk like afterthoughts, some not at all. There is no modesty, no shame. Just bodies, beautiful and bare, decorated with vines, tattoos, jewels. Freedom. The air thrums with it.

"Damn," Caomh mutters beside me, tracking a group of lithe, glowing figures. "I was born in the wrong kingdom."

I roll my eyes. Gaia laughs.

"I sensed a kindred spirit," she teases. "We do things... differently here."

"My kind of kingdom," Caomh replies without hesitation. "When this war's done, maybe I'll stay."

Gaia chuckles, but her gaze is knowing. "We both know you won't."

They fall into easy conversation, Caomh curiously inquiring about courtship rituals and relationship boundaries while I trail behind, overwhelmed by color, sound, freedom. It's dizzying. Beautiful.

And then—we arrive.

A vast platform stretches before us, and behind it, metal bars—cages. Dozens of them. No blood, no screams. Just quiet. The faces within are calm. Expectant.

I turn to Gaia, questioning.

She only shrugs, eyes twinkling. "We had hope you were coming."

Just like that, a guard steps forward and unlocks the cages.

And just like that, the prisoners—her people—step out, free. No fanfare. No speeches. Only movement. They pass me with nods and quiet murmurs, slipping into the protection of our ranks.

"The King is set to arrive soon," Gaia says, voice suddenly cool. "Take them and go."

There is no time to thank her.

I turn, guiding them back through the gates of Nadur, the towering trees casting long shadows across our path. As we leave, unease unfurls in my gut, coiling like smoke. I reach outward with my mind, hoping the beasts I lulled to sleep remain dreaming. But something... *shifts*.

The air is wrong. The tension unnatural.

"Cao?" I whisper, my voice cracking.

His eyes lock on mine—shuttered, then sharp. Too sharp.

And then the earth *erupts*.

From the underbrush, a serpent bursts into being, its size incomprehensible. It rises like a tidal wave, its head eclipsing the jungle canopy. Obsidian scales shimmer with sickly light, each one sharp as glass. My breath catches. *It's him*. The one from my dreams. The nightmare given form.

My heart slams against my ribs. The screams around me feel distant, warped. Time unspools. I reach, *reach* for the minds around me—for connection, for safety, for grounding, and find nothing. My power doesn't respond. It lags behind me, as if bound in chains.

Locked out.

"Olivia, *move!*" A voice pierces the ringing in my ears, but I can't find the face behind it.

The serpent's tongue flicks, tasting the air. And then, it sees me.

It *knows* me.

It charges.

The earth trembles beneath it. Trees split. I stumble back, but something grabs my arm—a rough hand, Caomh's—hauling me off balance. It's too late.

The serpent strikes.

Its coils whip around me with impossible speed. Cold, slick scales slam into me, pinning my arms, crushing the air from my lungs. My legs buckle. My vision swims. Light fractures and narrows until only shards remain. I can't breathe. I can't *think*.

The last thing I feel is the press of scales, and a thought—unbidden, cruel—slithering through the dark:

Maybe it's fitting that I die to a serpent.

Apophis in the Canopy

The thick, tangled brush where forest gives way to jungle rises before us like a living wall, veiling everything beneath its canopy in shadow. Whatever waits down there... it's hidden well.

"You're sure she's here?" I ask, scanning the layers of green, trying to see through the veil. Below, Lorkan soars over the undergrowth, a ripple of muscle and wings in his wyvern form, silent but alert.

Jet doesn't hesitate. "Eileamaid was raided for its prisoners. Nadur is the next closest Court. If she's doing what I think she is..." He trails off, but I already know. "She'll be heading there. To free them."

My pulse beats in my ears, loud and hot. The image of her blurs behind my eyes—Olivia, the woman who once trembled at her own power. Who chose chains over risking us. Who let herself be taken because she couldn't bear the idea of dragging others into her pain.

But the woman I saw across that battlefield... she wasn't hiding anymore. That final look—the one she gave me before disappearing in the Kings grasp—that was *her*. The woman I love. But now she wears her strength like a stormcloak. She faced the King, freed Caomh, freed Jet, freed *me*...and instead of running home, instead of collapsing into safety...

She ran toward more fire.

Toward Nadur. Toward the prisoners.

Toward the war.

"Isn't that too obvious?" I mutter, my concern heavy, thick as the jungle air. "Wouldn't the King know?"

Jet exhales behind me, his voice low. "You *know* her, Jeyr. She wouldn't risk it *any other* way. If she took the quiet route, the King would just move faster—slaughter the captives before she could reach them."

I clench my jaw, torn between admiration and dread. It's what I love about her—her stubborn, aching need to save everyone. And it's the thing that keeps me up at night. Her recklessness, her sacrifice. Every breath she gives to others takes her further from me.

"Any word from Caomh?" I ask, needing the steadiness he always brings.

Below, Lorkan shakes his wyvern head, a sleek ripple of muscle and scale. The gesture is small—but it sends a jolt straight through me. Caomh is never far. Never silent. He's always been a tether, a compass in the mess.

And now... nothing.

I grip the pommel at my hip tighter, eyes narrowing on the jungle as the knot in my chest pulls tighter.

Where are you, Hummingbird?

As if the Fates—or maybe destiny itself—heard the cry in my chest, the jungle *shudders*. Trees groan. Earth splits. A sound, low and thunderous, rolls through the underbrush.

Then I see it.

The world collapses before me in a breath.

Apophis.

The name tears from my throat before my mind even catches up.

Jet and I lock eyes, and with a nod we winnow from Lorkan's back into the fray.

A monstrous serpent, its obsidian scales gleaming like wet stone, tears through the jungle with brutal grace. Trees topple in its wake, roots ripping from the ground like screams. Its massive coils twist and slam, repelling every blade, every burst of power thrown its way. Chaos bleeds around it—Bane's soldiers crash into desperate defenders, their cries swallowed by the roar of destruction. And at the center of it all—held high, crushed within the serpent's embrace—is a figure.

Small. Still. Caught mid-breath.

A girl.

Wavy brunette hair lashes across her face as she fights to breathe, her limbs limp within the beast's crushing grip. She doesn't scream. She doesn't plead. She only stares out into the chaos, eyes wide, lips parted as if the air has abandoned her too. My body reacts at the sight—my heart races, my breath shortens, and my search for Olivia becomes frantic, knowing she is in danger.

I can't move. My thoughts blur with panic. The serpent coils, the forest burns, and Bane and Dominhall look on like specters carved from shadow.

Where is she?

My gaze searches—wild, useless—until it finds Caomh, blade flashing as he carves toward a group of children pressed behind the shattered remains of a barricade. He moves like a man possessed. I scream his name across the battlefield.

"*Caomh!* Where is she?!"

He spins, face drenched in blood and sweat, eyes burning.

Then he shouts—raw and furious: "*You fucking idiot—she's the brunette!*"

And only then do I *see* her.

Her green eyes locked on mine.

Action surges through me like a storm breaking free.

Lightning answers my call—ripping down from the heavens with a deafening crack. It tears through the canopy, shattering branches, splitting sky and earth alike. The serpent shrieks, its massive coils recoiling from the strike, body twitching with the sudden surge of pain.

A flicker—panic, wide-eyed and primal, crosses Olivia's face as she truly *sees* the creature for the first time. Kyzan circles beneath her, a blur of fangs and fury, striking again and again, but his fangs can't pierce its hide.

I reach her in a single breath. She collapses into my arms, her body limp, lungs wheezing. My heart stops.

"Hummingbird?" My voice breaks on her name. Her breaths are shallow, gurgled, and I feel the shattered bones beneath her skin pressing against my power like jagged glass. I press her closer, pour healing into her ribs, her lungs, into the space where pain has hollowed her out.

A roar—low, thunderous—rattles the jungle.

Lorkan.

He dives through the breach I carved, a blur of silver fury. The serpent, stunned and uncoiled, doesn't stand a chance. Lorkan sinks his teeth deep into its neck, twisting. *Crunch.* Bone and sinew snap. The serpent's hiss cuts off as its massive head collapses, thudding into the earth.

But death does not still it.

The serpent thrashes in its final spasms, tail sweeping through bodies like a battering ram. Fae scatter, screams rising. Olivia jerks in my grip, barely conscious. I hold her tighter, heart pounding.

We need to run.

We need to *leave*.

And then—I feel him.

Dominhall.

His presence slices through the fray like a blade dipped in oil. I look up to see his arms rise, magic already gathering in the air, dark and ruinous. I don't think—I *move*. I shove Olivia behind me, shielding her body with mine.

"Hummingbird, my love..." My voice is low, urgent, trembling beneath its calm. "Now would be a really good time to make his army fall asleep. Or hallucinate. Or vanish into thin air. *Anything.*"

She trembles behind me. Her fear, wild and electric, crashes into me like a wave.

"S-s-snake," she stammers.

I turn, cupping her face, forcing her eyes to mine. "The snake is gone. Do you hear me? *Gone.* It can't touch you now. Come back to me, Hummingbird. Hold on to me. Focus on the ones still alive—the ones we're saving. Their souls, not his."

And then—her arms wrap around me.

Tight.

Desperate.

Real.

A sob nearly escapes my throat, but I bite it back. I anchor myself to her touch, to the way her presence washes over me like warm rain on frostbitten skin. Even now. Even broken and breathless, she grounds me.

I whisper, forehead to hers, "I've got you. Just breathe. We leave together."

I felt as her body relaxed into mine, heard her inhale my scent. Me as her anchor, I watched as the humanoids collapsed in panic much like she had experienced only moments before. I watched as her power hit rank by rank. With it, I watched those who could winnow out do so. Those who were straying behind had others helping them. The King, momentarily crippled by her power, lifted his hand, and I took it as my cue to get the hell out.

Killing him was not an option, not yet.

The world still trembles with echoes of battle—serpent roars, the clash of steel, the thunder of falling trees—but here, in this shadowed hollow of the forest, silence begins to settle. Breath by ragged breath, bodies appear around us, winnowed from the fray, until the clearing fills with survivors. Fae and half-breeds alike stand watchful, their faces carved with awe, exhaustion, and the wary edge of disbelief.

And then—her.

With Olivia's arms snaking around my waist, the sight that dragged me here fades, replaced by the only thing that matters. I turn, ignoring the scrutiny of the crowd, and gather her into me, lifting her effortlessly. Her legs swivel, finding their place around my hips, her body folding against mine as if we were never parted. She burrows into my shoulder, and in that silent surrender, I feel the weight of her burden begin to ease.

It's not the right time. It's not safe. But it feels like coming home. Finally, I could shield her, erase the tremor in her voice.

"You did it, my love," I murmured, each word heavy with unspoken gratitude. With this victory, she hadn't just saved herself, but countless others, including my brother and my closest friend. The impossible, achieved.

"It's not over", she whispered, her voice muffled against my shoulder. A sigh escaped my lips, acknowledging the battles yet to come. "No, but this feat, my love, deserves its moment."

Her reply hung in the air, a blend of quiet reflection and humbling self-awareness. Words clamored for release, emotions yearning to be acknowledged. The tremor remained, ever so faint, mirroring in my own heart. I lifted her chin, tucking a stray strand of brown hair behind her ear. Her glistening green eyes, the eyes of my warrior queen, held a captivating fire.

Gods I missed you.

A jolt ran through me as her voice echoed in my mind, "I swear I heard you."

Her eyes blazed, meeting mine with a fire that mirrored the intensity within me. "Because you did," she confirmed, her voice a husky whisper.

Standing before me was a woman transformed, forged by loss and power. A million questions hung on my tongue, a million moments we'd missed. We'd both evolved, carrying scars etched onto our souls.

"We'll find the time," I murmured, cupping her face. "But right now, all I want to do is kiss you."

"What's stopping you?" she challenged, a spark of defiance dancing in her eyes.

"Nothing," I breathed, closing the distance between us. The world dissolved as our lips met, sending a tremor of longing through me. I held her close, savoring the familiar sweetness, the unspoken words carried on each kiss.

Suddenly, Caomh's voice intruded, "This reunion can wait. We have more pressing matters."

I glared at him, not breaking the kiss. *If I want to kiss my mate, I will.*

Olivia pulled away, her urgency cutting through the haze of desire. "He is right, the King's coming," she warned, "He'll try to stop us at Slanachad."

She leaned her head against mine, her thoughts silent but her anxiety a palpable hum around her. As she straightened, the girl who crumbled in my arms moments ago vanished. In her place stood a queen, her spine a steel rod, her presence radiating power. All eyes turned to her, their fate hanging on her next words.

"We need to separate. The King and his forces will try to stop me from saving more Fae and creatures like yourselves. Jet, you go with Lia and lead the way. Lorkan, Caomh, Jeyr... would you—"

Lorkan nodded, still in wyvern form, and I took Olivia's hand. "If you think I'm leaving you, you have another thing coming."

"You saved me from becoming a burnt carcass; the least I can do is cover your back," Caomh added.

"If you think I'm not coming, you're mistaken." The guard, recognizable from the ball, stepped forward. I caught a glimpse of Olivia's smile as she nodded in approval.

I try not to think about how I had only a split second—an interrupted kiss—after yearning so long to be with her. I try not to think about how I just pulled her from the crush of a serpent, only to find us thrust straight into another battle, denied even a moment to simply be reunited.

I straighten my spine, forcing myself into readiness as the others prepare to move again. But the truth is, my eyes track only her, memorizing every new feature as if she could be taken from me at any moment.

Olivia

THE WEIGHT I TAKE FOR YOU

I sit at the edge once more, the perimeter of the makeshift camp, watching the sea of Fae—each one radiant in their own unique, jagged way. My limbs ache with restraint, every inch of me begging for retreat. Not battle. Not chaos. Just stillness. Just... quiet.

It surprises me, how often my thoughts drift back to the room that was once my cell. The one that made me flinch at every flicker of firelight, where the scent of lilies turned my stomach and the walls bled memories I couldn't scrub clean. And yet... there's something about the seclusion that calls to me now. The solitude. The blessed silence.

Anything to escape the crawling sensation under my skin, my powers tugging at every passing soul, reaching before I've granted them permission. The press of minds, the voices, the pain... It hums, it scratches, it aches to connect. I've never been in a crowd this size. Maybe not ever.

I was the girl who wandered moonlit paths alone. Who found comfort in shadows, in whispers. Who was kept in solitude—and made it her home.

My gaze drifts over those I once called mine.

Caomh is in his element—stern and sure, command etched into the line of his spine, but there's a restlessness in him too. His eyes flicker constantly, scanning the crowd. Searching. Always searching. Not for threats. For someone.

Colden, like me, lingers on the fringes. Watching. Not engaging. His eyes meet mine across the firelight, and I let his voice in.

Need me?

It's quiet. Simple. Steady. He never presses. Just stands guard over the version of me most haven't met yet.

I shake my head. He nods once and moves on.

Jeyr moves through the wounded like a soft wind, steady hands, quiet words. He doesn't look for attention. Just healing. Still, I feel the bond between us pulse like a heartbeat out of rhythm. He wants to be beside me. I feel it tugging, warm and aching.

But I don't call him.

And, gods help me, I'm relieved he's occupied. Just for now. Just while I try to gather the pieces of myself scattered in the dirt.

Lorkan is nowhere to be seen, which usually means he's everywhere. I feel him though. Close. Watching in one form or another. After decapitating a serpent the size of Blacktown, solitude is earned. I shudder at the memory—bone and blood, weight and fear.

Then there's Jet.

The moment I see him, something shifts.

The reunion still thrums through my chest, but beneath the warmth lies something unfinished. A conversation swallowed by smoke and survival. Guilt gnaws at me. And grief—his grief—pulls at the edge of my awareness like a tide.

It's enough to drag me from the pull of dissociation.

I step toward him. His frame is solid, unmoved, but the silence in his mind strikes me harder than a scream. The Jethro I remember used to laugh like a spark, always reaching toward light.

Now... there's only shadow.

My hand hesitates as it hovers, then lands on his shoulder. A simple touch. He stiffens at first, then turns—slowly.

His eyes meet mine. What was once fire is now ash.

He tries to smile. Fails.

My fingers drift to his cheek, a feather-light brush against the sorrow etched into his skin. He leans into the contact, his eyelids fluttering shut like the weight inside him is too much to carry upright anymore.

And then I see it.

His grief opens to me like a wound. The image of Gwynn flickers in his mind—her body lifeless, draped across a field of flowers that haunt me too. The same as in my dreams. The same as the nightmares carved in serpent scales.

"What—" I start, the word dry in my throat.

But he cuts through the silence before I can finish.

"Bane," he says.

It's not a word. It's a wound.

I feel it slam into me like a storm—raw, jagged, final. The loss is too much for words. So I don't use any.

I pull him into my arms.

He doesn't speak. He doesn't need to. He just holds on, and I let him. I become the quiet he needs. The space where pain can just be.

He lets go.

And for a fragile moment, he lets it out.

And in turn—I take it.

Every inch of it. The blistering guilt. The jagged shards of loss. The quiet fury that curdles behind the silence. The emotion mortals reduce to a single, brittle word: grief.

But grief is not a word. It's a volcanic eruption, ancient and merciless. It runs deeper than language, deeper than bone—buried beneath the earth's crust and molten enough to level cities. And I take it. All of it. I draw it into the hollows of my chest, let it root there. Let it burn.

One day, I know, I'll release it. Not in mourning. In reckoning. I'll hurl it like a blade into the heart of our enemy. Because Jethro's love is pure. And no king—no fae tyrant—deserves to walk free while hearts like his bleed in the dirt.

Jeyr is the kind of man who heals with a touch, who shields with a whisper. But Jethro? Jethro burns. And still, he stands.

"He'll pay, Jet," I whisper, voice thick with the weight we now carry between us. "But not at the cost of yourself."

"He will," he replies. A rasp—cool and ragged. The sound of vengeance chilled over time, sharp enough to cut.

I nod.

The promise hangs between us, silent but absolute. An oath stitched in ash and memory.

"Want to go for a walk?" he suggests, and his hand stretches out, and that gesture is a lifeline. Like how I was reading him, he was reading me.

It flashes me back to a simpler time, our first time walking the beach together. A time where we spoke of how, in time, the emotions a fae felt just turned into stone. Not because they disappeared, but because they were never dealt with. Just burned lower. Because even with a life promised forever… time flickered faster somehow. And the problems that came with it—they never seemed to cease.

I take his hand.

And I feel it—his powers pooling gently beneath his skin. The touch of sunlight to my palm, like I had reached out and grabbed it. I could have sobbed—damn, I was near close to—with how rung out I felt. With the pressure of having to keep myself composed. Keep it all in.

But Jet knew.

He didn't say a word, just tugged my hand softly and led me away from the convoy.

I heard Jeyr whisper into his mind, *Keep her safe. Keep her unseen, brother.*

Jethro simply nodded, and I felt the cloak of power pool over us. The glamour shimmered faintly, then settled, like mist drawn tight to skin. And then we moved through the forest, unseen.

With each step, my heart found its rhythm again—matching my ambling feet. The breeze brushing my face, the smell of pine and moss slowly settling my breath. And the farther we got from the crowd, the easier it became to breathe. The relentless tugging. The overlapping voices. The pull of every soul in that camp—faded.

And I was left with just the familiarity of an old friend.

One I realised never asked anything of me.

He was just there. And his ache… matched mine. Though we grieved for different reasons—his for a love he lost, and me for a life I never really wanted to call mine. The loss of who I once was. The anger. The exhaustion. It was all so similar—and yet so different. But we both felt it.

Eventually we came to a small waterhole, water trickling over rocks, gentle and unhurried. The sun filtered down through the trees, casting soft light over the rocky bed. And like the light called to him, he moved—taking me with him.

We sat on the warm stone. The water's song filled the space between us.

His shoulder leaned against mine.

And then, after a while, he spoke.

"I have been alone for most of my relationship," he said quietly. "Gwyn was gone longer than we were ever together. And yet, little huntress… I don't know how to be alone. I don't know how to stop storing memories in my notebook to tell her later. I don't know how to stop thinking 'Gwyn would love that,' every time I see something strange or sweet."

He huffed a laugh. It wasn't amused.

"It's so pathetic, you know? Because missing her when she was gone is so different to now. Because now I'll never get to tell her how a black cat came into my room and pulled the same face she used to make when tasting brussel sprouts. Or how Caomh threw his fourth shirt in the fire after losing it over another one of his communications."

His voice wavered.

"It's all so... insurmountable. Stupid things. Small things. Things I barely got to voice to her."

He paused.

Then, softer—more broken:

"And now the only memory I have of her is her—dead. On a bed of lilies. With his handwriting on it."

His voice went thin as the last words left him. My chest cracked with the weight of it, and my eyes welled. I squeezed his hand—somehow still tangled in mine—and let his pain pour into me.

He turned then, pressing his forehead to my shoulder.

And I felt it.

The wetness.

He didn't sob. He didn't wail. He just let go. And I knew, even without reaching for the memory—this was the first time he'd cried.

I didn't say anything.

There was nothing right to say.

Not yet.

And maybe that was for the best, because his words came again, hoarse and low:

"I just feel like I should have made her stay. I got her back... and then you..."

A pause.

"You got captured."

My heart stopped in my chest. My eyes closed. Because suddenly the soft light and stillness around us felt like a punishment. I wasn't meant to be in this peace. Not if it had cost him that.

Somehow, it all came back to me.

I never wanted to be the pinnacle of disaster. But if I were to bury myself in my own pity—I was.

His words stopped there. And he let his emotion fall over me like a storm.

And I took it.

Because it was mine to carry, too.

Eventually, his tears faded, and my shoulder dried—whether by his own sunlight or the one basking down on us, I couldn't tell. The sun no longer hid behind clouds or trees. It touched everything. Even us.

I was the first to stand this time, letting my hand slip from his.

I pulled gently at the loose threads of ache I'd gathered from him, releasing them into the air, letting him feel peace—for now. The grief would return. It always did. I knew that from my own losses. But for this moment, he could breathe.

I found my voice, steady enough not to crack, though the swell in my throat warned me it was close.

"We better get back."

His lip quirked, the faintest trace of a smile tugging at one side of his mouth. He stood, brushing off invisible flecks of dust, stretching to his full height.

"Yeah. More people to rescue. More people to kill. Isn't that right, little huntress?"

I didn't know what he meant by it. There was something in his voice, undertones I couldn't name. I didn't try to read it. I'd already closed that part of me off from him, sealed the door before I could second-guess it.

My lips pressed tight. "Something like that."

This time, when we walked back to the convoy, we didn't hold hands. His power still cloaked us in shadow and quiet, shielding us from watchful eyes. But I felt the shift between us. The friendship we had in the manor, those late-night laughs, the casual, wordless comfort—it wouldn't be the same.

And I couldn't blame him.

My part in Gwynn's death wouldn't disappear. Not in his eyes. Not in mine.

If he held anything against me—resentment, regret, even hate—I wouldn't argue it. I wouldn't fight it. I'd just carry it.

But if I could hold Bane still, if I could be the one who bound him down while Jet took his head...

Maybe then.

Maybe then, I could claw back a fragment of what we once were.

Maybe then, I'd be worthy of the love I used to know.

The convoy was not as we left it.

Now the fires were blazing as the sun slipped below the horizon, and the air hummed with voices—song, laughter, spirit. People told stories, some sung softly, others loudly as food cooked over open flame. While some remained on patrol, vigilant at the borders, the heart of it—the families—buzzed more than it had before our journey to Nadur.

I stood once again at the outskirts, watching. Taking it in.

It wasn't until a familiar figure noticed me that I was pulled from my thoughts.

Lia.

She darted from her post—like me, she lingered on the camp's edge, watching without really watching. One moment she was leaning against a tree like she had nowhere better to be, and the next, she was striding toward me like a shot.

"Took your time," she called, not bothering to hide her smirk. "Thought you'd left me with a bundle of strangers whose eyes looked like they were one bad joke away from playing pin-the-dagger-on-the-donkey."

I huffed. "What?"

She looked from me to Jethro, and something in her—her usual unbothered stillness—started to shift. She got... fidgety. Like her skin was suddenly too tight.

"Nothing," she said quickly, eyes flicking back and forth between us, as if she suddenly didn't want to speak anymore.

"Jethro, meet Lia," I said, gesturing between them.

Jethro offered his hand, his gaze lingering on her for a moment too long. It wasn't cruel—just... piercing.

"She was in the prisons with me," I added, and that seemed to shift something in him. His eyes narrowed slightly, voice dropping as he spoke.

"From the Kingdom of Puinseann, are we?"

His tone wasn't loud, wasn't aggressive, but I felt the change. The subtle darkening of his energy. I'd never once feared the light master beside me. But at that moment, the way the hairs lifted along Lia's arms, the way discomfort rippled off her—I felt it.

My instincts flared.

I turned to her, locking eyes. My voice came out firmer than expected, but still soft enough to not draw attention.

And you, I said into her mind, *listen closely. Under no circumstances do you breathe a word about your... lineage. Not to Jethro. Not to anyone. The risks are too high.*

The weight of her secret hung between us, thick and silent.

She swallowed. Fear battled with the defiance in her eyes.

I understand she whispered.

Then louder, with a faint shrug of indifference, she said, "I don't know. I was born in the prisons. I don't know my lineage."

Not all a lie.

I felt it—truth and falsehood stitched together, sewn with survival. But Jethro didn't miss the waver. He watched her with that same narrowed gaze, no longer offering his hand. His light—usually warm—now felt like shadow pressed tight to skin. He dropped his hand, gave me a sharp nod, and walked off.

Toward Caomh.

I followed his path with my eyes just in time to see Caomh catch the change in him, the tightness, the new shadow settled across his shoulders. He looked past Jethro, straight to Lia. His jaw ticked. A new death-glare activated.

Lia glanced back, sensing it too.

"They don't trust me," she said dryly. "Nor like me."

Her eyes returned to mine, flat, distant.

I exhaled, rubbing a hand across my jaw. "Don't worry, Lia," I murmured. "I'm starting to feel the same sentiments."

I sigh as the family I once knew look at me and at the girl beside me with more distrust than warmth. Lia grabs my hand and ushers me away from their stares.

"Eh, they worship the ground you walk on, but they're a little scared of you. And me? Well, they both hate me and distrust me. It's quite an ego boost, being so important in their minds."

She says it as if the Fae in the circle ignoring her don't bother her in the slightest. And to be fair, I can't tell from her body language alone if it does or doesn't.

As we move, I feel Lia's hand slip away. I turn to see why she's stopped—when a familiar scent hits my nose. Jeyr. My gaze finds him leaning against a tree, eyes flicking from me to Lia. But this time, the stare is nothing like his brothers'. His gaze is intense, fixed solely on me, taking me in from head to toe.

"Ah, another place I don't feel welcome. I'll see if the Ice Man also sends me away." Lia pivots and slips off—probably to wherever Colden is hiding—leaving Jeyr and me...

It's all a blur.

And I refuse to let my mind drag me back to that moment, to how he first found me wrapped in that monster's grip, if this is to be the first time we're truly *together* again. But it is the first time in a long time. And it feels different. He feels different.

"Hummingbird." His voice hums over the space between us, lips quirking before his steps eat away the distance. His hand closes the gap first, thumb and forefinger tilting my chin so he can take me in. His fingers slide over the blunt cut of my hair, and I don't dare think about how the new colour might look slipping through them.

"Jeyr," I breathe, his name spilling out like the ghost of a dream that has haunted me far too long.

"I am right here."

That's all it takes. I lurch into his arms, and he catches me, strong hands grabbing my legs, wrapping them around himself. I bury my face in the cove of his neck, counting the beats of his pulse, breathing him in like the scent could wash away all the months of absence.

He backs up until the tree supports his weight, sliding down with me still in his hold, curling himself around me.

"Gods, I have dreamt of this moment for so long."

And I know he has. His memories bleed into mine—every thought of how he blamed himself for not burning the world down to find me. No matter who I've become, I can feel and hear the raw intensity of his self-hate, the belief that he failed. The failures he doesn't own are written over my mind as they are painted over his—in red, in bold.

I hold him tighter, hoping he feels that his guilt is not his to keep. The decisions were mine. He has so much more to live for. Whether it's the steady hum of chatter and soft songs in the camp, the smell of the fires, or simply the safety of his arms, exhaustion wins. And in his hold I am safe and sound.

Olivia

The Moment We Held Each Other

I wake to the low hush of the forest, the kind that comes just before dusk when the air feels heavier and the shadows stretch longer. My head is still resting against Jeyr's chest, his breathing deep and steady beneath my ear. He hasn't moved, not even to shift his weight against the tree. His arm is still looped around me, holding me there like he's been keeping watch over more than just the forest.

You're awake.

His voice threads through my mind, warm and sure, and my body goes rigid before I can help it. *What would he think, with this new power of mine?*

My eyes lift to his. The quiet between us sharpens. "You heard me," he says, not a question, just the inevitable truth hanging in the space between our breaths.

I look at my palms, pretending my pulse isn't hammering. "Sometimes," I admit. My voice is careful, the words steady when they want to splinter. "It's... new."

His gaze narrows, studying me like he's weighing how much to ask, how much to leave alone. I feel the faintest pressure at the edges of my mind, not invasive, just curious, like the brush of fingertips against glass. "How long?"

"Not long enough to be careless with it. Not long enough to know how to use it." My gaze drifts past him, to the faint glimmer of firelight flickering through the trees where the convoy waits. "And Caomh doesn't need to know. Not yet." I couldn't have him finding out not after that singular look he gave across the camp with Jet. If he decided later that I was his enemy, so be it. For now, all that mattered was keeping them safe... keeping these fae safe.

That earns the smallest shift in his stance, a barely-there tilt of his head. Not surprise—acceptance. "You have your reasons," he says quietly.

"I do."

He lets it settle there. No pressing, no challenge. Just the unspoken agreement slotting into place between us like it's always been there.

Jeyr stands, brushing bark from his palms, and offers his hand down to me. When I take it, his fingers wrap warm and sure around mine, holding just a fraction longer than they need to. "Come on," he says, the corner of his mouth lifting. "Ness is waiting. If we're any later, Caomh will brood himself into a storm."

We start toward the camp in silence, weaving between trunks while the fires grow brighter ahead. The Fae watch as we pass, their eyes flickering between me and Jeyr. I can't tell who holds their attention more—him, with his quiet command, or me.

It's only now that I notice what he's wearing. Armour fit for a king—tight layers of leather worked with wyvern scales, translucent as sunlight through clouds, colors shifting with each step. Threads of deep blue weave through the design, and on his chest gleams the emblem of the Court of Aimsir. There's no mistaking who he is: the Grand Duke, untouchable.

I glance down at myself—fighting leathers that hang loose, ripped from battles fought, singed by fire. My hair, cut blunt and left matted, a far cry from courtly grace. And yet Jeyr looks untouched by it all, like a man who has simply walked from his palace to stand beside me.

Ness waits at the far edge of the camp, her great head lowering when she spots us, tail swishing once against the ground. Jeyr runs a hand along her neck, murmuring something low that makes her rumble deep in her chest. Then he turns to me, his grip is steady at my waist as he lifts me into the warm curve of her back. By the time he swings up behind me, his body heat seeps through my spine.

"Sit close," he murmurs, his breath stirring the loose strands at my temple.

Ness starts forward at an easy pace, her stride rocking us in a steady rhythm. The forest folds around us, the glow of campfires slipping away behind. His arms curve around me, the weight of them as familiar as it is protective.

I let my eyes drift shut, listening to the measured beat of his heart against my back, and little by little, the rest of the world fades until there's only that sound and the rise and fall of his breath.

Ness's gentle sway cradles me, rocking me into a slow, delicate dance with sleep. Jeyr's warm, strong arms are an anchor, his whole body wrapped around mine. It's no surprise my own gives in—deciding in his presence that rest is its first demand, like a debt collector reclaiming what's owed after months of sleeping with one eye open.

"Sleep, my love," he whispers, his breath brushing my ear as he nuzzles closer. He knows. Knows that I need this, that my body is desperate for a reset. Still, even in the safety of his hold, a flicker of unease keeps my eyes open.

This moment feels stolen, and I want to savour every heartbeat of it. I want to steal another look at his face, trace the constellations scattered across the ocean-blue of his eyes. But time is a thief, and it slips through my fingers like sand. Soon, even the colour of his gaze will fade into the blur of sleep.

You will have a lifetime to look into my eyes, Love. His voice, soft and certain in my mind, follows a trail of kisses up my neck. Reassuring, yes—but doubt still clings to me like a shadow.

Jeyr's sharp bite, almost playful, yanked me back from the precipice of worry. *No dark spirals, Hummingbird.* His possessiveness, a double-edged sword, both comforting and unnerving. *It's you and me. If you go, I go.*

"This whole mind thing," I confessed, vulnerability bare, "I don't know how to shut it out. Don't know how to block the noise of others."

How about we think of something else? His mental voice held a playful lilt. *A nighttime story, perhaps?* Despite the unease gnawing at me, a smile curved my lips. We were adrift in a sea of unknowns, but there was solace in the sound of his voice, a melody that chases away the storm clouds for now.

What do you have in mind?

Jeyr's voice resonates in my mind, a warm rumble that sends shivers skittering down my spine. This closeness, this unbroken thread between us, feels like a forgotten luxury after the arid wasteland of my recent past.

Desire flickers—sharp, bright—but it's not the kind that fades when morning comes. I feel him testing the waters, the hesitant brush of his thoughts against mine, gauging how deep I'll let him in. But I want more than sparks. I want something that burns slow and sure. A love untainted. A flame steady enough to melt away the scars left by a possession that never truly held me.

The darkness is past. I dream of sunlight. Of a future that doesn't cast shadows.

He feels it—whether through the echo of my thoughts or that uncanny way he's always known me. His arm tightens at my waist, thumb brushing in steady, grounding strokes against my side. His other hand cups my cheek, fingertips threading gently through the loose curls framing my face. Each touch is a spark, but not one that burns. It's a warmth that seeps deep, a steady heat that asks nothing in return.

I close my eyes, sinking into him, letting that warmth become the walls of my world. The ache eases. The fractures in me knit a little tighter. And then—softly—he begins to weave a vision in my mind.

"We're in Aimsir Castle. You're leading me by the hand through the quiet corridors, your grip firm yet careful, as if letting go would risk losing me to the wind. You turn back to me with that smile—gods, that smile—that lights your whole face and crinkles the corners of your eyes.

"Where are you taking me, Hummingbird?" I tease, and you laugh. That sound... melodic, warm, threaded with joy. But it's the crinkle of your nose when you do that undoes me every time, making your beauty—which so often feels untouchable—suddenly human, suddenly mine.

You quicken your pace, sunlight spilling through a wall of windows to crown you in gold. Your hair bounces with each step, catching the light, your green eyes flashing back at me, flecked with gold that the day itself envies.

We stop before a door. You're breathless, giddy, vibrating with the kind of anticipation that's impossible not to catch. I should be annoyed that you've found it before I could show you myself—that you've claimed this secret I'd been saving. But all I feel is the pull of your joy, the way it leaves no room for my own selfishness.

And then you push the door open.

It's exactly as I'd imagined for you: a small, warm room lined with books, a low fire dancing in the hearth. Above it, a painting of our coastline—our little stretch of beach, were we first got to know each other, the beach between a hidden cottage in the forrest and a manor you turned into a home.

You guide me to the soft sofas, the kind that mirror those back in the manor, and the sound of Kyzan's familiar tip-tap follows at your heels. He curls up at your feet, content, like the world has settled just right again. We sip the deep, rich wine you love, the kind that leaves warmth blooming in my chest. With your back resting against me, we watch the mountains rise beyond the glass, the lake below catching the light in flashes of crystal blue. The quiet here feels whole—like the world has stopped long enough to let us breathe.

Music drifts low in the background. My lips find the slope of your neck, brushing over skin I've dreamed of too long, and a request leaves me in a whisper—dance with me. My breath fans across your skin, and I feel the ripple it sends through you.

You take my hand. We sway slowly across the woollen carpet, the fire casting gold across your freckles, turning your eyes into molten green edged with flame. I spin you once, twice, your hair catching the light so the brown deepens into copper, strands curling and flying around your face like the fire is dancing with you.

I can't stop my hands from threading into your hair, tilting your chin just enough to find your lips. The kiss sparks heat, not the fleeting kind, but the kind that takes root deep. My hands slide to your waist and, without thought, I lift you to me. Your legs wrap tight, your fingers moving against my shirt until buttons slip free and fabric parts beneath your touch.

The world blurs to firelight and the music's steady hum. I lay you back against the sofa cushions, our hands finding skin, unravelling each other slowly, like secrets we've waited years to share. The golden light spills across you, painting shadows I want to trace forever. My fingers map the curve of your silhouette, each rise and hollow etched into memory, until my mouth follows—soft, lingering, tasting.

My breath comes faster, though my hands stay steady at your waist, holding the shape of you there. I press my mouth to the warmth of your skin, letting my teeth graze, the restraint almost unbearable as I soothe where instinct begs to claim. I trail lower, your body arching into me, my palms catching the small of your back, thumbs brushing over the delicate ridges of your hipbones—just as they do now, here in the present.

My breath shudders.

My lips take that bundle of nerves between your legs, slow kisses and deeper pulls, until your thighs tremble and the air thickens with the sound of your breath, the heat of your need for me. I don't stop—won't—until you let go, until the only thing in your mind is me and my touch, the current of my lips, my tongue taking you, loving you.

You pull me to you and we pause, letting our eyes meet and linger, drinking in the way our bodies fit together like they were carved for it. Your hands find my face, fingers searching until they press into the dimples you've always claimed as yours. I smile—truly smile—because we made it, my love.

Our lips meet, unhurried, like we have all the time in the world. Your legs wrap around me, pulling me closer, and I find my place in you, the collision of our bodies tightening the bond between us until it's unshakable.

"Jeyr," I breathe, the word leaving me like a prayer, like an invocation meant to bind us beyond this moment. The scene unfurls inside my mind with such clarity that the world around me fades, the forest, the danger, the shadows—all dissolving beneath the pull of this vision. The longing for that moment, so vivid and impossibly real, threatens to undo me.

I had never dared to imagine such a thing, yet here it is—our story, our future—woven into the very core of me. Even in the heart of war, even with the ghosts of my past clawing at me, I clutch this hope like a fragile blossom in the desert, waiting for the rain. Much like I hold onto him.

Jeyr threads the images together effortlessly, his voice painting firelit nights and the feel of his fingers tracing lazy, reverent lines across my bare skin. I slump against him on horseback as we weave through a forest infamous for swallowing souls whole. Yet it's the most peace I've known since the dark days of my capture.

"Next time, don't tell a sex story when we are walking through the deserted forest–you are not helping my situation," Caomh grumbles, his voice cutting through the peaceful sounds of the forest. The light footfalls of Ness and the scent of pine fill my senses as I sit upright, my head cradled in the curve of Jeyr's warm shoulder, his arms wrapped around me securely, the gentle rhythm of his breath tickling the side of my neck. It is almost too peaceful considering at any moment this could be pulled from under me. I realise how much I had blocked him from my thoughts during my time being held captive. This closeness, this intimacy, is beyond my wildest dreams, a glimmer of hope in the darkness that has consumed me for so long.

"You were listening in? That was private," Jeyr hard-whisper scolds.

"No, but you both smelled like you were having sex, and our lovely little empath may have let her powers slip. I was walking with a hard-on for way too long." I feel my lip give, my attempt at feigning sleep slipping.

Jeyr scoffs behind me, jostling me. I feel his hands instinctively tighten their grasp to ensure I stay steady on the horse as we continue our ride.

"I keep telling you, I could think of one person who would happily scratch that itch," Jeyr sing-songs.

"I tried with Mr. hot 'n' icey over there. He says I'm not his type. Like seriously, I am everyone's type," Caomh counters. Oh, how I would love to have been around for that conversation.

I can't help but laugh, opening my eyes to see Caomh looking at me. "You're not my type," I answer.

"Oh, princess, we all know you find me attractive. If you and Mr. stormy behind you were not mates, you would be all over me."

I laugh some more. "Mr. stormy? I'm keeping that. You are attractive, but that doesn't mean you're my type, Caomh."

Jeyr, if possible, tightens his hold on me. "Let's not talk about what my mate finds attractive, thank you."

"Just you, Jeyr, just you," I answer, and I can't deny that his happy growl does something to me.

Caomh throws his hands up and groans. "Seriously, you two."

"You know, Cao, Jeyr has a point... there is a certain shifter who could satisfy your many varied likes," I coo, loving how Caomh only goes red in the face and more aggravated.

"I don't fuck shifters! End of!" Caomh yells.

Lorkan shifts from his Raven form in one fluid motion, and if looks could kill, the one he sends Caomh's way would leave nothing but ash.

"Good to know, Cay. No one said you would be the one to do the fucking," he replies, tone sharp enough to cut the air.

Cay draws in a breath, ready to fire back, but his voice dies before it starts when Lorkan turns fully toward Jeyr and me. His jaw is tight, and I can tell it's not Caomh's words that have him strung so taut.

"Princess," he says, his voice carrying weight, "the King is already at Slanachad."

The words hit me like a blow. My stomach drops. We're too late.

"The grand dukes were forced to kill fifty."

The air around us stills. Murmurs stir in the convoy, low and uneasy, while emotions—shock, grief, anger—bleed into me until they're indistinguishable from my own.

Behind me, Jeyr's presence presses closer, his breath heavy with restrained emotion. "It's against the healers' code..." he murmurs, the weight in his voice making the words drag.

"The King had Bliant in his grasp; Aison was not going to let his mate die," Lorkan explains, his tone roughened at the edges.

"How many are we working against?" Caomh asks, his voice steady despite the tension rippling through the group.

"The humanoid army is about two hundred. Then the King himself."

"What of Gliocas?" Jeyr asks, his gaze fixed hard on Lorkan, searching for the answer he doesn't want to hear.

Lorkan's shoulders stiffen at the name. "Bane is there, waiting for the King. No one has been killed yet; I think they're waiting to see where we go first."

"The position of my father?" Caomh asks, his voice level but shadowed with something darker.

"He is siding with the King," Lorkan says carefully, eyes flicking to Caomh to measure the reaction.

Caomh nods once, the motion slow and deliberate. Whatever runs through his mind, he keeps it locked behind that unreadable expression. Without a word, he resumes walking, the crunch of his boots on the forest floor the only sound he gives away.

Colden, silent until now, finally speaks. "So we go save Aison, Bliant, and their people?"

The answer comes in the form of a shared look between us all—a silent agreement. Aison and Bliant will not fall. Not today.

We move as one, the convoy shifting into motion, each step weighted with the knowledge of what lies ahead. Whatever waited for us at Slanachad—be it two hundred soldiers, the King himself, or Bane—we would meet it head-on. There's no other choice.

Jethro

THE DRAGONS INSANE WOMAN

"Jet, you and Lia take the children and their parents to the sanctuary, as well as anyone not strong enough or still recovering from injury," Olivia commands, and I feel my spine stiffen at once.

"No. I'm not going with your prison friend and missing the front line. We both know I have a score to settle." The words come out sharp, tasting of old bitterness. For a moment, her eyes widen—but it's fleeting. Her jaw tightens, her expression settling into stone. That look has me bristling, wondering if she'd dare use her powers on me. She's not the sweet, people-pleasing woman I trained all those moons ago. This Olivia... she looks like she could flatten every enemy—or friend—who stood in her way.

"We have the same purpose, Jet. You know the path to the Aotom better than anyone." She folds her arms, standing taller, the faintest tilt of her chin transforming her into something primal. Even without the fiery red hair, she's more huntress than diplomat now.

Jeyr stands beside her, and for the first time in years, he looks more like my brother. Colour in his face, peace in his eyes—even given the circumstances. He has the one thing I can never have again: his love, here in his arms. I snarl at him, knowing exactly what's about to come.

"She's right and you know it. Saving these men and women is the first priority, or all of this is for nothing."

And you won't leave your mate now that you have her. I fill in the words he doesn't say. Caomh won't lead them. Lorkan won't leave Caomh, and vice versa. That leaves me.

I grit my jaw, turning to the woman I'm supposed to share this long journey with. Her arms are crossed over armour that doesn't quite fit, gaps obvious enough that I could slide one of my daggers through with ease. She quirks an eyebrow at me, the unspoken challenge almost daring me to try. For reasons I can't explain, I take a twisted satisfaction in picturing her bleeding for me. She's survived countless suns in that cursed kingdom, and I know how it changed my wife over the years—how it hardened her will until nothing could break it. This one is just the same. Hard on the outside, and I have no doubt merciless when she isn't trying to charm Olivia.

I still don't understand what possessed Olivia to free a complete stranger from the prisons that hold the King's most wanted.

I take her in once more: jet-black hair falling past her waist, each strand impossibly smooth, as if brushed by an air shifter's power. Not a single piece out of place. She looks... other. Not just foreign. Other.

My senses buzz just by being near her, every part of me screaming that she needs to be as far from me as possible. And yet here I am, trekking the whole damn continent with her.

My fingers brush over my blades in a practiced ritual—muscle memory at this point. Who knows when I'll need them? A flash of daydream slides into my mind, vivid and uninvited: steel kissing the hollow of her throat, her eyes wide, her breath caught. Not many people inspire that kind of vision in me, but she does—easily.

"You've got a whole trek with my Light Bastard," she drawls, her tone toeing that infuriating line between teasing and mocking. "Maybe hold those killing instincts until we get there. I promise, I'll keep my mouth shut from here on out. Gods know I can go a millennia without so much as a word."

She rolls her eyes before strutting toward the convoy, where the lines are forming—fighters following Olivia and Jeyr, the rest beginning to fall into order. I try to ignore the murmur of plans rippling through the ranks.

My gaze shifts to the group I'll be leading—the young ones, the parents, those who need tending rather than battle. I force myself taller, set my shoulders, and start forward. Without looking back, I know they're following.

The convoy creeps along at a maddeningly sluggish pace, every step through the mountain ranges between Gliocas and Aimsir dragging like a chore. We've already thinned out the numbers as much as we can, taking the narrowest paths to keep exposure low. The terrain is unforgiving—jagged rock, treacherous snow—and I know it too well. Every twist and turn is carved into my memory from before I mastered winnowing, back when I was just a young Aire sneaking out with two others to steal a few hours away from training, from lessons about the gods, from our beloved King.

Back then, these mountains were freedom. Now they're just a reminder. I don't live life at this pace anymore. I winnow everywhere—always rushing, always on to the next mission. Sitting still has never been an option, because stillness leaves space for the one thought I can't bear: that the person I love is somewhere far away, doing what she insists must be done. Every crunch under my boot is a reminder I don't want.

Lia walks beside me in silence. She keeps her promise—no words, no smirk, no twitch of her lips. Her face is as still and pale as the snow that clings to the peaks. Even her hair lies tame, unlike the others whose hoods and strands whip with the wind. But every now and then, I catch the smallest fracture—her gaze lingering on the view, the faint inhale as if she's taking it in. Proof she's not entirely carved from stone.

"Stay close to the mountain walls," I call out. "And have someone beside you at all times."

The order ripples through the line, hands linking as they edge along the narrow pass. I don't know why I look back—what instinct makes me check on her—but when I do, she's standing still, too close to the drop, her head tilted up toward the peaks.

"Come on," I call. "Look too long and you'll end up staring at the sky while you fall."

She doesn't move. Doesn't even blink.

"Lia," I snap, "if something happens to the convoy because you decided to admire the view, I'll kill you."

Without looking at me, her voice cuts back, dry as winter air. "You've been looking for a reason to since you first saw me. I should think you'd be pleased."

Her eyes stay fixed on the ridge above. I follow her gaze, but see nothing—just white peaks, flurries spiraling at the edge, beautiful and silent. Silent like the cold that lulls you into thinking you're safe when you're minutes from freezing. The kind that claims you without mercy if you stay still too long.

I growl, stomping toward her. The convoy hesitates, glancing back at us, unsure whether to keep moving or wait. I grab her arm—and recoil at the jolt that shoots through

me.

Her head snaps to me. Her eyes are pits of black, lips curling to bare fangs. The hiss that escapes her is low and deliberate, thick with warning. She doesn't speak, but the distaste on her face says enough.

"We've got to keep moving," I grind out.

She shakes her head. I bite down on my frustration, but the growl still rips free. This woman makes something primal in me want to tear loose.

Suddenly, the skies above darken, and a colossal shadow sweeps across the mountain pass. For a split second, I think my mood has slipped its leash and I've lost control of my shadows. But the shouts from behind tell me otherwise—the Fae warriors have already spotted whatever cast that shadow.

I shove Lia behind me. She thrashes against my grip, her voice sharp with fury at being touched. "Don't touch me!"

I ignore her and lift my gaze to the sky, sword halfway drawn when the creature drops into view—wings stretched wide enough to blot out the sun. A puff of steam rolls from its massive nostrils, and I hesitate, my eyes locking on the gold-ringed pupils staring back at me.

The sound it makes isn't a roar at first, it's a low, displeased rumble, deep enough to rattle loose stones down the slopes. Children cry somewhere behind, parents hushing them in tight, panicked whispers, as the dragon straightens to its full height. Its wings unfurl further, the downdraft sending another cascade of rocks skittering off the ledge.

"No sudden movements," I murmur, more to myself than anyone else. Every muscle in me wants to move, but I don't dare provoke it. Lia, of course, seems oblivious.

"It's pretty," she says, far too loud.

The dragon roars—this time loud enough to shake the air—and adrenaline spikes hard in my veins. Killing it is the last thing I want. Dragons are rare, near mythical. No one's seen one in centuries, not since the ancient wars between the Queens' and Kings' lands, back when the Courts were still united, when wielding more than one power wasn't a crime. They'd been hunted for their strength in battle, and none had been found since. And now here one is, in front of me, and I'm seconds away from possibly killing it.

Its scales catch the light, a shifting tapestry of white and deep ocean blue. I call my power to my hands, light flickering across my knuckles, but the dragon sees it—feels it—and lunges. I blast, and it twists just enough to avoid it.

"You're going to hurt it!" Lia's sudden shove knocks me off balance. *Reckless.* **Insane.**

"Lia! Move!" I bark, scrambling to put myself between her and the beast. Golden eyes burn like molten coin, teeth bared, flame crackling at the edges of its jaws.

It lunges again, except something slams into me from the side, throwing me hard against the mountain wall. The impact drives the air from my lungs, leaving me gasping. When my vision clears, I see her—still there, still standing, and the dragon's blue fire curling between its teeth.

I push off the rock, ready to, gods help me...protect her. I don't know why. Moments ago, I wanted her dead.

And then the impossible happens. The dragon stops, its breath spilling over her outstretched hand. Lia doesn't flinch. Her voice, soft and melodic, pours out in a tongue I've only ever heard whispered in the oldest histories—a language forgotten by all but the dead. I can't make out the words, but I watch her lips shape them, steady and sure.

She stands there like she's speaking to nothing more dangerous than a woodland fawn. But it's a dragon. A fucking dragon.

Lia's hand moved, and I tensed, preparing to intervene. But then, to my astonishment, I watched her fingers scratch under the beast's chin.

"Did that crazy man try to blast you?" she cooed, her tone as one would speak to a kitten caught in the rain.

Me? Crazy? Does this woman have any idea she is crazy personified?

"Lia..." I warned, but the dragon glanced up at me in disdain before turning its softened gaze back to her.

I stood there, dumbfounded, as she continued to interact with the dragon, her hand moving over its large features. Mutterings behind me revealed that each Fae was just as stunned as I was.

"She is coming with us," Lia announced, already turning back to the path. The dragon followed, its massive body shifting with surprising grace as it fell into step behind her. I had to move out of its way, my hand brushing the mountain wall as its wingtip nearly grazed me.

The distance between us widened as I stood there, still trying to piece together what I'd just witnessed. Who the hell was this woman?

"You would like her, Gwynn," I muttered into the cold air, a sigh escaping my lips. Because I knew she would. My wife had always loved and fought for women like the one who had just befriended a dragon.

The convoy shuffled forward again, keeping their distance from the eccentric woman and her new companion. I kept us at the front, away from the crowd and its whispers, whispers about her powers, her strangeness, and how a straight answer from her was impossible without her suddenly getting agitated.

And then… nothing. Her silence was the loudest thing on the mountain. Not a footfall, not a breath, not a word—just a woman and her dragon, skirting the mountain's edge, the beast's great wings tucked in as it kept pace with her.

The cold bit through the scale leather of my vest, welcome and sharp. The fresh mountain air wrapped around me like an old embrace, dragging up memories I'd fought to bury. We both loved the cold. And as much as I tried to fight against them, my mind was cruel.

With the convoy beginning to relax behind me as we travelled toward what we hoped would be a safe haven to plan our next course of action, laughter and singing rose through the cold air. They kept each other's spirits high, but I couldn't join them. As soft flurries of snow drifted down from the mountains, a memory began to pull at me—unwelcome, but relentless.

The fire had crackled in the hearth, casting its amber light across the room. Gwynn sat close beside me, the flames dancing in her eyes. It had been one of those simple evenings—unremarkable at the time, but turned precious when life later stripped it away.

Her hand had rested on mine, warm and steady. We had spoken in low voices, the comfort of her presence wrapping around me like a shield from the world outside. I remembered the scent of her hair, the way it fell in loose waves over her shoulders, the quiet hum of her laughter threading through the air like music only I could hear. We had spoken of nothing important, and yet everything in that moment had mattered. I hadn't felt the weight of loneliness then. I'd been whole. She might not have been my mate in the way the Gods dictated, but she had been my equal in every way that counted to me.

Now that memory felt like a shard of glass—sharp, fragile, impossible to touch without bleeding. Gwynn, my beacon, had chosen to walk into the dark. She had gone to work with Bane, the enemy who stood against everything we fought for. The warmth of that firelit night had been snuffed out, replaced by a cold that never truly left.

Grief became my shadow. It settled into my bones, dulling the world until even joy looked like something far away. The laughter of others became strange to me. I had walked through days like a ghost, haunted by what I'd lost, driven only by the pull of vengeance.

Bane had taken her from me, whether by manipulation, persuasion, or some darkness I would never understand, and I had sworn that he would pay. That vow burned in me like an unquenchable flame, the only thing that kept me moving when nothing else could.

But in moments like this, walking behind another woman with black hair, my feet carrying me forward while my mind wandered elsewhere, the world seemed to fade until all I could see was that fire. That night. The warmth. The way she had made me feel... complete.

Gwynn would always be the light I had once followed. Even now, I navigated the dark with revenge as my compass—yet a part of me still longed for the simplicity of the life I'd had before the shadows claimed us both.

Caomh

ARROWS AND HARD TRUTHS

Slanchad's vast expanse of green fields stretched out before us, offering little in the way of effective cover. Lorkan soared ahead in hawk form, his usually prominent presence oddly muted in my mind. Colden walked silently beside me, his gaze scanning the horizon for any signs of danger. Meanwhile, Jeyr, Olivia, and Kyzan trailed behind, their footsteps barely audible against the soft earth.

Ness had ventured into the forest, her instincts guiding her as she sought out a path that would allow her to catch up with us later. As we pressed forward, the weight of our mission hung heavy in the air, each step bringing us closer to the confrontation that awaited us at Slanchad.

"For a mind master, you're remarkably obtuse," Colden declared, his words slicing through the quiet ambiance like a knife through butter.

I shot him a glance, his infuriatingly handsome face making it difficult to maintain my façade of anger. Deep down, I wasn't truly upset.

"For a commander, insulting others isn't the best strategy for making friends."

Colden huffed dismissively. "We won't ever be friends."

"Jealous that Olivia has other best friends besides you?" I teased, unable to resist needling him.

Rolling his eyes, he shot back, "Hardly. I was the one who notified your army about Princess Aella traveling with Tierney's son in the woods. I begged for assistance, for her to be saved, and for myself to be saved. I was only twenty when I got put on that post. But you forgot about her guard left in a kingdom of poison because I was not royalty. I just form ice and snow. She was rescued, and I was left, discarded, and had to find my worth in a kingdom that made me watch a man torture his wives."

His words hit me like a slap in the face, guilt washing over me as I realized the consequences of my decision to prioritize Aella's rescue. But before I could respond, Colden continued, his voice tinged with bitterness.

"Forget it. Because of that decision, I met Olivia."

As we trudged through the tall grass, my fingers clenched around the stalks, snapping them and letting the broken pieces fall to the ground.

"You're foolish because you're pushing away something out of fear of losing it," Colden persisted.

"You can never lose something that you have never had," I shot back defensively.

"But you have," he countered. "Maybe not in the traditional romantic sense of having. But I think losing it will feel just as devastating, whether you have had it or not."

I looked at him, but he remained stoic, his gaze fixed on the horizon. The fields were eerily quiet without the bustling activity of healers foraging for herbs. Slanchad had always been a sanctuary, clear of war, but the air felt different now. I used the shift in atmosphere to distract myself from Colden's words.

"You always spout off advice?" I deflected, trying to regain control of the conversation.

"I say it as it is," he retorted. "My freedom now has allowed it. I've been stuck in a body owned and commanded by a mind master like yourself for nearly fifty years. So excuse me for stating my thoughts."

"Why do you care?" I pressed, feeling the weight of guilt pressing down on me for the impact of my choices on a young man who had been nothing but a pawn.

"I don't care," Colden insisted, his tone firm. "I've just seen more heartache than love. If love is there, a love where you care more about them than yourself, you shouldn't sit back idly, letting fear separate you."

Colden shrugged, and I felt my heart race in my chest. I didn't have time to dwell on his words, though, as Lorkan's high-pitched screech pierced the air, sending a chill down my spine.

Through the swaying grass, the ominous forms of humanoids emerged, their arrows poised and ready.

"GET DOWN!" I bellowed, hoping my urgency would resonate with the others. I hurled myself into the concealing embrace of the grass, praying that the enemy wouldn't spot the bird circling overhead.

Screams erupted, filling the air with a cacophony of terror and chaos. Peering cautiously over the blades, I witnessed the humanoids contorting under some unseen force. Then, a searing pain seared through my shoulder, jolting me back into the harsh reality of the battlefield.

"Fuck, you've been hit. Get down," Colden's voice cut through the chaos, stating the obvious with characteristic bluntness.

Cay! Lorkan's cry filled my mind.

I'm fine. You stay out of sight.

A roar echoed above, the sky darkening as Lorkan, unmistakably shifted into wyvern form and swooped overhead. His violet eyes briefly scanned me before he veered off towards the humanoids.

Don't you get captured, Mo Chuisle.

You don't die on me, and we have a deal. His voice causing my heart to thump loudly in my chest.

I glanced down, assessing the arrow embedded in my shoulder, cursing my own recklessness. With a mental connection to Liv, I conveyed that I had been hit. Colden's hands were on my shoulder, deftly dealing with the cursed arrow, his touch surprisingly gentle amidst the chaos.

Caomh, stay back, Jeyr's command reverberated in my mind.

No.

Peeking cautiously above the grass, I surveyed the battleground. Lightning crackled ominously from the skies, striking down any humanoid in its path, while Lorkan's fiery breath reduced them to ash. I felt utterly powerless, a mere spectator in my own skirmish. A tug on my arm snapped me back to the present, and Colden steadied me.

"You okay?"

"Fine," I grumbled, attempting to take a step forward, only to find my legs betraying me. Colden's grip tightened, supporting my weight.

"Fuck, you're heavier than you look."

I wanted to retort, but my tongue felt thick and heavy in my mouth.

Mo ghràdh? Lorkan's deep rumble resonated in my mind, seeking reassurance. I tried to respond, but darkness began to encroach on my vision, swallowing me whole.

Olivia

TICKING TIME AND TAKING CONTROL

The fallen humanoids lie scattered in the grass, their bodies still twitching with the aftershock of the surge Jeyr and I unleashed together. For half a breath, hope claws its way up my throat—only to die as I see Caomh fold in on himself, his strength draining like water through cupped hands. Colden catches him, their weight unsteady, his mind screaming for help even though his lips don't.

Panic hits me like a pulse through my veins. My feet move before my mind catches up. Jeyr is there in an instant, fingers locking around mine, the familiar pull of his power dragging us to where we're needed.

Colden stays with Caomh, his shoulders tense under the weight of him, and I brace for the worst—ready to see the void in Caomh's eyes, that empty, soulless stare—only to find his lids closed, his breath shallow.

Jeyr presses his palm against Caomh's chest, feeling what my senses can't. "It's not the same poison," he says, steady voice betraying itself in the flicker of panic beneath. "But we still need an antidote. We have to move—one of the healers might have it."

His surface thoughts are calm, calculated, but I can taste the truth under them—we're bleeding seconds. Without Hecate, there will be no impossible salvation, no divine trick to save him like there was for me.

Lorkan soars close, his attention locked entirely on Caomh, muscles tight like he's daring the world to take one more step toward him.

"Colden, stay with him," I order. The hesitation flashes across his face, a stubborn flicker, before he gives a reluctant nod.

Jeyr's grip closes around my hand again, pulling me forward. The first line needs to be fastened. The king's presence hums through the air ahead, a warning note in a song I don't want to hear.

Slanachad unfolds before us in ruin. The green fields are gone, replaced by churned soil and the stench of rotting flesh. Death clings to the air so thick I choke on it, my power straining against the weight of it. But Jeyr's current buzzes against my skin—electric, steady, grounding. It keeps me from drowning in the smell, in the memory, in the fear. Keeps me moving toward the fight we can't afford to lose.

As we approach the castle, its smooth sandstone walls crowned with roses spilling fragrance into the air, serenity fractures at the sight of him—King Dominhall—his taloned hand wrapped around the throat of a slender figure. Panic bleeds from the captive's mate, their eyes locked on the one in the King's grasp.

Aison, the mate, holds a blade to a child's neck. Her sobs cut through me like glass, high and unrelenting. I slam my mental walls into place, forcing the flood of emotions back even as their thoughts claw at the edges of my mind. Aison's hand trembles, tears tracking down his face, his water-green eyes fixed on the man held by the King.

Bliant twitches under Dominhall's grip, his thick brown hair shaking with each failed attempt to pull free. His lips move in silent shouts toward Aison, his brown eyes wide with fear. The blade digs deeper into the child's throat, drawing a thin crimson line. Aison's corded arm strains, every muscle protesting against the act his body is forced to commit.

I tear my focus from him, because I can feel it—the weight of another gaze. Dominhall's eyes lock on mine, and the heat of his power licks at my boots, a living flame hungry for my soul. Jeyr moves in an instant, blinking us from danger, but the King's will follows like a shadow stitched to my own.

War shatters the air. The battlefield erupts in a roar, rocks hurtling toward us, flung by unseen force. Jeyr's winds rise to meet them, scattering stone like dry leaves in a storm. And still, Dominhall's presence presses into my mind, a constant, invasive clawing.

I shove him back. I seal my mate's consciousness away from his reach. The battle rages on in both worlds—the physical clash of power and the silent war in the mindscape. I strike with precision, sending weakness flooding toward him, but his healing magic rises like an unbreakable wall. Even so, my attack makes him falter for the barest breath, and fear flashes in his eyes—a fracture in the marble of his composure.

Warnings crowd my thoughts, humanoids advancing, eager for blood, but I silence them. There's no space for hesitation. Fear blooms in my enemies' chests as I push it into them, my gift cutting them down before they can touch those I protect.

Still, beneath the focus, a sharper dread coils inside me. Caomh's life is a thread pulled too taut, and I don't know how long it will hold.

A roar rips through the air, snapping Dominhall's attention away from me. Rage blooms in his eyes as he turns toward Lorkan, who stands between him and whatever victory he craves. Dominhall's hand falls from Bliant's throat, releasing him to the air.

In a heartbeat, Aison drops his blade from the child's neck and throws himself at his mate, gathering Bliant into his arms like he'll never let him go.

The idea strikes me in the thick of the chaos—dangerous, desperate, but possible. I push it into Jeyr's mind.

His head turns toward me, just enough for our eyes to meet through the storm. Lightning bleeds across the sky in time with the pulse between us. His lips shape the word *no.*

The bond between us strains, my will pressing against his. "Jeyr, now!" My voice cuts through the din, urgency wrapped tight with command.

He freezes for a fraction of a heartbeat—and I feel the shift inside him. My order settles into his bones, locking him into the choice I've made for him. Without another word, he blinks from the battlefield, reappearing by the Grand Dukes. He gathers them into his arms and vanishes again, leaving me in the fray.

The hollow where our connection stretches aches, his anger simmering hot along its thread...not anger at the danger, but at me. I'd commanded him. Forced him. Given my mate no choice.

But the moment doesn't allow for regret.

Lorkan is a blur of movement ahead, darting between buildings, shifting from hawk to wolf to something scaled and sharp. Dominhall's vines lash from the cobblestones, clawing at him, but Lorkan slips every snare. The King is surrounded by his two night-mares—the empath and the shifter—and it rattles him.

Jeyr's return slices through the chaos like a lightning strike. He's not alone. Warriors spill in behind him, those who refused to flee.

Winnowers—get everyone here to safety. Now! My command surges out, sharp as steel, my army snapping to it instantly. Fae blink in and out of the fight, dragging prisoners from cages, breaking chains, wrenching the bound and shackled from their captors.

But my focus is locked on the King.

I shut my eyes and reach into the threads binding him to his soldiers. The pull is suffocating—a quicksand of commands laced with poison. His will presses back, slick and insidious, trying to drag me into obedience. My hands tremble as I dig deep, forcing my power through every connection. Emotion pours from me in thick, unseen ribbons, the pressure in my third eye mounting until my skull feels ready to split.

I feel their feet falter. Their wills crumble. Tethers snap one by one.

Still, the humanoids advance—fever-eyed, weapons high, their devotion to him blind and burning. But I am past fear. I will fight until the last breath leaves me.

Bodies fall at my feet. The ground shifts beneath their collapse.

Lorkan keeps Dominhall's gaze fixed on him, darting and taunting, drawing the King further from me. Without him, I'd already be ash.

A shock jolts through my hand—*Jeyr.*

"Time to go, hummingbird." His voice is softer than it has any right to be, coaxing, tugging at the thread between us.

I drag my eyes from the carnage. The captives are gone. The King is still clawing for Lorkan. And in the space of a heartbeat, Lorkan's eyes meet mine.

Then the world folds, and we're gone.

The world around me seemed to freeze, caught in a moment of eerie stillness that belied the chaos raging within. Aison and Bliant hovered anxiously over Caomh's motionless form, their expressions etched with concern as they struggled to revive him. His lips bore a sickly blue hue, his breath barely perceptible against the cold whisper of the wind.

Despite the hushed tranquility that surrounded us, my mind buzzed with a cacophony of voices, each one clamoring for attention. I strained to filter through the noise, searching desperately for any sign of Lorkan's presence. But he remained elusive, lost to the unseen depths of the world.

The weight of the silence bore down on me like a heavy cloak, threatening to suffocate me with its oppressive embrace. It was a tangible reminder of the grief that lurked just beneath the surface, waiting to consume me if I dared to let it in.

I couldn't help but wonder if there would ever come a moment when I could allow myself to break, to surrender to the overwhelming sorrow that tugged at the edges of my consciousness. The thought sent a shiver down my spine, a chilling reminder of the fragility of the bonds that held us together.

My thoughts drifted to Caomh, my best friend, my brother not by blood but more than this family he had brought me into. We shared a bond that ran deeper than blood, forged through countless trials and tribulations. Yet, there were secrets between us, unspoken truths that lingered in the spaces between our words.

As I gazed down at his still form, I couldn't help but wonder what might have been if fate had dealt us a different hand. If his mother had been freed, if my own mother had succeeded in her endeavors, perhaps our paths would have crossed long before the moment in the town of Black Forest. But now, as I stood on the precipice of uncertainty, I couldn't help but feel the weight of our shared destiny pressing down upon me.

Aison's urgent voice pierced the heavy silence, a beacon of concern amidst the tumultuous aftermath of the mutiny. Yet, its clarity was lost to the lingering echoes of chaos, leaving his words to fade into the backdrop of my racing thoughts. As a Fae approached, their hands bathed in an eerie, acidic glow reminiscent of a forgotten era, a primal instinct urged me to retreat.

In that fleeting moment of uncertainty, arms enveloped me in a familiar embrace, offering solace amidst the turmoil that threatened to consume us. His presence was a balm to my frayed nerves, a reminder that even in the darkest of times, we were not alone.

"I am here, my love," his whispered reassurance brushed against my ear, a tender vow of steadfast support. But my heart clenched with apprehension as his gaze flickered towards Caomh's motionless form, his unspoken words hanging heavy in the air.

"But Cao..." I began, my voice faltering as the weight of our shared concern bore down upon us.

"I know," he murmured, his voice tinged with a haunting sense of resignation. We stood on the precipice of uncertainty, our hopes and fears intertwined as we grappled with the looming specter of loss. In that fleeting moment, as we hovered on the brink of despair, the question lingered like a shadow—had we arrived too late?

Lorkan

CLAWING TO YOU

Worry fuels each waning shift. Dizziness claws at the edges of my vision, black creeping in, but the tunnel offers no refuge—it only mocks me with the path my mind aches to follow. The King's obsession hunts me, his sick need to claim the one creature who can hold every power, who can wear any face.

Vines lash out, venomous tendrils snapping for my hide. I twist, shift, break free—hawk to raven to wyvern, my body tearing through shapes with a speed that feels wrong, almost monstrous. In wyvern form, my wings snap the air, skimming the jagged ruin of the castle. The curse slips from my maw as a roar, fire and fury spilling into the stormed sky. And I see it then—the flicker of delight on the bastard King's face. He thinks he can break me.

Iron hurtles toward me, the weapon searing even through scales thick as stone. The burn digs deep, rattling my bones. The sound that rips from me shakes the rubble, a roar that splits the night wide open.

Through the chaos, my eyes catch them—Olivia and Jeyr, gone with the mass of freed souls. That's my cue. I can't kill him today. Not yet. The weight of his power gnaws me hollow, and I am already burning too fast.

But none of that matters. Not the iron, not the King, not the blood soaking this cursed ground. Only one thought tears through me, louder than pain, louder than rage—my Mo ghràdh. His presence clings to me in every shift, his absence a fire chewing through my chest, a wound that will never close.

I summon the last of my energy to where I sense him. But with that final exertion, my body gives out, and I plummet. My wyvern form unravels mid-fall, wings warping into arms, talons twisting into fingers that claw at the empty air as if they could catch hold, as if they could soften the blow. They don't. The impact crushes the breath from my lungs, pain ricocheting through bone and sinew.

Dizzy and gasping, I blink through the haze to see the movement ahead. Fae are swarming around him. *My Mo ghràdh.*

I watch, chest burning, as Jeyr leans over him, trying to heal, only to be pushed aside when his power bends toward Olivia. She stumbles into the distance, swallowed by the thickets, leaving my view open. Aison and Bliant kneel beside him, frantic, calling for their fellow Puinnsean adepts to purge the poison.

Hands reach for me at last, but I shove them away. I will not be healed if he is not. Everything I have done—every rule broken, every battle fought—has been for him. Without him, I have no reason to drag air into my lungs.

The iron wounds in my side throb, but instinct drives me forward. If I had stayed scaled, perhaps I would mend faster. But my need eclipses pain. I claw through the dirt, dragging myself across the ground despite the stares of those watching my struggle. I reach him at last, lifting his head into my lap. His golden hair spills across my leather-clad thighs, catching fractured light. I've always harbored a fondness for it, the myriad shades of gold shifting like fire with every flicker. Scattered across his otherwise perfect face are small scars, freckles carved by battle—imperfections I've watched him scrutinize in the privacy of his chamber, vanity making him vulnerable. But he never knew. He never knew I would worship every scar, every strand on his head, if he let me.

I wonder—how long can this cycle go on? How many more times can I watch him teeter on the edge of death? There have been too many close calls already, each one etched into me like a blade. Over the years I've come to know the men he calls brothers, and I've claimed them as my own. I was there through it all, unseen. A shadow in his army. I never shifted where eyes could see, but I soared above them, guarding him in silence. They knew. They thanked me when I defended them.

But this—this is different. Too close. Too intimate. I can feel the heat ebbing from his body as if it were draining out of mine. His fragility presses down on me, stone-heavy, suffocating, and I can't breathe beneath the weight of it.

His lips turn blue, and I am trapped in the moment, my heart clawing, pleading with deities I have never believed in. Why would they grant me mercy now, when they never had before? The silence is proof of their indifference. Aison and Bliant move back, their whispers blurred into static by the denial ringing in my skull.

I close my eyes. Just for a breath. Because I cannot face what might come if I open them. The wait. The cruel, endless wait to know if he will survive.

His gasp for air mirrors my own, dragging breath into my lungs with a cruel rush of hope. His eyes flutter open—golden orbs locking onto mine, the foolish man already searching for answers, not even sparing himself a heartbeat to realize he was a breath away from dying, and haunting me more than he already does. Anger claws at me—unwanted, unneeded—because Caomh maddens me with his cursed sense of duty and honor. He can't take a quarter second just to look into me the way I do him, to thank whichever gods deigned to spare him this time.

"You didn't get stolen…" His voice is hoarse, each word scraping raw against the air, his breath brushing my skin and stirring something I can't bury.

"I made a promise, didn't I?" My voice betrays me, heavy with everything I try to hide. Despite all my attempts to keep steel in my spine, tears well and fall, burning tracks down my cheeks. Men aren't meant to cry. Men like me aren't meant to break. But when it comes to Caomh Conroy, I am nothing but ruin.

His hand lifts, trembling, wiping my tears away.

"I suppose I didn't die either," he mutters, so offhandedly I almost laugh. Instead, a scoff rips from me.

"Mm. But as always, you do it with a flair for dramatics." My words are meant as scolding, but they fall soft, powerless, because the fire in my chest is still smoldering, still reminding me how close I came to losing him again.

He winces as he shifts, careful, pained, easing himself upright. Instinct takes me before thought does—my hands steadying him, holding him until I know he's not about to collapse. Around us, the murmurs of the Fae dim, respectful, fading into nothing as they give us this moment.

I trace the contours of his face, memorizing him all over again, my gaze catching on the pallor still haunting his skin. "Mo ghràdh," I whisper, the word rasping from me. There must be something edged in my tone, sharp enough for him to study me in return.

His panicked gaze locks on mine, concern flaring as his eyes catch a trickle of blood. "You're bleeding!" he exclaims, voice tight with alarm, as though the sight of a wound on me is stranger than all the corpses we left behind.

I roll my eyes, dismissing his fretful reaction. "It's just a scratch."

"Jeyr!" Caomh's urgent call slices the air, sharp enough to summon gods, let alone my brother. His panic paints me as the one dragging myself back from death.

Jeyr approaches with Olivia at his side, both their faces breaking into visible relief as they quicken their pace. They kneel beside me, and Jeyr mutters with that dry bite of his, "Good to see you still issuing commands from hell's door."

"Fuck you. I'll be making commands past hell's door. Now save him."

Jeyr rolls his eyes but sets his hands against my side. Heat seeps through me as his healing power burns and stitches the wound closed. When it's done, nothing remains but the crust of dried blood. I turn my head to find Caomh staring at my bare chest like it's some offense.

"Better?" I ask.

He makes a noncommittal noise, something between a hum and a grumble.

Shaking my head, a wry smile tugging at my mouth, I push myself to my feet and extend a hand to him. His fingers hesitate in mine, but the faint squeeze that follows—gods, I tell myself it means more than it does. His breath comes sharp as he rises, and I guide him into the cove of my arm, his weight fitting against me as though he's meant to be there.

Caomh

BLANKET CRIMES

Panic grips my heart, a subconscious denial I've been clinging to since we were teenagers, sparring with our first swords. I've denied him for so long, convinced myself I could. But the moment he turns away, I curse myself. Love was never something I believed I would attain. Mindless sex with strangers was easier—no connection, no chance of being gutted when it all ends. I'd seen too much loss, too many people I cared for broken by it, and I convinced myself distance meant safety. If something ever happened to him, I told myself I'd be fine. Lies. Because with that single step away, I know the truth: his absence would ruin me. His silence would echo louder than any tick of an old clock.

My eyes trace his torso, scarred in ways I'll never know the full story of. I'd stopped letting him close to me long ago, guarding myself from the dangerous distraction he's always been. Protecting him became easier than admitting what I felt. But then he lets go of my hand, steadying me with a shoulder until I can hold my own. When he pulls back, the cold air rushes in where his warmth once was. My gaze drifts lower, betraying me—taking in the line of muscle carved into him, the dark hair at his chest, the sheer strength beneath his skin. Gods, if I placed my hand there, I'd feel every ridge, every depth of him. I slide my eyes up again and meet the violet fire of his stare.

His body vibrates with the telltale hum before a shift. He's going to vanish into the trees, retreat into the shadows where I once commanded him to stay. Habit now, more than my words. Since Puinnsean, since the chains and the cells, there's been no moment—none—where we've dared to speak of what remains unspoken. My fault as much as his. He's been waiting for me. Fuck, he's been waiting a century.

I grab his hand before he can leave, clinging as if this might be the last time. He pauses, looking back at me with heartbreak carved into his violet eyes. My body is wrecked, poison still burning its way out of me, strength dwindling by the second—yet in that moment, I could move a mountain just to make him stay.

I stumble forward, pressing him back against the rough bark of a tree, my weight collapsing into him more than forcing. He doesn't flinch, doesn't grunt. His arms are already around my hips, steadying me, holding me up.

I drink him in. The beard framing that sharp jaw, the dark curls tumbling to his shoulders, the lashes framing eyes that could only belong to Lorkan. My hands brace against the tree, refusing to move. If they touched him, they wouldn't stop.

"You'll regret being stuck with me, Mo Chuisle," I whisper against his lips. My nose brushes his, my body shaking as I fight this war within me—this impossible, inevitable pull he has over me.

His breath shudders out, his nose nudging mine as he shakes his head. "Never, Mo ghràdh."

And that is all I need.

I close the space and seize the kiss that's haunted me for a century. His lips crash to mine, and lightning surges through me, sparking to my very core. I sink into him on instinct, devouring his scent, his strength, his solidity—every piece of him I've denied myself. Years of yearning, fear, and hunger culminate in this single, blistering kiss.

When I finally tear myself back, breathless, our foreheads rest together, our chests rising and falling in frantic rhythm. And I understand. For the first time in my cursed, guarded life, I understand why someone would choose love above all else.

"So, you can get over the fact I'm a shifter?" he whispers, the corner of his mouth twitching, breaking through the haze of heat.

"Fuck off," I mutter, my lips brushing against the stubble of his jaw, "you know I love that you're a shifter. So very hot."

His chuckle rumbles through me, low and unguarded, and gods, it undoes me more than the kiss. I let my head fall beneath his chin, pressing into the warm hollow there. I've never been one to give up control, never been one to lean into someone else's strength. Power has always been armor, something to wield, something to keep me standing. But here—held against him, cocooned in the certainty that he won't let me fall—being small has never felt so good.

If I can call being poisoned a mercy... maybe this time I can. The mental fog that clouded me since the executioner's block has finally lifted. Gone are the restraints that severed me from my connections. With clarity comes the harder task—re-forging those lines over miles, searching for the faintest hum of a mind in the distance.

The first thread I manage to grasp is Aiden. His voice bursts through in static at first, then sharpens, cutting straight into me. *Where on gods' land have you been! I've been trying to contact you since the moment I heard you didn't get scorched by the king.*

Well, I was having some technical difficulties, I grit across the link.

Shit timing, commander. The kingdom's in mayhem.

I glance around at the fragile semblance of order here, the temporary calm after a near miss. *Yeah, no use pointing out the obvious.*

Word's out about the raids. The stolen illegals. Good thing for you, the King's slithered back to his own kingdom. Most likely rethinking his plans. But Bane—that serpent—managed to pull it off. He relocated the illegals from Gliocas and Neart straight into Puinnsean. Aimsir's been taken. Hecate, Althea, Aella... their fates are still unclear.

My eyes lift, landing on Jeyr. My chest constricts, and I close my eyes quickly, swallowing down the weight of it. I can't tell him yet. Not when Olivia is still within reach, not when the wound of losing her has only just been sealed. The last thing we need is Jeyr and Olivia storming off half-prepared.

Don't worry, Commander. I'll find them if it's the last thing I do, Aiden's voice vows, ringing fierce and steady.

I force my expression blank, letting no one glimpse the turmoil twisting inside me. *Make sure you do. Keep me posted.*

The line hums between us, but the silence that follows is enough. Aiden will do it. I know he will.

"Cay, you need to sleep."

Lorkan's voice slices through my thoughts, gravel-edged, threaded with concern. "The bags under your eyes rival the black of my raven's feather."

I look up at him, his longer dark hair curtaining his sharp face, violet eyes unyielding.

Before I can argue, his hand cups my chin, thumb and forefinger tilting my head, forcing me to see the exhaustion etched into my skin.

"Sleep, *mo ghràdh*," he says, the command gentled by the rasp in his voice. "We can't save the kingdom tonight. The King's nursing his bruised ego. We use this time to rest. To recover."

I open my mouth to protest, but he doesn't give me the chance. In one unceremonious movement, he hauls me up over his shoulder.

"Lorkan!" My fists thump against his back, a pitiful effort that earns nothing but a rumble of laughter from deep in his chest. His laughter rolls through me like thunder, shameless.

"Let me down!" I bark, heat rising to my face as I catch the sidelong stares of the Fae around us. Am I embarrassed? Or—gods forbid—do I like this?

I smack his rear in retaliation, a flare of rebellion against the indignity of being carted off like baggage. His shoulders shake, laughter spilling free, and damn it all—so does mine.

He takes me just beyond the campgrounds—close enough to know if something goes amiss, far enough that it feels like we've stolen privacy. I'd like to say that in all the years, I imagined us like this, imagined what it would be like if he and I finally gave in. But that would be a lie. I never allowed such thoughts; if they ever sparked, I stamped them out before they could burn me. And yet—now, in a forest brimming with Fae whose powers could unravel any veil of secrecy, I find myself wishing it could have been different. That having him didn't mean I had to bare myself in front of every watching eye.

"I love the Queen's lands," he murmurs, breaking into my spiral of thought, "but we never had nights like this."

I follow his gaze upward, to the moon—full and gleaming, stars breaking through in slivers of silver. "But we had the sunsets," I remind him softly. "I've yet to see a sunset more beautiful than those."

Lorkan hums his agreement, his breath warm against the cool stillness of the night. "I watched them every evening when you were gone. Not once did I miss it. Not once did I let the sun go down without me on our mountain, waiting."

My chest tightens at the thought, years lost stretching between us like an unbridgeable chasm. Words of regret press against my throat, apologies I've rehearsed a hundred times. But before they can form, his voice steadies me.

"Don't," he says gently, violet eyes on mine. "I don't need apologies, Cay. I care about now. I'll take this snippet of happiness—for however long the fates grant it."

The word *snippet* cuts me, sharp and fleeting. I want to argue, to demand more than slivers, but his hand on mine stills me. And when he leans close, when those eyes mirror the moonlight itself, hope sparks where grief used to dwell.

His lips brush mine—warmth against the night's chill, a tether I didn't know I'd been clinging to until it's there. I press closer, nestling against his chest, letting a shiver run through me. His chuckle vibrates in his ribs beneath my cheek.

"Wear bloody clothes, you fool," he scolds, affection hidden in his exasperation.

I grin up at him, wicked glint in my eye. "You love my body too much to see it covered. It'd be a crime."

His laugh deepens, arms pulling me tighter. "Then let's commit the crime. I'd rather you be warm and alive, even if I suffer the torment of cloth between me and your skin."

A heavy thud lands across my legs—a blanket. Jeyr stands a few paces away, rolling his eyes like an elder tired of children. "For the love of gods, cover up. If it helps, think of what one can do under covers."

I shoot him a mock glare, though I can't help the smirk tugging at my lips, and yank the blanket around us. Heat seeps in, mingling with Lorkan's, and for a moment the trouble of kingdoms and war recedes, leaving only this stolen warmth.

Jeyr

UNFASENING ARMOUR

I can't sleep. Fuck, how could I, after everything? Foolish of me to think having my mate in my arms would bring peace. It doesn't.

Olivia... gods, I knew she'd be different. Hair aside, she's not the girl I first met. I don't let myself dwell on the time lost—that cruel reminder of my inadequacy, of all the ways I failed to save her. My love hasn't wavered, if anything it's stronger. Holding her again is proof of that, a sense of rightness nothing else in this world could ever match. But still—there's the control, the way her powers drive me to obey without choice. That unsettles me. I'm not sure yet how to face it. And then there's her reckless edge—throwing herself into danger, facing beasts, squaring off against men more vile than Bane or Teiney. I've only just got her back, and she's already bartering her life with death again. I don't give a damn about the bodies she left strewn behind her; their souls were long past saving. I care about what it takes from her.

And now... now that her power has shifted, our bond has shifted too. Stronger. She doesn't know it yet, but I feel the tie in my mind, her pain flowing into me as if her body instinctively hands it over. Just as she curls into my arms seeking solace, her mind leans into mine, relinquishing its weight. I felt it when she bolted from Caomh, haunted. I felt it again as she listened in on his conversation with Aiden. I don't know why she listens. Another secret waiting to unfurl when she's ready. But I know what she knows: my sisters are missing. Hecate is missing.

I bite down hard, molars grinding as I watch the watchmen pace the perimeter, as others curl into their lovers' arms by the fire. Caomh thinks he can keep this from me—gods, he never trusted me with secrets before, and now I finally have privy to his mind. He doesn't want me flying off the handle, doesn't want Olivia chasing ghosts of my sisters. He doesn't know us at all. Maybe once we acted on impulse. Not anymore. These past months have carved patience into us, taught us to bide our time, to play the long game.

Olivia takes the knowledge in silence, already planning. Always planning. I'm grateful when exhaustion drags her down at last. It gives me a moment to see her without weight between us. Her freckles—little stars scattered across her nose—her curls, still unruly even in sleep. I can't help brushing one aside, watching it spring stubbornly back into place. Defiant, like its mistress. My lips twitch at the thought.

But the beauty is fleeting. Her brow tightens. The bond goes taut—then I'm pulled under, straight into her nightmare.

It hits like a lash across my own spine. My body seizes, fangs biting my gums as I choke down a growl. This is what I used to feel at a distance, across mountains. But now I'm in the room with her. I feel the whip, the sickness of heat that has nothing to do with desire. It's clammy, choking. I feel the tremors shaking her body. I hear her thoughts—gods, her thoughts. The desperate carving of a safe place in her mind, the game she played to survive.

It's only a sliver of what she endured, but it's enough to hollow me. Enough to vow—again, fiercer than ever—that I'll shield her from this darkness. That she will never be alone in her battles again.

I wrench myself free of the tether, gasping. She thrashes faintly, whimpers slipping past her lips. I gather her close, desperate.

"Liv," I plead, shaking her gently, "my love—Hummingbird. Wake up. It's a nightmare. Just a nightmare. Wake up."

Her soft cries pierce me, each one a dagger. I tighten my hold, burying her in my chest, letting my scent surround her. My voice trembles but I force it steady, a lifeline in the storm.

"Hummingbird, it's me. Focus on me. You're home now."

The nightmares that seize her mind halt abruptly as her eyes snap open. The frantic search of her surroundings stops the instant her gaze finds mine—*Jeyr.* I hear my name echo through her thoughts, a fragile plea, and I roll, no longer at her side but hovering above her. My fingers trace the soft silk of her cheek, her eyelids fluttering beneath my touch as a tear slips free. I catch it with my lips, a silent prayer that this tiny act might ease her suffering, though I know it cannot.

For a heartbeat, fear claws at me—what if my touch awakens the memories I wish she could forget? But Olivia reads me, always reads me, and instead her hands weave into my hair, tugging me closer. A surge of longing burns through me, raw and unrelenting, though the wariness in her eyes remains—a shadow, a scar, the remnants of Tierney's cruelty etched too deep to fade so quickly.

"Am I too damaged for you?" she whispers as she pulls back, reluctance heavy in the space between us. Her eyes cloud with doubt, her mind spilling insecurities that weigh the air down like storm clouds.

Gods, my heart breaks. To think she doubts her worth, her strength, her beauty.

"No, my love," I breathe, conviction laced in every word. "Never. You could never be too damaged for me. If anything, I failed you. I didn't find you soon enough. I didn't shield you from—" My voice falters, sharp and raw. "From him. But know this: every choice you made was survival. Every step you took was strength. And I could never, ever be anything but in awe of you. Of your resilience, your spirit."

Her lips tremble as she breathes, "Show me." The words are so faint they could be mistaken for wind, but I hear them. Gods, I hear them. And though some part of me longs to wait for a perfect moment—safe, quiet, without shadow—I cannot deny her now.

I cup her face, my thumbs brushing along her jaw, and kiss her. Gentle at first, reverent, a vow pressed to her lips. She melts into me, and as our bodies fold together in that silent embrace, I promise her again what she already is: my mate, my heart, my soul. No darkness will ever put out her light.

But then I catch it—the flicker of panic in her eyes. I shift back, pressing my spine against the cool stone of the mountain edge, and guide her to her knees. The fog coils thicker around us, cloaking us in secrecy. She moves closer, tentative but determined, her hands wandering over the leather and scale of my armor. I curse inwardly, the cruel irony of fighting gear designed to protect, not to surrender.

She laughs, a soft, startled sound, her short hair shaking as she looks up at me, waiting for direction.

"If I had a spare change of clothes," I whisper, groaning low, "I'd be ripping this off you."

As if we have all the time in the world, she begins undoing my armor. Buckles slip free beneath her careful hands, the vest sliding from my shoulders with a muted scrape of leather. The shoulder plates and forearm guards follow, falling away one by one until only the dark undershirt remains between her and me.

My breath stalls in my chest, caught in that fragile space between us. It feels as though if I take in too much air, this will vanish—that an alarm will sound and reveal the stolen nature of this moment.

Her lips brush the curve of my neck, moving down to the line of my shirt. Her hands tremble as they slip beneath the fabric, fingertips meeting bare skin. She gasps at the contact.

I glance down at her hands, quivering, fragile. I cover them with my own, swallowing them whole in the size difference. The instant our palms meet, her hands steady, pressing against me with more certainty.

"Hummingbird," I murmur, voice low, raw. "I'll have you as little or as much as you want to give. You have me, my love, in any way you are ready for. I. Am. Yours."

Her green eyes shimmer, lit with emotions I don't need her powers to feel.

"Can I?" I whisper, my hand brushing the hem of her shirt tucked into leather. Her breath fans hot against my lips, and she nods. But I need more. *Words,* I press into her mind. *Let me hear what you want.*

Another feathered breath spills from her mouth, trembling against me. "Yes, Jeyr. You can have me."

I nod, kissing her softly before stripping her free of cloth and leather. My hands roam reverently, sliding over her ribs, counting each breath, pausing between her breasts where her heart hammers at the speed of a hummingbird's wings. When I reach her thighs, I remove the blades strapped there, laying them carefully beside us.

And then I pause. Moonlight kisses her skin, milk-white and flushed rose at the peaks of her breasts. My breath mists in the night air as I lean closer, the cold pebbling her nipples.

"So beautiful," I whisper, and I watch the color bloom deeper at my words.

I draw her onto my lap, and the press of her bare skin against mine sends a shiver down my spine, my head tipping back at the sheer sensation of her. I reach for a blanket, draping it over her shoulders as she trails kisses along my neck, holding me in this stolen eternity.

She grinds against me, and I catch her hips in my hands, guiding her touch, sliding up her sides, across her back. She falters when my palms find her scars.

"This okay?" I ask.

Her nod comes with a kiss, deep and hungry, silencing any doubt. I flatten my hands, pressing her closer, her breasts flush against my chest as we take from each other what we've been starving for. I angle my hips upward, meeting her, and she pushes back—sinking onto me with a gasp.

Her head drops to my shoulder, teeth sinking hard enough into my flesh to leave a mark. The sound that leaves me is feral. Her eyes widen at what she's done, but I claim her neck in answer, sinking my own canines into her, marking her as mine.

Mine.

And she doesn't flinch. She kisses the mark, her lips trailing fire up my jaw until they find mine again. The sweep of her mouth matches the roll of her hips, our breaths twining together, wild and broken, like the lights dancing across the mountain peaks above.

"I love you," I breathe into her, the words spilling out like a vow, our eyes locking in a gaze that strips us bare. Tears shimmer in her lashes, and I cup her face, brushing them away with my thumbs as our bodies continue to move, chasing heat, chasing wholeness.

"I love you, Jeyr. I never stopped," she whispers, the words trembling into the night air.

Gods, those words undo me. My arms wrap around her instantly, pulling her flush against me as my hand tangles in her hair, anchoring her to me, so I can claim her lips. I kiss her like I'm starving, like the months apart weren't centuries but seconds that stretched too long. She needs to feel it—how I never doubted, never wavered.

My other hand trails down, slow, deliberate, as if daring myself not to rush, slipping between our bodies. The heat of her calls to me, and I tease, letting my fingertips barely graze her until I feel her shiver. I want my mate to know what it feels like to be undone—what it feels like to be worshipped, so there is never a comparison, never a question. Only me. Only us.

Her breath catches, her hips rocking instinctively against my hand, and I groan at the rhythm we fall into together. My thumb circles her clit, steady, patient, until I spark my power through the contact. Small shocks roll across her nerves, timed to the sway of our bodies, and the sound that rips from her throat—half gasp, half moan—shakes me to my core.

I feel her tightening around me as her pleasure builds, her nails digging into my back, her body convulsing in my arms. She bites down on my lip, hard, to stifle the cry that threatens to escape, and I relish the sting, the metallic tang of blood only making me hungrier. Her tongue soothes the wound with a desperate sweetness, and gods, I could lose myself here forever.

Her release crashes through her, her body clenching around me, dragging me under with her. I follow, surrendering, her aftershocks wringing me tighter, branding me as hers as much as I claim her as mine.

"Forever, Hummingbird," I rasp against her lips, forehead pressed to hers, my voice raw, breaking. "However long that is... we are forever."

Her head knocks softly against mine as she nods, unable to speak, the agreement written in the tears shimmering in her eyes. We stay there, locked together, breathing the same air, our ragged exhales tangling into fog that curls between us in the cool night.

When I finally ease us down, I take my time dressing her first, hands steady but reverent, like every buckle and strap is sacred. She watches me map her body with my gaze, watches how it heats me in the chill, and she doesn't stop me. She never stops me.

At last, I shift, stretching out on the ground with her weight settling over me. She fits perfectly, the warmth of her skin grounding me in a way nothing else ever has. Wrapped in each other, we drift, her heartbeat in my ear the last sound I register.

The sun creeps over the horizon, its light touching my face, coaxing me awake. But for a moment, I don't move. I keep still, letting her sleep, because this—her safe in my arms—is the only dawn I'll ever pray for again.

Jethro

ENEMIES DAUGHTER

I f I could ever class myself as finding happiness again... it's now, closing in on the wyvern hive. The buzz of wings, low growls, and deep rumbles make the mountain itself feel alive. But this—this is home, and returning is the only relief I've had in months.

The trek up is hell, each mile dragged out beside the stone-faced Lia, who hasn't said a godsdamn word since we left. She just watches her dragon soar overhead as the path narrows too much for it to walk beside her. I feel like I'm stuck in some dream—or nightmare—because every single glance she casts my way leaves me unsettled.

Caomh managed to slip me enough of a word through our bond: they're on their way here too. I don't know why they're heading to our sanctuary so soon. I expected more raids, more time bought. Doing the math in my head only leaves one answer—they hit Slanchad. Which means something went wrong. That thought I shove down, refusing to sink into it... not yet. But the worry lingers, bleeding through me the way grief always does.

"It's a dead end," Lia finally speaks, her voice edged with frustration.

My teeth grind. We've followed this narrow path for hours, and she chooses now to talk?

"You think I'd take you all the way up here for a dead end?" I mutter back, sarcasm dripping like venom.

"I never said you were smart, Light Master," she counters, tone flat, exasperated.

I opt for silence, ignoring her, which only aggravates her further. Behind us the Fae shift uneasily, their murmurs threading through the rising tension.

"If it wasn't for the fact I know you wouldn't risk all these men and women," Lia says, voice quieter now, "I'd think you were bringing me here to kill me."

A humorless hum escapes me. "What a shame. I've got a thousand witnesses—and a dragon who'd rip my head off before I even tried."

"Don't worry light master, I don't doubt you will find the moment to do what you desire." Her eyes roll. Arms crossed before she speaks again " So, care to share why we are here standing in front of a rock, or can we go to a path that actually works."

"Would you shut up," I snap, the words ripping out harsher than I intend. My patience shreds in the cold air, thin as the mountain mist.

Gwynn had never pushed me this far, never needled me to the bone the way this raven-haired bitch does. Lia, with her swirling eyes and a mind I can't quite read, has me raw and ragged in a way I hate admitting.

For a flicker of a moment, her gaze softens. It almost looks like understanding—but then the storm rolls back in, sharp and wild, flashing a warning I can't decipher.

"Can you manage to be patient for just one moment so I can get us all in safely?" I snap, my frustration bubbling over. Lia recoils at the sharpness in my voice, and I know—if it weren't for Olivia's insistence—I would've left this mission, and her, behind long ago.

I step toward the wall she's so helpfully called a dead end and press my palm against the stone.

"You're not strong enough to break through that rock, it's too thick. I can help." Her voice needles, smug and useless, and I feel her edging closer.

I spin on her, glare sharp enough to slice. She stops short, instinctively backing away as she catches the intensity in my gaze.

"I **said** patience, Lia." My warning rumbles low.

She raises her hands in mock surrender, her dark eyes flashing, but I turn away before she can add more words to grate at my skin. I pour my power into the rock. Ancient runes flare to life, glowing faintly against the surface before a cascade of clicks answers. The wall shifts and slides aside, stone grating on stone, revealing the cavern mouth.

The sound changes instantly, soft chatter, a rush of water. The cavern breathes around us, vast and alive. Waterfalls spill from high ridges, mist veiling the inner depths where wyverns roost, their scales catching glimmers of light. Small caves dot the walls, already claimed by Fae who have sought refuge here. At the highest ledge, my uncle's carved home looms, shaped by his bond with the beasts who made these mountains theirs.

These wyverns are not the pampered pets of royals. Wild. Territorial. Impossible to breed. They choose their mates as stubbornly as swans and grieve with a violence that can tear the skies apart when they lose them. This is no place to stumble, no place for weakness.

The waterfall shields us from prying eyes above, its frosted spray cloaking the nest. But the peace fractures the instant Lia's dragon wings overhead. The wyverns shriek, their cries piercing, claws scraping as they shift, readying for an intruder.

"Damn it." The curse rips from me.

Lia vanishes from my side like smoke, leaving me with a cavern on edge, dozens of wyverns thrumming with unrest. My jaw clenches as urgency coils hot in my gut—any slip here, any provocation, and this sanctuary will turn into a blood pit.

I face the group behind me, their eyes wide, fear rising. My voice is sharp, commanding. "Into the caverns. Avoid the wyverns. Hug the west wall and find Lumier. Tell him I sent you."

Their assent comes quickly, feet scattering into the depths. My hand brushes the hilt of my blade as I remain where I am, eyes fixed on the cavern above, bracing for what comes next.

I watch as Lia's dragon's shadow eclipses the waterfall's glow, and the wyverns, instead of caring for the thousands of Fae streaming into the cavern, launch toward the sky in a storm of wings.

A sharp inhale burns my lungs. I winnow to the mountain peaks, heart pounding as I catch sight of her astride the beast. Lia's ecstatic cries slice through the thin mountain air, black hair streaming like a battle banner against the snow-white sky. The dragon beneath her moves with terrifying grace, a predator at ease, while the wyverns circle, restless, their eyes flicking from the creature's massive form to the slip of a Fae woman balanced on its back.

She is riding a fucking dragon.

The beast rumbles low, smoke curling harmlessly from its nostrils. I know that signal too well—either peace, or the promise of fire. My fingers twitch toward my blades as stone grinds under talons. A wyvern lands behind me, the air shifting with the weight of its wings.

I glance over my shoulder and meet Jorax's golden stare. For a moment, the boy I once was surfaces, and despite myself, I smile. Reaching forward, I stroke his scaled chin, and the old bond hums between us. His growl softens, the mountain's tension easing by a hair.

"The dragon's no threat," I murmur, though my gaze remains locked on Lia, radiant and reckless atop the creature. "But the girl... she needs watching. Safe, but watched."

Jorax answers with a rolling roar, the sound echoing through the peaks. The message carries, and one by one, the wyverns peel away, retreating to their ledges, their suspicions tempered—though not gone.

Lia, observing the exchange, murmurs something to her dragon, prompting it to land a safe distance away from Jorax. I approach, my hand resting on my wyvern's side, offering silent support as he eyes the towering creature before him.

"The dragon cannot remain in the caverns; she's too large and will unsettle the nest," I explain, bracing for Lia's response.

Her eyes darken with frustration. "You just don't want me in there, do you?" Her voice carries a hint of accusation as she dismounts and approaches me with deliberate steps.

"The world might be a more peaceful place without you, yes. But Olivia's orders are to keep you alive. You can leave the dragon here and tend to her needs while staying inside the cavern for safety, or you can choose to sleep out here. Makes no difference to me which you pick," I reply bluntly, my patience wearing thin with each passing moment.

Fury ignites in her eyes. Darkness pools around her, a chill seeping through my armor as thunder rumbles overhead. Still, I don't back down.

"I can't decide whether to burn you first, shock you with lightning, scramble your mind beyond repair, or simply poison you right here and now," she hisses. "I thought you—" She cuts herself short, tone shifting, almost like she thought she knew me. It stiffens my spine. "Fuck, I should have known. Like all men, you just see me and want me to suffer. And for that, I wish I could make you suffer under every power I hold."

"Who are you?" I growl, low, dangerous, fighting against the cold that emanates from her very being.

Her face becomes stone. I seize her chin, forcing her gaze to meet mine. "Tell me."

Her eyes flash. "You know what? Fuck Olivia. Because what's going to hurt you more than my powers? You knowing who I really am." Her voice grates over me, cold, ancient, distant. Her eyes are dark pits of nothing.

"Tell me who you are." My voice drops further, sinking into the abyss she's created.

"Bane's daughter."

My body reacts before thought—blade drawn, pressed to her throat. Her dragon roars in protest, but I ignore it, my focus fixed solely on her. "I should end you right here.

Deliver you to his doorstep, the same way he delivered my wife. On a bed of bloody fucking lilies."

Her defiance falters, melting only for a second before her eyes go blank. "You should," she whispers, certain.

I pull the blade back. The cut seals instantly, blood gone as if it never existed. Jorax steps closer behind me, his presence heavy, his growl matching the tension as he stares down her dragon.

"You stay out here. This cavern isn't for you. I won't have Bane's offspring mingling with my kin."

Lia nods, voice flat. "My own father imprisoned me. He's just as much my enemy as he is yours."

"If Bane locked you away, that tells me all I need to know," I snap.

"He doesn't know," she admits, her hands twisting nervously. "He doesn't know about my powers. I've hidden them from him."

I study her, stone still, searching for a lie. There's nothing on her face, but blood ties are blood ties. She is his, no matter how she denies it.

I turn on my heel, fury burning through me. Olivia will answer for this—what in the hells was she thinking, bringing Bane's heir into the one place I swore was safe?

"Come, Jorax." My wyvern moves to me, and with one powerful beat of his wings, we are airborne, leaving Lia and her dragon behind.

"Nephew," my uncle greets as I step into his chamber, the rock walls glistening with fractured beams of light that catch and shimmer in his blue eyes. The sight of him, steady and alive, tempers some of the anger still buzzing through my blood after what I've just learned. He closes the space without hesitation, arms wrapping around me, squeezing tight.

"I'm sorry about—" he begins, but the words scrape raw against me. My stomach clenches, and I cut him off before he can finish.

"Please. Don't mention it," I snap, sharper than I intend, but I can't stand to hear condolences—not from him, not from anyone. There's only one person who should choke on apologies, and it isn't my uncle.

He doesn't push. Just pats my back, a silent acceptance. "Was that a dragon I saw?" he asks instead, voice lighter, shifting us to safer ground.

I let out a heavy breath, running a hand through my hair. "Seems to have taken a liking to a... friend of Olivia's," I answer, though the skepticism in my tone makes the word *friend* sound more like a curse.

My uncle tilts his head, those starry eyes of his cutting into me the way they always do, as if he can sift through my soul with a look. "And we don't approve of either—the dragon or the friend?" His voice is soft, but it's a probe all the same.

"The dragon has chosen to align herself with a woman who should be seen as enemy," I growl. "She's as dangerous as Salasgath, and the attitude to match."

That earns a low chuckle from him. Mischief sparks in his eyes, and it grates against my frayed nerves. "Enemy, you say? I seem to recall a time you were taken with another woman you swore had an attitude sharp enough to cut steel," he says, far too amused.

My temper flares hot, sharp enough to strike sparks off stone. I spin on him, voice rough. "Do not even suggest such a thing. That woman will never be a friend of mine. She's fortunate I haven't dealt with her myself."

The venom in my tone leaves no doubt—whatever my uncle thinks he sees in me when it comes to Lia, he's wrong.

Observing my reaction, my uncle only nods, sage as ever, as if he understands the fire in me without needing the words. "Strong words from the boy who used to drag home every wild creature he laid eyes on," he says, a smile tugging at his lips. "I still remember when the palace courtyards turned into a damned menagerie—panthers, snow leopards, even that snow bear you swore was 'tame enough.' Perhaps I should've put my foot down after the first beast." His chuckle rumbles low, tinged with mock exasperation. "Now look at us—three wild things that believe they own the halls, eating half the kitchen dry."

The laugh that escapes me is rough but real, breaking the tension that's sat heavy in my chest since the mountain. For a moment I let it stand, the memory of home softening the edge of my anger. My uncle has always been that—solace, kin, blood I can trust.

"Just don't let Lorkan hear you call them *pets*," I warn, mouth quirking despite myself. "Gets under his skin."

My uncle grins wide, the lines around his eyes deepening. "It's going to be like the old days, with all you boys back here again." His voice carries nostalgia, but beneath it, I hear the truth: he took us all in once, the broken ones, the discarded ones. Made family where there was none.

"Tell me," he continues, mischief flickering now. "Have Lorkan and Caomh finally buried the hatchet? Or shall I start a betting pool? Either they've torn each other apart by now, or they've made peace and—" his eyes gleam with amusement, "—decided to be together."

I chuckle at the notion, recalling the tumultuous knot that has always been Caomh and Lorkan. "Who knows? They've always had a complicated dynamic," I say, laughter slipping out rougher than it should. It hides the longing under my ribs, that ache for a love I once knew. Every time I'd taken it by the horns, it ended in loss. Left me wondering what might have been if the fates had been kinder.

"So, about this girl—aside from her temperament, why such strong feelings?" my uncle presses, his sharp gaze cutting through my flimsy evasions.

I hesitate. To speak her name is one thing. To speak her bloodline is another. Keeping it hidden might be the only thing that spares her life when there are plenty who'd happily mount her head as a trophy—if only for being Bane's kin. Myself included.

"It's imperative that her identity stays concealed," I finally say, the words tasting like iron. "Olivia wouldn't take kindly to interference."

His expression hardens. He knows enough of empaths to know Olivia wouldn't bend once her mind is set.

He nods once, and I let out a ragged breath. The words burn my throat raw. "She is the daughter of Bane."

My uncle's eyes flare wide, his voice a low exhale of disbelief. "The elusive daughter—no one has ever seen her, not a whisper beyond rumor."

I nod grimly. "He kept her imprisoned her entire life. Olivia freed her when she escaped."

"Only that wretched man would lock away his own blood." My uncle shakes his head, grief sharpening into contempt. "What do we know?"

"She's unpredictable. Powerful. Too powerful. She holds more than one ability and hides it poorly. Much like she does her temper."

His sigh is heavy, like stones grinding against one another, his blue-silver hair caught in his fingers as he begins to pace. "So he succeeded."

My brows knit. "Succeeded in what?"

The chamber grows colder with his pacing, the light flickering against the rock walls as if stirred by the weight of his thoughts. "During the war, those with multiple powers were marked, hunted, erased. But there were whispers... rumors of some being taken instead. Vanishing from their families' arms. Mothers, fathers searched the lands, never finding bodies, only silence. Some claimed they could still *feel* them, hidden in Puinnsean's depths."

His words send a chill down my spine, dragging old shadows out of their graves. "We assumed them dead, casualties of the conflict. But I harbored doubts," my uncle continues, his pacing sharpening, boots grinding against stone. "Bane was a man consumed by ambition, willing to stoop to any depths to seize power. When Tierney emerged from the war adorned with those soul stones, a gleam of malevolent triumph in his eyes, I knew something sinister was at play. The witches vanished, the empaths slaughtered—I suspected Bane was conducting twisted experiments, all in pursuit of ultimate dominance. He preyed on the King's insecurities, whispering poison, biding his time until he could claim supremacy."

My gut twists, bile sharp in my throat at the thought of Bane's depravity. "Of course he would. The bastard would subject his own daughter to such horrors." My voice comes out low, gravel scraping bone, because saying it aloud makes it all too real.

"It's imperative we keep her true nature concealed from both the King and Bane," my uncle says firmly, his tone cutting through my anger. "We must learn where her loyalties lie. But don't forget, she may well be as much a victim as the rest."

I drag a hand down my face, the weight of it all pressing like iron. His faith, his optimism—it grates against my own dark certainty. "I fear the poison in her veins runs deeper than either of us realize," I mutter, the admission bitter on my tongue.

My uncle regards me with a mixture of understanding and admonishment. "There are many among us who bear the burden of tainted blood, yet we do not judge them for the sins of their ancestors," he reminds me, his gaze steady and unwavering. "Our kingdom stands for freedom and equality, a return to the old ways where all Fae are treated with dignity and respect. We fight not for power or dominion, but for the fundamental rights of our people."

I let out a long sigh, knowing he's right. The division of the courts has always been our kingdom's fatal flaw. It doesn't just exclude half the Fae for their lineage—it cripples the very balance of survival. Neart is mostly desert and sea, the King using this to his advantage, their men traded into armies for shipments of food and water. Michael is our eyes and ears there, but even that comes at cost.

"Well, then," my uncle says, clapping a hand to my back, his solemnity already shifting to that sparkle in his eye. "Let's show these Fae an Aotrom welcome."

I watch as he strides down to the communal cavern, his energy already drawing others toward him. If there is one thing my uncle loves—perhaps more than the weight of all his wisdom—it's a good party.

Olivia

THIN AIR

The climb up the mountain was brutal, reminding me just how out of shape I'd gotten since... well, since forever. Jeyr kept offering to give me a piggyback ride, but I stubbornly refused, even though every step felt like it might be my last. My powers were like a leaky faucet I couldn't turn off, draining me with every flicker of thought. The few days we spent chilling at the camp were a joke; I might as well have been eating air for all the energy it gave me. All I wanted was a break, a chance to catch my breath and figure out how to put up some mental barriers to block out everyone else's thoughts.

The rest of the group wasn't doing much better. Parents were practically dragging their kids up the rocky path, anxiety etched into every line of their faces.

"I'd kill for Thanos right about now," Jeyr said, his hand pressing gently into the small of my back as he tried to boost me up another step.

"Think he'll be at the wyvern nests?" I panted, feeling like I might pass out from lack of oxygen at any moment.

"Don't know. Depends on whether he made it out before the King's goons wrecked my home," Jeyr replied, his voice heavy with guilt. I knew he was blaming himself for not being able to protect his people.

"You did what you could for your people," I said, trying to reassure him between gasps for air. It was tough, but we were in this together, and somehow that made it a little easier to keep putting one foot in front of the other.

His silence spoke volumes, painting a vivid picture in my mind's eye of the moment when Aella had to make a choice he couldn't. I felt the weight of his burden, the anguish of witnessing the consequences of his hesitation.

Reaching out, my fingertips grazed his cheek, seeking to offer solace in the face of his unspoken turmoil. "She bears a heavy burden," I murmured softly, my heart aching for the pain Aella must carry. "To know that she took the lives of two mates, their sister, and an unborn child... all because you couldn't bring yourself to do it."

But even as the words left my lips, I knew that Aella's actions had likely been driven by a desperation born of necessity, a moment where there was no time for hesitation or second thoughts. From the images flashing through his mind, it seemed clear that she had acted swiftly, perhaps not even giving him the opportunity to make that difficult decision.

Jeyr's jaw tightens, the flicker in his eyes telling me I've cut too deep. He doesn't say anything, but I don't need words when the hurt bleeds through him like smoke through cracks. His silence is heavier than shouting, heavier than any blade I've carried, and gods it twists something in me.

"Hey," I murmur quickly, reaching for his hand before he can tuck it away. My thumb traces the back of his knuckles, roughened by years of fighting, still trembling faintly from the effort of carrying everyone else's grief. "I didn't mean it like that. You're not the villain here, Jeyr. You never were."

He exhales, long and ragged, as if he's been holding that breath since the day it happened. His eyes finally meet mine, and I can see how much he still blames himself for what Aella did.

"You couldn't have stopped her," I continue, softer now, letting the words fold around him. "She acted fast because she thought she had to. You were still thinking, still weighing lives like you always do. That's what makes you you. That's why people follow you."

A faint crease forms between his brows, his doubt etched there for me to see, but his hand doesn't pull away from mine. Instead, his fingers curl slowly, deliberately, locking around mine like an anchor.

"You did everything you could," I whisper, leaning closer so the words are only for him. "And I'm still here. With you. That has to mean something."

His shoulders slump as if the weight he's been carrying finally shifts, even if just a fraction, and though his gaze stays fixed on the trail ahead, his grip doesn't loosen. If anything, it tightens.

Jeyr

RECKLESS MATES

"G*rand Duke, exterminate the illegals."*

The King's command reverberated through the storm-laden air, sending a shiver down my spine. My heart pounded hard in my chest, matching the rhythm of the tempest that raged around us—a tempest that mirrored the turmoil within me.

Maros's gaze flicked to mine before turning to Tynon. His lips shaped the silent words I love you, and they hung in the air, heavy with finality. I racked my mind for a way out, desperate for anything that could spare us from spilling the blood of our own people.

Before I could act, lightning cracked from the heavens, striking down three tree Fae with brutal precision. My grip tightened around the hilt of my sword, but I knew the storm had not answered to me. Still, the King's gaze seared into me, his expression inscrutable, as though he already knew where the true strike had come from.

"Good. Now let's see if you can do that to your own mate," he taunted, his words slicing through me like daggers. Rage burned hot in my chest, but beneath it, I was what I had always been—a healer, not an executioner. He knew that. He knew my heart was not made for slaughter, even if my hands could wield the storm. But I could kill him, I thought. I wanted to.

King Dominhall's lips curved into a knowing smile. "I wouldn't try. No weather element can kill me. And your healer's heart knows nothing of being a killer."

My sword stayed firm in my grip, but my arm trembled under the weight of his truth. A guard rushed up, panting, cutting through the tension with frantic words.

"Bane has sent an alarm. It's the Empath—she got free."

The King's eyes blackened before he vanished into thin air. A chill slid through me, sinking deep.

I turned to the palace window and found Aella watching, her face carved in stone, her strength unflinching. She looked every bit the ruler this Court deserved. And I couldn't stop myself from thinking—she should have been chosen by fate to lead, not me.

Olivia's touch drags me back, her hands cradling my face with a tenderness that speaks louder than words. In her eyes, I see my own war reflected, and for a moment—one fragile, stolen moment—her presence steadies me.

"We are going to make him pay."

I nod into her palms, press a kiss to each before finding her lips. But the kiss breaks too soon, torn apart by the thunder that rumbles over the mountain. My body goes rigid, hand flying to my sword as I tear it skyward, parting the clouds.

What I see makes my mouth gape.

Their shadows are nothing compared to their true forms—their sheer size makes a wyvern look like a babe fresh from its shell. Gasps ripple through the convoy as I act on instinct, dragging Olivia against the mountain wall and bracing her there, shielding her with my body.

Caomh! I cry through the bond, desperation thrumming like lightning in my veins.

You think I wouldn't notice the dragons? His voice snaps back, taut with urgency.

Olivia's hand finds my arm, pushing me aside. I start to protest, but she only shakes her head, fingertips pressed to her temple.

Caomh, can you hear the dragons?

You mean the roar? Everyone heard the fucking roar, little empath. But no—I can't speak dragon. His frustration cuts sharp through the tether.

One of the beasts banks low, its vast wings carving the air as it closes in on us and the convoy. Its scales flicker, swallowing and bending the light, shifting like liquid armor. It chooses to stay visible, gliding down with deliberate grace, until its molten-gold eyes are level with us.

A shiver knifes down my spine. Those eyes lock on Olivia.

You have got to be fucking kidding me, Caomh mutters, his voice jagged with envy. *She gets Kyzan and Ness—and now she gets the dragon?*

Ignoring the chaotic thoughts swirling around me, I remained captivated by the dragon's piercing golden eyes.

"What is he saying, Liv?" I questioned, tension mounting with each passing moment.

Olivia, frozen in time, staring into the beast's eyes, engaged in some silent, otherworldly conversation. Every Fae stood in petrified silence, too scared to move a muscle. The second dragon descended, moving towards the ranks where I knew Caomh and Lorkan stood.

What's happening? I asked, my voice fraught with worry.

It's looking to Lorkan, but he can't communicate with it, Coamh replied, frustration mounting.

What if he shifts? The unsettling thought lingered in the air.

What if he shifts, and they see it as a threat and bite his neck? The fear in Caomh's voice echoed our collective apprehension.

"Guess there is one way to find out." Lorkan spoke allowed and I watched him leap, Caomh's arms trying to catch him but failing. I watched as he fell down the edge, getting smaller without any signs of a shift.

Caomh screamed down the mountain at Lorkan's falling form. But then I was the one screaming as Olivia moved around me, and jumped. My voice taken by the wind as I stood in the edge cursing that I didn't have fucking wings. Didn't have my wyvern, and cursing at my reckless mate for jumping of a bloody cliff. The dragon huffed, and then dove, the dragon's scales shifted with a resounding click, and it swooped beneath her. She landed on its back, gripping for purchase, and then they were diving. Olivia on one dragon, the small dragon joining to dive after Lorkan, who was still falling. His shift began to take shape, but the ground was closing in on him quicker than the shift to dragon form allowed.

"How are we with the most reckless, crazy Fae in all the land!" Caomh's voice echoed our collective dread.

I couldn't reply, my heart ready to leap into the abyss along with them, and the mountain trembled beneath the weight of impending catastrophe. But for a fleeting moment I did think of a punishment for my mate living to cause my heart to combust with wory,

Olivia

CLIFF JUMPING

There had been many moments in my life where I found myself questioning its reality. A series of unfortunate events that left me wondering if I was merely an amusement to the fates. Whether it was being kidnapped twice, staring death in the eye countless times, or encountering creatures that seemed drawn to me... I couldn't help but feel like my life was a little too dramatic. Yet, despite my yearning for a quiet existence, I found myself standing on the edge of a cliff.

The haunting voice that rumbled through my mind, urging me to jump and trust it, should have given me pause. But I was beginning to realize that those series of unfortunate events had driven me a bit mad. So when that voice commanded me to jump, and those golden eyes dared me to trust them, I did just that—I leapt into the abyss.

There was a moment when the air rushed past me, my hair whipping my face in a mockery of punishment for my idiocy. In that split second, my heartbeat seemed to stop, as if bracing itself for the impending crash landing. The world around me felt suspended in time, as if it, too, was waiting to see the outcome of my reckless abandonment to trust a creature who whispered in my mind, *My Queen, are you ready to take what's yours?*

Some ancient part of me thrummed in its presence and needed to know what it was I could take. Was it this world? Take it back and set it free? The leap of faith that maybe—just maybe—having a dragon on our side could be a turning point in all of this.

I counted the seconds in which I was suspended in free fall.

One.

Two.

Three.

The trees rising from the earth appeared to be closing in.

Four.

Five.

Shouts above had me fighting the force to see Jeyr leaning over the cliff edge shouting my name. Another name was called into the drop—Lorkan.

Six.

Below me, a dark figure twists, light beginning to ripple weakly over his body. Scales try to form, slow and fractured, as if the shift is dragging him apart more than remaking him. My chest caves with panic—he's still falling.

Seven.

With a thud, I collide with the hard back of a scaled creature, my body sliding before I can fully comprehend what's happening. A blink later my mind snaps into focus, and I scramble to find purchase. To my astonishment, I am perched on the back of a beast that makes Ness's size laughable. The wind screams past as we soar, wings tearing the clouds, and the realization hits me—I am on a fucking dragon. A shocked laugh tears free, wild and unbelieving.

But then the deep roar resonates in my mind, rattling bone and blood alike. *Can you stop with the shock and focus on staying put?* The dragon's voice thrums through me, ancient, commanding. I obey without thinking, gripping tight to the ridged scales as he banks into a dive.

And then I see him again.

Over the dragon's wing, Lorkan plummets, still mid-shift, the earth racing up to claim him. His thoughts claw into mine—*I—I thought I could. But I don't know this form.*

"Help him!" I plead, forcing the bond open wider, bridging the creature beneath me to the man falling below. "Tell him how to shift, he doesn't know how!"

Lorkan! The dragon's voice bellows, ancient and relentless, shaking the marrow of my bones. *Listen. Focus. The power is in you. Feel it. Claim it.*

His panic lashes, a whirlwind of doubt and fear, but beneath it—I sense the ember. The hidden core. Waiting.

Close your eyes, I shove the words into him, desperate, the urgency burning me raw. *See the wings. Feel the fire. You are not falling—you are rising. Let it take you. Let it be you.*

The ground claws closer. Branches spear upward. My dragon folds his wings tight and plunges alongside him, the air splitting with the dive.

And then—scales race across Lorkan's skin, wings ripping free in a violent, beautiful snap.

With a final surge of determination, Lorkan embraces the power clawing within him, his body writhing through the breath-taking transformation as scales ripple and wings rip free. The ground is a merciless blur beneath us, clawing closer with every second. His wings snap open, catching air with a mighty flap. One beat. Two beats... but the momentum isn't enough. Time is a blade at his throat, the forest floor rising faster than his wings can bear him.

A sudden shadow cuts across him—another dragon. Smaller, swifter, its wings slicing the air as it dives. My breath stutters in disbelief as its talons strike, clamping down onto Lorkan's shoulders with vicious precision.

Blood blossoms instantly, spilling across his skin, and a scream tears itself from my chest, raw and broken. "No! You're hurting him!" My protest ricochets off the sheer cliffs, lost in the avalanche of sound as rocks splinter loose, thundering down the mountain in violent answer.

The dragon beneath me rumbles, voice ancient and deep, slipping into my mind like thunder through bone. *Hold on, Queen Arouz. That is my son—he will not harm him.* His name presses against me with the weight of inevitability, Faldr, a presence both commanding and steady. Golden eyes blaze as he dives after them, wings cutting through the storming air, determined to aid where his son's grip falters.

Yet, as I bore witness to the scene unfolding before me, doubt begins to gnaw at my loyalty, the tendrils of uncertainty weaving their way through my thoughts. I can both see and hear the unmistakable pain coursing through my friend, his anguished cries echoing through the forest.

"Let him go!" I scream, the words torn from my throat with a raw intensity that mirrors the agony in my heart. The sight of blood seeping from where the younger dragon clings to Lorkan's flesh cuts straight through me, every drop falling like a cruel reminder of the violence unfolding. It feels as though even the forest itself shudders in answer to his cries, the trees trembling, rocks loosening, the world itself echoing his suffering.

Amidst it all, Caomh's panic floods my mind like a torrential downpour, his desperate search for answers a relentless assault on my senses. I grit my teeth against the sheer force of his worry, the pressure threatening to overwhelm me. With a heavy heart, I reluctantly close off our connection, shielding him from bearing witness to Lorkan's valiant struggle to beat his wings against the tide of adversity.

Pathetic shifter, channel your power from your heart and not your mind. Draw from your mate, now! the dragon's voice commands, rattling my skull.

I don't... he begins, but the dragon cuts him off, firm, unyielding. *You do! There is enough of a connection there, not solidified, but it is there. Now, connect with him and draw the power.*

I feel Lorkan's mind, a singular focus on one person, his heartbeat echoing in my senses. His connection with Caomh thrums through the distance like a tether straining but unbroken. I hear his mind whisper to Caomh, pleading for him to find him, to let his power guide him. There is no other explanation, nothing else it could be. Then the distant whisper comes, soft but unshakable.

Have it, Mo Chuisle.

Closing my eyes, I surrender to the swell of my empathic power, letting it drown me, letting it strip me bare. The bond between Lorkan and Caomh burns bright in the dark of my mind, a taut string pulled between them, thrumming with a rawness I can almost taste. Distance does not dull it—if anything, the separation sharpens the ache. With every beat of Lorkan's wings, I feel the fire in his veins, the defiance that drags him upward against the claw of gravity.

The roar of wind, the hammer of my own pulse—none of it hides the rhythm of his wings, their cadence pounding like a vow. The smaller dragon loosens its grip at last, claws withdrawing, leaving Lorkan bloodied but unbound.

My breath hitches as I watch his wounds knit together, scars stitching shut in the space of heartbeats, as if the very air wills him to endure. Hope stirs in me like a fragile bloom in frost, reckless but stubborn, insisting on life even as shadows close in.

Then, Faldr's voice cleaves through my thoughts, ancient and undeniable. *Hold fast,* he commands, and with a sudden heave of his wings, he carries me higher, past Jeyr and the wide-eyed Fae who gape below.

"Olivia!" Jeyr's call lashes across the distance, but Faldr's will thunders through me instead. *Tell your mate to draw from you. He can winnow the convoy to the peak. He need only follow the pull of his mate.*

My lips stumble on the words, relaying the command to Jeyr even as doubt flickers in his mind. Faldr snarls through my skull, shaking my marrow. *Pathetic—have you all forgotten your instincts?* The fury of it rattles me into motion, and in my desperation I reach deeper, past thought, past fear. My hand presses to my chest, searching for the tether that binds me to Jeyr.

I find it—an inexorable tug, a current that consumes me. The world blurs to silence. I pour myself into him, every shred of me slipping through that thread, filling him until I feel the storm crown him like flame.

The elements bow to his call—lightning answering his pulse, thunder rolling to his breath. He is a beacon in the dark, his body the conduit that could lift us all.

Tell them—every Fae, hand to hand. He is the vessel. Wait for my word. Faldr's command thrums in my skull, and I obey, my voice raw as I pass it through the ranks. Colors fracture across my vision, bleeding into one another, dizzying, divine.

Then comes the plunge. Wind claws at my face as Faldr dives. *Now!* His roar splits the air, and I echo it, hurling the word to Jeyr through the tether.

But the colors are too much. The current unravels me. My gift spills too freely, flooding him, flooding everything. *Draw back!* Faldr bellows, but I am already slipping, confusion binding me tighter than chains. Lightning screams across the sky, thunder shakes the mountain, and I collapse against scales sharp as glass.

Darkness takes me whole.

Jethro

THE SIPHON

I watch the world move around me, mindlessly flipping a dagger in my hand, its golden-and-silver hilt catching the shimmer of the light orbs drifting through the cavern. I tell my mind not to stray to the woman alone on the mountain tops, not to picture how easily this blade could slide between her ribs. I tell myself not to look for the shadow of her or the dragon that might cut across the cavern's mouth.

But the gods like their cruel games.

The mountain groans with a sound that rattles bone, dust and stone skittering loose from the cave ceiling. Wyverns roar, their cries echoing like thunder, talons scraping as wings beat the air. They abandon their nests, surging toward the cavern mouth. The bonded beasts wait, eyes catching mine, ready for their Fae riders. My breath steadies, my hand tightens on the dagger, and I'm no longer a shadow in the corner. I'm captain of the Aotrom army again, and the weight of command slams back into my chest.

What the hell am I waiting for—more than falling rock, more than the mountain's warning?

Lia's dragon roars. The sound tears through the stone, rattling the cavern walls and showering us in debris. Gods. If that woman brings this mountain down—

I whistle, sharp and cutting, the command threading the chaos. Jorax answers instantly, my Wyvern surging forward. I vault onto his back, the sting of icy wind tearing across my cheeks as we launch. Precision carries us through the cavern, water from the waterfall drenching me as we cut past it, the cold soaking into bone. Behind me, Fae move as one, grim-faced, whistling for their bonded wyverns. Wings unfurl, talons strike stone, and the sky fills with them, answering my call.

Breaking into open air, Jorax spreads his wings wide, the wind snapping hard against us as I take in the sight—

And my breath stalls.

Thousands of Fae perch along the jagged ridges, faces stricken, eyes pulled not to us but to the sky. Four dragons command the peaks, their sheer presence choking the horizon. Lia kneels by her beast, her dark hair whipping like a flag in the storm. Beside her stands a smaller twin, restless, twitching wings a mirror of its kin. Beyond them, a black-scaled monster crouches, vast enough to drown the cliffs in shadow. And there—panting, wings trembling from the strain, a dragon of indigo scales lifts his head. His violet eyes burn bright, unyielding, locked on the darkness towering above him.

Above it all, lightning crackles across the sky, sending shivers down the spines of the wyverns, their instincts driving them to lower their altitude, wings twitching nervously as electricity dances through the charged air. In that moment, understanding ripples through me like a stone cast into still waters. The storm ahead is more than just thunder and rain.

I scan the tumultuous skies, searching for Jeyr amidst the swirling chaos. My heart quickens its pace. Only when Olivia was captured have his newly found powers ever torn the skies this violently. My thoughts run rampant, searching for Jeyr, for Olivia, and snagging on the weight of what I left hanging between us. I had my reasons for letting things change, and I know Gwynn's death isn't on her—not completely. She didn't kill her. But in my grief I wonder—if she had fought that day with the power I've seen in her now, if she had unleashed what I know she carries, would Gwynn have ever gone back searching for answers? Answers that never came, leaving me with nothing but questions. And now it feels as though my grief, and the anger I nursed beneath it, has manifested into tragedy.

My eyes sweep the chaos, catching on the absence of one brother. Panic twists until—there. Jeyr.

He lies curled on the back of the black dragon, limp and inert, nothing more than a vessel for the energies writhing through him.

Caomh's voice cuts through the storm, sharp with desperation. "Stop the connection! Push the power back into her, Jeyr!"

Jeyr shakes, clutching Olivia's frame. "I am trying!" His words are choked, ragged, rough—like the lightning tearing through him is shredding his throat from the inside out.

With a heavy heart, I watch as he strains against the overwhelming force, every muscle taut with effort, every breath a war against the storm threatening to consume him.

Perched atop Jorax's back, adrenaline floods me, my body coiled to leap into action. But truth be told—I'm clueless. None of us have ever dealt with anything like this. Sure, I've heard the old tales of Companachs sharing their powers in dire moments, one feeding the other like a torch passing flame when one runs low. But seeing it in the flesh? That's something else entirely. And Jeyr—he's not sharing. He's bleeding Olivia dry.

Frustration gnaws at me, hot and sharp, tangled with fear. My friends are unraveling before my eyes, and I don't have a godsdamned clue how to fix it. But giving up? That's never been in my blood. With a scowl that feels carved into my bones, I brace myself for whatever's coming, ready to tear the world apart if that's what it takes.

Jeyr is straining against the torrent ripping through him, his body trembling like a vessel too small to contain the storm. Shaking, he gathers Olivia tighter in his arms. The dragon shifts, lowering its body so they slide to the stone below. Jeyr stumbles, hand bracing against the mountain, but never once does he let her frail form slip. His eyes—bright, unrecognizable—flash upward.

The dragon's gaze tilts, not to him, but to Lia. Still kneeling. Her eyes... gods, they're not eyes anymore, they're a cosmos. Otherworldly, brimming with power she has no right to wield alone. And yet, without a mate, without a tether, she stands.

Before doubt can take root, she moves. Rising with a grim purpose, Lia lifts her hand to the sky. The storm obeys. Power bends, the crackling chaos above funneling through her body and into Olivia's silent form.

The sky answers her command. The clouds part in a slow shudder, like the hand of time itself brushing them aside, revealing the vast stretch of blue behind. It's fast and slow all at once, a cosmic shift, as if the gods themselves lean in to watch.

Lia staggers, her face pale, every ounce of strength bleeding from her frame with each siphon she pours into Olivia. But she doesn't stop. Not until color stirs back into Olivia's skin, not until breath lifts her chest.

Jeyr, still trembling from the drain, moves to shield her, his arms wrapping protectively as Olivia begins to stir.

Silence blankets the mountain peak, heavy and unreal. Only the hush of the wind and the rasp of our breathing remain. Around us, the Fae stand motionless, their wide eyes locked on the sky that moments ago raged with fury—now clear, impossibly calm.

Jeyr

BURNING OUT

Never before have I experienced such an overwhelming surge of power coursing through my veins. It is as if Olivia is injecting me with a potent drug, pumping energy into my body. My very being absorbs it eagerly, and the skies themselves respond to the call of this newfound force. Following Olivia's command, I harness the power to effortlessly move thousands of people from the mountain's edge to our destination.

However, the channeling doesn't relent. I fight against it, desperately trying to push back, but Olivia's influence is unyielding. It is as if she has closed the doors, preventing me from redirecting the power. I burn from the inside out, the intensity unbearable as lightning laces through my body. My healing abilities struggle to repair the damage inflicted by my weather powers, but my singular focus remains on Olivia.

Despite my resistance, I sense her weakness, feel her life force draining away. The connection persists, denying me any chance to push the power back. Relief only comes when a hand touches me. The energy drains like a punctured hole in a pressurized can, and as the link severs, my body slumps in exhaustion.

When I force my eyes open, I see a girl with hair that seems to shift in hues as the sunlight catches it. I turn—Olivia lies pale, lifeless on the ground.

Shaking, I draw her closer. "Hummingbird, wake up," I plead, pressing my lips to hers while pouring my healing into her. Her heartbeat—slow but steady—is the only thing that reassures me.

"Her dragon says she's burnt out, but she won't wake until her body recovers," Lia explains gently at my side.

"What happened?" I exhale.

"She channeled into you but didn't keep the lines open both ways. I won't repeat the other choice words he had about the lack of primal training we all have." She rolls her eyes as if she isn't speaking of near-death.

I gather Olivia in my unsteady arms and attempt to rise. More arms surround her weight, and I find myself staring into the purple eyes of Lorkan, newly shifted back.

"Let me help. Jet, is there a place where these two can rest?" His voice is calm, certain. My mate shifts from my arms to his, and my instincts snap in protest, my hands reaching—but Caomh and Colden grip me, steering me to follow.

"She's okay," Caomh says, his voice lighter than the tension warrants. "But when she wakes, please scold her. I have yet to meet a more reckless person." I manage a huff of laughter in return.

Jet smirks, eyes glinting mischievously in the cavern's dim light. "I don't know about that. You left me with the mad woman. She walked up to a dragon like it was a kitten lost in the woods."

Caomh groans, "I enjoyed being away from her."

"That woman just saved me. And my mate. some respect," I snap, my voice carrying a weight that stiffens them both.

We move in silence, our footsteps echoing against cold stone. The cries of wyverns outside bleed faintly into the caverns, stirring a pang of longing for stables long gone. If I had the energy, I'd be searching for answers, but Caomh and Colden flank me close, making clear I'm in no condition to stray.

We reach the carved halls where light orbs dance across the stone, scattering like stars.

Luminier emerges from shadow, concern etched across his face. "Come. I have a room ready." He gestures us on. Lorkan trails after him with Olivia in his arms, and with Caomh and Colden bracing me, I stumble forward.

The room is small but warm, a double bed raised on wooden pallets. Lorkan lays Olivia down gently, her curls spilling across the pillow, her chest faint with shallow breaths. I manage the last steps before collapsing beside her.

The others retreat, the door sliding shut on its iron rollers. Silence cocoons us.

I wrap myself around her, pulling her close, hating the cold of her skin against mine.

Sleep drags me down at last, lulled by the hum of a hidden city of Fae and wyverns, and my Hummingbirds heart beat lulling me to sleep.

Lorkan

HOT TUB TANTRUMS

Walking through the bustling paths of the cavern, I felt the itch of thousands of eyes, the whispers of who I was- the face to the myth. I had fought many battles, though I was a ghost in those, the only men who knew of me were the who Caomh wanted, and he only let me fight if my true face was never to be seen. I swallowed the lump in my throat at that thought, I know I spoke of here and now, forget the past but it didn't mean the years of being nothing but a shadow of existence didn't mean It didn't leave scars from small thread cuts.

I shake my head, trying to shake out my own thoughts that were too loud, rolling my shoulders for ache of my muscles. There was never a time in my life I had felt this kind of ache from a shift, it felt like I moved the mountain with my own strength, instead I fell from its edges and shifted into the imaginable. As if sensing my discomfort hands fell to my side, his breath fanning my hair. I could feel him asking for permission to my mind, wanting to know what what leaving me unease.

I let my hands rest against his as they gently rubbed at my chest. "You're hurt," his whisper reached me between my shoulder blades as we paused at the edge of a ledge, gazing up at the waterfall cascading down to the earth below.

"I am fine, because of you," I replied softly, matching his tone. I knew he preferred to communicate through our mental link, but I wasn't ready for that level of... intimacy right now. That had been our place of safety as a child, but now with what I knew...it wasn't something I was ready for.

"Are we going to talk about it?" Caomh's voice broke the silence, pulling me from my thoughts. I shook my head in response, knowing there was so much to discuss that I feared would only burden him further. I just needed more time, more time with him to claim him as mine before the world came crashing down around us.

"I will only accept that answer for now, Mo Chuisle. Not every day your partner turns himself into a dragon." *His partner.* The weight of his words hung heavy in the air, and I turned in his grasp, needing to see the look in his eyes.

Golden eyes met mine, moving in the orb lights with every dancing shred of emotion, . His hair was pulled half up in a bun, waves of it cascading down to his shoulders. With his shirt off, I couldn't help but laugh. "Feel better?" I poked his bare chest, a playful grin tugging at my lips. His eyebrow quirked, a hint of amusement dancing in his gaze. "You know it. Come to our quarters. I have whiskey ready, hot baths, and the promise of good company."

And this is why I hadn't shared what weighed on my mind. The knowledge of a dragon lurking within me felt like a ticking time bomb, threatening to explode our fragile peace. All I wanted was a night with my partner, where we could share whiskey under the soft glow of candlelight. The bath seemed like an added bonus, a chance for us to be together without the looming shadow of destiny overshadowing our every moment.

"The joys of being Lumineer's adopted sons," he remarks with a broad smile, shedding his clothes with the easy confidence of a mountain lion. It strikes me, not for the first time, how effortlessly he moves, as if stripping down is second nature. Truth is—if he could walk this earth naked all the time, he would.

I've never seen him completely bare before—shirtless, countless times, more times than I've ever seen him clothed, but never like this. I stand momentarily stunned as he strides toward the tubs, steam rising in thick curls like an open invitation. He casts a glance over his shoulder, playful, daring—and maybe, just maybe, not meant only for him.

The last time I saw him like this, we were carefree teenagers, racing to the spring outside his childhood home, nothing but our underwear clinging to us. Back then, he was all long limbs and untapped promise. Now, he is a carved statue come alive, golden muscles honed and defined with purpose. When he shakes his ass, knowing full well I'm watching, laughter bursts out of me before I can help it.

"Come on, Lor, the water isn't enchanted; it won't stay warm forever," he teases, beckoning me.

I chuckle, setting about removing my armor—a task that is anything but swift. Caomh's grunt of disapproval confirms what I already know: my armor is stubborn, cumbersome, meant to withstand battles, and moulded to shift with me.

"It's a shifter's armor; it's not meant to come off easy," I mutter, defensive.

"Hecate would insist on a clean escape route," Caomh quips with a wicked grin. "When I find her, I'll ask for improvements."

I shake my head, warmth rising in my chest. The sound of his bare feet pattering closer pulls me still, and then his hand is at my chest. I gasp, my eyes lifting to meet his golden gaze.

"Cay..." My voice fractures, low, reverent, undone at the sight of him standing before me, unadorned, his beauty undeniable. If I were a poet, I'd say he was sculpted by gods.

"What? I'm just helping," he says lightly, mischief sparking in his eyes.

"What you're doing is distracting me," I breathe, my heart hammering as his hands find the clasps of my armor, undoing them with practiced ease.

His lips brush mine—soft, fleeting. We don't speak as he undresses me, his touch reverent, steady, as if this ritual belongs to us alone. It makes me wonder how it might have been, if all those years ago he had let me stand at his side in battle, not just as the shadow in the trees. If, after victory, I had returned to his tent and let him undress me like this.

His lips trace patterns over my skin, his eyes drink me in like I am something sacred. I know he doesn't limit himself, that he has dallied with all manner of beings across the years. I pretend it doesn't affect me, that I don't seek his company just to be near him. I have never crossed his threshold uninvited, never stepped into his privacy behind closed doors.

And yet—I have tortured myself in silence. Watched him take others home, watched him kiss countless fae of every kind. Never once me.

The younger version of myself believed I could shape myself into anything he desired, no matter who caught his eye. But time taught me otherwise. I stopped trying to be everything for him. If he truly wanted me, it would be as I am: a tall, scarred male, marked by the echoes of every face I've ever worn. Being a shifter means carrying those scars—the ones that never quite fade, etched deep in my skin, a history of battles fought and survived.

And now, here he is, undressing me as though none of that matters.

As the leather falls away from my body, Cay's eyes rake over the ink that winds across my skin, the patterns designed to mask the scars that mark my arms. My chest, though, remains bare of ink. Unlike the others, who received their tattoos together as a rite of passage, I chose to mark myself alone. Always the outsider. Always in the shadows. But belonging—it clawed at me. So I carved my own story into my flesh.

Cay's hand traces the designs, gentle but searching.

"Lorkan... what the fuck are these? Who did this to you?" His voice is sharp, edged with concern, his golden eyes trying to dig answers out of me.

I sigh, the weight of his gaze pressing too heavy. He nudges me to turn, and his eyes fix on the canvas of scars across my back. Not how I wanted him to see me. Not like this. Call me sentimental, call me vain, but I wanted more than pity. I wanted the hunger he gives others. The lust. The desire. Ignoring his protests, I stride to the tub and sink into the water, its lukewarm embrace offering little comfort.

"Lorkan," he calls, voice softening, pleading.

I close my eyes, shift briefly into my fire form, and the water heats, hissing as steam curls around us. It stings my skin, but it soothes the ache in my muscles.

"They're nothing, Cay. Just old scars," I mutter, my voice rough with resignation. "Either join me in the bath or go drink your whisky."

"If you think I'm going to ignore the fact that my partner is covered in scars, you've got another thing coming." His words cut, frustration thick. "I can overlook it for one night, sure, but knowing that someone—or a whole army of someones—did this to you? That makes me want to burn kingdoms."

My jaw flexes. I drag a hand over it, then slam the water in frustration, sending waves spilling over the tub's edge.

"I'm sorry you can only look at me like I'm some scarred monster. Not exactly a turn-on, Cay. Would you rather I shift? Hide what's underneath? Pretend I'm nothing but the armor I wear?"

The silence after is brutal. Heavy. Suffocating.

"Lor..."

"Forget it." My voice cracks with anger and exhaustion. I scrub at my skin, trying to rid myself of the day and of him seeing too much.

"Lorkan."

I ignore him, ducking beneath the water, soaking my hair. When I resurface, he's there—kneeling by the tub, hands braced on the rim, eyes burning into me.

"If you think I don't find you attractive, you've got another thing coming." His voice cuts through the silence like a blade.

I fight to ignore him. Fight the way my heart wants to tear itself out of my chest.

"Mo Chuisle," he says, gentler now. "Look at me. Please."

Damn him. Damn the way he says it. Slowly, reluctantly, I turn. His hand finds my chin, tilts my face up. Water runs down his knuckles in shining trails.

"I have always—and will always—find you the most beautiful person. I mean the man in front of me. The real you," he whispers, every word steady, unshakable. "The reason I said I would never sleep with a shifter is because I won't. Not in another form. Not a raven. Not a wolf. Not a dragon. I'll be with you, Lorkan. Only you. It's you I want. It's always been you. I could never... be with anyone who even resembled you. Not when you exist."

I silence him with a finger against his lips, feeling his breath hot against my knuckles.

"Do. Not. Ever. Mention past lovers around me," I rasp, every word steel.

His smile is slow, tender, as he moves my hand aside. Then his mouth is on mine, deep, certain.

"They're in the past," he murmurs between kisses, "and they'll stay there. There is only you, Mo Chuisle."

I can't help but groan, the weight of his confession lifting a burden I've carried for far too long.

He shifts, sliding into the tub with a contented sound, his back pressing into my front. Instinct takes over—I wrap my arms around him, pulling him close until his head rests perfectly against my shoulder.

"You scared me today, Lorkan," Cay whispers into the dim-lit air, his voice tinged with a vulnerability that cuts straight through me. I tighten my hold on him, silently admitting that I, too, had been strangled by fear. My body had plunged headfirst into the decision before my mind could catch up, instincts ruling everything. I've never feared falling to my death before; I always had my hawk, my raven—wings to catch me, comfort in their certainty. But becoming a dragon? That stretched beyond any boundary I had ever dared. A wyvern had always been the largest I let myself become. Fear locked me mid-shift, and if Cay knew how close I'd come to shattering on the rocks below... I don't even want to imagine what it would have done to him.

He shifts again, settling in the bath to face me.

"Sorry, mo ghràdh," I murmur, my apology a breath carried into the stillness.

"Please never dive to your death again; my old heart can't take it," he pleads, his voice trembling with emotion.

A laugh breaks from me, and I press a kiss to his cheek. "You're not old. Not really." My fingers trace idle patterns across his skin, finding steadiness in the living proof of him. In fae terms, he's barely middle-aged, maybe not even that.

"I feel it. If I were human, I'd be gray-haired with ghastly wrinkles," he muses, self-deprecation softening his tone.

"You'd still be hot. A silver fox for sure," I tease, lips tugging into a grin.

He shifts once more, bracing his back into my chest, ass pressing into my groin—and he knows exactly what he's doing. I can feel the smirk without even seeing it. Despite it, his body unwinds, the tension leaving him.

"Mmm, you know it," he hums, smug and content.

I start washing him, slow deliberate strokes until he's melting into me. "Need the whiskey while in the bath, damn it," he grumbles playfully.

"Shhh." My lips find his neck, trailing kisses along the slope of it. "Need to be drunk to be with me?" I tease, my voice laced with affection.

"No. But the extra buzz would give me confidence," he admits, honest in a way that makes my chest ache.

"For what, mo ghràdh?" I murmur, though my thoughts already brush dangerously toward his mind, toward that place that is both familiar and forbidden.

His response echoes inside me, soft but potent, and I groan inwardly. Gods, I wonder how long I can stretch this moment, how many more nights like this fate will let us steal before it all comes crashing down.

Olivia

Deep Dive

I have never been one for swimming. Despite growing up near the ocean, the fear of what lurked beneath the surface kept me tethered to the safety of the shallows. Yet one day, I summoned the courage to venture farther, past the first break wash. The sensation of my body bouncing in the waves was both liberating and terrifying, the ocean's rhythm dictating the movement of my limbs as I drifted into deeper waters. At first, it was exhilarating—I felt weightless as I bobbed up and down—until a wave rolled over me. In that moment, I understood the suffocating press of being held beneath an insurmountable weight, my body burning as it fought desperately for one last breath.

I wake gasping, my body heavy and my mind consumed by panic, as if I'm trapped again beneath that relentless wave. In the darkness, arms reach for me, and instinct kicks—I fight, my hand connecting with a face and drawing a groan.

"Hummingbird!"

I pause, disoriented, breaths ragged. The same arms gather me again—gentle, firm—anchoring me against a hard, warm chest. Soft lips brush my thundering pulse.

"That's it, hummingbird. Settle." The one voice whose hoarseness can soothe the spiral in my mind.

I match my breaths to his, and the tension begins to dissolve, his power flowing through me like a tide, easing the ache in my joints and quieting the noise inside.

"You live to scare me, you know that?" he murmurs, exasperation braided with concern.

I sigh, apology and resignation in one. "Sorry."

"Will there ever be a day I stop worrying about you sacrificing yourself or walking into unnecessary danger?" His words hang heavy in the dark—clipped; if I weren't his mate he'd have me pinned with the fury in his eyes.

Even without light, I close my eyes and listen to his heart.

"I'm not scolding you, my love, but I have a request," he says, gentle and unyielding.

I hum.

"I need you to fight for you. You've been fighting—finding ways out of cages you never should've been in—but from now on, I need you to live. No matter what happens in this war, I need to know you won't give yourself away. There's no point in going into battle if I don't have a life with you on the other side."

He lifts me like a doll, firm and careful, settling me in his lap, my legs around him. He holds me tight to his chest until every beat of his heart thrums against mine—the here, the now, living proof.

"It's war, Jeyr. We can't have a life without putting everything into breaking Bane and Dominhall," I say, the truth pressing down like stone.

His head tips to mine, voice rough. "I know. But I'm struggling to find a reason to fight if you're going to burn yourself out. I know it's selfish, but I want you to fight to live. For me. For you. For us."

My heart aches. He has shouldered his own demons, and still he asks me to stay. I nod, letting him feel it—the unspoken depth of my love threading the dark, a quiet promise.

"I love you, Hummingbird. I know we aren't promised time. I know to cherish what we get. But please—stop trying to make it shorter."

I feel his head shift, seeking my lips, capturing them in a tender kiss. In the darkness, with sight stripped from me, every other sense sharpens—every touch, every sound becomes amplified. I am acutely aware of his hands, deft as they work at the stubborn fastenings of my armor, his breath quickening with the slow rise of excitement. My own hands wander his bare chest, tracing the cut of muscle, the warmth of his skin, even as he rids me of the corseted plates that have always been my shield. His touch sets fire beneath my skin, a flame I have no desire to douse.

Fucking perfect, his inner monologue rumbles through my mind, and I preen at the raw honesty of it. *I am never letting you go.*

His mouth claims one of my breasts, lips and tongue worshipping, reverent and hungry. The trail of kisses moves to the curve of my neck, where he bites—sharp and possessive. A gasp tears from me, pleasure and pain twined into one, only for him to kiss it away as if sealing his claim.

"Mine," he whispers, voice low, a brand against my spine.

Shivers scatter through me, need surging, my thoughts begging for his lips again. As though he hears, his mouth finds mine in a kiss that steals sound from me, leaving only a moan, just as his hands push at the last of my clothes.

In one effortless motion, he lifts me, flips me, presses me down into the mattress. Fabric rustles, discarded and forgotten. I can't see his eyes in the dark, but I feel the intensity of them as surely as I feel his lips trailing fire down my body, until the air itself trembles with anticipation.

My hands reach blindly for him, desperate for skin, but his canines graze the inside of my thigh, dragging a whimper from me, leaving me writhing in place.

"Patience, Hummingbird," he hums, velvet and maddening, his voice a caress in the black.

A broken sound escapes me, heat flooding even though he barely touches. But I *feel* his anticipation, hear the fragments of pleasure sparking through his thoughts. Then his mouth is on me—kissing, tasting, his tongue teasing from my entrance to that bundle of nerves that makes my hips buck wildly, betraying me. My hands clutch at his hair, torn between tugging him away and holding him closer, caught in a battle I know I'll lose.

With a growl, Jeyr pins me—legs hooked over his shoulders, his grip on my thighs iron. He feasts on me, each nip and lick a relentless undoing, until the pool of heat in my belly surges beyond control. My body trembles, legs shaking in pleasure I can't contain, my orgasm tearing through me as he hums against me, savoring.

One hand frees my thigh, sliding up my body, lingering between my breasts where my heart pounds like a drum.

"My Hummingbird," he murmurs into me, voice reverberating through every nerve. The hand on my heart glides lower just as he rises over me. Lightning sparks crackle faintly in the air, flashing enough to let me see his eyes—electric blue, blazing.

"There is something I want to try... if you will let me?"

I nod without hesitation, my trust absolute.

He smiles, kisses a trail across me—my breasts, my cheekbones, my lips—before his hand finds me again. The faint fizz of power gathers, and when his fingers press against my sensitive nerves, small shocks pulse through me, not pain but exquisite fire. My body arches, taut and trembling, my head falling back as the currents ripple through me.

His mouth finds my throat, his groan hot against my skin, and I know—he *feels* what

I feel. My reaction thrums through him, flooding both our veins with lightning.

"Gods, Olivia," he breathes, as though my name itself is his prayer.

I understood, this was hurting him too, in the best sort of ways, but his hard length that was flinching as my arousal shot through my body told me he would come just from this alone.

"Jeyr, please." I begged and he thanked me, angling me, one leg getting pulled to his side, his hand massaging my thigh as he slowly, pushed inside me. Like he wanted to savour it, remember the feeling. But it was something I knew we would both never forget. I was already convulsing around him, the feel of him, our connection making me claim him as mine. Tears fell down my cheeks, my emotions unable to be bottled up. Jeyr just simply kissed them away, lips moving to mine as he slowly and languidly kissed me. His groan vibrates through my chest, the sound pulling another whimper from me as I clutch at his shoulders.

"Jeyr," I breathe, not to remind him who he is, but because for so long, that name lingered on my lips unspoken.

He kisses me again like he's starved, like every moment apart has led to this. I feel it in the way his lips drag against mine, the way his hands move over my body like he is trying to memorize me all over again. His touch isn't hesitant anymore, it's hungry, searching, reverent all at once.

"Gods, Olivia..." his voice cracks as he sinks into me again, slower this time, deeper. His forehead presses to mine and I feel his breath stutter, his body trembling with restraint. "You feel—fuck, you feel like home."

His hands glide down my back, tracing every scar with a reverence that leaves me breathless. No longer do I feel self-conscious beneath his touch; he claims each mark as part of a masterpiece, his devotion turning old wounds into something cherished, as though love itself can rewrite the story etched in my skin.

"Then stay here," I breathe, lifting my hips to meet his, urging him to let go. "Stay in me. With me."

The plea shatters his control. His rhythm grows surer, hips pressing against mine with a force that makes the bed creak beneath us. But there's no rush this time, no frantic desperation like before. He's learning me, paying attention to every gasp, every arch of my body, every shiver that ripples through me when his thumb brushes over the tender peak of my breast or when his teeth catch lightly at my throat.

I can't help but moan his name, nails raking down his spine, marking him the way he marks me with every thrust. His growl answers mine, low and primal, vibrating against my skin as if the sound itself could brand me.

"You're mine," he murmurs against my mouth, not as a claim but as a truth we both already know. His hips roll deeper, slower, making me cry out at the intensity of it. "Every scar, every shadow, every breath—you're mine."

I pull him closer, our lips crashing, sloppy and desperate now, my body clenching around him as the storm in me breaks. Pleasure rips through me, my thighs trembling around his waist as his name falls from my lips like a prayer. He follows me into the unraveling, his body seizing, his face buried in my neck as he pours every ounce of himself into me.

When the storm settles, we're tangled together, his weight heavy but welcome, his hands still roaming as though he can't stop touching me. He presses soft kisses to my jaw, my cheeks, my temple—each one quieter than the last, like he's telling me without words that he'll never stop worshipping me.

The only sound that fills the room is the distant bustling behind the cavern walls and the steady rhythm of Jeyr's breath curled around me.

"We made it to the caverns then?" I whisper into the darkness, my voice small.

"With a little more fanfare than was needed, but yes," he replies softly.

I groan, hiding my face in his chest. "I am embarrassed."

"Don't be," he murmurs, lips brushing my hair. Then a beat of silence, his tone dipping with quiet warning. "But let's not exchange powers like that again."

I feel the weight of his words. "I... it felt good not to hear so many thoughts. And I think..." my throat tightens, guilt rising sharp in me, "I think I leaned into that, wanting to push the noise away."

His arm tightens around me, his chest solid against my back. "I'm hoping we can spend some time here training. Caomh and the other mind masters can help you. You're not the only one who needs it. I have an entire weather system going on in here, and I'm barely in control. It's latched to my emotions—half the time it feels like the storms know me better than I know myself." His words carry that rare, soft vulnerability that makes my chest ache.

"Maybe I can help with the emotional side of it all," I whisper back, daring to lift my hand over his. His response is a kiss to my temple, grounding and warm.

"Worth a try."

His mouth moves lower, brushing over the curve of my shoulder. My body shivers, though not from cold. His hands track lower, reverent as they trace the disfigured scars scattered across my back. I tense instinctively, but his lips follow the path of his fingers, pressing tender worship into jagged lines I've long despised.

"Olivia," he whispers, the weight of my name heavy on his tongue. "Do you trust me?"

The words steal my breath. My throat closes, the reflex to guard myself sparking like a defensive flame. But when I turn my head to meet his eyes, the storm in them is gone. All I see is him—steady, waiting, patient.

"Yes," I whisper, because it is the truest thing I've ever said.

He pulls away only to cross the room. I hear the low scrape of a drawer, then the quiet clink of something metal. When he returns, the flickering light orbs glint against an old set of tattoo needles, the kind etched with history, with ritual. My pulse skitters.

"Only if you want this," he says, voice low, reverent, almost breaking. "I want to give you something more permanent than scars. Let me?"

I nod, my voice lost, my body thrumming with the enormity of his offer. He waits for the tiniest flicker of consent before settling behind me again, his knees bracketing my hips. The first touch of the needle grazes my skin, but instead of pain there is only warmth. His healing seeps into every stroke, numbing, soothing, weaving flesh and ink together.

I close my eyes, surrendering.

His breath fans against my neck as the slow, deliberate lines take shape. I imagine it even before he whispers it into my skin: a dragon. My dragon. A creature of power etched across the jagged ruins of my back, turning what was once shame into something unbreakable.

"You're not broken," he murmurs as he works, every word syncing with the careful pricks and swirls of the needle. "You're fire. You're mine."

When he finally leans back, his hand soothing over the fresh ink, I feel it—not the ache of scars but the permanence of love inked into me, alive and whole

Jethro

The Mirror

Navigating the spiraled paths of the cavern, I make my rounds, checking on the Fae, how they're holding up—especially since my brothers are all off wrapped up in the company of their loves. Maybe this is what it was like in those early days with Gwynn—when war had us all rattled, but my eyes still lit on that wild woman who poured fire into them. Back then, I thought I was untouchable. Now I'm much the same as the rest of them, scorned and marked by loss.

The cavern stretches wide, the walls alive with wyverns clinging like gargoyles, perched high on ledges, their eyes glowing faintly in the dark as if daring anyone to test their keep. Privacy here is a joke—stone amplifies every whisper—but luck's on our side. Most of the survivors know one another already, so sharing camps comes easier than I feared.

I weave through the bustle, the underground hum reminding me of a city that refuses to die. Food stations sizzle, smoke curling into the cold air, and clusters of Fae gather round fires, trading stories, laughing in bursts that sound too alive for all we've been through. Someone's pulled out a fiddle, the notes sharp and bright against the cavern walls, and for the first time in too long, the sound feels like something close to hope.

Even after stepping out from under the shadow of death, companionship keeps pulling me back into the heart of it. Commanding my uncle's army, wrangling Caomh's smaller forces—it isn't just duty anymore. It's a tether. A way to stitch back the fellowship I lost the day Gwynn slipped into Puinnsean's border, chasing her truth instead of fighting at my side. The thought stings, sharp as salt in a wound I never let close.

"You were always at home here," my uncle's voice cuts through the monotonous churn of my thoughts, falling into step beside me as I make my rounds. Or—if Caomh were here—he'd say I'm just looking busy. I glance at my uncle, force a thin smile.

"Yeah," I murmur, a pang of nostalgia tightening my chest. "I was just thinking how much I missed this place. The sound of the halls with music..."

He grunts, his agreement weighted with the same solemnity clouding my own mind. "If only it wasn't before war. But there's something about the hope of a fight that stirs the spirit, isn't there?"

I don't bother to reply. Hope isn't something I have the spine for right now. Keeping my emotions locked down is the only way I stop the shadows from leaking out around me, prowling at my heels like they can smell my need to do nothing, to be left alone. Though—truth be told—my overwhelming desire to kill someone is a kind of shining light compared to wallowing as a hermit. Go figure. Murder as motivation. Guess we all reach new lows.

Then my uncle shifts the conversation, his tone heavier. "She's out in the weather, you know. Hasn't come down for food."

My muscles tense, instinctive and sharp, at the mention of her. I follow his nod up to the cavern's peak, my jaw clenching with that familiar mix of frustration and something dangerously close to concern.

"What a shame."

He huffs, unimpressed. "She's part of the army you and your friends dragged here. From what I hear, she's saved more than a few lives—your friends included. If you're a proper leader, Jethro, you'll check on all those under your command."

My teeth grind so tight I half expect them to crack. The words I want to spit claw at my throat: *she can look after herself perfectly*. And if she froze, if she starved, if another of Bane's blood rotted off the earth—I'd struggle to find fault in that.

But my uncle's gaze stays on me, steady, immovable.

I break it off first, turning on my heel. I make my way to the supplies without another word, his warning hanging in the air. Gathering what I need, I whistle for Jorax, the sharp sound slicing through the cavern's hum.

His answering call reverberates back, steady and familiar. I steel myself as I sling the supplies over my shoulder, knowing this won't be an easy confrontation. But duty is duty. Even if tonight it looks a lot like hauling food to the last bloodline on earth I'd rather see survive.

The rain pelts against my skin, relentless, strands of hair not caught by the leather strap in my hair whipping about in the wind. I pause, chest tightening in spite of myself, as my eyes fall on her.

Gone is the raven-black dye, stripped away by the weight of the power she's taken in. She is transformed. Her hair, now white streaked with ultraviolet hues, moves like it belongs to the storm itself—alive, fluid, radiant in a way that isn't soft but dangerous. Not ethereal. No. She is serpent: each lock gleaming like iridescent scales, beauty edged with venom, a creature born to dazzle and devour in the same breath.

She stands quiet, rain running down her skin as if even the storm bends to witness her. There is a pull in it, and I hate it. Hate that my gaze lingers when it should turn away. Her very existence is a symbol of death, a reminder of the bloodline I loathe most—and yet, gods help me, I cannot look away.

It isn't until she speaks that she betrays awareness of me watching. "No use bringing food if you're going to stand in the rain and let it get soggy."

Her tone is maddeningly ordinary, smooth where I expect edges, flowing like her hair in the wind, and all the more unsettling for its calm.

I leave Jorax crouched behind, his eyes still fixed on the dragons who watch the storm with her. My steps are slow, deliberate, as though the ground itself wants to delay me. Each pace draws me nearer, until the droplets glisten on her sharp cheekbones and jaw, a temptation I curse myself for noticing.

I force the sack into my hands to keep them steady. "Bread and soup," I mutter. "The soup's in the flask. Still hot. Did you need anything else?"

She takes the bag but doesn't look at me. Instead, her question cuts sharper than any blade. She takes the bag but doesn't meet my eyes. Instead, she asks, "Do you think Olivia is a madwoman?"

The question jolts through me. I study her, searching for the trap in her words. "Of course not. Why would you ask that?"

She turns her head just enough to watch me from the corner of her eye. "So the woman who can control souls, who can command minds and hearts—and at one point, I believe, commanded your whole army—isn't mad. Then why do you call me mad? Why do you let everyone else call me that?"

The ground feels unsteady beneath me. She is a mirror, holding every word, every judgment, up for me to choke on.

"Is it because of my bloodline? And only now that you've discovered it? Or because I wear sharp words the way you and your men do, to keep myself safe?" Her voice is steady, each syllable a strike. "You never branded Olivia a monster for her powers. No, you revered her. But me? I am just the woman who stroked a dragon like it was a kitten in the street. Forget that I helped save your brothers and sisters, as you call them."

Her pause hangs between us, the storm filling it.

"So you know, Lightmaster—I was *born* with these powers. Born in a prison cell. My mother died giving birth to me. So yes, maybe you're right. Maybe I am the spawn of demons. You try living your whole life in captivity, your veins bled dry by men testing how many powers you carry. I am the product of what was done to me. But I am free now. A madwoman, yes. One you will *need* on your side in this war. You're lucky I hate your enemies more than you do."

"Lia..."

"It's fine, Lightmaster. We don't need to be friends. Only allies. After that, I'll leave. Maybe find somewhere I belong—if such a place exists. Thank your uncle for remembering me kindly."

She lifts the sack, turns, and the dragons shift aside to clear her path, wings folding in solemn deference.

I mount Jorax again, his talons scraping stone, his body coiling to take flight. As he surges upward, I glance back. Her hair gleams like a beacon, her hands resting steady on the two dragons at her side. And in that moment, from the sky above her, I feel the truth sting like salt in a wound—

I am the one who feels small.

Olivia

FAMILY DINNER FIGHTS

The cavern breathes around me, alive in ways I hadn't allowed myself to notice from the confines of my chamber. I step out into its vast heart, and the world unfurls—stone arching overhead like the ribs of some ancient creature, light-orbs drifting in patient constellations. Wyverns cling to ledges like guardians carved from shadow and scale, their low rumbles vibrating through the very walls as their eyes follow me while I move. And woven through it all, the pulse of thousands of Fae. Their hope, their grief, their stubborn will to keep breathing. It rushes at me, a tide of feeling so raw it almost buckles my knees.

And then—her.

Hecate.

She stands at the far end of the cavern, dressed in armor like the other Fae. Gone is the woman who mulls in the kitchen over her spells and an apron covered in the wash of wine and produce; now, she is the woman my mother painted, the empath's protector, the last of her kind—a warrior, and my childhood protector. My heart stutters, tears blur my vision, and for a moment I forget to breathe. *I thought I lost you.*

My steps falter, every ounce of me drinking in the impossible sight of her alive. Her eyes find mine across the space, and the smallest, sweetest smile lifts her lips. A smile that breaks me open.

I run. I don't remember deciding to, my body simply obeys the ache of my soul. When my arms wrap around her, the sob that tears out of me is half joy, half the mourning I've been carrying for too long. She smells like smoke and salt, like travel and survival, but beneath it all she is Hecate—my Hecate—and I cling to her as though touch alone might anchor her here.

"I thought—" my voice cracks against her hair.

Her answering hum vibrates through me, soft and steady. "I know. But I am here." Her hands hold me as if they can restore lost time, and her emotions flood into me—by choice. The woman who guards her feelings so closely now lets me feel her grief, her loss, her relief to be reunited at last.

Behind me, laughter shatters the hush of the cavern. I turn just enough to see Jeyr, his massive frame crumpled into something small and tender as he gathers his sisters against him. His electric blue eyes brim with unshed tears, his smile wide and broken all at once. The bond between them thrums like a song in my chest, their joy radiating until it fills the cavern brighter than any orb of light.

For the first time since the war began, the air doesn't taste of fear. For the first time, I let myself believe in something softer than survival.

Home.

I turn from Hecate to Jeyr and his sisters, my mate looking whole again—radiant even—with all those he loves gathered in one place. Aella's relief drains the instant her eyes find me. Whatever warmth had softened her face vanishes, replaced with a blank mask, though her disdain hums so loudly through me I almost flinch.

"The cavern has been speaking of you," she says, her tone even, eyes moving from Jeyr to me. "Of you both, and what you have done."

I am grateful Jeyr cannot hear thoughts the way I can. Her words alone cut deep enough. Though he doesn't hear them, I know he feels the weight of her disapproval, the judgment she doesn't bother hiding.

"Luminier said once everyone was out of their chambers, we would meet in his dining hall. Now that we're all here—those of us still alive—we need to decide the fates of our people."

Hecate rolls her eyes, as if to say what I cannot, her small act of defense warming me more than I expect.

Jeyr presses a kiss to Althea's forehead before he moves to me, giving me the same tenderness, his hand wrapping around mine. He spares Aella no more than a glance. "Shall we?"

I nod, hoping the press of my hand steadies him, clears the shadows of memory I feel tugging at him—the last time Aella carried the burden of a choice he couldn't make. Despite her bitterness, I am grateful for her. She may hate me, and that I can endure. What matters is whether she can still stand beside me when it counts.

The climb to the Grand Duke of Aotrom's chamber spirals upward, stone steps carved smooth by centuries of feet. The chamber itself is vast, carved open to look out over the wyverns. A stone table dominates the space, its surface engraved with the map of our kingdoms. Kitchens, hearth, and bedchamber flow together into one, every part of it built for gathering, for planning, for war.

Questions stir inside me—what history echoes in these walls, what stories live in the grain of stone, how many lives were decided at this table. But the one I would ask—Jethro—stands beside his uncle, his expression set hard, no trace of the warmth he once carried. The smile, the laughter, the arms that had once felt like safety are nowhere to be found.

Jeyr's hand rests at the small of my back, a silent support.

Aella's eyes fix on me with a steadiness that leaves no room for doubt: if she could strike me from the room, she would. The weight of it presses close, making every breath feel heavy.

Colden steps nearer, his presence sharp at my side. His gaze locks with Aella's, and for the briefest moment, her mask falters. Shock flits across her face, her lips parting in a whisper of his name.

Colden tenses, his distaste radiating through him. I catch his hand, pressing a pulse of reassurance. *We got out,* I tell him silently. *We're okay.*

His reply is bitter, cutting. *No thanks to her.*

Reluctantly, I let go and step toward the table—only to be halted when Lumineer raises his hand to stop me. "Empath, you are at the head of the table."

I hesitate, shaking my head in protest, but the man with azure hair persists, his tone gentle yet firm. "You are the last empath, are you not?"

"Well... yes, but—"

He offers a sweet smile, bowing with reverence. "Daughter of the late Queen Arouz, and rider of the dragon Faldr."

The words settle on me like a crown of iron. I resist, but Jeyr's hand at the small of my back guides me forward. True, I am the last of my kind...but I am tainted, human blood running with the Fae. A hybrid among purity. I don't belong at the head of anything, not a court, not a kingdom. My dreams are of revolution, not thrones, of tearing down walls, not sitting on pedestals. Yet here I am, steered by my mate into a seat that feels too much like a throne and nothing like a place among equals. I hate it.

The head of the table looms empty, a void meant for someone else, and now all eyes are on me. Beside me, Jeyr stands like a pillar, Colden a frostbitten shadow at my other side. Caomh and Lorkan take their seats nearby, while Jet, Aison, Bliant, and Lumineer form a ring that feels less like protection and more like confinement. Hecate and Aella settle opposite.

And then she arrives. Lia sweeps into the chamber with a flare that sets every Fae on edge, her presence unsettling the balance before we've even begun.

"Am I fashionably late to the party?" she drawls, directing the tease toward Jethro as though the rest of us don't exist.

"Lia, your grace," Lumineer says, rising with a bow.

She recoils at the title, eyes flashing red, voices inside her flaring in unison. My empathic instincts move before my reason does—I rise and wrap her in calm, soothing the fray. It isn't my duty to make her likable, yet I want it for her. I want them to see what I see: the survivor, the girl who lived the hell I barely endured, the girl stronger for it. If they hate her, then let them hate me too.

"I propose," she begins, her tone smooth and sharp, "that while we are gathered, we dispense with the formalities. I am no queen, nor do I care to be one. Our aim is clear—stop the king's war, and restore the courts to what they were, where all fae may walk free."

She speaks the words I wish I'd had the courage to voice, the words I swallowed when I chose to bow and comply.

"That is not what we desire," Aella snaps, sharp as broken glass.

Lia's gaze doesn't flinch. She turns to her, unblinking. "And what do you desire, Aella? To wield power? To strip your brother of his throne?"

"No!" Aella's denial falters, her face too rigid to be honest.

Lia tilts her head. "Are you resentful that he carries the crown while you remain in his shadow?"

Aella's mask cracks, rage spilling through. "Who is this woman!?"

The truth has been laid bare. The doubt Aella has carried, the belief she might rule better than Jeyr, is dragged into the light.

Lia presses harder, pushing against the calm I wrapped around her, scratching at its edges with the will of her own mind.

"That's enough," I cut through, my voice steady with authority I don't feel but know I must wield. Silence folds over the chamber. I draw in a breath, weaving my power to soothe the room into stillness.

"For those who haven't met her," I say, voice carrying into the quiet, "this is Lia." I gesture to the empty chair opposite mine.

Her gaze finds mine for the briefest heartbeat, and in that flicker I see it: her hatred for the spotlight mirrors my own. We are two girls who learned to live in shadows, thrust unwilling into light.

And gods, I can't help but empathize.

Settling into my seat, I catch Jeyr's familiar smile, a silent reassurance that steadies the anxiety pressing at the edges of me. His gaze lingers, carrying me the way a harbor carries a ship, reminding me I am not drifting entirely alone.

Lia, clad in new fighting leathers, stands with a poise that shouldn't belong to someone so freshly freed from her prison. Her eyes, sharp as a blade tip, fix on one figure at the table. She doesn't shrink from their scrutiny. "I'm not exactly accustomed to gatherings like this," she begins, her hand sweeping across the stone table, her voice clear but edged with dry humor. "To say I'm unfamiliar with interactions beyond those who wanted something from me would be an understatement. But since we're all gathered here for a common purpose, I suppose it's time you knew me as Ameliana Bane."

The name strikes the table like flint against stone, sparks leaping in every startled inhale. Gasps ripple, though not from Jeyr or Jet—Jet merely raises his brow toward me, his thought spilling sharp as smoke: *And I didn't kill her. Aren't you proud?*

Lia doesn't falter. "I know what you're all thinking—literally," she adds with a pointed smirk. "Except for Olivia and Colden, those two are blessedly impenetrable. But I'll be plain. I'm not here to infiltrate your army. I'm here to kill my father, his army, and then the King. Because the moment he knows I live, he'll want me dead too."

Caomh's hand clenches tighter on Lorkan's arm, his voice cutting in, thorned and bristling like a Manticore. "Why would the King want you dead?"

Lia shrugs, the movement too casual for the weight of her words. "Because I'm like him. I carry every power from this kingdom in my blood."

My throat goes dry. I close my eyes, pinching at my thigh under the table, fighting the urge to pinch the bridge of my nose. We hadn't spoken of strategy, hadn't set what truths could be revealed. And now here she is, laying it all bare. If it were up to me, her identity would have remained locked away—safeguarded until trust was earned.

Her gaze slides to me, softening just for a breath, and I hear her thought hum into me like a low chord. *They had to know, Liv. If we hid it and they found out later, they'd never trust me at all.*

The weight of eyes turns to me. Caomh, Lorkan, Jethro—their stares hot and hard as coals. Aella's distaste curdling in the background. Even Hecate's steady gaze, probing. Their questions aren't about her—they're about me. About whether I'm someone worth following if I would've held such a secret.

My fingers twitch against the stone table, resisting the urge to curl into fists. I want to scream that I am not the monster she is accused of being—that we are both, in different ways, stitched together from pain. That if they damn her, they damn me. But I sit, and I swallow it, because war doesn't afford the luxury of purity.

Bliant saves me. His voice cuts through the silence, a whisper shaped like a lifeline: "How is that possible?" His eyes rest on Lia, pulling the focus from me.

Hecate, though, isn't distracted. Her gaze flicks between the two of us, something ancient and knowing flaring in her stare. She exhales, barely a murmur. "Blood and magic."

An expectant hush settles over the room, every gaze fixed on Hecate, awaiting an explanation. "Strong magic," she continues, her voice gaining strength, "stronger than mine. No single witch could accomplish it. But perhaps... an entire army, stolen from a kingdom. Maybe."

Understanding dawns in the eyes of those present, though many questions remain unanswered. There is a collective realization that Hecate's people, along with the Empaths, have suffered a fate long believed to be death.

Hecate continues, "Much like how I got you past the walls of Puinnsean, Caomh, and Jet, was only a small essence of what has been done to—" Hecate gestures to Lia, who is watching her intently.

"I made you appear to have the power of poison in your blood to seep past the walls. When you drank the vial, its contents entered your blood, and your composition resembled that of someone from Puinnsean. It was temporary, and because you did not have the combination of blood, soul, and magic, you could not possess the power, but appear of the bloodline." She pauses, gauging if people are following. The furrowed brows indicate she needs to continue.

"In order to possess multiple powers, there are several avenues," she explains, her voice steady. "Biologically, when the fates align and the souls of two parents harmonize, their offspring may inherit an equal share of their powers and genetics. Then there is godly magic, where souls bound within instruments in purgatory can be released and combined with another soul, subject to the whims of divine intervention. Finally, there is the method employed by the witches of Anam—an intricate fusion of blood, souls, and copious amounts of magic." Hecate's gaze lingers on Lia, who meets her stare with unwavering intensity.

"Cut to the chase, Hecate," Caomh interjects, his voice rough, catching like stone. Lorkan's hand rests gently on his knee, a silent attempt to pacify him.

"Very well," Hecate acquiesces, her tone clipped. "In simpler terms, all the missing witches and mixed-race fae were imprisoned, their souls extracted from their bodies. Through a complex manipulation of magic, these souls were then amalgamated into a single being." She turns to Lia, her expression somber. "You claim to have been born this way, suggesting they attempted to combine the thousands of souls into your mother's womb, infusing you with their collective essence while your own soul was still forming."

A heavy silence falls over the room as Lia and Hecate exchange a meaningful look. "Did your mother survive?" Hecate asks softly.

Lia shakes her head. "I arrived prematurely, as far as I know."

Hecate nods solemnly. "And you would have healed yourself, harnessing the power of them all."

"So what you are saying is—" Lia begins, but stops short.

"That she is the Queen of lost souls." Hecate turns to me. "And she is the Queen of mind and souls."

All eyes swing to me, and I feel like I am in a pressure cooker, Caomh's stare the most intense. "You," he whispers, realization flickering across his face of what I had done to him after his rescue. His expression curls with disgust that feels like the searing burn of lily-infused water on raw scars.

"I was going to tell you, Caomh, but you have connections to so many Fae. I didn't want anyone finding our location."

"You used your powers against me. We don't do that, Olivia." Caomh's voice slices through the tense silence, his use of my name sending shivers down my spine. Lia reacts instantly—she rises from her seat, fists clenched in a silent show of support.

My heart wrenches as his words cut deeper than any blade. Memories of our earliest days flare—of Caomh insisting that within our circle, family and friends alike, there must be a sacred law: never wield our powers against one another without consent. That vow had once bound us closer than blood. And here I am, the one to shatter it.

The realization presses down like stone, threatening to smother me. How could I betray something so fundamental? The trust I built with him teeters on the edge of collapse, and gods help me—it isn't the first time. Since our reunion, I've done it more than once. Duty, cause, survival... each time I convinced myself it was necessary. But the truth still burns: I've used my gift against those I love.

I raise my hand in surrender. "I had to protect you, me, everyone. I promise not to do it again." My voice shakes with desperation.

Lie, lie, lie, Lia's mocking tone twists in my mind. And Caomh's stare tells me he knows it too. That look—sharp, unyielding—splits my chest open with grief.

"I could not communicate with Lorkan, Olivia. More than once. That is not acceptable. I never blocked you from Jeyr. Never."

His voice is thorned, his truth undeniable. Guilt crashes over me like a relentless tide. I can't hold his gaze. His walls slam up, barring me from the mind I once walked freely. The silence that follows is suffocating, the entire chamber waiting on the edge of breath.

Finally, I let the weight of truth fall. "I gained extra powers the moment I killed Tierney," I confess. "His banded wrist contained the souls of my mother and her mate." The words taste of ash, dragging tears I choke back. I remember the letters, ink smeared with grief, words drowned in tears that never lessened the pain of two loves torn apart. And now those souls are no longer trapped, no longer bound to Tierney's cruelty—they are inside me. A weapon forged of their love and their torment. Me.

Caomh's voice dips to a whisper. "Who was the mate, Olivia?" His stare bores into me though I can't lift my head.

"It was your mother."

The words leave me steady, though my insides quake. When I finally look up, I see shock first, then disbelief, then a sorrow so deep it steals the air from the room. His small nod says everything: he understands, but our bond is fractured, and the trust we once had may never be the same.

"I understand there's a wealth of information that needs to be shared," I press on, ignoring the wetness that rolls down my cheek. Because I hold his mother's soul, and in some twisted way, in another universe... we would have been raised as siblings—if I were born at all in that dimension. The thought burns, but I force myself forward, determined to break the silence that threatens to suffocate us all. "But before we delve into that, we need to formulate a plan for how we're going to approach this impending war."

Caomh's reception of me is a force I can almost touch, his animosity clinging to the air like thick smoke. It isn't going to change today. Not without me forcing my powers into him, and gods, I will not do that—not to him, not again. The taste of his hatred sits heavy on my tongue, bitter, choking, reminding me that no matter what truths I want to bare—about our mothers, about the love that once tethered them together—I can't. I want to plead, I want to crack open the weight between us, but I won't. Not now.

Instead, I anchor myself to the one thing we all share: the necessity of ending this war. Of bringing justice to the women who bore us, who lost everything to the men who wielded blades and called it fate. My resolve sharpens, even as my heart frays. "Here is the plan I have in mind..."

The words spill from my lips, but soon my ears ring, my own voice muffled, as if the stone walls themselves refuse to carry it. I am here at this table speaking of strategies, but my heart is not here. My mind drifts back to that cursed manor, to the silken bed of Lord Tierney where I lay in tears, soul-heavy and broken, reading of the fate of soulmates. Each story more tragic than the last, each tale another blade in the ribs of hope. No matter the plans I forge, no matter how I try to claw at the seams of destiny, some truths linger like rot: that the fates do not break the bonds—they simply hand us over to the cruelty of men who do.

At some point, my voice falters, Lia's sharper tones filling the silence with her own thoughts. At some point, while I drown in the weight of choices past and choices yet to come, we agree to something—an outline, a strategy. I will try to recall the details later, when I am not compressed by the ache of my own existence.

The meeting ends with the scrape of chairs against stone. Caomh is the first to rise, Lorkan shadowing him like a loyal echo. As Lorkan passes me, he leans in, his breath a soft brush against my skin, his words firmer than air should allow. "I will talk to him, my Queen. But only to give you a chance to make amends."

I nod, swallowing the lump in my throat, my gratitude unspoken. Lia strolls off alone, pausing only to murmur that I should come see her and the dragons soon. I haven't since our arrival, though Faldr's voice still hums in the back of my mind, a living ember of knowledge I am not yet ready to touch.

Caomh

"Cay, you would have done the same... When did she have time to divulge all that?" Lorkan's voice breaks through the thick air between us.I stare at him, disbelief rising sharp and hot. That's what he chooses to say? Where are his soothing words, the ones that usually ground me? Gods above—I can't even think the words, let alone say them aloud—Olivia harbors my mother's soul.

"So, you're on her side?" I snap, whirling in the cramped confines of our sleeping quarters. Just this morning, I had woken to something close to happiness, his arms curved around me, his warmth against my back. And now? Now family feels like betrayal. Olivia crossed a line—my line—and she knew it.

"No, Mo ghràdh," Lorkan says gently, his voice finally carrying that familiar balm. "You know if there's a side to choose, it's yours I'll take every time. But Olivia is family. She saved you. And I find it very hard to hate the one who saved the person I cannot live without."

The bite in my anger softens, though it doesn't vanish. His arms slip around me from behind, his chin resting on my shoulder. The simple weight of him, steady and sure, leeches some of the fury from me, like it always does.

"I don't condone her separating us—not ever—but she's right. If she'd left those connections open, the King would've found us. And she hasn't had a chance to explain about your mom's..." He hesitates. "Just... give her the chance."

I grit my teeth, resentment flaring again. "I couldn't contact you, Lor," I hiss, turning my head but not moving from his arms. "I tried. Over and over. To make sure you hadn't been taken from me. Don't you understand?"

A heavy sigh rumbles through his chest, his lips brushing the side of my neck. "I understand," he murmurs. "I have nearly lost you more times than I can count, Caomh. You were locked in that prison and you cut me off, Mo ghràdh. I know what it's like to lose your voice in my head. I know how it hurts. But she never severed me from you. When I was falling—when I tried to shift down that mountain—it was Olivia who made sure I still had you. She gave me you."

I close my eyes, letting his words settle, though the ache still burns in my chest.

"There are no easy choices in love and war, Mo ghràdh," Lorkan whispers against my skin, his breath a vow and a plea all at once.

I grumble in agreement, the weight of my own choices pressing down on me like a leaden cloak. I have made decisions that led to entire armies vanishing, and now their souls are twisted into the making of a deranged princess. Lorkan turns me to face him, his hands cupping my cheeks, lifting my gaze to his violet eyes. The intensity there makes it difficult to hold onto my anger. I know fury well—it has fueled me for years, through the loss of my mother, friends, through surviving a world that never felt safe for the one person I cherished above all else.

He brushes a strand of hair from my face, thumbs tracing my cheekbones, sparking a different fire beneath my skin. My heart races as he leans in, lips hovering just short of mine.

"We have now, and I know our Queen will do everything so we have a future," Lorkan murmurs, his voice wrapping around me like warmth. "She wants to destroy the world that kept us apart, Mo ghràdh. She has the spirit of your mother in her and will make sure we have what your mother always wanted. Freedom to love."

I close my eyes, letting the words sink deep. And then his lips touch mine—soft, tentative—and I am gone, lost in him.

...I remember the night before. After our bath, after the slow kisses, after we mapped and relearned each other's bodies like sacred ground, exhaustion claimed me. I slept in his arms, and for the first time, I was warm enough, safe enough, to let sleep take me without fight. No restless nights wondering what it would be like to be held by him, no hunger left unanswered. Just the truth of it—real, mine. And even in sleep, I wanted more.

When I stir, he is pulling back, that sad smile shadowing his mouth, leaving me to wonder what weight he still carries. I don't pry, though every instinct begs me to reach into his thoughts.

"Let's go build our army," he says instead, practical as ever, breaking the quiet.

I groan. "Can't we build our army after I finally get to ravage you? Surely they can wait an hour or two."

His laugh—Gods, his laugh—is music. "It will be me who does the ravaging, Mo ghràdh. But not rushed, not with war waiting outside the door. I've waited a century, I can wait a few more hours. Come on."

I groan again, but a smile tugs at my lips. The word *our* sounds different in his mouth, and so does the word *bed*. I let the sound of our laughter fill the chamber, shaking loose the last of my chains, leaving only the promise of freedom—and of us.

Perched on an elevated platform, I watch the intricate dance unfolding below in the caverns. Fae of every kind, each bearing their own distinct gifts, shift and settle into factions, shaping themselves into a collective front. It feels different from the preparations for war years ago—back then I was not the man I am now. I was a boy barely half a century old, before that only a quarter, still hiding the one I wanted safe. I still think of it, even as my hand tightens around his. Down below, most Fae eagerly pledge themselves to stand united, their anger and need for justice burning bright, and I hope—gods, I hope—that intention will be stronger than the grief of those we have already lost.

The vulnerable, the young, the pregnant, the injured—remain deeper in the cavern's belly, where stone walls promise safety. Healers huddle together in their corner, pooling herbs, spellwork, and hard-earned wisdom. Jeyr, Blaint, and Aioson stand among them, shaping an impromptu infirmary. Urgent wounds are tended first, and the quiet sharing of healing techniques becomes its own kind of alliance.

Above, Jethro has resumed his post in the skies, commander of the Wyvern army. His shadow cuts across the cavern mouth as his voice bellows guidance, helping each fae find their destined companion. For many, the very idea is bewildering—terrifying and glorious in equal measure. The screams of failed matches echo through the stone, sharp reminders that bonds cannot be forced. Healers rush to soothe torn wings and bleeding hands, tending to wyverns as much as warriors.

It is treacherous, this ritual of choosing, much like love itself. Wandering the endless chambers of wyverns, reaching for one that feels right, only to learn too late that its red flags come with teeth. But the triumphs ring louder than the failures. Cries of joy echo against the cavern walls as new bonds are forged, pairs taking to the air in exultant flight. Their shadows sweep the rock as they soar toward the mountain peak, ready to learn what it means to be part of a wyvern army.

As we walk hand in hand to the training grounds, eyes follow us—but mostly, they follow Lorkan. He towers over even the tallest of Fae, and even without knowing his lineage, his presence demands recognition. His violet eyes sweep the crowd, cataloging every face, every flicker of power. I can feel the familiar zap humming through him, a secret code etched beneath his skin, always ready to shift, to adapt, to blend into any battlefield.

In the center of the grounds, where some fae grapple and others stare in open shock at the man beside me, Lorkan clears his throat. The low, rough grumble cuts through the air, and my body betrays me, standing taller, reacting to him in ways I try to hide.

Later, Mo ghràdh.

"You." His finger points to a man from Nadur—buzz-cut hair, jawline sharp enough to make painters put brush to canvas, sea-foam eyes sparking with pride at being chosen. He steps forward just as Lorkan turns and points again, this time to a small woman with rose-gold hair cropped in a pixie cut. Her bright blue eyes flash with the kind of confidence that warns the world not to underestimate her.

"I know your powers," Lorkan says, voice steady as stone. "But you don't know each other's. Fight. Learn their style. Learn how they move. When you are too tired to lift your fists, *then* you'll work together. Find out how your powers combine."

My gaze lingers on him—hair tied back, jaw firm, every line of him speaking command. He holds no title here, yet his presence is that of a general, a captain carved from battles.

"Sir..." the Nadur male scoffs, crossing his massive arms over his bare chest.

"*what?*" the rose-haired woman spits, stepping forward, chin high, daring him to finish the thought.

"Fight," Lorkan commands, no mind-powers, no tricks—just his voice, deep enough to rattle the training grounds.

The man shrugs, lifting his sword, casual arrogance dripping from every motion.

"*No weapons,*" Lorkan calls.

The woman's smile curls, sharp and sinister, her eyes gleaming as if she's been waiting for this very moment.

The rose-haired woman doesn't hesitate. Her fists clench, a sheen of frost crawling down her arms, glimmering pale-blue against her skin. The ground hisses where her feet strike, every step cracking with ice.

Her opponent answers with a whip of green—vines erupt from the dirt, writhing toward her ankles, leaves sharp as blades. He grins, smug, as the first tendrils lash at her legs.

She tears them apart with brute force, the frost along her skin hardening like armor. Her strength is not just muscle; it radiates, bone-deep, every strike of her fists cracking vines in two. She lunges, quick despite her size, landing a blow against his shoulder that makes him stumble.

"Good," Lorkan growls from where he stands, arms folded, eyes sharp. "Strength against poison. Cold against life."

The Nadur male snarls, throwing his hand out again. More vines shoot upward, thick and thorned. He exhales, the scent of something bitter and metallic hitting the air—an irritant, a weaker poison carried in the sap. The girl's smile only sharpens.

"Poison won't work on me," she hisses, her voice like cracking ice. Frost spreads across the vines as her hand closes, freezing sap mid-flow until it shatters in a spray of green shards.

The man curses, sweat running down his jaw as his plants wither under her chill. He stumbles back, caught off guard, but his roots dive deeper, pulling from the earth itself. Thorns erupt around her feet, barbed and grasping. One snags her leg, tearing skin.

Her response is a roar, raw power shuddering through her frame. Ice cascades outward, freezing the entire patch of vines in a heartbeat. She kicks, and the frozen thorns shatter like glass.

The crowd watching leans in, a ripple of excitement running through them.

"Enough!" Lorkan's command silences the cavern, the sheer authority in his tone dragging both fae to stillness. He steps forward, violet eyes alight, every inch the commander he denies himself to be.

He gestures between them. "You see it now. Alone, your powers clash until neither of you win. Together..." His hand slices through the air. "Plant and frost, poison and ice. Vines ensnare, ice freezes. Roots spread, frost strengthens. One slows the enemy, the other breaks them."

The two fae glance at each other, panting, reluctant respect flickering in their eyes.

Lorkan's jaw tightens, his voice low, meant for all gathered. "Learn each other, or die alone. That's the truth of war."

Silence hangs heavy. Then the rose-haired woman smirks, offering her hand to the Nadur male. He hesitates, then takes it.

I look once more at the man who is now mine. After knowing him for so long, I never thought there would come a point where he could still surprise me—but the years apart had carved him sharper, deeper, with knowledge I had never accounted for.

His eyes catch mine, steady, violet and unflinching. I almost scoff at the cockiness flickering there.

"Don't underestimate those who sit back and watch," he rumbles, the faintest tease threading through the gravity of his tone.

"I suppose I'm learning not to underestimate anyone," I answer, a reluctant smile tugging at me.

His lip quirks, just a sliver of amusement, and my gaze betrays me, tracking its movement. The urge to be brash and kiss him here—in front of everyone, in front of the whole damned army—is overwhelming. Instead, his arm slips to my shoulder, a brief squeeze, before he lets go.

"See everyone?" His voice carries, rough and commanding. "Never, ever underestimate someone. We don't always know who we are going up against, so we cannot walk into this war with cockiness or sureness. Just because you wield more than one power doesn't mean you're strong enough to win. There will always be someone sharper, someone who adapts faster. Remember that."

He pauses, letting the weight of his words settle over the training grounds.

"Each day," he continues, "you'll be assigned a new partner. Learn their battle. Let them learn yours. Know their weaknesses, and your own. That is how we survive—together." After some time watching, I glance to Lorkan. He meets my eyes, reading the thought I don't bother to speak, and gives me a nod.

"Alright, known Companachs," I call out, voice carrying across the training ground, "I want to see you working as pairs against other Companachs."

We had already agreed to keep them together—the distraction of splitting them across ranks wouldn't do us any favors. Before, when one felt their partner's pain lashing through the bond, it had weakened both. But now, working side by side, the difference is undeniable. Their strength builds in tandem, their rhythm almost impossible to break.

"Until the other army comes in and separates them. Like they have for centuries."

Olivia's voice cuts through, calm but sharp, arms crossed as she surveys the field.

I turn to her, holding her gaze. "Strength together is going to overcome the opponent."

She *tsks* softly, shaking her head. "I may be younger than you by... what is it, ninety years? But trust me, Caomh—the first thing Bane and the King will do is assess the Companachs and tear them apart. You need to train them for it. Let them be distracted, let them struggle, let them learn how to harness that bond even when they're forced apart."

Before I can form a reply, she turns, vanishing back the way she came, leaving the echo of her words heavy on the air. I shift my gaze to Lorkan, catching the sudden tightness in his face.

"She isn't wrong," he says quietly.

I hold two fingers up, my jaw tightening. "That's twice you've taken her side. Don't make a habit of it, Lorkan—or we're going to have problems."

Olivia

DROWNING IN SELF PITY

Y ou're weak queen, *shut them out!* Faldr roars in my mind as I perch on him, over-looking the Fae engaged in wyvern training. The incessant buzz of their thoughts remains unabated.

You're mixing your empath powers with your telepathy, a voice echoes in my mind. *When you're reading their emotions, you're inherently listening to their thoughts.*

I grumble audibly, struggling to sense the delicate balance between both powers. Since Caomh isn't exactly part of the Olivia fan club, I decide to seek guidance from the old creature who decidedly knows everything—the one who often enjoys labeling me an idiot. Right now, I feel like a bit of one, so I welcome his candid perspective.

I only call you an idiot, my queen, because you don't listen to what's inside. You fight your instincts, and all it does is make it harder for you. You need to be at one with your powers, stop fighting them.

"But you just told me to shut them out!" I retort, a note of frustration in my voice.

The people, my Queen, not your powers! Faldr clarifies, his immense wings slicing through the mountain air. He banks suddenly, causing me to startle and cling tightly. In the distance, I hear Jeyr's distant worry, asking if I am okay. Fudging the truth, I assure him I am fine, even as Faldr carries me farther away from the Fae engaged in training.

"Where are we going?" I yell over the mountain wind's howl, my nose tingling with cold and my ears popping from the change in altitude. *Find you some inner peace,* Faldr remarks, and I feel the urge to roll my eyes. "I will have peace when I figure out how to control my powers and bring down the injustice that is in this kingdom. Until then, I am putting one foot in front of the other and getting through."

A puff of smoke leaves Faldr, and I sense his frustration. *You would not expect anyone else to work in the conditions you have made for yourself. Surviving is not thriving.*

I gaze into the distance, gritting my teeth against a retort. All I know is surviving. Faldr is quiet as he glides around the cloud tops of the mountain ranges. The snow peaks are almost deserted of any life. I feel my body shift with him as he glides down to the mountain's edge, and I gasp as he ducks, seemingly about to hit the mountainous wall. Instead, we dive into darkness. I look around, catching the slight glimmer of fire bugs, signaling that we have entered another cavern large enough for Faldr to fit through. I squeal as we descend, my heart racing as we change altitude. Then, I feel the air catch in my throat at the sight.

A small glen on the inside of the mountain reveals itself, a waterfall cascading to the stony ground, steam billowing from the tops. Despite the cold conditions, small shrubs grow in the cracks of the rocks, flourishing with the spray of water.

"This is..."

My home.

Faldr lands softly, his size making no sound as his body lowers to the ground. I take it as an invitation and climb off his scaled back.

Get into the spring, he commands.

I blink at his demand, rough and showing no sign of backing down. I look down at my fighting leathers.

Get in the water. If you think I haven't seen a naked body before, you've been mistaken. It's a body, get in.

I huff, not really wanting to find out what it would be like to defy a dragon. I take off my clothes and walk to the water, my body covered in goosebumps from the frigid air. I feel the heat coming off the spring in an instant. I haven't soaked properly in days. How Jeyr is around me is a question I will ask later. Maybe... not really.

Bathing is a privilege in war. Get in.

I dip my toe in and feel the fizzle of heat zip through my body, my breath visible as I let it out. I can feel the hot gaze on my back, making my scars and the tattoo that covers them feel all the more visible under his gaze even with the dragon that claims them. I slowly wade into the water but feel my body stiffen as it covers my breasts.

I see the hand come to my face and stroke away the hair that blows in the wind. "Clarity," her whisper of my mother's name, said with such deep affection. Somehow, I know my mother is smiling even though I am seeing through her eyes. I feel the love blooming through her bloodstream as if it were my own.

"Amery."

My mother's hand comes to curl at the back of her neck. I watch Amery's head get closer, the moment it touches my mother's, I wish I am not seeing through her eyes. I want to see her; instead, all I can do is feel. I feel the swell of power, the amber hues tangling between the points at which they touch. My mother leans in, and I feel the power of their kiss, how they both feel what it does to one another.

"I love you," my mother whispers against her lips.

"And I love you," Amery whispers back, and just like that, they hug each other tighter and disappear with a power surge that leaves me breathless.

I feel my eyes open, realizing that immersion is all in my mind.

I turn in the water, the sparks of light of red and gold bouncing around me, their pattern much like little fireflies dancing around one another. Trying to catch my breath, I look to Faldr, who remains expressionless, looking at me.

"What was that?"

They wanted to show you their love. Part of it was the love of their power, which together was stronger. You need to be able to love and control the power like they did. You have to do that before you can have that feeling with Jeyr.

I blink, looking away. I feel that love with Jeyr before; I still feel that love for him, but there is a small, very small disconnect, especially since the power draw and the number of things that have happened between then and now.

I blink, looking away. I feel that love with Jeyr before; I still feel that love for him, but there is a small, very small disconnect, especially since the power draw and the number of things that have happened between then and now.

You both once had a power each, Faldr rumbles in my mind. *You had learned to love your empathic powers; you made those around you feel good. You worshiped and nurtured your powers instead of hating them. Jeyr loved his powers because they kept you alive. You were once, body and soul; he healed the physical hurts, you healed the emotional. Now, you are soul and mind; you can heal or break them. Jeyr, much like you, has his journey of self-discovery and learning to love that he can do both—physically harm someone with his new powers of the weather elements or heal them. But I cannot train you both to draw on powers until you learn to love those you have. I made a mistake before, and I will not do it again.*

The fireflies of power bounce around me, much like the bouncing of my thoughts? How do I love what I hate? I hate that I have the power to hurt. That monstrous, weak part of me that can so easily manipulate.

Faldr has the audacity to chuckle. *Head under the water, my queen.*

My face twists in shock, and I should be surprised to see a dragon roll his eyes—but I'm not.

I obey, submerging my head beneath the surface. The darkness slithers over me like a snake. It grabs hold of me and drags me into the nightmares of the past.

I witness my father clutching his chest. I see men crumple under the weight of my power. Then, I watch Cooper die because I did not wield my power. I feel every lash on my back as I suppress my abilities. I drown in the misery of hating what I am. The anguish of how I distanced Caomh from those who loved him—even if it was to keep him safe—consumes me. My body thrashes, and I choke on the water as the memories take an unrelenting hold.

Jeyr

DRAGONS BE DAMNED

I plunge into the water of the hot spring without hesitation. I don't know if I should be grateful or furious that Olivia's new power opens a path into her mind, but it leads me straight to her. I feel her distress like it is my own, tugging me from miles away. I hear the dragon inside her, feel its presence as clear as thunder, aware of their conversation whether Olivia knows it or not. He tells her to submerge her head. I wait, teeth grinding, trusting the ancient beast against every instinct screaming at me.

Then her body thrashes. Bubbles break the surface. She is drowning.

Faldr bellows in my mind, *Let her fight! Let her confront what haunts her.*

"Fuck you!" I roar back, every muscle taut. "She's fought her demons alone for too long!"

This is the truth spring, the dragon snarls. *Those with troubled souls face their nightmares until they relinquish self-hatred. If you take her struggle from her, she will never learn.*

But the tug on my heart is relentless. Tug. Tug. Tug. My throat burns with her struggle, my lungs ache like hers are filling with water.

"Fuck you, Faldr," I growl, fury laced with terror. "That's my mate. Find a new way to help her find peace."

I dive.

The water swallows me whole, ink-black and boiling against my skin chilled by mountain air. My demons come, swift and merciless—the screams of my father, my brother's lifeless eyes, the weight of every moment I failed her. Every single day I played it safe while she suffered. The memory claws at me, tries to drag me down. But the only thing I want—the only thing I have ever wanted—is her.

My hand finds her at last, slick skin beneath my grasp. Her panic flares as my touch becomes another obstacle, her body fighting even me. I ignore it, tightening my hold, wrapping my arms around her waist. The shadows try to anchor us in the depths, but I kick, forcing every ounce of power through my body. Air whirls, wind gathers, and together it propels us upward.

We break the surface. The cold slap of mountain air steals my breath as Olivia gasps, choked by water.

I haul her onto the stone ledge, lowering her gently. Her body convulses as she coughs, the water spilling from her lungs. I channel my power, warming her trembling frame, coaxing her breath steady. Slowly, painfully, she relaxes, her chest rising and falling again.

I brush aside the wet strands of her golden-red hair, revealing the unruly trellis of true red curls beneath. In her mind, her past flickers like a cruel picture book—image after image of her hell loop. Choices that broke her. Choices she never wanted to make. I wish I could shoulder them all, take every wound into myself, carry the weight so she doesn't have to.

I cradle her cheeks in my hands. "My love," I whisper.

At the sound of my voice, her body softens, though her eyes remain shut. I feel the fear trembling through her—the terror that I will not love her for who she has become.

I lower my forehead to hers, my words a vow against the silence. "I will always love you, Hummingbird. No matter who you become, I will always love you."

Her body relaxes further, and she whispers, "He said I can't control it because I hate who I am."

The croak in her voice slices through me, sharp as any blade, and when a tear slips past her lashes, it burns my chest as if it were my own. I don't move away. I stay exactly where I am, anchored, until her hands slide to my sides, holding me in place.

"Why do you hate yourself, Hummingbird?"

She inhales too quickly, the breath short, stabbing at her own chest. I feel every inch of it, though I keep that knowledge to myself. "Too many reasons," she sobs.

"Start with one. If there are more, let them come."

I resist the urge to pull her so tightly she can't breathe, forcing myself to stay steady, to give her the space to spill what she carries.

"I am both weak... and a monster."

"How are you weak, my love?"

Another sob breaks from her, raw and jagged, her grip on my leathers tightening. Her gaze avoids mine, like she can't bear for me to see her face.

"I am weak because I let him take me. I could have done more—I should have done more—but all I could think was not to risk any of you. Then... then—"

The word splinters into sobs. I see the images flooding her, the memory of what "then" means. Faldr is right—we can't put this off any longer.

"Then I let him touch me. I didn't fight, not really. I didn't want him to feel my powers let go, that's what he wanted. But I should have. I should have shattered his heart with the pain he gave me."

My fist slams the stone beside us. "I felt your pain, my love, kingdoms apart. If that man didn't crumble from it, it only proves how sick he was."

"I could have done more. I could have. I was... weak. So weak." Her body trembles with the weight of it. I wipe her tears, my thumb gentle against her skin.

"What you are," I murmur, "is the strongest woman I know. No one killed that monster. He only grew stronger with every soul bound to his wrist. You played the only game you could to survive. And you won, Hummingbird. I know it doesn't erase the hurt, or the fear, or the pieces of yourself you wish you hadn't given—but it means you are still here. That makes you a warrior, not a monster. You adapt. You change to survive. Now you have to love that part of you too. Love it enough to thrive in it. We'll find shore, my love. But you are not alone anymore."

Her eyes open, evergreen glow piercing through the blur of tears. I pray she can see the love in mine, feel it enough to loosen even a fraction of the hate she clings to.

"I hate that I also loved the power," she whispers, her voice shaking. "The power to overrule him. To manipulate him. I loved stabbing that knife into him, even though he did love me. I liked it, Jeyr..."

I smile, slow and sure. "Good."

Her brows crease. "What does that make me?"

"A warrior, my love. Your compass led you to do what you had to do. We'll both face choices that wound us, but hear me—I love you. All your sides. It's kind of hot, really. You're not a monster; you're my revengeful mate, the one who will do whatever it takes to keep me, and everyone we love, safe. These powers are what will win us this war. And I want you to love them too."

I lean down, my lips brushing hers, letting sparks of electricity roll from me into her skin. I kiss her cheek, her neck, the hollow of her collarbone.

"I love every inch of you, Hummingbird. The hollow here—" I press a kiss against her bone, smiling when she shivers. "The freckles scattered like constellations across your skin." Another kiss. "The way you think, always of others first. The way you care, even when you shouldn't."

She huffs a laugh, her breath tickling my jaw as my mouth traces her skin.

"I love the way you attract every mythical creature in existence—though, I'll admit, the dragon has some serious work to do in the charm department."

Another laugh breaks through her tears. I kiss lower, to the scar between her breasts, laying my mouth gently there.

"And I love this. Because it reminds me you survived. That you still choose to be here, with me, even when the world isn't what it should be."

Her hands thread into my hair, keeping me pressed against her heart.

"Most of all, I love this," I whisper, lips grazing her skin. "The way it beats for me. The way it races every time I'm near, like it's dancing its own rhythm just for me. My Hummingbird. My mate."

She tugs me down until my chest is flush against hers. Her lips crash to mine, urgent, demanding, and a growl breaks loose from my throat. Her intent sears through me.

"Got room for two on the wyvern?" she murmurs against my mouth. "We should go to our room. Bathe. Preferably not in a magical spring."

I smile against her lips, electricity humming in the space between us. "Always full of good ideas."

Jethro

I Spy, Endless Power

I watch Lia attempt to weave herself into the ranks of the Fae training, but the effort is pointless. Every warrior turns their back on her, whispers slithering through the air—*Bane's child, queen of stolen souls.* She doesn't lash out, doesn't argue. She just nods once at each rejection, shoulders tightening though her face remains unreadable. For a woman branded mad, she wears composure like armor. But I notice it—the way her muscles lock every time another Fae refuses to spar with her.

I keep to the shadows, light bending around me, my power cloaking me from sight. She leaves the training grounds and winnows to the mountain's summit. I expect to find her hunched, broken by the cold bite of rejection. Instead, she stands tall, arms spread wide as if the mountain itself belongs to her. Her dragon crouches behind her, silent and watchful.

The wind stirs at her call, strands of her pale hair whipping free as she closes her eyes and listens. Then she moves, fire in her palm, water coiling like a serpent, earth grinding up from the stone, air spiraling at her fingertips. Ether hums in the spaces between, threads of it weaving through her like she was born to command it. While Fae below sweat and stumble with their singular gifts, she barely breaks a breath.

And I hate that I can't look away. Resentment burns through me, yet fascination coils tighter. Every time I meet her eyes, memory betrays me—my wife among the lilies, gone and buried, and somehow the echo of her beauty rises in Lia's face.

Stones lift, vines snake across the mountain peak, weaving into walls that bloom with flowers both healing and deadly. Nadur, in all its breadth. Most believe it's nothing but a gardener's trick—speaking to plants. But I know better now. Nadur controls monsters if it wants.

Snakes slip across the stone, answering her like hounds to a master's call. And then the sky breaks with a cry. A giant eagle descends, white-capped head proud, talons digging into her wrist until blood flows. She doesn't flinch. The snakes vanish, the eagle stays, bound by her command.

She speaks without words, and the beast obeys, lifting into the air. When it returns, a fish dangles from its claws, dropped neatly at her feet.

Lia sits. A tree unfurls at her back, leaves broad and shifting in the mountain wind. She cooks the fish in its own wrapping, scent curling upward until it reaches me, and for a moment, I almost step forward. The eagle waits patiently as she shares its portion before turning her gaze over her shoulder.

"You must have quite an appetite with all that watching. Tiresome work being a spy. Want to try?"

Her voice should not command me. And yet my body twitches forward before I catch myself. I step from the shadows, jaw set.

"Or worried I might have poisoned it?" she adds, venom sharp in her tone.

"I suppose I don't need to bring you provisions then." My words are clipped, cold. I fade back into the shadows, ignoring the look she pins me with as I vanish.

And still, even unseen, I feel her eyes follow.

Jeyr

Seeing Ghosts

Excitement hums through my veins, alive in every beat of my heart as Olivia's grip holds me tight and Thanos cuts through the clouds. Her lips graze the bare line of my neck, and shivers spark across my skin, pulling from me a hunger that belongs only to her. All I can think about is our bed, the press of her body against mine, the things I've waited too long to do. The urgency thrums through me, fierce and unrelenting.

For a breath, I let myself imagine it—her laughter against my lips, the warmth of her hands running over me, the quiet nights where nothing exists but us. That picture is what I want more than any victory in this war.

Thanos huffs his irritation, his wings flaring wide as if Olivia's affection is beneath his notice. I can't help the low laugh that escapes me, smug at having unsettled him. "Is it wise that we pissed him off?" I ask, knowing full well I'd do it again.

"He's fine... mostly." Olivia waves her hand, dismissive as ever, and I watch the dragon tilt his massive head like he's tallying every fault she's ever made. She doesn't see it, but I do—the way she refuses to bend to anyone, even when the oldest of creatures rumbles their displeasure. Gods, she's young, younger than all of us, but she carries a kind of knowing that no number of years can teach.

I glance at her, this woman who survived when she should have broken, who still dares to love when she should have turned to stone, and I know—wisdom isn't measured in centuries. It's in her.

The mountain ridge rises to meet us, and ahead, Lumirwen and Elduin lie sprawled beside Lia. The girl looks like she's been carved from the mountain itself—skin pale, hair white, leathers black as the cliffs. An eagle perches near, Kyzan watching with sharp eyes that flick to us the moment we approach.

"She's upset," Olivia murmurs, her body tightening against mine. I study Lia, face blank as always, and nearly say she looks fine—but I know better. If Olivia feels it, then it's true.

I release a breath. Whatever plans I had for our cave, for her pressed beneath me, have to wait. Olivia squeezes me once, a silent promise, and when we land, she presses her lips to my cheek. "Don't worry, Jeyr," she whispers, mischief in her tone, "I'll make it up to you."

Her words flare through me, sharp and hot, and I groan, leather tightening over the want she stirs so easily. It takes every scrap of restraint not to throw her over my shoulder and take her away. Instead, I call to Kyzan, who perks at his name. "Come on, Ky. I'll find us food."

The wolf pads to me, and I let the distraction pull me forward. But my thoughts? My thoughts are already back in that cave, with her.

The training grounds, once alive with the crackle of powers colliding and the shouts of drills, fall quiet now. Most of the army drifts away to their quarters, the weight of the day pulling them to rest. Yet around the great fire, a pocket of life lingers—music threads through the smoke, laughter rises in bursts, bowls of broth and bread pass from hand to hand. The grounds themselves still bear the marks of the day: scorch-lines etch the stone where fire met shield, patches of ice glimmer faintly, and the tang of ozone clings to the air from lightning cast too wide. Even in silence, the earth hums with the residue of what was unleashed here.

I spot Lorkan and Caomh still in the mix, which surprises me. After the heat between them earlier, I half-expect they'd retreat to their chambers. Instead, they stay—together. Caomh has his shirt off, his head resting against Lorkan's shoulder, chest ink catching the firelight as if it has its own pulse. Lorkan whispers something into his ear, his hand tracing the tattoos in slow circles, and for the first time in what feels like years, my brother looks truly at ease. A small smile tugs at me. Whatever waits for us outside this cave, at least here he has this.

Jethro sits apart, a dark silhouette against the flames, his stare locked on the fire like it's the only thing worth answering to. The weight around him keeps others away; no one dares disturb him. But I have never been one to leave him to his brooding. With three bowls of food in my hands, I lower myself beside him. Kyzan pads over too, snatching his portion with a wolfish hunger that makes me huff a laugh.

Before I can speak, Jethro knocks his shoulder against mine. "Let's not ask that question," he mutters. His meaning is clear enough—some silences aren't mine to break. I let it lie, though I wonder if it's Gwynn he thinks of, or the war, or both. The fire crackles, spitting sparks into the cavern air. I cradle the bowl in my hands, but my appetite is gone, my chest too tight. Jethro sits heavy at my side, silent as stone, though I know he feels the questions pressing against his teeth. I am about to break the silence when the air shifts.

A shimmer. A flicker, like heat bending light.

I blink, and the breath stops in my lungs.

Tynon. Maros. Tatine.

They step out of shadow, hand in hand, Tatine's swollen belly unmistakable even beneath her wool dress. Maros still wears his fighting leathers, boots scuffed raw; Tynon looks worn but whole. They are not ash or ghostly memory—they are here, *alive.*

The bowl slips from my fingers, broth splattering on the stone, and I stumble to my feet. Jethro grabs my arm with a grunt, his violet eyes narrowing. I shake him off, chest heaving. "You see them, don't you?" I demand, desperate. His frown deepens, but the way his jaw tightens tells me enough—he does.

They smile at me. Gods, they smile. Warm, steady, as if months of grief and guilt have been a dream.

Tynon's voice is the first to reach me, low and steady. "Your sister shocked us enough that our hearts stopped. But the King was distracted. Althea healed the worst of the lightning's strike."

The explanation twists like a blade. Relief crashes into guilt, sharper than any steel. My head bows, shoulders bending beneath the weight. I should have stood in their place. Should have shielded them. Instead, it was Althea's quick mind that saved them, not me.

Silence hums until Maros speaks, his voice gentler than I expect. "We heard what you did, Jeyr. Refusing him. Defying the King. That was no small thing."

Tatine's hand smooths over her belly, eyes bright as embers. "We're here now. And we'll fight with you."

The words snap me upright, my throat raw. "No." My voice is harsher than I mean, but the thought of Tatine's child in danger sets fire to my blood. I step closer, shaking my head. "You carry life. I will never ask you to risk it. If what you want is peace, if you want only family—take it. No one here will chain you to this war."

But they do not retreat. Tynon steps forward, Maros steady at his side, their arms twined tight. Their faces hold no anger, only a fierce light that makes me ache.

"Then answer us this," Tynon says. "What are you fighting for?"

The question stills me. My fists clench at my sides, but the truth is already there, rising through the ash in my chest. "For Olivia. For my mate. For justice against the ones who wronged her—and all like her. For those born with more than one power. A gift of the gods, not a curse."

Their smiles deepen, quiet but sure. Tatine's voice trembles as she adds, "Then we fight for the same thing. For us. For this child. For the chance to see a world where they will not live in hiding."

The fire pops between us. My chest loosens, though the sting of guilt remains.

Olivia

RE BOUND

In his arms, his bare chest on full display, the tattoos I adore stretch across his skin, each line etched into him like a story only I know. Over his heart, just above where our bond thrums against his pulse, a new addition takes my breath away. A hummingbird. I've caught glimpses before, in the frantic moments when having him close mattered more than pausing to look. But now, I drink it in. Black ink alive with hues of red and green, wings mid-beat, the bird seems ready to lift from his skin altogether.

"I needed something to make you feel close," he whispers against my lips.

I close my eyes briefly, pressing the moment into memory. He has practically etched my name across his heart, while I still keep our bond hidden from the world. The urge to brand myself burns within me—not for ownership, he never makes me feel owned—but to claim the truth of my choice. To show I am his mate. I want the mark, whether it's a scar, a bite, or his name written in blood across my soul. I crave it.

Jeyr's eyes darken, and I know the gates to my thoughts are open. "We can arrange that, my love," he says, his voice low and rich, curling heat low in my belly. Goosebumps ripple across my skin, my body already answering him.

His lips press to my neck, teeth grazing until the sting flares sharp, soothed at once by a kiss. My breath hitches, and then his voice follows, a truth I've longed to hear: "You once said yes to being my wife..."

A tear slides down my cheek, hot and certain. I nod, my voice breaking as I whisper, "Today, tomorrow, any day, Jeyr Aimsir. You say when, and I will be yours in every way.

The way it was always meant to be."

He lifts his head, searching me with that fierce, beautiful intensity. How he ever doubts me is beyond sense, but even gods are not free of insecurities. His hand cups my jaw, thumb brushing where the tear has fallen.

"Do you mean that? Because if you do, I have every urge to throw you over my shoulder and marry you right now."

I laugh, even as my chest aches with love. "Caomh would be so proud—his brother married without a shirt. But... I did promise I'd make it up to you... and I really, really want to do that."

His groan rolls through me, rough and wanting. The mattress dips beneath us, the furs warm against my back as his mouth trails fire up my skin. Leather peels away, cool air rushing in to meet the heat of his touch.

Gods, the way he worships me. It never loses its power. Each time feels like a spell, a potion poured straight into my veins.

"My mate, my soon-to-be wife," he hums against my ribs.

I smile into his kiss before he can draw another breath, then roll us in one smooth motion until he's beneath me. Surprise flickers in his eyes—then hunger darkens them, ceding the reins. He lets me take them. Cherishes that I take them. With Jeyr, I feel the power to set the tempo, to chart the rise and fall of our bodies. And he—always—molds himself to fit my rhythm like a perfect puzzle piece.

His hands slide to my hips, guiding them against the hard ridge of his cock, but that isn't what I want. Not yet. I kiss his mouth once, slow and claiming, then lift my hips, smiling as a groan tears from his throat at the loss of pressure.

I trail kisses down the planes of his stomach, loving how each muscle tenses beneath my mouth.

"Livy..." My name, raw on his lips, only spurs me on. This is the man I crave. The man I will have.

Another sound breaks from him, low and wrecked, as if he already knows where I'm headed. My lips follow the lines of his hips, down, down, to where he's thick and hard. His body arches as my breath ghosts over him; his gasps come quick and uneven, his heart a steady thunder I can hear even without my power.

I drag my tongue from base to tip, fighting the smile that wants to bloom at the profanity spilling from Jeyr's mouth.

"Love. Please." He begs, and the sight of him—powerful, beloved, trembling at my mercy—sends a thrill through me no saint would admit to. But I am no saint.

I open the channels between us, feeding him every pulse of my desire. He gasps. His cock twitches in my hand. I give him mercy—just a little—sliding my mouth over him at last. He jerks beneath me, cursing.

"Oh gods. Oh gods. What are you doing to me—"

Showing you you're mine, I think, and his answering growl tells me he's heard.

I work him with my mouth, tasting him, feeling the pulse of his veins, the tremor of his thighs, the desperate sound of his moans fueling me on. I pull back to circle my tongue over his tip, teasing, then let him go entirely.

I kiss my way back up his body—lips, teeth, tongue—hovering above him to drink in his face. His blue eyes are gone, swallowed by black desire.

"Can I take control now," he rasps, "or are you going to keep driving me wild?"

I don't need to think. "Have me, my love."

He flips us, swift as a storm, settling me on my back. He wraps my legs around his waist, slides a finger inside to test me.

"Mmm. So wet."

He drags his finger through my slickness, then zaps me lightly with his power. Lightning arcs along my spine and I arch, gasping. He brings his fingers to his mouth, licking up the glowing sheen.

"Tastes like home," he hums, and now I'm the one whimpering at his mercy.

Strong, gentle hands hold me as he pushes inside—firm, deep enough to make me gasp, pleasure blooming sharp and bright. He begins slow, shallow strokes, one hand sliding down to circle my clit, timed sparks of magic striking just right.

"Look at me, love. Let me see your eyes."

I open them, and his worship nearly undoes me. His thrusts turn harder, deeper, hitting that perfect spot. I pour every ounce of my pleasure into our bond and feel his crashing back into me.

An arm snakes beneath my back, and suddenly I'm lifted, chest pressed to his. The new angle tips my head back, bares my neck. He can't resist. His teeth graze the hollow where neck meets shoulder, lightning shooting down my spine with each bite, pleasure and pain twined.

Every roll of my hips, every slide of his skin on mine feels charged, the air itself sparking. His hand fists in my curls, tugging just enough to make my eyes roll back. The other traces my scars, cups my breasts, rolling my nipples between calloused fingers, then slides to my throat—firm pressure, enough to spike my heartbeat as our movements grow frantic, desperate to claim and be claimed.

I bite my bottom lip. His growl rips through me and I shatter, dragging his mouth to mine in a kiss as fierce as the climax that takes us both. We glow—sunrise on water, light refracting off every surface—as we fall over the edge together.

He is mine. I am his.

Later, in the cooling bath, his hands massage my scalp, washing my hair with a tenderness that nearly rivals the high of sex. When the water has gone tepid, he dries me, gathers me into his arms. Wrapped in Jeyr's embrace, sleep finally finds us both.

Caomh

WHISKY AND BLUE BALLS

I awake to an empty bed, a maddening void that echoes the tantalizing touch of his hands tracing the contours of my tattoos and the sweet whispers of affection that wrapped us in an intoxicating embrace the night before. We were eager to return to our shared sanctuary after those moments of where heated stares and flirty touches became all to much, now? I find myself bewildered—What kind of enchantment is at play here? Finally, I have the person I crave, the one I truly want in both life and the confines of our bed. Yet, to my dismay, *bed* seems to translate to nothing more than kisses and sleep. *Kissing and fucking **sleep**.*

It is a curious concoction of passion and slumber that leaves me perplexed. I reflect on a time when my sex life was undeniably active, although it always feels somewhat hollow. Some label it as merely scratching an itch, a phrase that resonates with an unsatisfying emptiness. I can't help but shake the feeling that those who use that expression are dealing with an itch one would rather avoid altogether. Thankfully, I manage to steer clear of such discomfort.

Now, with Mo Chuisle by my side, I possess not just a desire but a *need*. His kisses have the power to weaken me, his gentle touches promising an explosion of pleasure if only they linger a bit longer. Yet each time passion escalates, it invariably culminates in kisses and caresses everywhere but where my desires yearn for. And then, we sleep.

I pound my fists against the bedding in frustration, acutely aware of his absence. The silence echoes, void of his thoughts, leaving me with a gnawing unease that I often drown in whisky. It occurs to me that I haven't tasted the amber liquid in far too long. Despite the early hour, I crave a drink. Disgruntled, I throw my legs off the bed, realizing I am still naked from the night before, lying beside the man I love, *untouched*.

Whisky. That's what I need.

I march through the caverns, the soft morning light filtering through the waterfall as breakfast preparations for training are underway. The scenery could be breathtaking, but my anger overshadows any beauty. I reach Hecate's room and barge in without bothering to knock. She spins around, red eyes flaring as she hastily finishes changing into her tunic. At that moment, I can't summon even a hint of attraction toward the witch, despite the fact that, in hindsight, I know she possesses a certain allure. Gods, what is happening to me?

Hecate hisses until she takes in my disheveled appearance. "What do I have the honor of seeing you this early, Caomh Conroy?"

"Whisky, or I'll settle for wine," I grumble.

Hecate shoots me a deadpan look, as if my request is absurd. "Haven't you ever woken up in the morning and needed a drink, witch? If I asked for a mimosa, you wouldn't be judging."

Hecate huffs out a laugh, rolling her eyes before retrieving a bottle from a bag on the floor. "I don't know why, but I had a feeling this would be needed when I packed to come here." She holds out the bottle, and I could weep—it's my favorite. I take it without hesitation, but not before kissing her on the cheek.

"Have I ever told you that you're my favorite of the group?"

I receive another huff in response. "Fuck off. If anyone from the land of Anam is your favorite, it's the shifter. You're just mad because he's giving you blue balls."

My eyes widen. "Is it that obvious!?" I whisper-yell.

"I can smell your sexual frustration a mile off. Also, asking for hard whisky at sunrise is a dead giveaway that you need something to blow off." She smiles at my expense.

I flip her off, because she only reminded me how much *blowing,* wasn't happening, then take a swig of the golden goodness that is my favorite whisky. Fueled by the strength of my happy juice, I bid my goodbye and saunter toward breakfast.

The makeshift food station buzzes with a mix of warriors and families, everyone vying for their share. No hierarchy governs this scene; it's a simple rule of first come, best dressed. Standing in line, I casually swig whisky from a canteen.

"I go just for a morning, and I come back to find my man already drinking the day away?" Lorkan's voice resonates with disappointment.

Rolling my eyes, I turn to face him, pointing a finger into his chest while still clutching the canteen. "You left me *alone* in bed, *again*."

Lorkan, with the audacity only he possesses, flashes a smile. "Miss me, Mo ghràdh?"

I can't bear to look at his smug face. Turning away, I allow the Fae to fill my bowl with food. After offering my thanks, I move away from Lorkan, heading toward the cavern exit in search of cold, fresh air.

Though aware of his footsteps trailing behind, I choose to ignore him, much like he has ignored me.

"I wasn't ignoring you, Cay. I was training with the dragons," he calls out, attempting to justify his absence.

"And that couldn't wait until I woke up? Maybe I could have witnessed your dragon-ry in action, or at least received a kiss good morning—or something more. The something you've been promising me, that hasn't happened."

I leave the side passage to the mountain edge and gaze at the sun-kissed peaks. The serenity is short-lived as Lorkan catches up with me.

"There's no rush," he murmurs, coming up behind me. His lips find the pulse point on my neck, and despite my frustration, that touch alone leaves me feeling more intoxicated than the whisky in my canteen.

"Tease," I grunt, moving away despite how my body calls to him. I find a smooth rock to perch upon and start to eat.

"I want to make sure I have enough training under my belt, Mo ghràdh. We can't stay here in hiding forever."

Oh, how I wish we could.

I close my eyes, attempting to quell the rush of emotions that surge within me. It has taken merely a week, a mere blip in the grand timeline of a century, to unravel the tightly wound threads of denial that I had spun around my true feelings. I have steadfastly convinced myself that my affection for him is no more than friendship. My duty, I believed, was to shield him at any cost, and now he is set to stand by my side through it all. Call me crazy, call me immature, but the desire to savor the time I have with him overcomes any rational thought. It takes everything in me to dismantle the walls I've built, choosing instead to embrace the motto that it's better to have than not have at all. And so, here we are—*having*, even if it's only a sliver of what I truly want.

As I gaze at an eagle cutting through the sky, Lorkan settles beside me. The side of his body finds mine, "Cay."

"What." My voice comes out hoarse, scraped raw by the emotions clawing at my throat. Moments like this usually send people stepping back, leaving me with my drink and the labyrinth of thoughts that spiral through every possible future.

My mastery over the mind always leans toward delving—connecting to the thoughts of countless Fae, bridging them all into a web I can move through. The glimpses of potential futures are never reliable, fleeting shards of choices and consequences, but they're enough to let me strategize, to occasionally shift the tide of wars.

But now? Now I know Lorkan won't let me drown in the what-ifs. When I glance at him, I sense a dozen possibilities—some that pull me in like a current, others that make me want to fight until my last breath to stop them.

"Do you think I don't want to?" he says, voice low, violet eyes unflinching on mine. "Because I do. But just having any part of you—it's enough for me, Cay. I just don't want it to be a rushed night."

I grunt, a sound that's both understanding and irritation. I get it, but that doesn't mean I have to like it.

"How was dragon-ry?" I ask, shifting the conversation, focusing on stabbing my spoon into the stew in my bowl. I can *feel* the look he gives me, but I ignore it on purpose. He indulges me anyway, describing the strain of learning to fly in that form—the way muscles ache in places he didn't even know existed, the brutal weight of wings that feel impossible to lift.

"Honestly, it feels almost impossible they can fly at all. It's sheer strength in their wings, the power in their backs, that keeps them in the air. Wyverns are different—they're nimble, their flying feels like instinct. But a dragon? Every move is like dragging stone. Once this is done, I never want to be a dragon again. All I'll want is a long soak and a massage," he finishes, exhaustion lacing his voice.

I arch a brow at him. "That can be arranged, you know."

He laughs, the sound deep and easy. "You are insatiable."

"Only for you, Mo Chuisle," I murmur, lips quirking. "Only for you."

Jethro

SIDING WITH THE ENEMY

We gather once more around the war table, the carved map etched into the stone like an open wound that refuses to close. Wax drips from guttering candles, their flames throwing uneven light across strained faces, shadows leaping over cheekbones and jawlines sharpened by exhaustion. The chamber hums with low murmurs, the restless scrape of armor, the uneven shuffle of boots against stone. I lean into the table's edge, feeling each tremor ripple through it, each whisper of strategy that rises and falls without anchoring into something solid.

The silence that follows is taut, stretched thin as a bowstring—until Lia breaks it.

"We take them in groups," she says, her tone flat, unbothered, stripped of the weight her words should carry. "The ones not fighting. To the Kingdom of Anam."

The suggestion hangs, deceptively simple. My jaw clenches. Of course she says it like that, as if uprooting families is no more than a passing thought. As if children clinging to their mothers, elders barely able to walk, are just pieces on this carved map to be moved where she wills.

Aella leans forward, ice flashing in her lone eye. "Send them with the wyverns," she offers, her voice clipped but certain, as if the answer has been under our noses all along.

Lia's laugh is low, humorless. She tilts her head, a pale curtain of hair sliding over her shoulder. "I am no general, princess, but even I know that a fleet of wyverns would draw the King's gaze faster than any army."

The dismissal stings. Aella straightens, spine rigid, her voice hardening into steel. "And what proof do we have that you'll deliver them safely? That you won't turn them over the moment it suits you?"

Lia's eyes flicker, the barest flash of power shimmering beneath her skin, though her voice remains calm. "You have proof enough. The families already here. Did I not deliver them unscathed? Have I made any move to harm them?"

Aella doesn't yield. She never does. Her chin lifts, her words slicing as cleanly as any blade. "That doesn't mean you're not scheming behind our backs. We would be fools not to wonder what you plan to do with that much power."

The curl of Lia's lip is pure disdain. "Bit rich, isn't it? Considering your entire rebellion is about freeing those with more than one power." Her gaze sweeps the table, daring anyone else to challenge her.

Aella falters, but only for a heartbeat. She clutches the oldest weapon in her arsenal—the accusation the courts have hurled at Lia her entire life. "You're just like him. Like the King. Like Bane."

The words land heavy. But Lia doesn't flinch. Instead, her power ripples, controlled but seething. "That's old, princess. That's the voice of the rotting courts still clinging to your tongue. Yes, I am of his bloodline. But I belong to no court. I fight so I—and every soul like me—can live without fear of execution for simply existing."

The air shifts with her words, the table vibrating beneath my hands. I let the shadows stir, let them creep close, until their whispers curl against my ear. "She's right," I say at last, the sound cutting across the chamber like a blade cleaving wood.

Lia's head snaps toward me, surprise loosening her careful mask. For once, she isn't composed—she's unguarded.

Aella seizes the crack, her venom quick to strike. "Oh, of course. Just because you like this white witch."

At that word, witch, Hecate's chair screeches back. She rises slowly, crimson searing through her eyes, the temperature in the room spiking. "Careful, princess." The warning is low, steady, and sharp enough to flay.

Shadows coil tighter at my back, answering the insult hurled across the table. "I don't like her," I snap, each syllable hard enough to bite. "Not even a little. But look around. Do you see anyone else here with her kind of power—anyone willing to bleed for us the way she already has? I am an army commander. If I have a weapon, I'll wield it."

Aella's lips part, her retort a half-formed thing, brittle with fury. "So you trust her?"

"Olivia does," I counter. "And I trust Olivia's judgment. It's carried us this far."

For a heartbeat, silence. Then Lia's gaze finds mine again, sharp and unreadable, lingering too long, pressing too close. I break it first, though the jab in my gut refuses to ease.

Aella retreats into silence at last, though it tastes of surrender held on a knife's edge, brittle as thin ice.

The decision comes down like a decree: Lia, Jeyr, and I will lead the groups to Anam. The longest jump I have ever attempted—and the risk of it thrums in my veins, heavy, inevitable. I will test it first with Lia, scout the terrain, carve out the safest landing point. The dragons themselves whispered Anam into our plans, and Hecate has already declared she will follow, to lay wards over the kingdom again.

Chairs scrape. Boots echo. The chamber empties in restless waves of voices and muttered dissent, alliances thin as smoke. I stay behind, palms pressed flat against the carved stone map, tracing its lines as if they might bleed into me.

We have a plan. Yet it feels like setting foot on a path with no clear end—one more step toward a chasm we cannot see until it swallows us.

And I am left with this truth: I must trust her. The woman I would rather see buried beneath a mountain than standing at my side.

Olivia

MOMENTS CHERISHED BEFORE WAR

"Do we trust him not to kill her?" I voice aloud as Jeyr undresses for bed, the weight of the day pressing down on my shoulders. It is the first day when the caverns feel anything but joyous. Families are nervous about the change of location. Aiden warned Caomh the army is on the move, and Aimsir is now a new training ground—too close for comfort. All our warriors are here, Fae from every court watching over their kin. The dragons' suggestion to relocate families to a kingdom free of war is deemed necessary. The risk of leaving them unattended is too high, and we don't have the time to court a queen into alliance. My home kingdom, whatever state it is in, technically belongs to me as the last empath. If it can give sanctuary to families in need, then I will relinquish what the gods claimed was mine.

"He won't." Jeyr's voice is steady, but his eyes hold lingering sadness. "He has a chip on his shoulder, for all the right reasons. She's just a reminder of what he's lost—and who caused it."

I bite my lip. "I know… I just worry. She's never had anything resembling care. I brought her here, and all she receives is hate. She acts strong, but I feel that hurt."

Now he stands bare before me, his body carved like marble and yet warm, alive, mine. He strolls toward me in a way that should be sinful. I try to keep my eyes on his, but fail—badly. He chuckles, lifting my chin to meet his gaze. "I love your heart, my love. Things will change. You can't control fear. She is trying to prove them wrong, and you can't meddle with that."

I sigh, leaning back on my palms, tilting my head to the ceiling. His groan fills the space at the sight of me so exposed to him. I never dared to dream of this when I was captive—the simple act of being naked with the one I love, unafraid, open to him in comfort, not necessity. The memories of what was done to me will never fade, but here, with Jeyr's soft touches and kind words, the weight of the past eases.

Jeyr crawls over my body, sparks of lightning coursing through me with every point of contact. His hand maps me from hip to breast, then cups my face. His eyes burn electric blue, brighter than the dark that surrounds us. I wrap my legs around his taut torso, shivering at the rumble that escapes him.

His fingers find proof of how ready I am. He takes them away, brings them to his lips, and trails his tongue along the slickness he's stolen from me. My breath stutters at the shutter of his eyes. "Mmm, my hummingbird... always so sweet."

I can't take it anymore. I use my thighs to pull him closer, forcing his hips to thrust into me. The smooth glide of him filling me makes my back arch, greedy for him deeper. Tomorrow begins the first move of war—having him between my legs may not be a luxury I can cling to again for days. I plan to savor it.

Animal sounds tear from Jeyr's throat as he rocks into me, slow at first, holding himself back. I feel it, the love behind each measured thrust. But bravery rises in me—I am not bound to the past in this bed. I am only his.

"Let go," I whisper.

His eyes flash, wide, deciphering. I see the doubt, the fear of hurting me, of summoning ghosts best left buried. But the very presence of that fear erases mine. I nod, giving him everything.

Strong arms slip beneath me, palms bracketing my shoulder blades, pulling me up. In a blink I'm in his lap. I almost protest—I want him in control—but I don't need to. His hips piston upward, hard and fast, shockwaves tearing through my spine. His teeth find the curve of my neck, biting, not to break skin but to brand me with pleasure.

He pounds into me with a rhythm so perfect it borders punishment. My cries meet his groans, our bodies colliding with a sound that echoes against cavern walls. He lets go, and I shatter with him, fire rolling through every vein.

Lightning cracks above us, the cavern itself lit by his power, reflecting our storm. He gathers me into his arms as we collapse onto the bed, holding me so tightly not even air could divide us. His breath whispers over my skin, the softest lullaby.

And just like that, we sleep—fused, spent, whole.

I wake to the press of tension on my chest, heavier than any weight of stone. The walls of the cavern are supposed to keep us safe, but this morning they tremble with voices raised, arguments thrumming so loud it feels like the rock itself can't contain them.

Beside me, Jeyr still sleeps, his breath steady, until I shift and nudge him. His eyes flick open, the blue deepening as his frown forms. He feels it too—my unease, the storm outside our chamber door. Without words, we rise, dress quickly, and move toward the noise. His hand brushes the small of my back as we walk, a silent promise: I'm here.

The community chamber is alive with discord. Fae press shoulder to shoulder, faces carved from stone and fire. Fear hums in the air, jagged, desperate. The debate is no secret—the plan to move families, the old, the wounded, away from danger. But fear makes enemies of allies.

"She is not to be trusted!" a Fae shouts, his voice cracking against the cavern ceiling. A man we pulled from Eileamaid, scars still fresh across his arms. His finger stabs toward Lia. "I am not going anywhere with that monster."

The word monster echoes through the chamber.

Lia stands at the center of it all, still as a statue, her pale hair catching the firelight like a halo made of ice. She doesn't answer him. Doesn't rise to defend herself. Her silence is louder than their shouting, and it unsettles them more than any outburst would have.

Aella lingers near the wall, her arms crossed, her gaze sharp as a blade. She catches my eye, tilts her chin. The smugness in her look says what her tongue does not: *I told you so.* I bite back the urge to argue, to strip that smirk from her face.

Jeyr's hand lingers at my hip, but I slip away, stepping forward into the ring of hostility. Dozens of eyes follow me. I can feel their doubts prickling against my skin.

"Is she not like you?" I ask, my voice carrying over the din. "Exiled, hunted for what she is?"

The man snarls, ready to bite back with lineage and bloodlines, ready to throw her father's sins into her face. My anger flares, heat licking at the edges of my control. I draw breath, ready to argue, to bare my teeth and rattle off every reason why they should trust her—why they *must.*

But before I can, a shadow cuts forward and stands at my side.

Jethro.

His presence is iron, his voice steady as it rolls through the cavern. "I know every one of you has reservations. I hear them. I share them." His gaze sweeps the crowd, hard enough to pin even the loudest dissenters into silence. "But I will not lead you astray. We opened these caverns to you—our most guarded secret—and still we trusted you, every one of you, despite not knowing who you truly are." He lets that sit, lets it sting. "Now you must extend that same trust. For the safety of your children, your families. Lia's power is the only thing that will move you unseen. Without her, you risk everything."

The words ripple through the crowd. No cheers, no relief—just low murmurs, reluctant acceptance, the heavy shift of bodies resigning themselves to a choice they don't want but know they have to make.

I glance back at Lia. Her eyes are dull, her emotions a knotted tangle, rusting chains twisted beneath the surface. I wonder if she even knows how deep her scars go, if she'll ever be able to untangle them.

She doesn't speak. Doesn't argue. She only turns on her heel, white hair catching the firelight once more, and disappears into the shadows of the cavern.

The space she leaves behind feels colder than stone.

Jethro

ROTTEN DOUBT

Power hums and coils around me as I stand above the peaks of my mountain home. Lia's energy spills like a storm today, sharper, stranger. Her face, usually carved of stone, is set even harder—as if no feature dares to shift. She stares into the mountains, eyes locked beyond the horizon, as though she could pierce the veil and glimpse Anam itself.

We wait. And then Hecate comes, unhurried, as though this is only another morning. Her gaze flits from me to Lia, reading what we refuse to say aloud. She doesn't touch, not yet—she only steps close enough that her warmth brushes Lia's skin. I see Lia stiffen, though the motion is slight. Hecate leans close, whispers something too soft for me to catch, and the smallest ripple eases Lia's rigid stance.

Hecate shifts between us, her eyes bright, wet with feeling. "So," she says, her voice catching, "you two ready to take me home?"

Her tone cuts me. Gwynn and she had too little time together—two witches born of different lands, two powers meant to intertwine. I take Hecate's hand, her grief as raw as mine. For a breath I close my eyes. Wind brushes my cheeks, the sun parts the clouds as though Gwynn herself peers down for this one fragile moment. *Home,* close enough to touch.

Lia nods, her stare unbroken, fixed on some horizon only she sees. Hecate takes her hand, and at once an image floods my mind: a kingdom of temples rising among the forest cliffs, crowned by mountains, haloed in mist. I seize the picture, focus my light, and let it blaze through my veins. Breath leaves my lungs in a rush—then the shift. My feet strike leaf-littered earth. But there is no dizziness, no hollow drain. The power still thrums in me, hungry, ready for more.

I open my eyes—and freeze.

The kingdom is northing but ash.

Temples lie gutted, their blackened bones jutting against a sky veiled in smoke. Ash swirls in cruel spirals, taunting with the memory of what was. The air reeks of fire and sorrow. Water at the mountains' base runs dark, thick as ink. Even the trees refuse to rise, as though mourning the souls who once dwelled here.

A sob tears from Hecate, raw and jagged. I cannot look at her; I cannot move. The truth strikes me: empaths, witches, dragons—all slaughtered, taken, broken. The land itself lies hollow, stripped of love.

Lia sinks to her knees. Her hair, white as bone, glows against the ruin. Her hands press to the soil, and the earth groans beneath her touch. Tears slip down her cheeks, liquid gold that falls into the dirt. The ground trembles. Then fire bursts forth—blue, violent, devouring.

"Hecate!" I seize her arm, pulling her close as the blaze rips through the ruins. Buildings, trees, bones—they ignite, vanish in blue flame until nothing but cinders remain. Fire licks the water's edge, dancing even upon its surface, burning away the black oil slick. My chest clenches. Is she finishing what her father and the King began? Is Lia the ruin of all things good?

But then—silence. The flames gutter out, leaving the world still, the air heavy with the stench of char.

Rain falls. Sheets of it, drenching us to the bone, running through my hair and over my skin until I shiver with the weight of it. Lia still kneels, her tears falling with the storm.

And then the earth moves. Light bursts through the soil, rainbow shards scattering in the rain. Souls rise, free at last. Green spears pierce the darkened dirt. Trees unfurl, racing skyward in spiraled towers. Vines lace together, bridges of living wood. Flowers bloom in jubilant bursts. Before my eyes, a city rises from ruin—the city of pines, alive once more.

Hecate lifts her hands, trembling, lips moving in words older than stone. Magic answers her. The land bends, welcomes her home. Here, her soul sings. Here, her power is whole.

I can only stand and watch. History reshapes itself before me, yet I am the lone witness who will speak of it. The two women at the heart of it all—Lia and Hecate—will never tell. Their pain runs too deep.

Together, their voices—one of flame, one of root—finish as one. The wards shiver into place with a sound like breath rushing through a cavern. I do not know what protections Hecate has laid, only that they hold.

A cry echoes from the cliffs—the creatures of Anam, stirring, waiting, calling. Life answers life.

Lia staggers to her feet, her eyes raking over what she has wrought. In mere moments she has turned a graveyard into a sanctuary. A haven for the fae yet to come.

And then, with nothing left to give, she collapses.

"How is she?" I ask.

Hecate kneels under a shelter of wisteria and vines, grapes dangling heavy above her head, her fingers stroking Lia's hair. Lia hasn't stirred in two days. Her body glows faintly, breathing slow and shallow. The kingdom she built hums around us, alive with her power, though she lies still as stone.

"She is healing herself, but slowly," Hecate says, her voice low, steady. "She is lucky she didn't kill herself. She was teetering on the edge of burnout."

A frown pulls at my brow. "Why would she—"

"Because she just wants life," Hecate cuts in, her eyes flicking to Lia's face. For once, Lia looks her age—young, almost fragile, stripped of the terrifying force she wielded on the mountain. "I am no empath. But I am old enough to know when someone grieves. She grieves a life she'll never have, because everyone cages her, fears her. What she did here? It was her proving she can be more than that cage."

The words bite. I let them sit inside me, unsettled, while my gaze drifts across the island. The lake sparkles, clear now, teeming with fish that hadn't swum here in centuries. A river winds its way toward the rising city of pines, water skipping over rocks. Along its banks, new shoots push through the soil—vegetables, herbs, life. The very foundations of survival, conjured by her hands. It looks like paradise, but the thought curdles in my chest.

Then I see them—white lilies, blooming on the steps. My breath catches, fury surges. Before I think, light flashes from my palms, searing them to ash. The scent burns my nose.

Gwynn's face swims in my mind, surrounded by those flowers. My grief, my rage, rise raw and jagged. Poisonous beauty. Always her mark.

I turn sharply, jaw clenched, refusing to let this place seduce me into forgetting what Lia is, what she carries in her veins. Dangerous. Always dangerous.

"I'll go back," I mutter. Hecate doesn't try to stop me. Lia still glows faintly in her sleep, untouched by my choice.

The moment I step into the caverns, the air is taut with panic. "Where are they?" voices demand before I even clear the entrance. Caomh appears at my side, Lorkan at his shoulder. Olivia and Jeyr rush forward, their eyes fixed on me with sharp urgency.

"She's fixing structural problems," I say, jaw tight. "She pushed herself too far. She's recovering from burnout." I do not say she rebuilt a dead kingdom from its ashes.

"Is she okay?" Olivia presses, her eyes burning with worry.

"She's fine," I snap, brushing past them. Their stares track me like daggers. Caomh's hand clamps my arm, his eyes fierce.

"Do we need to worry about her?"

I hesitate. Her safe haven, her brilliance—yet the suspicion claws at me. "She is keeping her word," I say finally. The words taste hollow, my tone betrays the uncertainty I won't admit. Caomh reads it anyway. His gaze searches mine, but I give him nothing more. He lets go, though I feel his unspoken questions cling to me.

The hall hums with whispers as warriors glance my way, their eyes asking why I returned alone. Why Lia isn't with me. Doubt spreads like rot, and gods help me, I feel it too. At full strength, she could move them all herself. Efficient. Perfect. Too perfect.

But one blink, and she could deliver every fae straight into the King's grasp. One choice, and she could make Anam her own kingdom. She could take Olivia with her, twist her, claim her. Have we all been blinded?

Olivia imprisoned beside the Grand Duke's daughter—her miraculous survival, her sudden heroics. Was it all too convenient?

I clench and unclench my fists, whistling for Jorax. His wingbeats come swift, familiar, pulling me back to another heartbeat, one that no longer exists. The pang strikes sharp.

I climb onto his scaled back. He surges upward, wings carving the sky. He knows the drill—patrol the perimeter, eyes sharp for danger. I close mine, the wind stinging my face, and try to silence thoughts tearing me apart.

I often think I should be okay with her loss. Our romance began as a whirlwind—because that's who my wife was, a force, a beautiful glowing force. After, our love became small captured moments. And as much as I try to forget, the thoughts always come rushing back.

I let myself be carried back to the training room of the manor, *the scent of steel and sweat sharp in the air. Gwynn's dark curls clung to her brow, damp with exertion, as she circled me with a smile meant to unnerve. "Come on, Jethro, show me what you've got," she taunted, blade raised, eyes sparking with the fire that had always undone me.*

I lunged, and she spun away, quick as flame, the slap of her boots echoing off the stone. My strikes were heavy, measured, each one designed to test her guard. Hers were fast, cunning, sharp with that mischief that lived in her veins. She darted in and out of reach, laughter spilling free, mocking my weight, my precision. Gods, her laughter—it struck harder than any blade, reminding me why I loved her. She was life in motion, unyielding, untamed.

"Watch your left," she called, though the warning was only meant to distract. Her blade tapped my ribs, the sting light but the victory hers. "You'll have to try harder than that, my lord," she teased, curls flying as she ducked beneath my arm.

Heat rose in my chest, half from exertion, half from the way she moved. Strong thighs carried her in a dancer's rhythm, the swell of her breath straining against her tunic, skin flushed with the thrill of the fight. The spar blurred, became something else entirely. My hand caught her wrist mid-strike, twisted her arm behind her back, drew her against me until her laugh broke into a gasp. Our blades clattered to the floor, forgotten.

"Yield," I growled against her ear, though we both knew she never would. She turned in my hold, her lips meeting mine with a force fiercer than any strike. The training floor became our battlefield, our sanctuary. Her back pressed to the mats, my body braced above hers, every movement rough with want, tempered with the reverence only she could draw from me. She bit my lip; I answered with a thrust of my hips. Her nails raked across my shoulders, claiming me. Every kiss, every touch was war and worship in one, until we lay tangled on the stone, breathless, conquered and conqueror alike.

And when the echoes faded, it was her head on my chest, her hair damp against my skin, her laughter soft as the night settled. In that moment, I believed we could fight the world and win, as long as we did it together.

The memory fades, and I open my eyes. The cold wind chills the tears that streak my face. I bow my head, releasing a ragged breath.

She loved to fly. Always had. She had a way of making creatures love her more than me—Jorax included. Gwynn never bothered pairing with a wyvern. Her answer was always the same: *"Why get my own, when I can share yours?"* Impractical, yes, but it made my heart swell.

I hate the sound that rips from me when the thoughts return—the image of her dark curls whipping in the wind, that one stubborn strand always clinging to her bottom lip. Gods, I loved taming it. Or pretending to. It was our private joke: I could never tame her. No one could. Once Gwynn set her mind to something, only the gods could stop her. Or Bane.

At that thought, a roar tears from my chest, rising to the heavens.

I had just gotten her back. Gwynn had come home. *For good,* she said. A witch of the queen's lands, yet bound by duty to the witches of Anam, she still carried the cause in her veins. I had Olivia to thank for that, though it was unintentional—she had brought my wife back to me. And as always, the moment Olivia slipped from our grasp, duty pulled Gwynn away again. Behind enemy doors. Away from me.

Once, I found that fire endearing. She was a fighter, like me. I never stopped fighting. I commanded the rebellion, small battles, small victories. We saved the illegals, hid them in shadows, gave them safety. But it was never enough for her. Gwynn wanted more, needed more, even if it meant walking willingly into Bane's hold.

The worst of it was—she fought that war alone. She gave Caomh scraps of intel, enough to keep him satisfied, enough to keep our soldiers one step ahead. But I knew her. I knew she was holding more. From him. From me. And even now, even in death, those secrets burn like a blade in my ribs. Bane made sure they died with her.

Maybe she had answers about his daughter. Maybe she could have told me whether to trust the pale witch who stirs my blood with hatred every time I see her. The one I want to kill but cannot.

I never was a hunter. I killed to protect, to survive. But I would be lying if I said the thought hasn't come: to trap her, bind her, drag her back to her father. Deliver her as he delivered death to my wife. Spill her blood the way Gwynn's was spilled.

But revenge isn't the answer. Gwynn would never want that. She would want me to keep fighting—for the cause that bound us, for the freedom that brought us together.

Still, the temptation lingers. It gnaws at the corners of my mind, feeding on grief, on rage. I remind myself I am better than this—that her memory deserves more than another cycle of blood and ruin.

And yet... deep in my chest, a fire will not die. The flame of justice. The hunger for retribution. Burned into me by the loss of the only woman I ever loved.

Jorax banks beneath the stars, the night a tapestry of black and silver. The mountain looms before us—dark, immense, its cliffs jagged as old scars. Yet there she is. A single blaze against the shadow. Her hair glows, pale fire at the edge of the abyss. She sits like a sentinel on the cliff's lip, armor clinging to her legs, a wisp of a shirt barely shielding her from the cold.

She does not move. She does not falter. From this distance I cannot see her face, but I feel the weight of her stare. Sharp. Merciless. A blade pressed to the hollow of my throat.

I dismount as Jorax tilts, boots crunching against stone. He vanishes into the night, his wingbeats fading, leaving me with only her. If not for that unearthly hair, she could be mistaken for marble—some god's cruel carving.

"Couldn't wait around for me, then?" Her voice slices the air. Flat. Unmoved. A phantom's whisper laced with venom.

"Not everything revolves around you, Princess." My reply is steel, clipped short. "The island was ready. I wasn't waiting on you."

She laughs—low, humorless, the sound scraping like gravel over stone. "If you knew my life at all, Jethro, you would know nothing revolves around me." Her words tumble, ragged edges tearing at the night. "The King believes power makes us gods. That all must bow. That fear is love. He thrives in it—revels in the solitude, mistaking silence for devotion." Her head tips back, white hair spilling down like starlight. "But I don't. I feel it choking me. Every hour. Every heartbeat. The voices of those who want me dead—they never quiet."

Her gaze spears me, unflinching, cold. "Even yours. I know you want to kill me. So don't pretend otherwise, Light Master. I am already damned enough to know the world still turns because I breathe."

The shadows stir in me, restless, hungry. A part of me aches to deny her. A darker part aches to agree. I keep my silence, jaw locked, because if I open my mouth, I might not stop.

She exhales, bitter as smoke. "Why waste words? I am what they say. Monster. Manipulator." Her voice drops, almost a confession. "When the war ends, I'll vanish. I won't stain Anam. I won't touch the Queen's lands. I'll find some corner of this wretched earth, carve my freedom from it. And if I die trying..." Her pale shoulders lift in a humorless shrug. "Then at least I'll die chasing the dream that haunted me since chains first kissed my wrists."

The wind keens through the peaks, cold as bone. And I—I cannot look away. Every instinct screams that she's danger. A storm cloaked in skin. A living blade that could cut us all to pieces.

And yet—gods curse me—I believe her.

Lorkan

Understanding limitations, understanding Power

The night sky stretches wide above the clearing, starlight spilling over the massive figure of Faldr where he waits, coiled and watchful. His silver-scarred scales gleam like a blade catching the moon, and his eyes glint with something sharp—impatience, annoyance—and it needles at me, sparking heat in my chest.

Are you ready, boy? Faldr's voice rumbles into my mind, the disdain in it a low, curling snarl.

My hands fist at my sides, jaw tight. "As ready as I'll ever be," I mutter, low and rough, letting the edge bleed into my voice. I know he hears the defiance there. I know he thinks little of me—always has—but I refuse to let it get into my head, not now.

"Remember," Faldr drawls, dragging out the word as if savoring it, "shifting isn't just flailing until your hide sprouts scales. It is about calling that blood in your veins to heel and not making a fool of yourself. Try to look like you belong to my kind."

I grit my teeth, swallowing the sharp retort that burns my tongue.

I force my lungs to slow, drag in a long breath and let the heat crawl under my skin, through my bones. My body answers, reluctantly at first—then all at once. Bones snap and twist, muscle shreds and knits back together, and the pain blazes white-hot. I bite it back, the hiss tearing from my throat anyway, but I do not stop. I will not stop.

When it is done, I stand in the clearing on four taloned feet, breath sawing out of my chest. The night air steams around me, and my shadow cuts sharp against the earth. Faldr circles me with the slow precision of a commander judging a recruit, his gaze dragging over every inch of my scaled form.

Well, he rumbles at last, smoke curling from his nostrils. *You didn't turn yourself inside out. Congratulations. Don't get cocky.*

A grin bares my teeth, sharp and full of challenge. *Your faith in me is touching, old man.*

Faldr's nostrils flare, but instead of biting back, he goes still. *You think you know what you are, pup? Think again.*

The words catch me off guard, enough to still the quip on my tongue. "Then tell me," I say, my voice low, steady.

Shifters are dragon-born, he says, and there is weight there, age-old and undeniable. *Once, your kind had only two shapes—Fae and dragon. You did not wear the skins of other creatures until much later, when your blood tangled with the rest of the Fae.* His tone softens, only barely, as if memory pulls at him. *But even then, we never forgot what we were. We were bonded—to the Companachs, to the land itself, to one another. Together we were untouchable.*

His massive head lowers, eyes narrowing. *Until the King burned Anam. Until he hunted us. Until that bond was torn apart and left your kind fractured.* The words rumble like distant thunder, full of old grief.

A sharp ache claws at my chest. I never knew that bond, never felt that belonging—but Gods, I want to.

Then we put it back together, I say, quiet but certain. *Whatever it takes.* Faldr studies me, the silence thick enough to press against my skin. Then, slowly, he inclines his massive head. It is no grand gesture, but I feel the weight of it. *Rest, Lorkan,* he commands, voice low and rough with something almost like approval. *Tomorrow you will learn what it means to truly be dragon.*

And then he is gone—launching into the air with a sweep of wings that stirs the treetops before he vanishes into the dark.

I shift back to two legs, sweat slicking my skin, my muscles trembling from the effort. My chest heaves, frustration and pride warring inside me. I am no hatchling. And I am closer than ever to proving it.

I call the shift again, this time to something lighter. Feathers sprout, wings unfurl, and the raven's form is a relief—fast and lean, the night wind kissing every edge of me as I leap skyward. The clearing shrinks beneath me, the cavern waiting below, but my blood still thrums with the echo of Faldr's words.

As I descended into the darkness, I couldn't shake the feeling of unease that lingered in the back of my mind. Tomorrow would bring new challenges, new lessons to be learned. But for now, I would take solace in the comforting embrace of the shadows, knowing that I had survived another day in this unforgiving world.

Caomh kneels in the dirt and gravel, sweat sliding down his temple, jaw locked tight. The cavern is silent, the only sound the occasional drip of water echoing from the limestone above. The faint glow of moss and lichen paints everything in greenish-gold hues, shadows dancing across the faces watching him. Olivia stands before him, chin lifted, her expression serene—but I feel the tension thrumming beneath it. Her mind is open, humming, ready, deliberately unshielded. She is letting him in.

The air hums, charged and heavy, the pressure making my own power spark along my spine, ready to lash out if needed.

From the edge of the cavern, Lia steps forward, her boots crunching softly over loose stones. Her hair—white as moonlight—glows faintly, a living thread of illumination against the dark. It frames her pale face like a halo, though there is nothing angelic in the sharp glint of her eyes.

"Better," she says, her voice cutting through the stillness like a blade. "But you're holding back, Conroy."

His golden eyes snap open, narrowing on her, but he doesn't speak. His shields hold, his control ironclad.

"You want to lead armies?" Lia presses, her white hair catching the dim light as she circles him, her glow spilling over his tense shoulders. "Then do it. Stop just keeping her out—take control. Command every mind here like the King does. Bend them to your will. Show Olivia she was wrong for caging your powers."

The words land like a blow. A muscle ticks in Caomh's jaw, the flicker of hesitation visible even from here.

Lia leans closer, her tone dropping low. "You fear her, Caomh. You hate her, a little, for doing what you refuse to do—use her power, even when it costs her. You don't want to become Tierney, the man who wifed your mother and made her soul his until she broke. And Olivia loves you for never being that man. But now? That's the only thing holding you back from breaking the King's hold and saving the person you would burn this world for."

Her words slice him open, and I see it in the change of his face, the tightening of his mouth, the flash of pain in his eyes.

Across the cavern, Jeyr moves. He steps forward, each movement deliberate, predatory. The glow from Lia's hair glints off his ice-blue eyes, which pin Caomh with a warning as sharp as a blade: *If you hurt her, you do not leave this cavern alive.*

But Olivia doesn't flinch. She inhales slowly, squares her shoulders, and nods once. "Do it, Caomh."

Something in him snaps.

Caomh's breath comes harsh in the stillness, each exhale loud against the cavern walls. The entire chamber feels suspended, waiting.

Then he breaks.

I feel it before I see it—a deep, thrumming pulse that rolls outward through the ground, scattering pebbles at his knees. Caomh stops holding back, and his power *erupts*. The air tightens, charged and humming, until it feels like the very stone vibrates with it.

My head jerks, a burning tether yanking tight through the bond I share with him. I nearly gasp at the force of it.

The power lashes outward in invisible threads, weaving through the cavern, coiling around every mind within reach.

Olivia gasps, her body jerking as he shatters through her defenses. Her knees nearly give out, but her chin lifts stubbornly. She meets his gaze head-on, defiance blazing even as her fingers tremble.

All around us, the crowd of Fae react as one. They straighten where they sit, their spines locking into place, jaws going slack as their eyes glaze under the weight of his will.

The cavern is utterly silent—save for the faint trickle of water dripping somewhere deep in the tunnels—every soul frozen, held in Caomh's grip.

A sick twist curls in my gut as I feel it through our connection: the sheer *scope* of him. He could make them do anything. Fall to their knees. Tear each other apart. Burn this place to the ground. He is strong enough to hold them all—strong enough to rival the King.

And he knows it.

Lia's pale hair glows like silver fire in the darkness as she smiles, satisfaction sharp as a blade. "That's it," she says, her voice low, almost reverent. "You could lead a battalion through hell itself with that kind of control."

Caomh's chest rises and falls once, twice. Then, slowly, he releases them.

The hold snaps like a taut rope cut clean. The rush of release makes the cavern echo with the sound of everyone breathing at once.

Olivia sags forward, catching herself on her knees, but she's smiling. "I can't get through," she says, wonder and pride tangled in her voice.

Caomh stands, gravel crunching under his boots, and rolls his shoulders back. "Good," he says, his voice rough and scraped raw. "Your next task is to break me."

All around us, Fae blink rapidly, rubbing their temples as if waking from a dream. A few mutter under their breath, unnerved by what just happened.

Caomh doesn't stay to answer their questions. His eyes lift to mine, unreadable, his face carved from marble, and then he's striding across the cavern toward me.

Before I can think better of it, I meet him halfway, my hand finding his. His grip is iron, but his thumb brushes once across my knuckles, an almost unspoken gratitude. Without a word, I lead him away, out of the circle of firelight, away from Lia's glowing, knowing smile and Jeyr's predatory watchfulness.

The sound of water drips behind us as the cavern swallows the crowd's murmurs, leaving only the echo of our footsteps and the faint hum of power still clinging to him like a second skin.

Steam coils in heavy ribbons through the chamber, clinging to the carved walls until they glisten like hammered gold in the glow of the sconces. The bath is deep and wide enough for two warriors to drown their demons in, and yet the air feels too small for what coils between us.

Cay straddles my lap, his thighs braced against my hips, skin flushed from the heat. His fingers knead into the base of my skull, thumbs pressing until I feel the pain and pleasure blur into one another.

"These knots, mo chuisle," he murmurs, voice low and hoarse, "they could tie down a dragon."

A breathless laugh escapes me, strained, unsteady. "Bloody dragon has me doing the impossible," I rasp, tipping my head back to give him more access.

His mouth brushes the damp skin just below my ear, and a hum rumbles through his chest. "But you're doing it," he says, and there's pride there — quiet, unflinching pride that threads through me like a lifeline. "Better than any of us dared hope."

I tilt my head until our eyes catch. The glowstone light paints his lashes in gold, carves his cheekbones into marble. My chest aches at the shadows there. "What is it?" I whisper.

He exhales, a long breath that fogs the air between us. "I judged Liv," he says, his words sharp-edged, careful, "for the way she wields her power. For slipping into minds without permission. For using her gift to steer people where she wants them. I told myself it was a line I'd never cross." His throat works. "But tonight... I crossed it. And gods, it felt good. Too good."

My hands slide down the hard lines of his thighs, holding him steady on me. His head bows until his forehead rests against my shoulder, his confession barely a ghost of sound over the quiet lap of water.

"I could have gone deeper," he breathes. "I wanted to. Wanted to own every mind in that chamber. To make them all move as one, bend until they broke. And for a moment..." His fingers tighten on my neck, not in pain but in fear. "For a moment, I didn't care if it was right."

I smooth the damp hair from his brow, my voice quiet, steady. "But you *did* stop. That matters, Cay. You know the difference between using power and being consumed by it."

His golden eyes lift to mine again, close enough that I feel the heat of his breath against my mouth. "You trust me not to become like him?"

My answer is immediate. "I trust you with everything I am, mo ghràdh."

Something inside him eases — the iron set of his shoulders loosens, the storm in his eyes calms. Then he kisses me, slow and deliberate, a vow pressed against my mouth.

And for a moment, the day is forgotten — my gripes about failing as a dragon, his hunger for something more, both drowned beneath the heat of this room. There is only skin and breath and the quiet way we find each other again after so much battle.

I rise from the bath with him in my arms, steam trailing from our skin as we cross the stone floor. The furs are warm, soft underfoot, and I lower him onto them with care, as though he might shatter if I let him go too soon.

And then there is no space between us.

Our mouths find each other like a promise and a punishment, teeth catching, lips bruising. His hands roam over me, desperate, claiming, and mine answer in kind — tracing the lines of muscle, the dips of his ribs, the sharp edges of his hips. We roll together across the furs, the heat of the chamber nothing compared to the heat between us.

It is messy and wordless, our breath coming in gasps, our bodies straining like we are trying to erase the distance the war has carved into us. When my nails bite into his shoulders, he groans into my mouth, and when his teeth graze my neck, I arch against him until the pressure building in me. It is messy and wordless, our breath coming in gasps, our bodies straining like we are trying to erase the distance the war has carved into us. My nails dig into his shoulders, leaving crescents that rise red against his skin. He groans into my mouth, the sound vibrating through me, and I drag him closer until there is no space left between us.

His hands roam with unrestrained hunger, mapping every line of me as though re-learning a favorite weapon. I feel the scrape of his teeth at my jaw, then my throat, sharp enough to make me gasp. He nips, soothes the bite with his tongue, and I shiver as if struck.

We roll again, the furs tangling around our limbs, his body pinning mine to the floor for one breathless, perfect moment. My back arches, meeting him in a rhythm that builds with every shift of his hips. There is nothing gentle about it—this is not worship but a claiming, a desperate need to feel alive, to feel each other.

"Look at me," he rasps, voice rough and frayed, and I do. His eyes blaze gold, wild and reverent all at once. He holds me there as though daring me to look away, to break this fragile, blistering tether between us. I am lost in his eyes, caught in the molten gold that reflects every raw thought he isn't saying aloud. He is just as lost — his breath stuttering, his lips parted, his expression undone. Our cocks slide against one another, hard and aching, slick with heat. The friction is maddening, driving me closer, until I can barely remember where I end and he begins.

We move together in a rhythm that feels older than either of us, hips rolling, thighs flexing, our hands everywhere — in hair, on shoulders, gripping and clutching like we could hold this moment in place if only we pressed hard enough. His teeth catch my jaw, my throat, and I gasp, my head tipping back as the pleasure punches through me, sharp and bright.

The glow of the chamber catches on our damp skin, turning sweat into molten light, painting us in shifting shades of gold and rain-soaked silver. His hand cups my face, forcing me to look at him even as the tension winds tight in my belly.

"Don't look away," he rasps, voice frayed, and I don't. I *can't*. The bond between us hums like a drawn bow, pulling tighter, closer, until every pulse of blood feels like it might snap us into place.

When release takes me, it is with a cry that echoes off the stone, my body arching as my vision whites out. His follows a breath later, a low groan torn from his chest as he shudders against me, spilling hot between us. For a moment we are nothing but heat and light and the thunder of our hearts, the world beyond the chamber forgotten.

He collapses against me, both of us shaking, chests heaving, the aftershocks rippling through us like rain across still water. I thread my fingers through his hair, feel the wet strands catch against my knuckles, and pull him closer until there is no space left between us.

We curl together on the furs, sweat cooling on our skin, our legs tangled, his forehead pressed to mine. The faint glow of the sconces catches in his lashes, and I know that when I close my eyes, I'll feel this moment humming through me — not just the relief of release, but the truth that we are closer now, closer to snapping into place, closer to being whole.

And as sleep drags at me, I know this is not the night he lost himself — this is the night he chose me, chose us, and let me see every shadow and every flicker of light inside him

Jethro

POWERS NOT ACCEPTED

As the fae gathered on the mountain plains, a bitter taste filled my mouth as I watched Lia's presence among them. Her mere existence seemed to taint the air, casting a shadow over the solemn scene. I stood back, seething with resentment at the sight of her standing alongside Olivia, her expression unreadable.

Despite the gravity of the situation, Lia exuded an air of indifference that grated on my nerves. It was as if she thought herself above it all, untouched by the turmoil that surrounded us. Her disinterested gaze swept over the gathered fae, a stark contrast to the genuine concern etched on the faces of those around her.

I trust you, Caomh's voice intruded on my thoughts, drawing my attention to his side where Lorkan stood. I clenched my fists, suppressing a growl of frustration at the sight of Lia lingering nearby. We exchanged a tense glance, silently acknowledging the weight of the decision we had made to lead the groups with her.

Jeyr moved gracefully through the ranks, his easy charm and genuine empathy a stark contrast to Lia's aloof demeanor. Despite his reluctance to embrace his royal title, he commanded respect with his natural charisma. Olivia's gaze followed him, a small smile playing on her lips. She caught me watching her, and I felt her try to soothe the itchiness that was riding inside me. But one glance at the woman beside her had me forcing myself to tear my gaze away from Lia, unable to stomach the sight of her any longer. She was a constant reminder of everything I despised about this war, a symbol of the chaos and uncertainty that plagued our world. And as the Fae prepared to embark on this perilous journey, I couldn't shake the feeling that Lia's presence would only lead to further destruction.

"I know you do, Cao. I'll get everyone there, one sign that she steps out of line, I will end her," I muttered through gritted teeth, my frustration boiling beneath the surface.

Caomh nodded, his gaze meeting the Princess of Puinnsean. "Cay, give her a chance. The dragons trust her," Lorkan's voice interjected, his attempt to soothe us met with skepticism.

"I thought you said that big black-scaled bastard was mean. Why should we trust him?" Caomh shot back, unable to conceal the bitterness in his tone.

Lorkan laughed, "I also know a prickly bastard who has asshole tendencies, and I trust him in my bed," he quipped.

Despite myself, I couldn't help but crack a smile at Lorkan's remark. Our once silent brother was starting to show his real colours now that he had who he wanted by his side. But as the weight of Lia's presence hung heavy in the air, I couldn't shake the feeling of unease that gnawed at my gut. Whether we liked it or not, Lia was here to stay, and only time would tell what consequences her presence would bring.

Olivia's calls cut through the air, her voice steady as she orders the groups into lines. Nervous glances pass through the ranks, tension like a pulled bowstring. I find my way to Lia despite myself, my boots crunching on the gravel as I close the distance.

She stands there, arms loose at her sides, watching the Fae with that maddeningly blank face. When one of the younger warriors stumbles into place, her lip curls, and—gods—she actually rolls her eyes.

"At least try to make them feel like they aren't marching to their deaths," I snap, my voice low but sharp enough to cut.

Her head tilts, eyes gleaming, unbothered. "What, you want me to coddle them? Pretend they're my friends?" Her tone drips with sarcasm. "Sorry, Jethro, I don't perform well for audiences."

My jaw grinds. "If you so much as breathe wrong—"

She cuts me off with a lazy flick of her hand. "You'll gut me, slit my throat, cut off my head like a snake," she recites, her voice flat but mocking. "We've established this part already."

My glare doesn't waver. "Glad we're on the same page."

Then she does the one thing I don't expect—she steps closer. Her hand finds mine, warm, sure. My stomach knots at the contact, an unwelcome jolt that ripples down my arm. I hate that my pulse jumps.

"We need the connection," she says simply, no bite to her tone now, just quiet certainty.

The first group joins hands. Power surges, smooth and cold, coiling around my own like a leash. My breath shortens, the world bending under the weight of it—and then the ground rips away.

The landing hits hard, gravel biting into my palms as I catch myself. The air here is alive, thick with pine, with flowers, with the bite of fresh water and herbs. All around us, Fae stand stunned, blinking up at the towering tree-lodges, the light slanting down like gold.

Hecate waits at the treeline, patient as a statue. "Go to Hecate," I call out, gesturing the Fae forward. "She'll tell you where you're sleeping tonight."

They move slowly, murmurs rising in a hush. No one thanks Lia. No one even looks at her.

She doesn't move to follow them. For a heartbeat she just stands there, face tipped toward the night sky. And then—damn me—I see it. Her hand lifts, brushing her cheek, and for a fraction of a second I swear I see the wet track of a tear in the glow of the lantern light.

I tear my gaze away, fury boiling in my chest, not at her, but at myself. At the fact that I noticed. At the fact that some quiet, buried part of me wants to know what could make a woman like her cry.

The landing knocks the breath from my chest, but this time the ground beneath us is soft—springy moss and wild grass that glow faintly under the early starlight. The scent hits me next: salt air, blooming night-flowers, the sweetness of fruit heavy on unseen branches. This is no hollow chamber carved from rock. This is a living sanctuary.

The last of the refugees stumble to their feet around us, murmurs rising as they take it in. Towering trees rise in spirals toward the sky, their leaves shimmering with soft gold light. Vines drape like ribbons over boughs, heavy with blooms. Pools of crystal water glitter where moonlight touches them, fed by streams that sing over the stones.

Beside me, Lia straightens, her glow matching the soft illumination of the land she's made. She looks... otherworldly. I force my gaze away, angry at myself for even noticing her beauty in this moment. Angry that I feel it at all.

"You need to rest," I say, the words rougher than I intend.

She scoffs, but her shoulders sag a little. "Look who's talking," she tosses back, and I catch the faintest tremor in her fingers.

"Commander Jethro." A voice draws my attention—Liza, a half-light Fae with soil still on her palms, bows her head. "There is food and water prepared. Please take strength before you winnow again."

I nod, accept her offered hand, though my legs are steady enough. My eyes pull back to Lia despite myself. She stands apart from the others, alone, while every pair of eyes in the clearing lands on her. No one approaches. None offer the same kindness they do me.

Her chin lifts, proud as ever, but there's something brittle in it this time. "I'm going back," she says, voice low but carrying. "I'll see you soon, Commander."

The title lands heavy in my chest. Before I can reply, she's gone, vanishing into air and light, leaving nothing but a ripple of magic that stirs the moss at my feet.

The Fae around me shift, whispering. I drag a hand over my jaw, shove down the feeling gnawing at my ribs. I told Caomh I'd slit her throat if she so much as looked treasonous, and yet—gods help me—I hate the way it feels, watching her vanish alone, unwelcome even here.

I turn away before the feeling can root itself too deep. There are orders to give, mouths to feed, things to do—anything to scrub her from my thoughts. But as I follow Liza toward the tables set beneath the fruit trees, I know it won't work. Lia's shadow follows me even here, in this impossible place of light and abundance.

Lia

THE ONE THEY HATE

Nausea rolls through me in hot and cold waves as we land, the world tilting before it rights itself beneath my boots. Somehow, I manage to stay upright, landing with a grace I didn't think I still possessed. I force my expression into something cool, unreadable—because apparently my particular brand of unhinged frightens people. Anything I do does, no matter what I do, I am still like the King, created by my father.

The voices clamor at the edges of my mind, but I shove them back, walls slamming into place. I cannot let them see me falter, cannot let them smell the weakness on me. They think I am powerful. Fine. I will be. It's the last weapon I have left.

No one thanks me. They never do.

Why do I even crave it?

Why does my chest twist when I watch the others—when I see the grateful glances tossed toward the Companachs, the light master, the mind master? They command, they lead, they are touched without fear, smiled at without hesitation. Even Caomh, whose relationship with Olivia frays at times, still checks her well-being with the devotion of someone who would burn the world if she asked him to.

"Where is he?" Caomh's sharp voice slices through the clearing, all warning and fire.

I roll my eyes, bite down hard against the back of my teeth to keep from spitting something truly cruel. "He was tired from all the winnowing," I say, spinning to face him. "The Fae wanted to feed him before he winnows back."

"If you're lying—"

"Yeah, yeah," I snap, cutting him off, "you'll make sure I burn at the stake like the illegal I am." The words are acid, but they hit their mark. His jaw locks, golden eyes sparking.

If he didn't belong to the shifter, I might have regretted saving him. Then again, Lorkan might be an ass sometimes, but at least he isn't cruel.

Movement catches my eye—Olivia parting from her mate, starting toward me—but I shake my head before she can open her mouth. Let her stay where she is. I'm not worth the whispers she'll earn for trying to bridge the chasm between us. She doesn't need my kind of misery. The kind where every look brands you dangerous, contagious, a wretch to be avoided.

I turn my back on them all and make for the ridge where the dragons rest.

Faldr and Elduin are locked in sleep, their massive sides rising and falling with each rumbling breath. Beyond them stands Lumirwen, quiet and watchful. She tilts her head as I approach, and for a heartbeat, I swear there's recognition in her silver-flecked eyes.

She exhales warm breath across me in greeting. Something in my chest aches.

"Not now, Lumirwen," I mutter, turning away from her nudge. My voice is tight, brittle.

She doesn't press. Just stands there, silent and patient as I pace to the edge of the cliff. The mountains stretch forever, endless and indifferent. My fists clench so hard my nails dig into my palms.

It's too much.

A scream tears out of me before I can stop it, raw and ugly, ripping from somewhere deep. It echoes back from the peaks like a chorus, mocking me. Lumirwen startles, takes a half step back, but I am already moving—running, boots skidding over rock as if I can outrun the clawing, festering thing in my chest.

I run until my lungs burn, until the tears streaking my face mix with the rain that begins to spit from the sky. Until my legs buckle and I collapse to my knees, chest heaving, throat raw. Was this all that was waiting for me beyond the prison walls? More Hate, a torment that is totally different from the physical shit they did to me. There I lived with hate, hate for my torturers, now? It was like I was walking in a world where *I* was the one people hated. Like I cut them tens of thousand ways to discover their secrets.

Lumirwen finds me there, quiet as a shadow. She lowers her massive head until her eyes are level with mine, and I crumble the rest of the way, pressing my forehead against her warm scales.

"Take me away," I whisper, voice shaking. "Anywhere but here."

She lowers herself in answer, and I climb onto her back with shaking hands. Then her wings unfurl, catching the wind.

We launch.

The ground falls away in a rush, the camp, the war, the whispers shrinking to nothing below us. The wind bites at my wet face as we climb higher, higher, until the mountains are only dark teeth against the horizon.

And then the sky opens.

The northern lights flare, ribbons of green and violet and silver sweeping across the heavens. They paint Lumirwen's scales in wild, shifting colors as we soar through them, a kaleidoscope blazing above and below.

For the first time in what feels like forever, the voices go quiet.

I cling to her back and let myself breathe, let the beauty of the world wash over me. The loneliness is still there, the ache, but it feels lighter somehow—like the wind is carrying a little of it away with every beat of her wings.

For a few precious moments, I let myself believe there is still something worth saving in this broken world.

The night is velvet-black, the stars sharp enough to cut. I curl into Lumirwen's side, her scales warm beneath me, the steady rise and fall of her breathing rocking me as sleep begins to creep in.

It feels almost sacrilegious—this peace.

I drink in the night sky as if it is a luxury I'm not supposed to have, my eyes tracing constellations I never saw from the confines of my cell. In those endless days, I used to dream of the stars—of a moon that was more than a rumor, of skies that weren't black stone above me. The stars were freedom then, the promise of something beyond the walls that caged me.

Now they stretch above me, endless, brilliant, a gift I hardly know how to hold. My chest aches with it. Not sadness. Not despair. Gratitude—so sharp it burns my throat.

For the first time in too long, I dare to imagine something past the pain. A future. A tomorrow that is not merely survival. And when I think of Lumirwen's loyalty, of Olivia's stubborn, unshaken belief in me, I know I cannot give in yet. Not when they have chosen to stand with me.

Sleep takes me at last.

But it is not peaceful for long.

A sound ripples through the air—low, steady, rhythmic. Like the strange drums some of the Fae use in their celebrations, except this sound carries no joy. It snaps me awake, heart pounding, every muscle tense.

Lumirwen is already alert, her wings flaring slightly, the glow of her eyes cutting through the night.

Swarm.

Her voice thrums through my mind like a bell, sharp enough to rattle my bones.

Cold dread lances through me.

Swarm of what? My thoughts are frantic, reaching for hers. *Who is coming? Should we wake the others?*

Another voice answers instead—my own, cruel and cold. *Why warn them? Do they warn you when they spit their curses behind your back? When they whisper that you are a monster in a pretty cage?*

I clutch at my head, nails biting into my scalp, trying to block it out. The chorus in my skull rises, hissing, snarling, dragging me toward that familiar pit of darkness.

Lumirwen doesn't wait.

My breath is ripped from my lungs as she surges forward, leaping from the cliff edge and snapping her wings open.

The wind tears at me, threatening to rip me away, but talons rip through my fingertips and I dig them into her scales, anchoring myself as best I can. The air is icy against my skin, my eyes stinging as tears—gods, real tears—stream back over my face.

I risk a glance over my shoulder.

The horizon is black. Not with night, but with movement.

The world tilts as dread pours through me. My power lashes outward, tasting the minds in that oncoming wave—and recoils.

The King's beasts. His soldiers. His hounds.

They have found us.

Olivia

Not Ready

I shoot upright, breath ragged, the shiver of dread crawling beneath my skin. Sleep flees as if it never touched me. My heart thrums like a war-drum, loud enough that I swear Jeyr must hear it.

"Hummingbird?" His voice is thick with sleep, groggy, yet already his arm reaches, pulling, trying to draw me back to the shelter of his body. His lips press to my brow, warm and steady. "What's wrong?"

But this isn't a dream. Not one of the terrors that haunt me. This is real. Too real.

I tear from his arms, scrambling, hands clumsy on the buckles of my armor. Leather straps slip, metal clasps bite at trembling fingers. Kyzan rises too, his hackles lifting, a low growl vibrating through the stone chamber. He paws at the door, desperate, sensing the danger before words can shape it.

"Olivia." Jeyr's voice sharpens, commanding now, the softness burned away. He swings out of bed, already dragging on his shirt, his eyes piercing through the half-light of the cavern.

I close my own, pulling in a breath, forcing the trembling in my hands to still. My power stretches, ribbons of thought unfurling into the cavern, brushing against dragons, wyverns, Fae alike. My silent warning threads through their minds: *be ready, be armed.* The ripple comes back to me—fear, disbelief, but also the heavy pulse of resolve.

When I open my eyes, Jeyr is already armored from the waist up, his composure the steel edge I cling to. He buckles his vambraces without looking down, his gaze locked on

me.

"How many?" His tone does not waver.

"I—I can't tell." My throat tightens around the admission, tears threatening to burn. Not now. Not when they need me steady.

He steps close, close enough that his breath brushes my cheek. His fingers catch my chin, tilting it so I cannot look away. His voice is soft, but unbreakable. "Look at me. We're as ready as we'll ever be. Together."

The word clings, fragile and fierce. *Together.*

The confession slips from me before I can stop it. "I don't want to lose you." Barely a whisper, torn from the deepest part of me.

His arms fold around me, armor hard but embrace unyielding. "You won't," he vows against my hair, though the echo of his own fear slips through the cracks. "Not again. Not ever."

The swell of his anxiety pulses through me—his guilt, his near-breaking from every moment he's already lost me. But beneath it is something stronger. A vow. A vow he will not let fracture.

His hands find mine, halting my clumsy armor-work. "Here," he murmurs, fastening each buckle with deliberate care. The surety in his touch is steady, protective. So different from the hands that once forced armor upon me in another court, under another's gaze. Those hands had been predatory, cold. Jeyr's are fierce but gentle, securing not only my body but my soul.

When the last strap tightens, his blue gaze lingers, fierce as a blade, tender as a kiss. His lips find mine, not in parting, but in promise. Not a goodbye, but a vow.

We'll get through this.

I only pray my luck has not run out.

The mountain plain is alive with motion, a thousand small sounds weaving together into one tense symphony—footsteps crunching on rock, armor snapping into place, the deep hiss of wyverns shifting their massive weight. The air is tight with urgency, and beneath it all I can feel it—the rising tide of fear, bitter and metallic on my tongue.

"Assemble the archers on the eastern ridge!" My voice cuts through the clamor, ringing across the narrow pass. Fae scatter to obey, their determination hardening as they take position. Beside me, Jeyr stands like an anchor, his hand brushing mine briefly as if to remind me that we are still here, still breathing, still fighting. His blue eyes never leave the horizon.

Something brushes against my senses, a pulse of power like the prickle before lightning strikes. My breath catches. "Lia. Lumirwen. They're close."

Fae glance skyward at my words, and whispers ripple like wind through grass. Then she appears—Lumirwen, a flash of white and silver as she dives through the clouds, her wings sending dust spiraling into the air as she lands. Lia dismounts, white hair catching the dim light, her presence sharp and unyielding.

Caomh's voice erupts before anyone can speak, his fury a blade slicing the air. "This is your doing, Lia! You go for a mystery flight and the fucking kings army is at our doorstep!"

I move forward, my hands half raised. "Caomh," I say sharply, my words clipped to keep them steady. "Not now. The enemy is coming. It's a coincidence"

He doesn't back down, golden eyes blazing. "Coincidence?" His lip curls. "There is no such thing."

Jeyr's hand slides into mine, his presence pulling me back from snapping. But I can feel his conflict too—his loyalty to me battling his loyalty to his brother.

And then the sound comes, low at first, then growing until it shakes the very mountain under our feet. A steady, ominous rhythm. The beat of wings.

Every head turns. Every breath stills.

On the horizon, a line of black begins to form, thick as smoke. *The swarm.*

Caomh rounds on Lia again, but his voice breaks on her name. "If I lose my mate because of you—" His words turn raw, jagged. "I'll spend every breath I have making you pay." His finger juts out to Lia, who swallows and nods. Her emotions just as raw as she drags her eyes away and looks to the oncoming battle.

I feel the sharp ache of it in my chest, an echo of something I know too well. Fear, not for himself but for the one person who means more to him than life.

Lorkan moves then, his hand catching Caomh's arm. "Cao," he says softly, his voice rough.

Caomh's golden gaze finds his, and the snarl fades from his mouth. He grabs Lorkan's face between his hands, desperate, almost feral. "You fight with me, Mo Chuisle. You win with me. And when this is over—" His voice cracks, then steadies. "We stop pretending.

We stop running."

Tears streak Lorkan's face, and he kisses him, fierce and unrestrained. "I love you," he breathes against his lips. "You are my mate. We've been bonded since the day we met, whether we said it aloud or not."

Caomh lets out a strangled laugh, brushing his forehead to Lorkan's. "You say that now. Wait until we fuck"

"Make love," Lorkan corrects, his voice shaky but sure.

"Semantics," Caomh mutters, though the hint of a smile finally breaks across his face.

Jeyr steps forward then, his voice carrying over the mountain wind. "Caomh, you take Elduin. Olivia and I will ride Faldr. Lorkan, shift. Lia—Lumirwen is yours, prove that you didn't bring this fight to us. "

The orders ripple outward like stones thrown into a lake, and the wyvern riders surge into motion. The Fae without mounts rush to the cliffs, bows strung, their faces pal, eyes frantic at the black line closing in on us.

There is no escape route. No fallback plan. War is coming to us whether we are ready or not. And gods, what I could have done for more time.

"Ready, Hummingbird?" Jeyr's voice is quiet, meant for me alone. I nod, my throat too tight for words. My power stretches outward, touching every soul around us, lending them courage, quieting the sharpest edges of fear. I feel them steady, their resolve harden like steel.

"That's my girl," Jeyr murmurs, kissing my cheek before we mount Faldr.

Faldr's growl rumbles in my mind. *Stretch your reach, little queen. Make them falter.*

My ribbons of power shiver, straining as I push them toward the approaching enemy line. My bones ache with the effort, my breath hitching.

Again, Faldr snaps. *Harder.*

With Jeyr's hand at my waist, his power spilling into mine, I reach further—until my chest burns, until I taste blood at the back of my throat. The world narrows to ribbons of power lashing from me into the night. Rain sheets across the sky, hail slicing like knives, and exhaustion rolls over the enemy like a tide. For a single, suspended heartbeat—the tick of a grandfather clock—triumph sparks in my chest. The King's wyverns falter mid-flight, riders jerk in their saddles, some tumbling from the sky.

Then fire blooms.

A thousand blossoms of molten death erupt against the night, searing orange and gold. Explosions tear the air apart, lighting the world in stark, hellish flashes before plunging us into blackness again. The next blast hurtles straight for the mountain below our feet.

"Down!" someone roars—maybe Jeyr, maybe me—but it's too late for the first line.

Water-wielders throw up walls, stone rises in jagged shields, colors of magic glinting like stained glass as they collide—but the impact still lands. The mountain trembles as the first explosion hits. The ringing in my ears is so loud I can't tell if I'm screaming or not.

When the smoke clears, I look down—

And there is blood. And fire. And the broken bodies of our first defense.

Their emotions hit me like a blade to the chest, sharp and unbearable. Panic. Pain. The last clutching threads of fear as souls rip themselves from ruined bodies. A thousand voices wailing all at once, clawing at me, begging me to stay with them, to guide them through the dark.

For one aching moment, all I want is to be there—kneeling among them, holding their hands as they pass, whispering them into peace. I want to cradle them, to weep for them, to tell them they are not dying alone.

Focus, Queen, Faldr snarls in my head, the ancient dragon's voice a crack of iron. "No point saving the dead."

My nails bite into my palms. The words cut—but they're true.

I tear myself free of the threads of the dying, force my power outward again, vicious this time, slicing across the sky. The next wave of enemy wyverns staggers as I lash them with fatigue, draining every ounce of strength I can rip from their bones.

Jeyr's presence steadies me, pouring his storms through my veins. Lightning cracks across the sky, slamming into the front line of riders, thunder shaking the mountain.

But the fear—oh gods, the fear still presses in, whispering at the edges of my mind. The dead are calling for me, and the living are begging me not to fail.

And I can't.

Not now. Not ever.

"My power—" My voice breaks. "It's only holding them for seconds."

"Then buy us seconds," Jeyr growls, summoning a wind so fierce it shoves enemy ranks back through the air.

I throw my power forward again, slicing ribbons of pain through the enemy line, but it's like shoving against an invisible wall. I slam into it over and over until sweat runs down my spine.

"I can't get in!" My scream rips from my throat, ragged and furious.

"Neither can I!" Caomh's voice answers, a mix of rage and fear.

Someone is shielding them. Someone powerful. And suddenly, every one of my gifts feels like they've been stripped away.

"Don't falter yet, Hummingbird." Jeyr's words are soft but unyielding as he presses something into my hand. I look down to see the bow and arrow, his blue eyes fixed on mine.

"we find another way."

Caomh

NOT TIME FOR AN ANATOMY LESSON

It is chaos—an unrelenting tangle of wings, fire, and death.

I reach for my power, the way I've done a thousand times before, expecting it to flare hot and sure in my chest. Nothing. Not even a spark. My teeth grind together as I throw my shields out again, holding the army's minds from being seized by the bastards on the other side, but I can't push further. Can't command them, can't unleash hell like Olivia asked me to.

Every attempt at control is cut, severed before it can form. Someone is out there—stronger than me, blocking me on purpose—and rage bites hard at my ribs. I've trained for this, broken myself open to wield this power, and now I am nothing more than a wall. I can keep us standing, yes, but I cannot move us forward.

Useless. Gods-damned useless.

Elduin growls beneath me, golden scales flashing as he veers away from the fray no matter how hard I pull at his reins. He ignores me, charts his own path high along the mountain's spine, keeping us from the thickest part of the battle. I snarl, shoving the command harder into his mind—but the dragon shakes me off, the motion nearly throwing me. He knows better. Knows my head isn't steady enough to lead him where he needs to go.

Then—*Mo ghràdh.*

Lorkan's voice cuts through the haze, deep and steady, a lifeline I hadn't realized I was begging for. *Jump. I'll catch you.*

I don't think. I don't weigh the risk. I just pat Elduin once and leap into the open air. The wind tears at me, cold and vicious, before I crash onto Lorkan's back with a thud that rattles my teeth. He grunts—his irritation a flash through our bond—and I drag a hand over the slick stretch of his neck scales in apology.

Careful, love, his voice purrs through me, warm even as we're hurtling toward certain death. *Last thing we need is an anatomy lesson on how a dragon gets hard.*

The laugh punches out of me before I can stop it, loud and feral. "Later," I snarl, half threat, half promise.

He surges forward at my words, wings snapping wide as we dive together. And this—this is what it should feel like. Our minds link without effort, without hesitation. Every muscle in his massive body moves as if it is my own, and for the first time all battle, I am *in control.*

We become a weapon. He banks left and I know before he does it why—because three of the King's masked soldiers are waiting for an opening there. I strike with my mental power, shoving a pulse of disorientation through them long enough for Lorkan's tail to sweep and send two of them flying off the cliff.

Below us, the first line of Fae has found its footing again, the shock of their fallen brothers burning into resolve. Water surges, fire answers, and the mountain glows with the raw power of those still standing. They are no longer prey—they are wolves, and they will bite back.

The King's soldiers close ranks, their masks catching the light. No faces, no courts. No chance to know who I am about to kill. Cowards.

"You hide behind masks?" I snarl into the wind. "Fine. Then I'll show you how death wears a face."

Lorkan growls deep enough that it rattles my spine, then plunges us back into the fray, violet fire spilling from his jaws as we rip through the enemy ranks.

The first wyvern and rider come at us, the beast banking back to snatch at Lorkan with its talons. Instinct takes over. I launch from his back, steel flashing as I draw my longsword from my hip. One clean strike and the wyvern's head tumbles, its body plummeting from the sky. The light dies in its eyes as the Fae rider grabs at me in desperation.

We fall together, air roaring in my ears, his knife catching the dim light—then massive talons strike. A griffin. The screech splits the battlefield as claws crush bone, blood dripping before the Fae is flung away. My chest heaves as Lorkan sweeps under me, catching me with a bone-jarring thud.

Cay, how about you don't leap off me like you can fucking fly? I'd rather you not become a pancake, Lorkan snarls.

"Yeah, well, I prefer your esophagus attached," I snap back, fingers tightening around my bowstring.

He huffs, smoke curling, and dives again, claws raking riders from wyverns. My arrows cut through the chaos, dropping enemies before they can regroup. Screams ring in my head—ours and theirs. Some are falling. Some are dying. But the shield I'd held is no longer needed, and I force myself not to think of who I can't save.

Out of the corner of my eye, Lia blazes through the battlefield, griffin at her side, power sparking like wildfire.

"What the fuck happened?" Jet's voice tears through the storm, his face wild as Jorax wings beside us.

"Lia happened," I grit out, loosing another arrow. "She came back from whatever adventure she thought was worth it—and those things followed her."

Jet's eyes go black with fury. "Then leave her to her own defenses." He doesn't wait for my reply—just dives, light blazing from his palms as Fae burn in his path.

The clash surges around me, chaos made flesh. Wyverns shriek above, wings blackening the sky, while the Fae army lashes out with everything they have. Powers collide, a violent symphony—light, fire, ice, venom—each note striking against the stone gorges until the mountains themselves seem to tremble.

Jethro's light erupts in a blinding burst, searing the enemy ranks and forcing wyverns to wheel back with screams that split the night. Overhead, their shadows claw jagged shapes across the rock walls, turning the gorge into a shifting labyrinth of teeth and fire.

Beside me, Aella lifts her hands, and lightning answers her call. Bolts tear the heavens wide open, ripping through wings and bodies, her power scorching the dark sky silver.

We are hemmed in, funneled into the narrow passageways of the mountain, every strike demanding precision. The walls leave no room for error. Talons scrape, blades clash, wyverns barrel through with fire boiling in their throats. But still—we hold.

Ahead, Lia commands the front, balanced on her dragon's back as if the uneven scales and violent bucking of battle mean nothing. Fire spits from Lurenan's jaws, sweeping across the gorge. And her griffin—summoned from gods know where—tears through riders, scattering them like leaves in a storm.

Her barrage of powers whips through the air, shifting seamlessly—earth to flame to wind to ether. Devastating. Terrifying. Useful. And yet fury gnaws at me. Reckless. She brought this fight to our doorstep. Even if her beast just saved my life.

Our riders surge forward, using her as a shield. I catch faces in the chaos—Aiden at the front, fire in his grin, fire in his hands. He winks, the cocky bastard, giving me the barest bow before spurring his wyvern back into the fray.

Through it all, Feldr roars. Jeyr and Olivia thunder down the gorge astride him, towering above even the largest wyverns. Olivia's eyes are sharp, scanning, searching for the one suppressing our power. She won't stop until she finds them.

And then—pain. Not mine. Lorkan's.

He falters beneath me, the echo stabbing my ribs. My heart lurches as I spot the arrow lodged between his scales. Gods. I hadn't even seen it strike. My hands tremble as I reach for it, terror clawing up my throat.

"Mo Chuisle." My whisper barely makes it past the roar of battle.

Pull it out, Lorkan orders, steady, unyielding.

I brace myself, grip the shaft. Silent thanks to the gods—it isn't barbed. With one wrench, it slides free. Blood spills hot over my palms, searing me with the reminder of what I stand to lose.

I'm fine. Keep fighting, he growls, voice iron despite the wound.

I force my breath steady, shove the bloody arrow into my quiver. Look up. And my stomach shatters.

Jeyr is falling.

Olivia

CURSE THE FALL

He was just there.

He was just there.

The hand gripping my hip through the chaos vanishes, warmth ripped from me in an instant. I spin, my heart lurching—just in time to see a wyvern's talons clamp around Jeyr, lift him skyward... and then drop him.

"No."

My breath seizes as his body plummets, his wind answering but not strong enough to stop the descent. He's falling too fast.

"FALDR!" The scream tears from me, raw with terror.

On it. The dragon's reply is sharp steel in my mind.

Faldr dives. Cliff faces blur past in jagged streaks, the rush of air like knives against my skin. My stomach flips as rocks scatter below, the earth racing up to claim Jeyr. All I can hear is the ringing in my ears, the thunder of my pulse, the sound of my mate groaning through the bond. His pain. Gods, his pain.

Faldr banks hard, a jolt slamming me forward on his back. "Jeyr!" I cry, again and again, voice breaking. His groans echo through the bond, guttural, alive—but slipping. Is this what he felt every time *I* was the one bleeding, broken, close to death?

I have him. Shut up and stay put. Faldr snarls through my mind.

But I can't see him. He's so close, yet I can't *see* him, can't touch him. The bond sears, flooding me with his agony. I hate this. I hate being helpless.

Arrows whistle past. My head snaps up. A horde of wyverns close in, riders already loosing their bows.

Down, Queen! Faldr's command cuts through panic, and I flatten against his scaled hide, air burning my face.

But Jeyr. Jeyr. His name beats through me like a war drum.

I lift my head just enough to see. Power surges out of me, sharp and merciless, targeting the rider drawing his bow. His scream cuts the air as he writhes, toppling from his wyvern. Satisfaction burns hot and fleeting.

Faldr lashes his tail, cracking into the nearest wyverns. Their cries split the gorge—before a second roar, deeper, older, answers. My head jerks back to see Lumirwen streaking from the sky, Elduin on her wing. Riderless, furious, Elduin rips through the enemy rear with a bite that snaps bone. Gore rains down. I look away, bile rising, forcing myself to focus.

Then—Lia. Balanced atop Lumirwen as if standing on flat ground instead of shifting scales, her griffin tearing Fae from the sky. She peels from the front to cover us, power blazing in every direction.

"Do you see him?" I scream across the wind, throat raw. Lia glances down, her white hair snapping like a banner. Her face twists. A nod—nothing more. Gods, it guts me. I could dive into her mind, rip the vision from her. But I know it'll break me. I don't dare.

Faldr climbs, wings hammering the wind, then veers hard into darkness. A cavern mouth swallows us whole. Fireflies spark like stars, their glow dizzying as we drop into a hollow heart of stone.

He lands with a quake, wings folding as he lays Jeyr out before me.

I'm on the ground in an instant, knees cracking stone as I drop beside him. My heart splinters at the sight—his skin ghost-pale, his gut bleeding freely, each cough wet with blood.

"If you die, Jeyr, I swear—I'll never forgive you. Heal yourself. Now." My voice breaks, command tangled with desperation as I seize his hand.

He manages a crooked grin before pain drags it away. Faldr's voice presses in: *Take his pain. Channel your power. Keep both lines open.*

The memory of what happened the last time I tried claws through me—but I shove it down. For him, I'll risk anything.

I clutch his hand tighter, drag his pain into myself, open the flood of my power back into him. "Pull, damn you. You said we were in this together—so *take it*. Heal yourself!"

At last—at last—I feel the tug. Hesitant at first, like honey sliding slow and reluctant. But he takes it. His eyes flicker, electric blue softening, shifting back to the aqua I first loved. Golden light threads his wounds, knitting them closed.

Relief chokes me.

"Not getting rid of me that easily, Hummingbird," he rasps, voice shredded but alive.

Tears sting my eyes. I press my forehead to his. "I'd fight the gods themselves to keep you. We haven't even had a human lifetime yet."

He winces as he sits, his palm cupping my cheek, eyes drowning me in everything he can't say. I kiss him, slow, deep, the panic bleeding out of me under the slide of his lips. "You scared me," I whisper against his mouth.

His head rests against mine, steady. Silent. *I know.*

But then Faldr intrudes, voice low, sharp: *I know you two are trying to reconnect. But my mate and child are out there, still fighting.*

The reminder cleaves through me. My heart screams to stay, to cling to this fragile peace—but the war waits. I nod, even as dread roots itself in my chest.

Because I know what I stand to lose.

BLOOD AND RETREAT

My heart hammers in my chest, each beat echoing the exhaustion dragging through my veins.

You have to stop using your powers, Lumirwen snaps, her command cutting sharp.

But what else do I have? The sword in my hand feels foreign, like it belongs to someone else. My powers are all I've ever had—too much of them, always too much—and now they're slipping through my grasp like water. I know I've burned too much since yesterday, but I can't stop. Stopping means dying.

Still, the battle is shifting. The sky, once thick with wings and fire, begins to clear. The King's wyverns peel back, shrieking as their riders wrench them into retreat. The cries of battle dull, leaving behind only the ragged sound of our warriors catching their breath. I can feel the disbelief ripple through our ranks, the tentative lift of hope.

"Good to see you alive," I manage when Jeyr reappears, Olivia clutched in his arms. Relief lances through me—relief I can't afford—so I mask it in a nod, my smile brittle. The suspicion in their eyes is heavier than any chain I've worn.

But even as I turn back to the sky, unease prickles along my skin. The wyverns are retreating too easily. Too soon.

"Surely it can't be over?" Olivia whispers, her words barely carrying over the wind. No one answers, because we're all thinking the same thing: it's never this simple.

Silence falls like a shroud over the gorge. No more cries. No more clash of steel. Just the hiss of wind through the peaks, too calm, too wrong.

Olivia's eyes flare gold as her magic stirs, searching the ridges. Her whole body goes still.

"Something isn't right," she murmurs, her voice a thread pulled tight.

Then her gaze locks on the shadowed mountain face across from us.

"Get the others out," she orders, calm but edged with urgency. "Winnow as many as you can to the safe house. **Now.** We'll hold them off."

Before we can question Olivia's orders, a horn blasts—low, guttural, and hauntingly familiar. The sound rips straight through my bones. A heartbeat later, the sky darkens with arrows, raining down in a merciless onslaught.

Panic tears through the ranks as wyverns shriek and tumble, their riders thrown screaming into the gorge below. The air fills with the stench of blood, the crunch of impact, the thunder of wings scattering. Our line scrambles, the order of battle dissolving into chaos.

Jethro streaks past on Jorax, light spilling from his hands in blinding bursts. Gravel edges his voice as he snarls to Olivia and Jeyr, then to me. "The first front was just to get close enough..." His eyes cut to mine, sharp as blades, and for one staggering moment I wonder if he'll simply end me here, let the arrows finish what he's always wanted.

His next words confirm it. "Once we get through this, you'll realize—the prison you came from before is nothing compared to what we will do to you to get information." His tone is venom, his promise iron.

The knife of his hate slides deep. No matter how hard I fight, no matter how much I bleed beside them, I will never be more than the monster in their eyes.

My head bows, shame burning my skin though I have nothing to be ashamed of. An arrow grazes my arm, hot sting blossoming as blood trickles down. I refuse to heal it. Let it mark me. Let them see what I choose. Because I do have a choice: save myself, and confirm their suspicions, or fight and fall proving them wrong.

I choose the latter.

Whispers slip into me—Olivia's mind, steady, commanding. *Withdraw. Get them to safety.* Her will unfurls through the ranks like a net. In my thoughts she plucks the image of Anam, as easily as lifting a painting from a rack, and presses it into the minds of those who can winnow. Across the mountains edges, Fae grasp hands, light flaring as they vanish in clusters. One after another, they disappear, leaving the wyverns to hold what ground remains, or scatter to find safety.

But the sky doesn't relent. More arrows descend, piercing scale and wing. The wyverns' roars turn into cries of agony, and the battlefield shrinks beneath the rain of death.

"Olivia!" Aella shouts, lightning sparking at her fingertips, panic sharpening her voice. "We must leave!"

Yet Olivia doesn't move. Doesn't yield. Her power thrums around us, steady as her voice. "I must retrieve them first."

Jeyr jerks his head toward her, his brow furrowed. "Retrieve who, hummingbird?"

Olivia's gaze cuts through the storm. "The empath," she says, resolute.

Olivia

NOT THE ONLY ONE

I should have seen it sooner. The pattern had been there all along, but the thought was too far-fetched, too impossible. How could anyone hope to turn armies when an empath shielded their emotions, smothered them into silence?

Wait... what? Caomh's voice cuts through the mayhem, his disbelief mirroring my own.

Arrows scream past us, a deadly rain slicing the storm-washed sky. Dragons and wyverns wheel frantically, wings clipping air so tight it thrums in my bones.

I'll explain later, I answer, urgency coiled in every word. *They are here. I can sense them.*

No—worse. I *can't*. They are absence. A hollow where my power should reach, her shield pushing me away.

My palm finds Faldr's scales. I pour the image into him, my vision of the void that gnaws at me. He grunts, power surging through the beat of his massive wings as he climbs higher. Jeyr clings to him, and I feel my mate's resolve press steady into mine, bracing me, fortifying me.

The horn blares again. My heart jolts as molten spheres launch from the cliffs. Fire splits the sky. Faldr tucks, veers, and the heat still scorches as it passes, singeing the air in our lungs. Below, a wyvern screams as it's torn from the sky, its rider burning before they hit the ground.

Focus, Queen! Faldr's roar slams through me, the weight of his command dragging me back to the moment.

Go! I hurl the thought outward, pulling every tether of power I have to rally them. *We'll retrieve the empath. Get the others to safety.*

We're not leaving you! Jet's fury lashes across the bond like a whip. *Not now. Not for her.*

He's right, Caomh echoes, grim and steady. *We all go to Anam together.*

They'll be safe, Hummingbird, Jeyr's voice wraps around me. Rain answers his call, sheeting down in torrents, cloaking us from sight, dulling the fire overhead.

But I feel it—the hum of power gathering, sharp and hungry. Shadows pulse with enemy energy as Faldr drives us toward the mountainside. The closer we get, the louder it grows, like static clawing against my skull.

It's a trap, I whisper to myself. Too late. The shield is working against me, hiding dozens—hundreds—of Fae in the rocks above.

Faldr roars, arrows biting into his hide, and Jeyr tears free, sliding along his spine to press his glowing palms against torn flesh. My chest clenches at the sight, at the quiet ferocity in him as he heals mid-flight.

I can smell it now, Faldr's voice cuts through the storm, low and grim. *Its bloodline is faint. But tainted.*

Before I can ask, he dives, talons shearing through a wyvern rider, his roar shaking the stone cliffs. The army scatters, but not far enough. Their weapons catch the light, and still they come.

The disturbance calls to me, a beacon pulling on the marrow of my bones. My own power thrums alive, a recognition I can't deny. I feel Jeyr's body tense behind me, his anticipation matching my own.

Thump.

Thump.

Thump.

The sound grows louder, reverberating through the cavern that opens before us. Each beat pounds like a countdown, every pulse of air feeding the dread coiling tighter in my chest.

Thump.

Thump.

Thump.

And then—there. A shield, familiar as breath, forged of silence. The same armor I once wore to bury what I felt, leaving nothing but a void.

Firelight flickers ahead, throwing shadows over stone. A figure waits, seated in the dark. Their eyes snap open, golden fire catching mine.

"Hello empath, I have been waiting for you."

Caomh

STOLEN TO DEATH

Rain hits like knives. My hands keep sliding on Lorkan's scales no matter how hard I clamp down. He shifts under me, steady as he can make it, breath going tight with the effort it takes to hold this new shape.

"Can someone tell Jeyr to turn the goddamn tap off?" I snarl into the whiteout, scanning for anything moving that wants us dead.

Lorkan just grunts. Not his chatty mood. He hasn't had this form long and it's chewing through him.

"Lorkan, I can find another way if you need to shift," I say, trying to keep it even.

I'm fine, he bites back. The quiver under the words says otherwise.

I push power toward him—meet a wall. "Let me help you."

I said, I'm fine. Final. Door shut.

I swallow the argument. Not the time. Not when the sky is spitting steel.

Lia flashes past on her dragon, scales throwing light, banking hard to miss a lombard shot by a hair. My patience snaps.

"Lia, you could help for once and use all that power of yours," I bark, jabbing a hand at the mess above.

She turns, eyes dark as fresh ink. "For once? Help yourself, mind master—if that's what you think." Venom, clean and sharp.

Lightning hits a lombard a breath later. It detonates. Rock rains down the mountainside.

Aella knifes by on her wyvern, circling once as she throws Lia a look. "That's how you work with a team, princess." Then she's pushing forward again, Aiden on her flank, fire bright in his palms as they arrow for the enemy massing at the pass.

"Any news on Olivia and Jeyr?" I shout to Jethro. His hand glows hard as he bats aside incoming shafts like they're gnats.

"Radio silent," he calls back. "All we can hope is they come out of that cave soon. I'm still drained from the winnowing. If I'm going to get us back, I need to hold what I've got."

A curse burns my tongue. If Lorkan would let me bolster him, maybe I could save enough to pull us all out. But he's stubborn—and right now, that stubborn keeps us airborne.

Jethro's gaze slices past me, goes flint. "Shit."

"What?"

"There's a whole army heading for the cave Olivia and Jeyr entered."

"Of course there is." My jaw locks. "Right. Everyone—get your wyverns to drop you. Looks like we're going old school."

Into the mouth of it, then.

I pat Lorkan's neck. "Once you drop me, shift to something that won't tear you apart and let's end them."

I can't, he says after a breath.

The word hits like a fist. "Why not? If you're not by my side, I can't protect you."

I don't have enough to shift back, he admits. *I either stay like this or lose my abilities.*

I choke down another curse. "Let me help you."

I... He stops, breath rough. Then, steadier: *No. You need that power so we can jump to safety. Jeyr's hurt and recovering. Lia's burnt out. Jet's burnt out. I don't know if Aiden, Aella, and Colden can make the jump—especially while they're burning through it right now. All we have is you. You're the only one with enough in reserve to get us out.*

He's right. For once, the thing that used to make me feel like not-enough makes me the piece that matters. I want to pour into him anyway—can't. Not if I plan on hauling what's left of us home.

I nod—he feels it in the way my weight settles. He banks toward the mountains to drop me near the cave mouth. I clock the line coming for it and feel my lip curl.

They're wrong. Humanoid, sure—but the canines are too long, the frames too big, the eyes all wrong. Silent as they move. Their smiles say they want the taste of us.

"Look, I'm all for someone wanting to consume me," I mutter, "but that kind of consumption is off the table."

Lorkan huffs, then peels away to draw fire. I hit the rock hard, roll, come up with steel in hand. Footsteps close in—Aella at my right, Jethro to my left, Colden and Aiden fanning wide. Lia is nowhere.

Answer enough.

Colden slides in front, palm up. "Brave fucker," I say, half under my breath, as spears of ice slam out from him—clean, fast, wicked. They punch through the front line—bodies stagger, impaled—and the bastards laugh, yank the ice free. Black blood slicks and dries in an instant.

Colden snarls, flicks fingers. Frost climbs their legs, locks boots to stone.

"Do that again," Aella snaps.

He doesn't even look at her. The freeze doubles down. Aella lifts her arm and calls the sky. Bolts slam into frozen torsos, crackling white.

They smile.

The light pours into them. Skin drinks it. Eyes light up with stolen shine.

"That does not look good," Aiden says, tone flat.

"You think?" I draw my sword up, settle my stance.

A breath of white shifts against the cliff. A shape resolves where there should be stone—Lumirwen, her scales a perfect match to the snow and granite. She had been there all along, waiting for the cue.

And then she's there—Lia. On her dragon, blade flashing like it was forged for her hand alone. Her beast banks low, pale hair and black leather streaking across the line as she slices through the first rank without hesitation. Quick. Ruthless.
Her griffin dives alongside, tearing a rider from his wyvern and dropping him like a broken toy.

Lumirwen positions her body to shield the worst of it, but the price is steep. White scales split red, her blood spattering the snow as she rips through the enemy.

"Fuck, we have to help them," I rasp, chest tight. Seeing a dragon bleed is enough to make bile rise in my throat—especially when my mate wears scales of his own.

Lorkan barrels toward her, talons wide, fury in every strike. I'm already moving, sword in hand, colliding with the nearest brute. Their strength is unnatural, every blow jarring my arm down to the bone. My elbow trembles, my wrist screams as I lock blades against him.

I go for the dagger. The one Lorkan pressed into my palm nights ago. I slam it upward, straight through the creature's chest. A roar tears free, and then—ash. He disintegrates into nothing, scattered on the wind.

I freeze, staring at the blade. Gods.

Lorkan's eyes meet mine for a heartbeat, and if dragons could smile, I'd swear he just did.

"Fucker even looks cute as a dragon," I mutter, clutching the dagger tighter. If this little relic can turn monsters to ash, then I'll be damned if I'm not glued to his side.

A cry tears through the din—Aella. She staggers, steel jutting from her ribs.

"Not happening," I snarl. Jeyr will never forgive me if we lose his sister.

I sprint, slam the dagger across a throat. Ash falls around her feet. Aella blinks at me, stunned, then breathes, "I want one of those."

"Not a chance," I grunt, bracing her as she finds her footing again. She can fry bastards with lightning. This dagger is mine.

"Are you two going to keep grinning, or maybe fight?" Colden snaps, ice already blooming at his fingertips.

"Sure, Colden," I shoot back. "I don't see you turning these ugly fuckers into ash."

And the pretty bastard smiles. A second later, a blade drives straight through his back. His gasp curdles my blood. The clang of swords and the shrieks of beasts dull to nothing. All I can hear is the wet choke in his throat, the sudden cough that sprays scarlet across his lips. His body jerks once, twice, and the sword slides deeper, the steel gleaming crimson as it pierces clean through.

"No—" I'm moving before I can think, dagger sinking into his attacker. Ash explodes.

Colden coughs, crimson spilling over his lip. Aella's scream rips the sky apart. For half a breath, he is still standing, blade raised, eyes sharp.

The world tilts.

"Colden!" I hear myself yell, but I am too far, too slow. His knees buckle. His hand loosens on his sword.

And then he falls.

He hits the ground hard, coughing blood, gasping as if air itself betrays him. The light in his eyes flickers, but he is still conscious, still aware enough to drag his gaze to us. Still fierce enough to speak, even as his life drains from him in thick, dark rivers of red.

"Don't just stand there—fight."

His words are broken, each syllable torn from him with unbearable effort. His breath rattles, blood staining his teeth. He is commanding us even as death takes him.

I drop to one knee beside him for the briefest moment. My hand twitches toward him, but I know—*gods, I know.* This wound is final. There is no healing this, no miracle, between the swords fatal strike and the poison flooding his system... His voice is already fading, the sound fraying at the edges. His body trembles once, then stills against the rock, though his eyes burn defiance to the very end.

I can't move. I can't breathe. My chest is stone, my throat raw with the scream I don't release.

I stagger back to my feet, sword trembling in my grip. I obey him. Because I owe him that much. Grief claws at me, raw and unrelenting, and for a heartbeat I almost let it pull me under. But then it hits—what this all means.

Olivia.

Her name flutters through my mind like a blade through silk, cutting straight to the truth I've avoided for too long. Colden—this man I left behind to a world of hell—took that torment and made it his own. And every damn step he took after, every scar, every breath, every fight... it was to keep her safe. To protect my sister when I couldn't.

The weight of it slams into me harder than any enemy's blade. He carried her survival in his hands, even when the world stripped everything else away from him. And now he's bleeding out on this cursed ground, giving the last of himself the same way he always did—without question.

My throat tightens, rage and grief coiling like a noose. I know, with a sick certainty, that Olivia will never see him again. She will never know the full measure of what he gave for her.

But I do.

And gods help me, I will carve it into the bones of every enemy on this field, so the world remembers his name.

Jethro is faltering under three opponents, and I throw myself into the fray beside him. My blade cleaves through one, the dagger Lorkan gave me burning hot in my hand as it turns another to ash. "Thanks, brother," Jet pants, his voice wrecked, before diving back into the melee.

Above us, Jorax and Thanos shriek their fury, ripping enemies apart with talons and teeth. Lia's griffin limps, injured but fighting, clawing enemies down despite the blood streaming from its leg. The battle rages, but every sound feels muted, wrong. Because Colden's dry humour will never ring out across these mountains again.

And in the corner of my vision—Lia. Bent double, clutching her abdomen, her sword slick with her own blood. She sways on her feet, too close to collapse, her power failing her. Two humanoids close in, grinning like wolves.

I move to strike, but Lorkan is faster, tearing through them, his scales dripping violet flame. He scoops her up, her body pressed against his chest, and roars as he carries her out of reach.

Relief punches through me, sharp and fleeting—because then cold steel kisses the side of my throat.

"Don't move that dagger," a gravelly voice hisses, low and familiar, and the world ices over once again.

Lorkan's roar answers, but I shake my head, desperate, pleading with him to stay back.

And then the voice slithers deeper, venom wrapped in words. *"Bane's daughter delivered you straight to me. Now I'll see what makes your mate bleed. I'll take him apart piece by piece, and you'll watch."*

I snarl, flipping the dagger, intent to kill—

—but another blade sings through the dark, and in a heartbeat it cuts straight across Lorkan's throat.

Time halts for the second time tonight.

His violet eyes go wide, full of shock. Blood gushes hot and fast, slick down his indigo scales. His wings falter. His roar breaks into silence.

I reach for him, hands going through empty air, the scream finally tearing free— but he is already falling.

Shifting midair, body snapping back to Fae form, limp, lifeless. His violet eyes roll back as he plummets into the abyss.

And with him—her white hair streaming like a banner of betrayal— she falls too.

I move, slicing the dagger into the person behind me, and I swear they chuckled as they disintegrated.

Olivia

THE MOCK WAVE

I stand frozen, breath caught in my chest, as my gaze locks with his.

Green eyes—my green eyes—mirror mine, sharp and knowing, but colder, emptier. His golden hair, shorn close to the scalp, gleams under the torchlight. His face is striking, almost human, but the aura that coils around him gives him away. Power. Ancient. Other. He radiates what I never could claim: He isn't human.

Half-breed, he says, voice low, smooth as cut glass. His frail frame doesn't match the disdain in his tone. In another world, maybe, without the King's leash around his throat, he could have been something else.

Empath, I answer, my voice steady though his scorn presses against me like iron weights.

You are a poison to our bloodline. A monster in our nature. His lips curl as the words slice through the air. I flinch, traitorous and small, and he sees it—he savors it.

Jeyr's hand slips into mine. His unease ripples down our bond, and for once, it steadies me. The other empath shifts his attention, his gaze raking over Jeyr with clinical malice.

Interesting. A healer and an empath. Once, you would have been a formidable pair. Now? Nothing but a disgrace. His voice drips with centuries of loathing. *I have watched kin fall. I have buried the ones who dared defy what we were meant to be. And you... you are their curse made flesh.*

I bite down on silence, waiting, listening.

I didn't believe them when they told me, he continues, bitterness threading every syllable.

I thought I could resist the dark. That I would not rot as the others had. That I would not wither into nothing. But then they brought me proof. They showed me you—the monster empath who can strip armies with a thought, who kills without care, who seeks to rule with fear. If seeing you was the price for freedom, I agreed. And when I am done, I will fulfill my sacred duty: to protect our people from you.

A laugh bursts from me, sharp and ragged, startling even myself. Maybe it's exhaustion. Maybe madness. Or maybe it's the only shield I have left. Jeyr squeezes my hand, wary, but I can't stop the hollow humor spilling out of me. *Do you know what's absurd? That this "monster ability" of mine is the very thing tearing down the tyrant who slaughtered your kin, my kin.*

His shoulders lift in a careless shrug. *The gods made us caretakers. Healers. That is our truth. Better to die true than live false.*

Better to die? I echo, tilting my head. *Then your gods have doomed us all. And what's your name, martyr?*

His lips part. Surprise flickers. *Gower. Marquis of Anam. Firstborn of the Queen's sister.*

Jeyr stifles a grin. I only smile faintly as I slip into his mind. His shields—thin mirrors of mine—crack like glass under my pressure. He realizes too late.

Good night, I whisper. And with one push, his mind folds. His eyes roll white, body collapsing against the granite floor like a puppet with its strings cut.

I glance at Jeyr. *Too harsh?*

His smirk is sharp enough to wound. *Not harsh enough. But gods, it makes me want to throw you to the floor right now.*

Later, I murmur, though my lips twitch. *Help me haul him out of here before his friends come looking.*

Together we lift him, lighter than he looks, his glow guttering like a dying flame.

Each step out of the cave feels like punishment, the echo of our boots on stone heavy with dread. The air outside is choked with smoke, the copper bite of blood so thick I taste it on my tongue.

Faldr's roar shatters the air. His great head whips toward the cliffs, pupils narrowing to slits as his mate thrashes, wings straining to leap after something beyond the ledge. My stomach drops.

Then I see it.

Lorkan.

His Fae form plummets, limbs loose, head lolling. And behind him—Lia, a pale streak of light diving after him.

"LORKAN!"

Caomh's cry tears free of him like it rips something vital from his chest. Gravel fills his voice, raw and jagged, and he lunges for the cliff before Jeyr tackles him, pinning him back by sheer will.

All around us, the battle rages. Jethro, Aiden, Aella—battered, bloodied, but unbroken—hold the line, their power flaring bright against the tide of humanoids. I snap, letting go of every restraint I had left. Pain floods outward from me in a torrent, ribbons of agony lashing through the enemy. One by one, they crumple where they stand, shrieking as my power crushes their will.

But it isn't enough.

"Get OFF me!" Caomh snarls, thrashing against Jeyr's grip. His eyes are wild, his body a bowstring ready to snap. "Give me a wyvern! A dragon! ANYTHING! I *have* to get to him!"

"Faldr," I whisper, my hand pressed to the dragon's hot scales. His massive form shudders, and with one mighty beat of his wings he launches skyward, leaving the ground a memory. He looks back once—at his mate, at his child—and then tucks his claws around Caomh, carrying him with terrifying speed down the cliff's face.

The fog parts beneath us.

And then—there they are.

Lorkan's body lies crumpled, Lia crouched beside him, her hands pressed hard to his neck. I can see her shoulders shaking even from here.

Faldr's voice rumbles through me. *We are done here, my Queen.*

"No—" My protest catches in my throat, but it's too late. He banks hard, carrying us away from the sight just as Bane emerges from the mist.

Bane's grin is carved from cruelty as he raises a gloved hand, mocking us with a lazy wave. His soldiers descend, shackles glinting. Lia screams and fights, throwing one guard back with a wild burst of power, but they are too many. They wrench her to her feet, bind her wrists, and haul Lorkan's limp body away like a prize.

Bane's arm slides over Lia's shoulders as though she's nothing more than a possession. He turns, dragging her with him, and vanishes into the fog.

Caomh's cry breaks then—raw, unhinged—and Faldr does not slow even as the sound of it cleaves the air.

When we land, there are no enemies left. No sound but the wind and the quiet sobbing of the survivors. Aella's eyes burn like twin suns, her lips bloodless. Aiden bows his head, and Jethro stands rigid beside him, his jaw clenched as if he could hold the entire world together by force of will.

And then—

I see Jeyr.

He's crouched on the blood-soaked ground, and my heart knows what I will see before I reach him. My hand flies to my mouth.

Colden.

Lifeless, sword still clutched in his pale fingers.

"No." The word is a gasp, a prayer, a curse.

I am running before I know I've moved, falling to my knees beside my best friend. His body is cool, his face eerily calm, as though he could wake at any moment and tease me for crying over him.

Jeyr's voice is hoarse. "I'm sorry, hummingbird. The blade was poisoned. There's nothing left for me to heal."

My fingers trace Colden's cheek, desperate to feel something—anything—of the power that had always steadied me. Nothing answers.

Memories claw up my throat: the man who stood by me through every dark hour, who dragged me out of hell the first time, who taught me how to breathe again. Gone.

Jeyr wraps himself around me, his body a cage as the sobs break free. "We will let him rest in Anam," he says against my hair, gentle but firm. "He wouldn't want you risking yourself for his body."

I nod against him because if I speak, I will shatter.

When Jeyr lifts me to my feet, I let him. But my hand is still stained with Colden's blood, and I know I will never wash it clean.

Caomh

FINAL VOW

I am hollow.

The world feels muted, as though someone has reached inside me and stolen the very marrow from my bones. My mind drifts—back to the island where I left him, back to the days I told myself my visits were nothing more than a check-in. A small fix. A taste to keep me sane. But it was never enough. It was never *just* a check-in.

My soul ached for him even then.

The longest stretch apart came after the war. He couldn't understand why I wouldn't let myself come back, why I wouldn't stay. And I couldn't explain it without risking everything—because I knew if I saw him too often, I'd never leave again. Each farewell splintered me until I felt like I was running out of pieces. We must have set some kind of record, the longest a pair of Companachs could deny their bond. But really, it was just me—me denying him, denying myself.

I told myself it was for the right reasons, that I was protecting him from a world that would never let us be what we were meant to be. I thought I could outrun the pull between us. I thought I could tame it into something that looked like friendship. Lorkan never called me a liar, but he knew. He always knew.

Now he is gone.

The thought shatters whatever scraps of control I have left. I feel it—our connection, the thread between us—fraying. Not breaking, not yet, but crying out for me to *claim* it before it is cut entirely. I can feel him, faint as a candle flame in a storm. Alive. Hurting.

Bleeding too slowly to heal. Every beat of my heart counts down the time he has left.

Across the lake, the mountains rise in quiet splendor, mocking me with their stillness. Dragons wheel high above, their shadows spilling over the water as Faldr and Lumiwen herd the wyverns higher, pushing them toward safety. Olivia's presence is a quiet hum behind me, her energy steady as a hearth fire, helping me keep my feet beneath me after what we've just endured.

But there are whispers. Always whispers. About the Princess of Puinnsean—the one who saved us, betrayed us, perhaps both. It doesn't matter what anyone calls it. She stole my mate from me. And I will kill her for it.

A shift of air at my side, a shadow I would know anywhere—Jethro sits beside me, saying nothing for a long moment. We watch the wyverns together, their wings catching the light like living banners.

"We'll get him back."

His voice is quiet, iron wrapped in silk, but it strikes through me like a blade.

"I don't know how you survived it," I admit, my voice hoarse, my chest tight. "The years without her."

He doesn't look at me right away. When he does, his mouth is a grim line, his eyes full of the kind of understanding no one should have to earn. "She chose to leave me," he says.

I huff a bitter laugh, dragging a hand through my hair. "I chose to leave him too many times. Gods, I... I did to him what she did to you."

Jethro's hand comes to rest on my shoulder. The weight is steady, grounding, a strange comfort. "You did," he says without judgment. "But your reasons were not the same. You thought you were protecting him. I understood Gwynn when she left—and I understand you now."

I swallow hard, fighting the sting in my throat. "I lost so much time."

He squeezes once before letting go. "Then don't waste what's left. We'll get him back. And when we do—you won't have to leave him again."

I let my head tip onto his shoulder, the words clawing out of me before I can stop them. "Can I at least get a piece of her?"

He chuckles softly, a sound more like steel being sharpened than true mirth. "First strike is yours. But I'll finish her."

The silence that follows is sharp, alive with the promise of blood. My rage no longer feels like it's eating me alive—it feels like purpose, like resolve. The memory of that humanoid's voice, that taunting grin as they shackled Lorkan, feeds the fire roaring to life in my chest.

A faint crunch of steps breaks the quiet. Jethro's head lifts first, but it's Olivia's voice that reaches us.

"We're waking the empath," she says softly. "I need you"

I don't move. Not yet. My gaze remains on the lake, on the place where the sky and water meet, on the thread of connection still humming between me and the man who is mine in every way that matters.

When I do rise, my fingers flex around the hilt of my blade. The war is far from over—but one thing is certain: they will regret the day they tried to take him from me.

* 9 7 8 0 6 4 5 9 6 4 8 7 5 *